PRAISE FOR RAMSEY CAMPBELL AND *ANCIENT IMAGES*

'Campbell is highly regarded for his sensitive use of language and psychologically complex characters . . . Disquieting, unnerving and thoroughly satisfying' *Dean R. Koontz*

'A powerhouse of a writer. *Ancient Images* is a taut, tight thriller, a real hackle-raiser' *Robert R. McCammon*

'The best horror writer alive, period. Each new book uncovers a little more of the real nightmare' *Thomas Tessier*

'More creepy and compelling than any excursion he's made in years. A brilliant, bad dream of a book' *Alan Moore*

'A storyteller who repeatedly leaves you stunned with the flick of a phrase, or an insight that can honestly be called awesome. The worst is *never* over. No one knows that better than Ramsey Campbell' *Jonathan Carroll*

'Carries us inexorably past levels of abnormal psychology into something that is much, much worse' *Stephen King*

'There's more than enough stuff here to make your flesh creep halfway to Honolulu' *Time Out*

'Writes brilliantly . . . a rare talent' *New Statesman*

'Campbell is unmatched at visions of large-scale creepiness' *City Limits*

D1324218

ANCIENT IMAGES

Ramsey Campbell

A Legend book
Published by Arrow Books Limited
20 Vauxhall Bridge Road, London SW1V 2SA

An imprint of Random Century Group

London Melbourne Sydney Auckland
Johannesburg and agencies throughout
the world

First published in 1989 by Century Hutchinson Limited
This Legend edition 1990
Reprinted 1990

Printed and bound in Great Britain by
Courier International Ltd, Tiptree, Essex

ISBN 0 09 967340 1

Acknowledgements

I should begin by thanking Forry Ackerman, whose *Famous Monsters* magazine acquainted me with Karloff and Lugosi before I saw any of their films. Decades later Dennis Etchison helped me add to my knowledge of them. In the writing of the book my wife Jenny was more important than ever; Edward A. Novak III, Tom Doherty, Harriet McDougal and Ann Suster also made helpful suggestions.

for Joan, my favourite mother-in-law
with all my love

1

At last the pain became unbearable, but not for long. Through the haze that wavered about her she thought she saw the fields and the spectactors dancing in celebration of her pain. She was surrounded by folk she'd known all her life, oldsters who had bounced her on their knees when she was little and people of her own age she had played with then, but now their faces were as evilly gleeful as the gargoyles on the chapel beyond them. They were jeering at her and holding their children up to see, sitting children on their shoulders so that they were set almost as high as she was. Her streaming eyes blinked at the faces bunched below her. As she tried to see her husband she was praying that he would come and cut her down before the pain grew worse.

She couldn't see him, and she couldn't cry out to him. Someone had driven a gag into her mouth, so deep that the rusty taste of it was choking her. She couldn't even pray aloud to God to numb her awareness of her bruised tongue that was swollen between her back teeth. Then her senses that were struggling to flee what had been done to her returned, and she remembered that there was no gag, remembered why it couldn't be her tongue that felt like a mouthful of coals whose fire was eating its way through her skull.

For an instant her mind shrank beyond the reach of her plight, and she remembered everything. Her husband wouldn't save her, even if she were able to call out his name instead of emitting the bovine moan that sounded nothing like her voice. He was dead, and she had seen the devil that had killed him. Everyone below her, relishing her fate, believed that she was being put to death for murdering him, but one man knew better – knew enough to have her tongue torn out while making it appear that he was simply applying the law.

The haze rippled around her, the gloating faces seemed to swim up towards her through the thickening murk, and again she realized what her mind was desperate to flee. It wasn't just a haze of pain, it was the heat of the flames that were climbing her body. She made the sound again, louder, and flung herself wildly about. The crowd roared to drown her cries or to encourage her to put on more of a show. Then, as if God had answered the prayer she couldn't voice, her struggles or the fire snapped her bonds, and she was toppling forwards. Her hair burst into flames. As she crawled writhing out of the fire, she thought she felt her blood start to boil.

She didn't get far. Hands seized her and dragged her back to the stake. She felt her life draining out of her charred legs into the earth. Hands bound her more securely and lifted her to cast her into the heart of the fire. In the moment before her brain burned, she saw the man who had judged her, gazing down impassively from his tower. The face of the devil that had killed her husband had been a ghastly caricature of the face of the man on the tower.

2

Sandy was on her way to lunch when she met Graham Nolan in the corridor. His grey mane gleamed as he strode towards her through the sunlight above London, his blue eyes sparkled, his long cheeks and full lips were ruddy with glee. 'Whatever it is must be good to bring you here on your day off,' she said.

'What the world's been waiting for.' He gave her a fatherly hug, and she felt as if he was both expressing his delight and hugging it to him. 'You've time for a drink, haven't you? Come and help me celebrate.'

'I was going to have a roll in the park,' she fed him.

'If I were younger and swung that way . . .' he sighed, and ducked as she mimed a punch. 'A stroll and then a drink, will that do you? Toby's collecting me when he's finished shopping. You wouldn't send me off to toast myself.'

'We're beginning to sound like a bread commercial. I think you're right, we'd better take a break.'

The lift lowered them five storeys to the lobby of Metropolitan Television, where the green carpet felt like turf underfoot. Beyond the revolving doors, taxis loaded with August tourists inched along Bayswater Road. Graham shaded his eyes as he followed her out beneath the taut blue sky, and kept his hand there while he ushered her across to Hyde Park.

A man whose scalp was red from shaving had attracted most of the tourists at Speaker's Corner and was ranting about someone who ought to be dumped on an island: if they couldn't survive, too bad. Graham made for the nearest park shelter and smiled apologetically at Sandy. 'Not much of a stroll, I grant you.'

'You can owe me one,' she said, and sat beside him on

9

the bench, 'since you can't wait to tell me what you've tracked down.'

'Guess.'

'All the scenes Orson Welles shot that were cut after the sneak preview.'

'Ah, if only. I begin to doubt we'll see those in my lifetime. Maybe my heaven's going to be the complete *Ambersons*, double-billed with *Greed* on the biggest screen my brain can cope with.' He blinked rapidly at the park, nannies wheeling prams, pigeons nodding to crumbs on the paths. 'I know you've indulged me already, but would you mind if we were to go inside now? I feel in need of a roof over my head.'

They dodged across Marble Arch, where the black flock of taxis wheeled away into Edgware Road and Oxford Street and Park Lane, and almost lost each other in the crowd before they reached the pub. Though he was mopping his forehead with one of his oversized handkerchiefs, Graham chose a table furthest from the door. Sandy perched on a seat wedged into the corner and stretched out her long legs, drawing admiring glances from several businessmen munching rolls. 'You haven't found the film your American friend was sure was lost for ever,' she said.

'*Tower of Fear*. I have indeed, and I wanted you and him to be the first to know. In fact I was wondering if you'd both care for a preview this evening.'

'Was there ever one?'

'Not even in the States, though my copy came from a bank vault over there, from a collector who seemed to prefer watching his investment grow to watching the films themselves, bless him. Mind you, I've my suspicions that one of my informants had a copy salted away too.' He sat back as if he'd just finished an excellent meal, and raised his gin and tonic. 'May all my quests be as successful, and my next prize not take two years to hunt down.'

'Was it worth two years?'

'My *dear*,' he chided her, knowing she was teasing him. 'A feature film with Karloff and Lugosi that no one living will admit to having seen? It would have had to be several times worse than the worst of the junk that's made these days to disappoint me, but let me tell you this: I watched half an hour of it before bedtime, and I had to make myself put out the light.'

'What, just because of –'

'An old film? An old master, I'd say Giles Spence was, and it's tragic that it was the last film he directed. He knows how to make you look over your shoulder, I promise you, and I think you'd be professionally impressed by the editing. I'd love to watch the film with someone who appreciates it.'

'Doesn't Toby?'

'He's sweet, but you know how he is for living in the present. I hope he won't feel outnumbered if Roger joins us, the American you mentioned. You met him at my last entertainment, you'll recall.'

'We exchanged a few words.'

'Oh, wary, wary. I wouldn't dare to arrange a match for the hermit of Muswell Hill,' Graham said, pretending to shrink back in case she hit him. 'Seriously, shall you be able to come tonight?'

He sounded so anxious that she took pity on him. 'I'll look after you.'

He glanced behind him, presumably for Toby, but there was no sign of Toby among the crowd silhouetted against the dazzle from outside. Above the bar the one o'clock news had been interrupted by commercials. Aproned women with sheaves in their hands danced through a field of wheat to the strains of Vaughan Williams, and a maternal voice murmured 'Staff o' Life – simply English' as the words appeared on the screen. Now here was the news footage Sandy had edited, the line of constables blocking a road into Surrey, the wandering convoy which the media had christened Enoch's Army fuming at the roadblock, the leader burying his fingers in his beard which was as massive as his head while a policeman gestured him and his followers onward to yet another county, children staring out of vehicles at children jeering 'Hippies' at them from a

11

school at the edge of the road. 'Scapegoats, you mean,' Graham muttered.

'I hope people can see that's what they are.'

'All you can do is try and show the truth,' Graham said, and jumped as someone loomed at him out of the crowd.

It was only Toby. He stroked Graham's head in passing, and leaned against the wall beside Sandy, wriggling his broad shoulders to work out tension. In his plump face, made paler by the bristling shock of ginger hair, his blue eyes were wide with frustration. 'Thank you, Dionysos, for this oasis in the jungle,' he said, elevating his glass.

'Trouble with the natives?' Graham suggested.

'Not with us at all. Hitler youths on their way to a bier-keller almost shoved me under a bus, and two gnomes in Bermuda shorts sneaked in front of me for the last of the pasta in Old Compton Street. "Look, Martha, it's like we get at home. Thank the Lord for some honest to God food instead of all this foreign garbage." They ought to have been thanking the Lord for my concern for international relations.'

'Never mind, love. Sandy'll be joining us tonight, by the way.'

'It'll be a sorry buffet, I warn you – whatever I concoct from the little I managed to save from the locust hordes.'

'The two of you are enough of a feast,' Sandy declared, raising her voice to drown out a man at the bar who was telling a joke about gays and AIDS. She thought he might be unaware of the periphery of his audience until he and his cronies stared at Graham and Toby and burst out laughing.

'I think we may adjourn to our place,' Graham said, 'lest my mood be spoiled.'

'Just as you like,' Toby said, his mouth stiff, blood flaring high on his cheeks. Sandy could tell that he wanted to confront the speaker on Graham's behalf. She ushered her friends past the bar, where the men turned their thick necks towards them. The joker's eyes met hers in the mirror between the inverted bottles. His face was a mask made of beef. When he smirked she said, 'You must feel very inadequate.'

'Queers and women's libbers, I can do without the lot of them,' he told a crony out of the corner of his mouth.

'Then you'll have to take yourself in hand,' Sandy laughed.

He understood more quickly than she would have expected, and wheeled bull-like on the stool, lowering his head as if he were stepping into a ring. She didn't even need to imagine him in drag in order to render him absurd. She shook her head reprovingly and urged her friends out of the pub. 'You make sure our Graham enjoys his triumph,' she told Toby, patting his angry cheeks.

'We'll enjoy it more for sharing it with you,' he said, and took Graham's hand as they crossed over to the park.

Sandy lingered outside Metropolitan as they strode rapidly past Speaker's Corner. The man with the raw scalp was still ranting, but only the sound of traffic appeared to emerge from his mouth. A tramp or a tangle of litter stirred behind a bench as Graham and Toby reached the nearest entrance to the car park that extended under the whole of Hyde Park. As Graham stepped out of the sunlight he glanced back sharply, but she didn't think he was looking at her. She was squinting in case she could see what he'd seen when Lezli came out of Metropolitan to find her. 'Help,' Lezli said.

3

At first Sandy thought Lezli was editing an old musical, brushing her green hair behind her ear whenever she stooped to the bench. Astaire was dancing on the moviola screen, and it wasn't until Cagney joined him that she realized that this was something new. It was *The Light Fantastic,* a television film where the players in an end-of-the-pier show found themselves fading into monochrome and dancing with the best of Hollywood. 'Only their rhythm's wrong, and the film's already over budget, and the dancers have gone to America themselves now,' Lezli wailed.

'Any chance of using some other vintage clips?'

'It took us months to clear these. I did tell the producer he should try, and he used words I didn't know existed. The worst of it is these aren't the clips we thought we'd be using, the ones the dancers were told to match.'

The point of the film was that the ghosts of Cagney and Astaire allowed the dancers to forget their bickering and their failures and realize their ambitions for a night, if only in fantasy, but now it looked as if the encounter turned them into clowns. Sandy examined the out-takes, which proved to be useless. She ran the completed scenes again, and then she hugged Lezli. 'Couldn't see for looking,' she said, and separated the main routine into three segments. 'Now how do we get them all to dance in the same tempo?'

Lezli peered and brushed her hair back and saw it. 'Slow our people down.'

'That's what I thought. Let's see.' She watched Lezli run the tape back and forth, trying to match tempi, until the dancers joined the ghosts, not imitating them so much as interpolating syncopated variations in a slight slow motion that seemed magical. The producer of the film came

14

storming in to find Lezli, then clapped his hand over his mouth. 'Light *and* fantastic. Thanks, Sandy. I thought we were up cripple creek.'

'Thank Lezli, she's the one who put the idea into words. Soon I'll be coming to her for advice,' Sandy said and went to the vending machine for a coffee, feeling even happier than she would have if she'd edited the film herself.

She enjoyed the urgency of editing news footage, but equally she enjoyed helping shape fictions, improving the timing, discovering new meanings through juxtapositions, tuning the pace. She'd learned these skills in Liverpool; she'd spent her first two years out of school working with children at the Blackie, a deconsecrated church with a rainbow in place of a cross, helping them make videos about their own fears. She'd moved to London to attend film school, she'd lived with a fellow student for almost a year and had nursed him through a nervous breakdown before they'd split up. She'd been a member of a collective that had made a film confronting rapists with their victims, and the film had been shown at Edinburgh and Cannes. When a second film that would have let people who had been abused as children confront their seducers had failed to attract finance, Sandy had gone for the job of assistant editor at Metropolitan. Later she'd learned that Graham had put in a good word for her, having seen the collective's film in Edinburgh and admired the editing. He'd introduced himself once she had begun work at the station, and they had taken an immediate liking to each other. He'd steered her towards jobs he'd thought would stretch her talents; he'd suported her when, infrequently, she'd thought a task was too much for her, and had been the first to applaud when she solved it; he'd given her the confidence when she needed it and asked for nothing but her friendship in return. In less than a year she was promoted and managed to land Lezli, with whom she'd worked in the collective, her old job. Now, two years later, she was twenty-eight, and some-times felt as if she was able to shape her life as deftly as she shaped films.

She might meet someone she would like to spend it with, but there was no urgency, especially since she didn't want children. It was Graham and her parents who were anxious to see her matched, though Graham was less insistent since she'd met a young architect at one of his private showings. Among the guests who had assembled to watch Graham's latest treasures, Dietrich's screen test for *The Blue Angel*, Walt Disney's menstruation film and a copy of *Double Indemnity* that began in the death cell – actors from the Old Vic, chairmen of art galleries, columnists and socialites and even minor royalty – the architect had seemed to feel out of place until Sandy had befriended him. He'd invited her out for a drink, and next time for dinner in Hampstead, where he lived. Afterwards they'd walked across the heath towards his flat as the wind blundered up from Regent's Park, bearing a mutter of traffic like the sound of a sleeping zoo, and the architect had questioned her about her childhood, whether she had misbehaved at school, how she had been punished and what she had been wearing . . . She might have played his game if the gleam in his eyes hadn't been so dangerously eager. She'd left him with their only kiss and had walked home to Muswell Hill, reflecting that the encounter had been both funny and sad. Such was life.

Though she enjoyed Graham's crowded private parties, not least because she knew they meant so much to him, she was flattered to be invited to tonight's small gathering. She must tell him to watch the film Lezli had edited, she thought as the underground train rocked her homeward. He always watched films she recommended, and that made her feel both special and responsible for him.

She left the train at Highgate and climbed to the main road. Traffic slow and apparently endless as a parade of baggage in an airport rumbled up from Archway towards the Great North Road. She turned along Muswell Hill Road, where buses were labouring towards Alexandra Park. In five minutes she was at Queen's Wood.

After the stuffiness of the train and the uproar of the traffic, the small wood felt like the first day of a holiday.

Beneath the oaks and beeches the velvety gloom was cool. Holly spiked the shadows among the trunks, tangles of brambles sprawled across the grass beside the tarmac paths that were cracked by the clenched roots of trees. Sandy strolled along the discursive paths, letting her senses expand until the wood glowed around her.

Her flat was at the top of a mock-Tudor three-storey house that overlooked the wood. She owned half of the top floor. The skylight above the wide stairwell was trying to fit a lozenge of sunlight into her door frame as she unlocked the door. Bogart came to greet her, arching his back and digging his claws into the hall carpet until she shooed him into the main room, where Bacall was sitting on the window sill among the cacti, watching a magpie. Both cats raced into the bright compact kitchen as soon as she opened a cupboard to reach for a can of their food. They ate daintily while she finished off last night's lasagna and the remaining glassful of claret, they rubbed themselves against her ankles while she washed up and told them about her day. They followed her into her bedroom and watched her change into a dress she thought elegant enough for visiting Graham, and then they chased her as she ran to where the phone was ringing.

She'd left it plugged beside the window seat between the gables that gave wings to the main room. She answered it and sat on the sky-blue couch, Bacall curling up in her lap. 'Roger sends his apologies,' Graham said. 'You don't mind sitting on your own in the one and sixes, do you?'

'I'm almost on my way.'

'She's almost on her way,' he called, and she heard Toby protest, 'If she comes too soon there'll be nothing worth eating.'

Sandy cradled the receiver and smiled wryly at herself. It seemed she had been looking forward more than she realized to continuing the argument she'd had with Roger at Graham's last soirée. He'd accused television of ruining films by shrinking them and editing them afresh, she'd retorted that some critics did them worse harm. No doubt they would meet again at the grand opening of tonight's film.

She was easing Bacall onto the floor when the phone rang again. A coin put an end to the pips, and a girlish East End voice said, 'Hello?'

'Hello.'

'Is Bobby there?'

'What number are you calling?'

The voice gave Sandy's number. 'Bobby who?' Sandy said.

'I don't know his last name.'

Of course you don't, Sandy thought, knowing that the girl had been trying to make sure nobody was home. 'We've a couple of Bobbies here. Which do you want?'

'I only met him once.'

'Well, is he the fat one or the thin one? Youngish, is he? Moustache? I know which he must be, the other's been abroad. Hang on and I'll get him for you,' Sandy said, wondering how much longer the girl would dare to pretend. 'He'll just be a minute. He's coming now. Here he is,' she said, and the connection broke.

'How rude,' she told the cats, and took them for a brief run in the wood, where they chased crumbling shadows on the paths. They gazed down from her window as she headed for the station. At Euston, where a distant giantess was apologizing for delays in the upper world, she changed trains for Pimlico. All the women on the train were sharing the compartment nearest the driver, and when Sandy alighted she grinned at them for luck.

A vessel loaded with containers coloured like building blocks was passing underneath Vauxhall Bridge, between the dark women that supported the road over the Thames. A bus with more lights than passengers crossed the bridge towards the Oval, and then the night was still except for the lapping of long slow ripples full of the windows of riverside apartments. Graham's apartment was ten storeys up, at the top of one of two tower blocks built companionably close together. One of his neighbours was stepping out to walk

18

her dog. 'You're Graham Nolan's colleague,' the woman remembered, and held the security door open for her.

As it thumped shut, Sandy heard a shrill sound. Perhaps the dog had whined, though the door cut off so much noise from outside it made the silent building feel deserted. The waiting lift rushed her to the top floor, and snatched away her hearing. She swallowed as she walked along the corridor, as if she could gulp down the silence. She passed two doors and turned the corner, and saw that Graham's door was open.

Toby must have gone out for more ingredients. She went to the door, which shared this stretch of corridor with an exit to the roof, and halted on the threshold, disconcerted to find herself shivering. 'Graham?' she called.

The small bedroom to the left of the main room had been converted into a projection booth. The beam of light from the projector splayed out of the square window, across the Persian carpet, the tables Toby had constructed out of steel and chunks of glass, the enormous semicircular couch that faced the view of the river. The screen was on the right-hand wall, between two elaborate brass standard lamps, but the beam was streaming into the master bedroom. She knocked loudly and called, 'Graham, it's Sandy,' and went into the apartment, shivering.

The kitchen was next to the master bedroom. The oven was on low, and she could smell pastry, but the kitchen was unmanned. She made for the projection booth, wrinkling her nose at an odd stale smell. The door to the booth was wide open. Perhaps Graham was preoccupied. She was about to call to him again when her hand flew to her mouth.

The booth was full of shelves of books about the cinema, but now most of the books were on the floor. Some of the largest were torn almost in half, as if they had been flung across the room, as several cans clearly had: she could see where a can had split the plaster of one wall. There was no film on the projector, which had been knocked askew.

Graham and Toby might have quarrelled, but never, she thought, like this. She backed out of the room, the smell of

19

pastry swelling in her throat until she had to fight for breath, and swung towards the master bedroom. The bed was made but rumpled, the duvet sagging where one of the men had sat on the edge. The beam of the projector shone over the bed, past a dressing-table strewn with jars and combs and brushes, and blanked out the window – except that the double glazing wasn't quite blank. Bewildered, she thought there must be film on the projector after all, or at least a strip caught in the gate, for a blurred figure was visible in the midst of the light. Then her awareness lurched nervously, and she realized that the figure of a man wasn't projected on the glass but standing beyond it, ten floors up, on the next roof. More dismayingly, she was almost sure that she recognized him.

She ran to the doorway of the bedroom. Of course, she had been shivering because the exit from the corridor to the roof was ajar. Now she could see the face of the man at the edge of the neighbouring roof, though she didn't want to believe what she was seeing. He was Graham, and he was waving his hands feebly as if he were terrified of the drop below him.

A wind fluttered the sleeves of his shirt and brought his grey mane wavering over his shoulder. He looked back, stumbled backwards a few steps, and panic grabbed Sandy's heart as she saw what he meant to do. 'Don't,' she cried, and knew he couldn't hear her through the double glazing. She dashed into the room and leapt over the bed, she wrenched at the catch of the window with one hand, waved her other desperately at him to delay him. Surely he could see her, surely he would wait for her to speak to him, to tell him she would go into the other building and open the door to the roof – But just as the catch slid out of its socket, he sprinted to the edge and jumped.

He'd already done it once, she told herself as he reached the edge. However wide the gap looked, he had managed to cross it safely, never mind why he was up there at all. The thoughts didn't slow her heart down or allow her to breathe, nor did they help him. As she sidled the inner pane clear of its grooves, he missed the roof above her, and fell.

She saw him fall into the beam of light. His hair blazed like a silver halo. His mouth was gaping, silenced perhaps by the wind of his fall, and yet she thought he saw her and, despite his terror, managed to look unbearably apologetic, as if he wanted her to know that it wasn't her fault she hadn't been in time to reach him. That moment seemed so unreal and so prolonged that she was almost able to believe the light had arrested him somehow, like a frame of film. Then he was gone, and as her breath screamed out she heard a thud below her like the sound of meat slung onto a butcher's slab.

She dropped the pane on the carpet and fumbled the outer window open, sobbing. Graham lay between the buildings, at the rim of a pool of light from a riverside street lamp. He looked small and pathetic as a discarded doll. His legs were bent as though he were running, his arms were outstretched on either side of his head, which seemed too large, its outline spreading. Sandy felt as if she were toppling out of the window towards him. As she staggered backwards, the building opposite seemed to nod at her, and a shape reared up on its roof.

It must have been a ventilator. When she managed to focus she saw the boxy funnel on which two weeds were flowering. She walked rapidly to the door and took a shuddering breath, and ran across the main room to the phone before the smell of pastry could make her sick. She swallowed several times while the emergency number rang. 'Ambulance,' she gasped, and gave the details in a voice that felt almost too calm.

She had to close her eyes in the lift, for all the way down she was sickeningly aware of its faint swaying. Stepping into the lobby felt like stepping onto dry land. She turned towards the entrance to the building, and groaned. Toby was coming in.

He was struggling to unlock the door while he balanced a carrier bag. He nudged the door open with his bottom and snatched the keys deftly out of the lock. 'Hi, Sandy,' he called. 'We're nearly ready for you. Graham will keep you amused while I finish in the kitchen.'

He saw her expression and hurried forward, tucking his package more firmly under his arm so as to reach for her hands. 'Sandy, what's the matter, you poor girl? Just tell me what we can do to help.'

'It's not me, Toby,' she said, hardly able to speak. 'It's Graham.'

His plump face was always pale, but suddenly his skin looked like paper. 'What? What about him?'

'He had an accident. He's badly hurt, or – '

She couldn't say it. She tried to steer Toby towards the door, then thought of telling him to stay here while she went to see, but he misunderstood: he pushed past her with a gentleness that felt like controlled panic. 'I know you mean well, Sandy, but please don't try to keep us apart. I have to go up and see for myself.'

She found her voice as he reached the lift. 'He isn't upstairs, Toby, he's outside. He fell.'

'But he was upstairs just now. I only went round the corner.' He stared at her, and his blue eyes dulled. 'Fell?' he said, his voice shrinking. 'How far?' Before she could answer he dodged past her, knocking his elbow against the wall, as if she might hinder him. He seized the security bolt with both hands and dropped the carrier bag; she heard glass smash. As he heaved the door open she ran after him, wanting to be with him when he found Graham. But she was halfway to the corner of the building when he vanished around it and let out a cry of anguish beyond words.

4

The woman with the dog had found Graham. Toby flailed his hands at the animal as he ran, almost falling as he leapt over a rope that was the shadow of a railing. 'Get away,' he screamed.

The woman tied the dog's leash to the railing and hurried back to Graham. 'You mustn't touch him either. You know me, I'm a doctor.'

Toby stooped and flinched from the sight of Graham's broken head. His hands were opening and closing, yearning to lift Graham to him. When Sandy put her arm around him he stiffened to hold himself together. She wished he would turn away from Graham, because then she wouldn't need to see Graham's face, mouth flung wide, eyes moist and sparkling faintly as if he might still be conscious inside the ruin of his skull.

The doctor peered into his eyes, unbuttoned his shirt and felt for his hearbeat, lifted one limp arm by the wrist, and then she stood up, her small tanned wrinkled face carefully neutral. 'I'm afraid – '

Toby moaned and wriggled free of Sandy's arm and fell to his knees beside Graham. He stroked Graham's blood-soaked hair back from his forehead and began to murmur, saying goodbye or praying. A shiver Sandy couldn't quite locate was gathering within her as she waited, feeling redundant but unwilling to leave him. She wondered why she couldn't feel the rain she saw falling on Graham's face, and then she realized Toby was weeping. The sound of an approaching siren made him crouch lower. When he gripped Graham's shoulders as if he would let nobody take him away, she went to him and held onto his arm.

The police car halted beyond the gap between the tower blocks, and two policemen with peaked caps pulled low climbed out. One had a disconcertingly small nose, the other a moustache wider than his face. The doctor met them and gave them details about Graham while they pushed their caps back and gazed up at the building. 'You called us, did you?' snub nose said.

'No, I was on the bridge.'

Sandy squeezed Toby's arm and stood up, wobbling. 'I called the ambulance.'

'You are . . . ?'

'Sandy Allan. I worked with him. I was supposed to be visiting.' Lowering her voice for Toby's sake, she said, 'I saw him fall.'

The moustached policeman lowered his gaze to her. 'All this is double-glazed, isn't it?'

'I believe so. Can we talk somewhere else?'

'Is it open where he came from? We'll need to take a look.' At the sound of an oncoming ambulance he muttered to his colleague, 'If that's for this, they'll have to wait for the photographer.'

After the evening chill, the heat of the building made Sandy uncomfortable. So did the swaying of the lift, and the smells of the policeman – sweat, talcum powder, pipe tobacco. A charred smell met her at Graham's door. She ran into the kitchen and switched off the oven. 'You seem to know your way around,' the policeman said.

'I've been here a few times.'

She sat down on the wide couch, feeling as if her legs had been about to give way, while he leaned against the window that overlooked the river. 'You said you worked together,' he said.

'At Metropolitan, the television station. I'm a film editor. I should let them know what happened. I don't mean for the news.'

She was talking too much, too haphazardly, and she wondered what that might imply to him. He had her dictate her name and address and phone number, then he moved to the bedroom door. In the projector beam he looked disconcertingly like an actor dressed as a policeman. 'Were you in here?'

'I was, yes. That's how I saw.' Now she seemed unable to say enough. 'He was on the other roof,' she managed.

He followed his deflating shadow to the window and gazed up. 'What were you doing in here?'

'Watching. What do you think?' At once she regretted snapping at him; if anyone was accusing her, it was herself – accusing her of being too slow to stop Graham. 'I mean,' she said wearily, 'I was trying to call out to him not to do what he did.'

'Had you some reason to suspect that he would?'

'Before I saw him up there? No.' It was beginning to seem even more unreal. 'What could have made him do it? I had a drink with him at lunchtime and he couldn't have been happier.'

'Happy enough to be reckless?'

'He wasn't like that at all.'

He continued to question her until he appeared satisfied that she couldn't help further, which only made her more convinced that she had failed Graham. 'Let's hope his son can shed some light,' the policeman said.

'Which son?'

'Wasn't that his son with him down there?'

'Toby?' Her keeping their secret might make him suspicious. 'They lived together.'

'Ah.' He stared towards the projection booth, where he had already noted the disarray. 'What kind of films did you make together?'

It was less the question or its implication than his innocent delivery of it that infuriated her, but losing her temper wouldn't help Toby. 'We didn't. Graham was the film researcher at the station. He used to find lost films. He'd invited me tonight for a private viewing.'

'What sort of film would that be?'

'An old horror film with Boris Karloff and Bela Lugosi.'

'Is that all? Why, I'd let my daughters watch that.' He

sounded relieved on Sandy's behalf. 'So the two of you were purely professionally involved.'

'No, we were good friends.'

'I'm sorry if this is painful for you,' he said in the tone of a rebuke. 'And where was his young friend while all this happened?'

She cleared Toby as best she could, while the policeman looked increasingly unhappy. 'Think carefully if you will,' he said. 'Could you have seen anything at all that might suggest why Nolan behaved as he did?'

She tried to drag her mind away from the memory of Graham's fall, but it was reluctant as a fascinated child. 'I can't think of anything.'

'He could hardly have been running away from an old horror film.'

'He wasn't running away,' she said, and found herself wishing that her response hadn't been quite so immediate: it seemed to cut short her ability to think. As she strained to imagine what Graham had been up to, Toby came in.

He stared blankly at the kitchen and the lingering smell of charred pastry, stared at Sandy and her interviewer. He stepped into the projector beam, rubbing his upper arms as though it might warm him, and stumbled into the booth. Minutes seemed to pass before he gave a cry of outrage and grief.

The snub-nosed policeman, who had brought him upstairs, grimaced as he kept an eye on him and made a fluttering gesture to tell his colleague what Toby was. 'There's nothing wrong with people showing their emotions,' Sandy said, her voice pinched.

'Depends what kind you mean.' The policeman wrinkled his nose. 'There are some we can do without, that are best locked up.'

'Maybe you've forgotten someone's just been killed. If you can't leave your prejudices outside, at least show some compassion,' Sandy said between her teeth, and told herself to stop: she might be making them even more hostile to Toby. It was Toby who interrupted her by appearing in the

26

doorway, knuckling his eyes. 'Who did this?' he demanded. 'Where's the film?'

'It was like that in there when I first came, Toby. I didn't see any film.'

'But he'd set it up. He was lining it up when I stepped out,' he cried. 'The can's still there on the floor.'

Both policemen scowled as if he were talking in code to her. When Sandy explained the moustached one said, 'How rare was this film?'

'Very. It took Graham years to track it down.'

'Have you any idea how much it's worth?'

'A great deal to a collector, I should think. Are you suggesting – '

'That he might have caught a thief red-handed? Would that have made him act as he did?'

Toby sucked in a breath so fierce it seemed to dry his eyes. 'He'd have chased the swine all right.'

'You're not telling us he'd have chased someone across the roofs at his age,' snub nose said.

'You'd be surprised. You don't have to be straight to win prizes at athletics.'

It was news to Sandy if Graham had, but Toby fetched a photograph album from a bookcase and flung it on the couch. 'Try believing these.'

They were photographs of a young Graham in singlet and shorts. In one he was snapping a tape with his chest, his full lips pouting with the effort. Sandy found the photographs heartbreaking, but the policemen looked unimpressed. Eventually snub nose said, 'How do you reckon a thief could have got in?'

'I left our door on the latch,' Toby said, his eyes brimming. 'He said to, and I thought it would be safe while he was home.'

The policemen exchanged resigned glances that said this was all too familiar. 'You saw Mr Nolan jump,' the moustached policeman said to Sandy. 'You actually saw him jump.'

Why must he repeat it? 'I said so.'

'Of his own accord, you're certain.'

'There was nothing – nobody else on the roof.'

'There isn't now,' snub nose said, gazing into the bedroom, and Sandy felt reality shiver, for she could see figures up there. Of course, she thought as he gave them a thumbs-up sign, they were police. 'Well?' he said.

'Well?' said his colleague.

He jerked his head at Sandy. 'The doctor said the same as her.'

So Sandy needn't have felt nearly as harassed, she realized, too exhausted to be angry. 'The place will have to be dusted,' the moustached policeman said, 'but Fingerprints may not be here until the morning.' He put on his cap and tugged the peak down. 'I'm sorry about your friend. We do tell the public not to have a go if they come across a crime in progress.'

He went out slowly after his colleague, as if he might think of something else to add. His slowness seemed to linger in the room, turning the air sluggish. The room was too bright, the darkness that buried the windows too black; the chafing of light and dark scraped Sandy's nerves. 'Would you like to stay with me tonight?' she asked Toby.

'You're sweet for asking, but I have to wait here for the law. If I didn't I'd want to be with Graham. You stay by all means if you don't want to be by yourself.'

'I'd better go home. My cats . . .' she said, feeling awkward and inadequate. She didn't move until the doctor came upstairs and offered her and Toby tranquillizers. 'I'll stay with him,' the doctor promised.

Outside the night air settled on Sandy's face like a chill mask that felt distant. She hailed a taxi and climbed in and hugged herself. Streets the colour of a dying fire swept cheerlessly by. When the taxi drew up in front of her house she paid automatically and trudged along the path. She climbed the stairs as the timer switch counted the seconds of light, she let herself into her hall and screamed as claws clutched at her out of the dark. The cat fled as she switched on the light and burst into tears. If she hadn't had to tell

Metropolitan what had befallen Graham, she thought she might have wept until dawn.

5

She couldn't sleep. Whenever she closed her eyes Graham launched himself towards her, and she clenched her fists as the hands of her mind tried to grab him. Worst of all was the look in his eyes, reassuring her that she couldn't have saved him. Even as he fell he had tried to be kind to her.

She sat on the bed and stroked the cats and stared out of her window until the sight of the dark filled her with vague panic. She brewed herself coffee and sat on the window seat. While she waited for the mug in her hand to cool enough for sipping, she felt gusts of wind at her back, the night snatching at her through the glass. She sat on the couch and stared at the wrinkling skin of the coffee, and the gables loomed at the edge of her vision, hemming in her thoughts. Why had she said that Graham had been killed instead of saying that he'd died? It was only in detective stories that the police pursued that kind of detail, she told herself; in reality they had more important tasks, such as making life unpleasant for people whose lifestyle they disapproved of. They should save their unpleasantness for whoever had stolen the film. Graham plunged towards her from the roof, and she put down the mug for fear of crushing it in her fist. She couldn't sit here all night in this state.

She called the Metropolitan newsroom and spoke to Phyl. 'Will you be putting out a report about Graham?'

'We hope to if we can fit it in. We'll have some kind of tribute going out tomorrow.'

'I thought I might come in now and help select the material.'

'Absolutely, love, if you want to. We can always use expert help.'

The streets into the West End were almost deserted. Lonely walkers tried to head off their own shadows under the street lamps, but the absence of activity in the bare glaring streets felt like her absence of reaction, her reaction delayed. 'What's the big news?' the taxi driver asked her, and kept quiet once she shook her head.

When she rang the bell at Metropolitan, Phyl let her in. Phyl was broad and over six feet tall, and seemed always both amused and regretful that most men found her daunting. She took Sandy's arm as they walked to the lift. 'Listen, love, I hadn't realized you were with him when it happened. Are you sure you want to do this now? Wouldn't you rather just sit and talk to me while I haven't too much work?'

'I want to be sure we do the best we can for him.'

'I understand,' Phyl said, with the faintest implication that she was choosing not to feel insulted. 'You knew him better than most of us did. You might want to draft a script for us. We've the interview he gave last year that wasn't broadcast because of the technicians' strike, and we need two minutes maximum.'

She gave Sandy the tape and stayed with her while she watched the opening. 'I'm only down the corridor,' she said eventually, and tiptoed out. Sandy had braced herself for the sight of Graham on the monitor, but it seemed she had been unduly apprehensive. At least she would be keeping Graham alive in the world for a little while longer.

The tape was of an episode of *Meet Metropolitan*, the show on which viewers could question television personalities. Graham had been surprised and delighted to be asked for. He chatted to the viewer as if the camera wasn't there, his enthusiasm rejuvenating him before her eyes. He began by enthusing about Metropolitan. 'They let me take however long and however much cash it takes, and they know I won't give them any film until I can swear it's complete. Only they can edit this out if they want to, but I wish we weren't in this display case for shrunken heads. I wish we were in any

31

of the cinemas I grew up in and fell in love with. This is never the place to watch a film.'

Sandy wouldn't use any of that, but here was an answer worth considering.

'You care and I do, but there need to be more of us who won't sit still for what's done to films. Films get squeezed into this fish tank where they can hardly breathe, or projectionists show them out of focus or don't bother lining them up properly, or the screen's the colour my handkerchief was when I was a snotty six-year-old, and if a film's missing a few bits, so what? Even if the censor hasn't had his way with it we can expect to lose a few seconds at the end of a reel because of how it's handled – I really think projectionists grow their nails specially to scratch films with – and when some television stations get hold of a film, well, saints preserve us. If it's been on before they'll make room for a few more ads – it's only Cary Grant hanging about in the desert, nothing's happening, forget the rhythm of the film, it's not Art like music is. Vandalism? Why, they're just giving the public what they want, most people don't write in to complain and that must mean they're satisfied. I'll bet you wish you hadn't asked the question, if you even recall what it was after all that.'

The young woman who'd requested him smiled forgivingly. 'Can we know what films you're looking for this year?'

'It doesn't go by years, my dear, it's a continuing process. Let's see if this whets your appetite. Can you believe that Karloff and Lugosi made a film together here in Britain that no one has ever seen? The Victorian ghost story it was based on seems to have disappeared, and the film was being condemned even before it was completed. That was in the thirties, when we were supposed to have had enough of horror films, but I've a feeling this one particularly upset some people in high places. I hope soon we'll have the chance to judge it for ourselves.'

He held out his hands as if he were offering a treasure to the camera, and the tape ended. Sandy rewound it and watched it again. Best to let him speak for himself and give the newsreader as little to say as possible. There wouldn't be time to mention how he'd lived with his parents in the apartment above the Thames, how he'd been given the worst report of his school year when he'd left to work on Covent Garden market with them, how he'd spent nearly all his wages on filmgoing, how his life had changed the day he'd found cans of film piled high on a market stall . . . She used half of his comments on the way film was derided, and most of his answer about the horror film. 'It was the last film he revived,' she wrote, 'but it was stolen before he could watch it. Anyone with any information should contact the police.'

Did that fit? The film ought to be found, as a memorial to him. She went out of the editing room, down the corridor to consult Phyl, and felt as if her feet were failing to touch the carpet. Dawn was shuttering the window at the end of the corridor. A cloud muffled the sun, and she saw the long drop beyond the glass, heard the thud as Graham struck the concrete. 'Phyl,' she called, and as soon as she heard her voice, the rest of her began to shake too.

6

The next time she saw Graham, he might almost have been asleep. His eyes were closed, his lashes two delicate silvery crescents. His full lips looked satisfied, though untypically prim. His long cheeks were faintly powdered, as if he had no further reason to conceal his femaleness. He was wearing his favourite blue suit. His hands were folded on his chest, no longer reaching out desperately. 'Thanks, Toby,' she murmured, and left him beside the coffin, where she could tell he was ready to weep.

It had been his idea that she should visit Graham before the funeral; she hadn't realized how much it would help her. The tranquillizers had only postponed her reaction further. Phyl had sat with her while she watched the broadcast about Graham, in which even her own script seemed to have nothing to do with her. Graham's fall had followed her home and back to Metropolitan, where she was able to work, though her head and her hands and the world had felt brittle. She'd agreed to Toby's suggestion so as not to upset him. She hadn't realized how renewing it would be for her to see Graham at peace.

He would want her to be at peace too. Allowing her failure to save him to grow cancerous in her was no way to preserve his memory, it was simply unfair to him. She lifted her face towards the sun as she came out of the under-taker's. A plane too high to hear was chalking the cloudless sky. A wave of birds rose from a grassy square, a football beat like a heart on a schoolyard wall. The world was coming back to life for her. 'You can still be proud of me,' she whispered, happy to imagine that Graham could hear.

By the time she rose from the underground at Marble Arch she was remembering Graham introducing her as if she were the brightest talent at his soirée, Graham in the

Metropolitan lobby performing a dance routine with her and refusing to stop until she identified the musical, Graham buying her and Toby dinner at a hotel on Park Lane and solemnly producing a magnifying glass to pore over his portion of cuisine minceur: 'That's what I call a *minute* steak,' he'd said . . . The thought of his fall made her wince and brought tears to her eyes, but so it should. She went into Metropolitan and worked on a tape of children being rescued from a crashed school bus.

She was rounding it off with the image of two of the survivors embracing so hard that they had to be helped into the ambulance together when Lezli came over, smiling tightly. 'Can you see the improvement? I've just got disengaged.'

'Lezli, I'm sorry.'

'Don't be. Best decision I've made this year. Let's have a coffee to celebrate.'

They took the lift to the staff restaurant on the top floor. 'Here's to trusting in ourselves,' Lezli said, raising her cup.

'Did you feel you hadn't been?'

'That's what men want, isn't it? Men basically just want one thing.'

'Sometimes we do too, don't we?'

'I don't mean horizontal dancing. I mean they want to undermine our confidence and make us dependent on them.'

'Let them try.'

'This one nearly did until I savaged his view of life. He kept going on about security as if it was me who should need more of it instead of him that did. He started barking and snarling when I asked him if he knew where all the money his firm invests comes from, though. Pop goes my Christmas on his family's estate that Daddy runs like a little kingdom, so that's a relief.'

'I see he's left his mark on you.'

'Only till I get to a sunlamp,' Lezli said, making a face at the ghost of his ring on her finger. 'Do you know the kind of shit he'd been storing up for me? He would have

35

wanted me to promise not to make any more films in case they drew attention to him as well. That came up because of Graham Nolan.'

'Did he know Graham?'

'No better than anyone else who reads about him in the paper.'

'Which paper?'

'Last night's.' She seemed to regret having mentioned it, especially when Sandy said, 'I'd like to see it.'

Lezli went reluctantly down to the newsroom and produced a copy of the *Daily Friend*. SUSSEX SAYS STAY OUT, SPONGERS, said a headline above the tabloid's version of the progress of Enoch's Army. She turned to the film column by Leonard Stilwell who, Sandy gathered, was the kind of reviewer who emerged from film shows bearing flaws like trophies. Lezli flicked the last paragraph with her fingernail and gave Sandy the comment to read:

'Another film world death to mourn, though Graham Nolan never made a film. Film buffs will be grateful to him as the perfectionist film buyer for Metropolitan TV. Pity his last months were wasted on a wild-goose chase after a fictitious film. Now he's with his idols where he deserves to be, and all of us film buffs will miss him.'

Sandy wondered if the writer had a special key that typed the word 'film'. She read the paragraph twice in case she had missed something. 'His remark about the wild-goose chase, is that what you meant, Lezli? Shows he doesn't know as much about films as he pretends to.'

'Well, I'm glad you can take it that way. Quite a few of us thought it was unfair to Graham.'

'If you're writing to the paper, count on me to sign.' But the mistake seemed trivial, and she didn't think it would have mattered to Graham.

She did her best to persuade Toby of that when he rang her at home to share his rage with her, but he wasn't convinced. 'I won't have Graham called a liar,' he vowed. 'The *Daily Friend* is instant litter, but its readers don't know it is. I'm going to make this parasite admit in print he was wrong.'

'Let me know if he does,' Sandy said, and thought as soon as she'd replaced the receiver that she should have put him in touch with Lezli. Still, her impression was that Lezli and her colleagues would stop short of complaining to the tabloid, and she couldn't blame them. After all, it was only a film.

7

The day after Graham's funeral she went to the latest Alan Ayckbourn, and found herself laughing longest at jokes Graham would have liked. After the performance she drank with friends in a pub off Shaftesbury Avenue. Both of the unattached men in the party offered to see her home, but she refused gently. She was feeling wistful and relaxed and private, carrying memories of Graham that seemed worth more than anything he might have bequeathed to her, not that she would have expected him to. But the next morning Toby called her to say he had something Graham would have wanted her to have.

She found Toby at the railing by the Thames, his face solemn as the lowing of boats on the river. He looked paler than ever; so, disconcertingly, did his ginger hair. 'It's soothing here, isn't it?' she said.

'I used to think so. Let's go up,' he said as if he wanted to get it over with.

In the lift he blinked every time the glowing numbers changed. He unlocked the flat and stood aside for her. Sunlight streamed into the main room, which felt cold and deserted. His steel and glass tables had gone. 'You aren't living here,' she said.

'I stayed the first night, but after that it began to get to me. I was having to keep all the lights on. Not because of Graham. I don't know what it is, except there's a dead smell about the place. Let me give you what I found and then we'll go.'

He took down several volumes of an encyclopedia, revealing a wall-safe between two bookshelves. 'Where are you living?' Sandy said.

'With my parents while I put myself back together. Would you believe they're trying to fix me up with a nice girl? If I don't move out soon they'll be turning me into a stockbroker like the old man, training it into the city five days a week with my bowler on my lap and my portfolio stuffed with lunch.' He pulled back his cuffs like a safecracker. 'Shush a minute.'

She was glad he felt able to put on a show for her, though she knew it was also for himself. The sunlight was creeping towards the bedroom, where a dressing-gown lay on the bed. The tumblers clicked, and Toby reached into the safe. 'This will mean more to you than it does to me,' he said.

It was a dog-eared red notebook. At the top of the first page Graham had written *Tower of Fear* in elaborate capitals. Each of the next few pages bore a different name and address and telephone number, all scored through lightly. 'I decided against giving it to the police,' Toby said. 'It didn't seem right to have the police upsetting more people for no reason. Graham said most of them were old and frail.'

'They're the ones he contacted about the film.'

'Most of them worked on it, I think. It's not as if any of them would have come here after the film,' he said with a hint of defensiveness. 'At least the police seem to have crossed me off their list of suspects, though they couldn't find any prints.' He closed the safe and walled it up with books. 'Maybe that notebook can prove our friend at the *Daily Friend* wrong.'

'Did you call him?'

'What I called him is what you should be asking, except it's not for your delicate ears. And I wanted to know if he cared to set his reputation against Graham's. He blustered and then he shut up. I expect to read an apology next week.'

'Did you tell him you'd seen the film yourself?'

'I only saw a snippet, old Boris up a tower watching someone being chased across a field at night, and to tell you the absolute truth, I wasn't anxious to see any more. Neither of us wanted to be the one who switched off the lights that night.'

'It must have been some film if it could do that to you both.'

'It must have been the film, yes. What else could it have been?'

She hadn't meant it that way, and his response made her feel unexpectedly nervous. The sunlight had reached the bed now, and she realized that a shadow on the duvet must have been the long shape she'd mistaken for a dressing-gown. Toby was right about the dead smell, she noticed, a faint stench like stale charred pastry that reminded her of the last time she was here. 'I'm glad you thought I should have this,' she said, slipping the notebook into her handbag, and made for the door.

She walked Toby to Victoria Station and left him at the barrier. On her way into the underground she thought he'd followed her, but there was nobody to be seen behind her on the escalator that sailed downward with a faint inconsolable squeal. She sat on a bench on the empty platform, the breaths of oncoming trains stirring the hairs on the back of her neck. She leafed through Graham's notebook, but couldn't concentrate; she found she had to keep glancing along the platform towards the tunnel. Some fault in the mechanism made the train doors reopen after she boarded, as if someone had leapt on at the last moment. The galloping rush of the wheels made her think of a hunt in the dark.

Someone was walking a dog in Queen's Wood. Sandy couldn't see the owner, but she heard the animal in the undergrowth. Once she glimpsed its ribs through a gloomy clump of bushes. Even if it was a greyhound, it looked in need of feeding. She would have shouted to the owner to call it off if its sounds hadn't stayed in the undergrowth as Sandy reached the gate.

Neither Bogart nor Bacall came to greet her as she unlocked her door. They prowled the main room while she examined the notebook, wondering if Graham might have indicated which of his informants he suspected had a copy of the film. Few of the names scattered across Britain and abroad meant anything to her. 'Come on if you're so anxious to return to the wild,' she said to the pacing cats, and took them out for a walk.

Perhaps the dog in the woods was a stray. No wonder the cats stayed close to her. She thought she saw its eyes glistening, but they turned out to be weeds blurred by shadows. 'I think we're safer at home,' she said to the cats, which raced into the house as soon as she opened the door.

She took the notebook with her while she baby-sat for the young accountants on the ground floor. She was beginning to think Toby had meant the book as a plea to her. She had a busy week ahead, editing a play whose male lead had fallen ill before his reaction shots could be filmed. She had made nothing of Graham's notes before the newspaper reviewer responded to Toby's call.

She read the paragraph in the lift at Metropolitan, newsprint soiling her hands. 'Sorry if any of my faithful readers thought I was getting at Graham Nolan last week. A very close male friend of his rang up to shrill at me for saying Nolan could ever have been wrong, but believe me, the last film Nolan tried to find wouldn't have been worth finding even if it existed. Even Karloff and Lugosi didn't want to own up to it, and anyway someone owns the rights, so if Nolan had really had a copy he would have been breaking the law. I say let him rest in peace now. He earned it.'

Sandy tore the column out of the page and placed it in her handbag before dropping the rest of the newspaper in the bin next to her desk. She felt tense all day, even more so when she let herself into her flat. She had time only to get changed and hurry out again to dinner in Chelsea.

When conversation at the far end of the table in the conservatory her friends had built onto their apartment turned to Graham, at first she didn't realize that it had. A headmistress with several combs in her hair was saying, 'Not that I'd wish it on him, but at least he went before he could infect the world with whatever the film was.'

Sandy wouldn't have listened if their hosts hadn't been trying to hush the woman surreptitiously. 'I'm sorry, what was that?' Sandy said.

The headmistress stared at her as though Sandy had entered her office without knocking. 'We were discussing the television fellow, the one who fell off the roof. I was saying that if he didn't want to go that way, perhaps he shouldn't have been so eager to revive horror films. Some of my children watch nothing else.'

Sandy paused to be sure of speaking calmly. 'He told me the film was a classic, and I believe him. Thank you very much for dinner,' she said to her hosts, 'and now if you'll all excuse me, I mean to prove him right.' The incident was almost worth it for the way the headmistress was gaping at her, but Sandy was perspiring with rage by the time she came up from the underground. As soon as she reached home she made the first phone call.

8

She caught sight of Roger as she came into Soho Square. He was marching up and down the pavement with his hands in the pockets of his green corduroys, tossing his broad head to throw back an unruly curl of blond hair and whistling snatches of the score of an Errol Flynn movie. He was as tuneless as anyone she'd ever heard. He began to hum a march, occasionally alluding to the melody, as he passed the office of the British Board of Film Censors. She sidled through a gap in a rank of motorcycles under the trees that shaded the grass, and called, 'Here I am, Roger.'

He choked on whatever note he was about to aim for and clapped a hand over his mouth, and watched her cross the road, his dark keen eyes smiling ruefully. 'It isn't every day you hear that kind of overture before a movie,' he said.

'True enough.'

He pushed his lower lip forward in a rueful grin, then looked more solemn. 'Listen, today's movie isn't the one I was expecting, may not be the kind you go for. Maybe we can go for coffee or a walk and come back here in time to meet your quarry.'

He was talking like someone rushing to finish a tongue-twister. 'What kind of film is it?' she said.

'Some kind of horror comedy. Gross, therefore funny, supposedly. Not Graham's kind of movie at all.'

'We disagreed sometimes. I may like it more than he did, and I want to be sure of catching your colleague.'

'No colleague of mine, let me tell you. Okay, I'll brave the movie if you will. You can hide your face on my shoulder if you need to,' he said, and added 'I mean, don't feel you have to' so hastily that she was immediately fond of him and at her ease with him.

He led her around the square to a film distributor's

offices. On the way to the basement he said, 'Did you happen to bring Graham's notebook?'

'Damn, I knew there was something. My cats were playing up this morning. I don't know what's got into them.'

'I can tell you about some of the guys in the notebook. Harry Manners was a character actor, must be in his seventies. Leslie Tomlinson will be even older. He was a stunt man before there was sound. I should have asked you to read out all the names when you phoned me,' he said as they stepped into the auditorium.

Not only the floor but the walls and the dozens of seats were carpeted in dark red. About twenty people, most of them men, lounged here and there on the seats. A few turned from chatting to greet Roger. 'Presumably we can start now,' someone on the front row grumbled – an old man with a sharp veinous nose, protruding eyes, large ears that reminded Sandy of the handles of a jug. Roger followed her into the second row and nodded at the man's back. 'Len Stilwell of the *Daily Friend*,' he mouthed.

As soon as the film began, Stilwell stooped forward and fumbled in his lap while peering up at the screen, at an actress with enormous breasts. Sandy thought he was adjusting his penis until she realized he was scribbling notes. A vampire with hair slicked back like Lugosi's sank his teeth into the woman's left breast, which deflated with a hiss that sounded disapproving. A man guffawed, then two more, while Roger showed Sandy his gritted teeth.

If there was an audience for the film, Sandy wouldn't like to live next door to them. She laughed when a vampire left his false teeth in his victim's neck, but even that made her feel as if something she was nostalgic for were being spoiled. A tottery doctor called Alzheimer kept missing the vampires' hearts with his stakes, hammering squelchily though he was blinded by squirts of blood, and she sensed Roger's embarrassment on her behalf. When the film tried to convince her that eye-gouging was comic she looked away and patted Roger's arm to cheer him up. 'The End' dripped off the screen at last. 'That's a relief,' she said.

Stilwell turned and looked down his nose at her. 'Just another bloody horror film.'

'Is that what you'll write?'

She meant it conversationally, but he seemed insulted. 'Who are you, may I ask? Where are you from?'

'I'm Sandy Allan from Metropolitan, and this is Roger Stone, who's written a shelf of books about cinema.'

'Well, a few,' Roger said. '*Shower Scenes*, you might know.'

Stilwell raised his nose further. 'Wasn't *Hitler at the Movies: Portrait of a Clown* by you? Some would say that was in decidedly bad taste.'

'Maybe, but not mine. Think about the way the movies have portrayed him.'

'I just write consumer reports, I've no time for cleverness. Nor to argue, I may add,' he said, and turned away.

'Don't go,' Sandy said. 'I wanted to ask you about something you wrote.'

He gazed at her like an indulgent teacher. 'What did you want to know?'

'Why you said what you did about Graham Nolan.'

She could have meant the tribute – her tone was neutral – but at once his ears grew alarmingly red. 'Why should that concern you?'

'I was a very close friend of his.'

'Not another one who thinks he was infallible! He was only a film buff, you know. Good heavens, we can all make mistakes.'

'Except Graham didn't in this case,' Roger interrupted. 'Sandy described to me what his friend saw, and there's no such scene in any other film.'

'You've seen every film ever made, have you?'

'I've seen every Karloff movie, and I mean to see this one. I'm researching a book about American performances in foreign films.'

'Make up your mind whether you mean English or foreign.' Stilwell lowered his voice as reviewers loitered on the stairs to listen. 'Let's just drop the subject, shall we?

None of us are going to prove anything, and you wouldn't be allowed to broadcast the thing even if it existed.'

'I'm not a broadcaster. I'm a film editor, and I mean to prove Graham right.'

'Who let you in? This show was only for the press,' Stilwell said for everyone to hear. 'If I were you I'd give up before I drew too much attention to myself.'

'Seems like you've already done that,' Roger said. 'Just tell us the name you left out of your column and we'll leave you alone.'

'I haven't the least notion what you mean,' Stilwell said, breathing so hard his nostrils whitened.

'You wrote that someone owns the rights to *Tower of Fear*. Who would that be?'

'How should I know?' The look he gave Roger to demonstrate his good faith seemed to rebound on him. 'Don't you stare at me,' he yelled. 'Behave yourself while you're in someone else's country. And as for you, Miss Allan, remember we have laws that protect a man's property.'

'But not to stop me proving the film exists.'

Stilwell swung round, his ears crimson, and stalked upstairs. 'I needn't have said that,' Sandy admitted to Roger.

'I shouldn't have let him needle me, but Christ, what a son of a bitch. I can't stand these guys who don't give a shit for what they write about and look down on anyone who does. And for someone like that to set himself up as more informed than Graham when Graham can't even answer back . . .' He slapped his fist with his palm and grinned apologetically at her. 'You'll be thinking I care too much.'

'Not at all,' Sandy said, though she had been a little disconcerted by the vehemence of his reaction, 'and I thought you performed admirably. We can always think of what we should have said, but there's never a retake. Let's have a coffee before I head back to work.'

Leaving Soho Square, they walked past the Pillars of Hercules, under the arch that was thick as a room behind Foyle's, and sat at a table outside Break for the Border.

'You were saying on the phone you helped Graham find out about the film,' Sandy prompted.

'In a small way only. I talked to some people.'

'Anyone I've heard of?'

'Jack Nicholson.' He fell silent while their waitress enthused about the actor, and when she moved away he said, 'We had a fine time partying, reminded me of my own easy rider days, but he couldn't tell me much. Except when he and Boris were working on *The Raven* they were talking about how kids would get to see it in America but here nobody younger than sixteen could, and Boris said there was a film he'd made he was quite glad to see suppressed.'

'Meaning *Tower of Fear*.'

'I guess. Then I talked to Ed Wood. Angora Love.'

'He liked to dress up in women's sweaters.'

'Right, and made a film about it that Lugosi narrated. Maybe you know Lugosi's doctor said Lugosi ended up on morphine because he used to be so anxious. Wood told me Bela once admitted to him that it was a movie he made in England that caused him the most grief. Now, he might just have resented it because it virtually got him barred from England for the rest of his career, but I talked to Peter Bogdanovich about it and he thought that wasn't the whole story.'

'He asked Karloff about it?'

'While they were filming *Targets*, yes. Bogdanovich interviewing Karloff sounds like a contest for who would be more of a gentleman, and he didn't get much out of him about this film except that he really didn't want to talk about it at all or even about the director, Giles Spence. I don't know if you realize Spence died the week they finished shooting, in a car accident somewhere up north.'

A breeze chased through the passage outside the restaurant, bearing a smell of bread rolls from the kitchen, and made Sandy shiver. 'I'm beginning to realize how little I do know about the film. What do you think it was about it that upset so many people?'

'It may just have come at the wrong time. There was

some kind of a debate in your Houses of Parliament that I keep meaning to check out. That's me, Slow and Steady Stone, except forget the steady part, more like easily diverted. Christ, I wish I'd gone to Graham's that night when he invited me. I might have been there in time.'

'I know how you feel.'

'Not that I'd have been able to do any better than you,' he said, so hastily that she leaned over the table and gave him a kiss. 'Uh, thanks,' he stammered.

'That was just to let you know you needn't be afraid I won't know what you mean.'

'Well, good. Me too. I mean,' he said, and gave up when she smiled at him.

'I'll have to be heading back in a few minutes. I wanted to ask if you've any idea what the film was about.'

'According to Graham, Karloff plays an aristocrat who owns some kind of haunted land, and Lugosi comes to England after his brother-in-law has been killed on the land. Usually it's the monster which is foreign, some kind of invader – think of Dracula. Spence may have stirred up some hostility by making the monster English, especially just before the war.'

'Was that what the original story was about?'

' "The Lofty Place"? Maybe. I understand it's almost as rare as the movie.'

A chilly breeze nuzzled her ankles, and she stood up. 'I must go.'

He accompanied her along Oxford Street and hesitated in the midst of the crowd at Oxford Circus. 'Did you want to dictate Graham's notes to me or maybe bring them round to my place?'

'Best offer I've had for weeks. How does Thursday evening sound?'

'Great.'

'I'll call you before then,' she said, and watched him down the steps into the underground.

When Lezli told her she looked pleased with herself, she wondered why she didn't feel calmer. It must be that she felt pursued by a pack of unanswered questions. Even walking home through Queen's Wood she felt tense, especially when she heard a child wailing in the gloom. The sound stayed ahead of her, and when she reached the house she realized she had been hearing the accountants' little girl. 'Home now,' her mother said as she wheeled her into the hall.

'He wasn't ill, pet,' her father reassured her. 'He was just an old gentleman having a lie down on the grass.'

His wink at Sandy presumably meant the man had been a tramp. She squatted by the pushchair and tickled the little girl under the chin until she had to smile, then she went upstairs, thinking that she wouldn't have expected the child to be so easily upset. That was children for you, she supposed, and she had enough to ponder. Whatever the child had seen, it had nothing to do with her or with the film.

9

He would feel safer once he drove through the wood. The only figures he could see in the fields around him were scarecrows, and there wasn't even a bird in the vast indifferent sky, yet he felt watched. If anyone were following him along the road, from the town or the great house beyond it, he would be able to spot them several hundred yards away. It was just his imagination that was troubling him, his damned imagination which had brought him here in the first place and which he was beginning to feel was almost more trouble than it was worth.

He'd thought last time he had got the better of his enemies when he'd sneaked down under the chapel, but could that have done himself and his collaborators some harm? He didn't understand how, especially since today his enemies had seemed genuinely unaware of what he had been suffering. Could he have worsened his situation by coming back here by himself?

He couldn't have brought anyone with him. However nervous and persecuted he felt, he didn't want anyone to realize what he'd done until it was out in the open, incapable of being suppressed. Nor could his feelings trap him here, he vowed, striking the horn to scare away his fears and proclaim that he was coming. Nothing but the by-products of his imagination could be waiting in the wood to head him off. As he heeled the accelerator he felt unexpectedly brave, as though he were spurring a steed into danger.

The shadow of the trees fell on him, a greenish shadow damp and chill as moss. Trees crowded about the road as it wound into a hollow and wormed upward again towards the sunlight. Perhaps the sun had gone behind a cloud, for the hollow seemed darker than it had earlier. As well as the dimness, a smell of earth made him feel buried until the car swung towards the promise of daylight ahead.

As the car reached a brief straight stretch of road beyond the first curve, he looked back. Nothing was following him except the smell of turned earth, though why should that be following him? Down here it seemed ominous, perhaps because of the hint of something more unpleasant underlying it, and the shadows that dodged between the trees, just beyond the focus of his vision as he glanced at the road ahead. The way was clear. He had time for one more backward glance before the next curve, to reassure himself that the shadows were only shadows. He turned his head and saw a figure running after him on all fours along the dim road, a thin shape moving faster than the car.

Shock wrenched his head round further, sending a blaze of pain through his neck. His feet jerked wildly on the pedals, and the car lurched faster. For a moment – for too long – he was unable to look away from his pursuer. He twisted round to see where he was going just as the car swerved across the road. As he stamped on the brake, the car smashed into a tree.

The impact shattered the windscreen and crumpled the bonnet like tin, but he was gripping the wheel so hard in his panic that he wasn't flung out of the car. Glass showered his neck and chest. When he tried to brush away the fragments he found he couldn't use his hands, which felt like bruises swelling hugely at the ends of his broken wrists. He couldn't use them to let himself out of the vehicle before it burst into flames as he feared it was about to. He jammed one knee under the door handle and shoved, and the door fell open so quickly that he almost sprawled headlong in the undergrowth.

He staggered alongside the car towards the road, every movement discovering new bruises and injuries that might be worse. The pain, and the shock of the crash, had almost closed his mind down. The wood seemed both darker and remote from him. All he knew was that he needed help, and the nearest place to find it was the inn he had passed on his way from the town to the wood.

Either he'd forgotten what had caused the crash or his mind was refusing to accept it. The accident, and the way it had wrecked his body, was all he could try to cope with. When the figure reared up to meet him from behind the car, his mind was as unable to grasp it as his body was incapable of defending itself. He stood there almost passively, gazing at a face that had no right to be called one, while the long blackened fingernails reached for his throat and finished what the fragments of glass had begun.

10

Sandy ate dinner with Graham's notebook propped in front of her. Halfway through the Greek salad she remembered what he'd told her at her party that had filled all her rooms and almost driven out the cats. 'The hunt's begun,' he'd said, 'and I can thank one of your profession.' He'd tracked down the assistant editor on *Tower of Fear*. The editor's name was Norman Ross, she remembered now, and there it was on the second page of the notebook.

He lived outside Lincoln. She took the phone to the window seat and gazed down at the dark that was climbing the trees. Bogart and Bacall prowled the far side of the room while she tried to think of her best approach. 'You aren't helping,' she informed them, and buttoned the number.

The bell sounded unreal, more like a recording. A child's voice interrupted it and gabbled the number. 'Who's there?'

'May I speak to Norman Ross?'

The receiver was dropped with a clatter. 'It's a lady for Grandpa.'

What Sandy guessed was a large family greeted this with ribald encouragement, in the midst of which a man said, '*Never* drop the phone like that.' Seconds later he was at the mouthpiece. 'Who's speaking, please?'

'I'm a friend and colleague of Graham Nolan's.'

'Sorry, doesn't mean a thing.'

'This is Mr Ross, is it?'

'It is, yes,' he said as if she had threatened his manhood. 'What are you selling?'

'I'm buying,' she said, and wondered how much might be involved: presumably one of the film archives would pay. 'I wanted to ask you about a film you worked on.'

'Which film?'

'The one with Karloff and Lugosi.'

'That thing again?' His response was so sharp it made the microphone buzz waspishly. 'Yes, I know who your friend was now. You're wasting your time, I'm afraid. My father isn't well, and in any case he wouldn't be able to help.'

Because of his irritability she had assumed he was the old man. 'He did help Graham Nolan, I believe. All I want is to ask your father what he told Graham. I can't ask him, you see. He was killed.'

'That's most regrettable, but still the answer's no. I won't have my father troubled. He's nervous enough as it is.'

'I'm a film editor too. Perhaps when he's feeling better we could at least talk about his work.'

'I doubt he would want to.'

'May I give you my number in case he changes his mind?'

'If you must,' he said, and interrupted her as soon as she had said it and her name. 'I wish you people would let this wretched film stay buried. Isn't there already enough horror in the world?'

If his father had overheard that, she hoped he disagreed. 'Do settle down,' she pleaded with the cats. She must stop saying Graham had been killed; she had seen him jump. She tried some more early entries in the notebook, but these old folk seemed to go to bed early, and the retirement home in Birmingham was unobtainable. She felt dissatisfied, on edge. Placing the phone well out of reach, she read Umberto Eco until she was tired enough for bed.

In the middle of the night she had to grope her way to the toilet, half asleep. She was in bed again before she realized that she had been creeping through her own rooms as if she mustn't let herself be heard. She assumed she had still been in a dream, though one that she couldn't remember. The stealthy creaking of the trees beyond her window lulled her to sleep.

The more she knew about the people Graham had approached, the easier it ought to be for her to get something out of them. In the morning she called Roger and read him all the names.

'Were you still thinking of visiting?' he said, sounding ready to be disappointed.

'Absolutely.'

'Can you stand a take-out meal if it's with some good wine?'

'I hope you aren't planning to get me drunk.'

'No, not at all,' he said, so solemnly that she had to make sure he knew she was teasing him.

She was still unable to raise any numbers from Graham's book. When she took the cats out they stayed together on the paths. Once she faltered, thinking that she saw a pair of eyes watching from among a knot of roots: pale eyes, empty of pupils. They were toadstools, she realized when she ventured closer. She kicked them to pieces, releasing a doughy smell.

She thought she knew what made her feel eyed that night – not that it was worth bothering about, she told herself. Nevertheless she rose early to buy the *Daily Friend*, and turned past the latest diatribe against Enoch's Army to Stilwell's film review.

'Spoofy schlock that tries to shock but turns out more yucky than yuk-yuk' was his comment on the vampire film. 'Worse news is another friend of Graham Nolan's is trying to dig up the film that never was. She cuts films for Metropolitan, so I shouldn't think any film buff would let her have it even if it existed, but advertisers might think their money could be spent on more worthwhile things. As far as this column's concerned, the subject is now closed.'

She was alive to defend herself, unlike Graham. All the same, she was dismayed to notice how many people in the underground were reading the *Friend*. At least nobody at Metropolitan seemed to be. The day proved too busy to let her call Stilwell or his editor, and in any case what was the use? Tracking down the film was the way to make Stilwell eat his words.

There was research she could do on her way to Roger's.

During one of her Sunday afternoon strolls around her district she'd noticed a fantasy bookshop on Holloway Road. She went straight from work.

The shop felt like stepping back into the fifties. Bookshelves of various designs held magazines and paperbacks that grew paler towards the window. An intense young man who looked as if he'd starved himself to buy a handful of the rarities stored out of reach of the sunlight pushed past her and left her alone with the stocky Scottish proprietor. 'Nearly closing,' the proprietor said.

'Do you have a Victorian ghost story called "The Lofty Place"?'

His lanky partner came out of a back room, and both men laughed politely. 'I wish we had,' the Scotsman said. 'That'd buy us a few beers.'

'It's a legend,' his partner said. 'It only ever appeared in one book, more's the pity. Conan Doyle admired it, so did Montague Summers.'

'Who was the last one?' Sandy said.

'A clergyman friend of Aleister Crowley's, and an anthologist.' The lanky man went to the shelves and selected a fat book printed 12/6 on its yellow jacket. Among the stories cited in Summers' introduction but not included in the anthology was 'The Lofty Place' by F. X. Faversham, 'in which a titled British family seeks to build a God-like vantage but is punished down the generations for its hubris, and which may be favourably compared to Mr Blackwood in its sense of landscape, and touches on the darker sources of English tradition.' None of that seemed to help. 'Can I leave you my number in case you find a copy?' Sandy said.

'If you like, but we've never seen one in all our years of bookselling. Maybe the darker sources of English tradition don't like to be touched.'

She gathered the Scotsman was joking, since his partner chortled. She left her number with them and made her way along Holloway Road into Islington. Upper Street and some of the side roads were dug up, smelling of uncovered earth, but the area seemed more gentrified than ever. A Jaguar was parked at the corner of the street off which Roger lived in stables converted into flats.

Cobblestones led under an arch and past a long communal garden. Roger's flat was halfway along, opposite a path boxed in by shrubs. She'd hardly rung the bell when he opened the door. He was struggling to unbutton the collar of his shirt, until she did it for him. 'Excuse the mess,' he mumbled.

In fact the main room, which turned into a dining kitchen on the far side of a counter, was compact and almost obsessively neat. Shelves on one side of the electric fire held books, their twins held video cassettes. Two identical armchairs faced the television, which stood in front of a wall papered with posters for silent films. Roger snatched a necktie off the floor, and she realized that had been the mess. He must have been undecided how to dress for her. 'You look smart,' he said.

'This is just what I wear for work,' she said, slipping off her denim jacket.

'Well, you always do.'

He was in the bedroom, hanging up his tie, moving rapidly as if he could outrun his awkwardness. 'I brought some Australian wine for you to try,' she said.

'I got Californian. Once you wouldn't have drunk either, right? Now they've earned their reputations.' He opened her bottle and filled their glasses. 'Here's to reputations.'

'Reputations. Let's hope mine survives.'

'Any reason why it shouldn't?'

'I can take care of myself, don't worry,' she said smiling. 'I meant Stilwell's little sally in the newspaper today.'

'How come? He didn't say anything about you.'

'He certainly did,' Sandy said, grabbing her handbag.

Roger frowned at the torn page and then rescued his copy of the paper from the kitchen bin, leafing gingerly through the stained pages until he found Stilwell's piece. 'See, they've edited that out of the later edition. Not so many people will have read that garbage about you after all.'

'Why would it have been edited?'

'Maybe he had second thoughts.'

'Maybe,' she said, but she felt dissatisfied. Roger interrupted her speculations. 'Take a look at the menu and I'll summon the feast,' he said.

Dinner arrived twenty minutes later, and they moved to the far side of the counter, the only area of the flat which didn't refer in some way to the cinema. 'You really care about films, don't you?' she said.

'Don't you?'

'Of course, when I'm working on them. But it's Graham's name I want to save more than this film.'

'I guess quite a few people would be happy if you were to save both. I know I would,' he added to soften any hint of rebuke.

'Tell me about yourself.'

'What do you want to hear? Grew up with the ambition to do something for Disney, and I got to play a mouse at Disneyland one summer while I was at UCLA. A hundred in the shade some days, and kids tromping on my feet while they had their picture taken, and I could have used some Disney animation by the end of the day myself. Next year I did movie reviews for a UCLA magazine, only I got barred from the trade shows because there was one guy who always came in after the movie had begun and one time I told him the male lead's girlfriend had just been murdered, so he reviewed it as an understated suspense story. Actually, it played better that way.'

'So that was how you got into films.'

'Well, more like hung around the edge of the frame. I graduated from UCLA and then I toured Hollywood with three unfilmed scripts. Lots of taking lunches and some invitations to try writing something else, and nearly a couple of options. Then a friend of mine landed me a continuity job on an independent movie, and one job led to another, and that's how I got to work with Orson Welles on his last film.'

He was talking at full speed, no longer aware of the curl

58

wagging over his forehead as enthusiasm carried him out of reach of his self-consciousness. 'Which you wrote your first book about,' she said.

'I thought someone should. It isn't every day you get to watch a genius at work. And then the book did so well the publishers came to me for another, and over a particularly drunken lunch I said I'd write a book about shower scenes in the movies.'

'A whole book?'

'Yeah, that's what *I* thought when I sobered up. So I wrote about persistent images in the movies, starting with how if you don't end up dead in any shower you take since *Psycho* you can guarantee someone will leap in pretending to be the monster.'

'I'm waiting for the person in the shower to turn the heat up all the way and let him have it in the face.'

'I wish I'd known you then, I'd have used that. So I wrote about how if you're shown a newspaper headline in a movie, chances are the story underneath is about something else entirely.'

'Or whenever anyone walks past someone reading a newspaper you know the one who's reading will follow them.'

'Or whenever someone's reading a book they always hold it as if they're advertising the cover.'

'Or whenever someone talking on the phone is cut off they always jiggle the rest as if that will somehow bring the call back.'

'Or if someone refuses at the top of their voice to do something the next thing you'll see is them doing it. Like, you know, a woman saying on no account will she stay the night.'

'Why, have you had that problem?'

'Well, you know, now and then, mostly then, I guess.' He reached for the Californian Chablis and stared hard at her glass while he filled it. 'That wasn't meant to be a sly pass just now, you understand.'

'I didn't think it was sly.'

'Good, okay. So you see another reason I was pissed at

Stilwell. I believe you can both be serious about movies and have fun speculating about ways to read them. Say, listen, I nearly forgot,' he said, and stood up so quickly she felt rebuffed. 'I got these for you.'

They were photocopies of entries in reference books for three of the names from Graham's notebook. 'These look pretty old,' she said.

'The British Film Institute was the only place that had them. None of these guys worked in movies very long after they made *Tower of Fear*.'

'But they would only have been young then. Why was that, do you think?'

'Another mystery for you to solve. Or for us, if you like.'

'I'd be glad of any help.'

'Fine. Well, I think I've shown you all I have to offer. Maybe you can use a coffee?'

'I wouldn't mind.' If he didn't care enough to make a move, nor did she. Maybe he'd seen too many films to be able to act spontaneously in real life. She drank the coffee stiffly, feeling frustratingly English and prim, and said, 'Thanks for the evening. I enjoyed it and I learned a few things.'

'Let's stay in touch,' he said, 'for Graham's sake,' and his pause made her so breathless it was infuriating, all the more so because she couldn't tell whether or not he intended it to mean anything. She thought it unwise to kiss him goodnight: she patted his cheek on her way out instead.

After the compactness of the flat, the vastness of the sky, blinking minutely down at her, came as a shock. His closing door took in the light from his hallway; darkness crouched forward on the path between the shrubs. Echoes dogged her as she hurried across the cobblestones. The furniture that sat outside shops in the daytime had been locked away; chairs perched on shadowy chairs beyond plate glass. As she made for her platform at Highbury & Islington, she glimpsed a man who must be very drunk further along the tiled ramp, crawling upwards to ground level. A train with a few snoozers propped in it took her to Highgate, and she jogged up Muswell Hill. She came in sight of home, and screwed up her eyes. She didn't recall leaving the top of the window of the main room open so wide.

The strip of darkness might be a shadow. High up in the house next to hers, a dog was barking as if it might continue until it lost its voice. She let herself into her building and ran upstairs. The time-switch popped out of its socket as she scraped her key into her lock, and the night leapt through the skylight at her. She stuck her hand into the dark and groped for the switch in her hall. Her fingernails scratched the plastic, the button snapped down.

She'd thought the apprehension she had felt as the time-switch left her in the dark would vanish once she switched on her own light, but the silence of the rooms seemed ominously unfamiliar. She eased the door shut, holding the knob of the latch between finger and thumb, and dug out of her handbag the whistle that was supposed to deafen any attacker. She pointed it ahead of her, finger twitching on the button, as she tiptoed along the hall.

She pushed open the bathroom door and tugged the light-cord just in time to see a movement so small it seemed stealthy. It was a drop of water losing its grip on the bathroom tap. She crept into her bedroom, where the reflection of the shaded lamp sprang into the gap between the curtains. She tiptoed down the hall to the door of the main room and flung it open, punched the light-switch, levelled the tube at the room.

A smell made her hesitate on the threshold, a faint stench reminiscent of stale food. Papers and the contents of her waste-paper basket were strewn around the couch: the cats had been having a fine time, apparently. The window in the gable end was open wider than she had left it. She tiptoed quickly to the kitchen doorway. Either the smell had lodged in her nostrils or it was stronger in the kitchen. The fluorescent tube jerked alight. The only food to be seen was in the two bowls on the floor – but where were the cats?

'Bogart,' she called, 'Bac – ' and drew a breath that made

her teeth ache. Graham's notebook, which she had left on the couch, lay on the carpet beneath the open window, or at least the cover did. The remains of the pages, shredded and chewed, were scattered over the floor.

Her fists clenched, almost setting off the whistle until she threw it on the couch. 'You little buggers,' she whispered, 'where are you hiding? Come out or I – ' She glared at the window, and saw that the top of the sash was marked by claws that had scraped off paint. She shoved the lower sash up and leaned out, her shadow lurching across the lit tree-tops as she tried to see past them into the gloom. She was still straining her eyes when the doorbell rang.

She dashed along the hall and slapped the button of the intercom. 'Yes? What?'

'I'm not disturbing you, am I? I saw your light go on.'

She vaguely recognized the man's voice. 'Who is this?'

'I live across the road. We've said good morning. I drive the Rover.'

'Oh yes, all right,' she said, furiously impatient, mostly with herself. 'Well?'

'You're the lady with the cats.'

Something in his tone made her catch her breath. 'Yes?'

'Do you mind coming down? I'd rather not – you know.'

She suspected that she did. She went downstairs apprehensively and opened the front door. He was tall and in his forties, and already pregnant with beer. He was rubbing his hands back over his hair so hard it tugged his forehead smooth. 'Sorry,' he said at once. 'I was on the main road, not doing more than the limit, honestly. They ran out in front of me. I'd have had a bus up my rear if I'd braked. I found the address on the collars and I didn't know if you'd want to – There you are, anyway.'

She thought he was staring at his toes, embarrassed by the threat of her reaction, until she saw that he was eyeing what he'd laid neatly on the doorstep: two plastic bags full of fur and blood.

11

The cat food must have been tainted, she thought. She'd
smelled it in her rooms, the smell of what had driven the
cats mad. The owner of the Rover had crossed the street
now, walking slowly as if that were apologetic or respectful,
leaving her to gaze at the bags. She didn't think she could
bear to open them. She carried them to the back garden
and took a spade out of the communal shed.

She dug for almost an hour in her patch of flowerbed
before she was convinced the hole was deep enough to
keep the bodies safe. The stray dog might still be roaming
Queen's Wood, and it might try to dig up the grave. She
peered through the railings whenever shadows stirred. Too
many bunches of roots appeared to be crouching bonily,
but she could never catch sight of a watcher, only flowers
shifting in the dark. Every time she peered she had to dab
at her eyes.

At last she finished digging. Holding each bag at both
ends, so as not to feel how broken the cats were, she laid
the bodies in the trench. 'Goodbye,' she said, 'you rest
now.' She gazed down at the glint of plastic, then she
replaced the disinterred soil gently and patted it smooth.
'Look after each other,' she said, and eventually went back
into the house.

The smell was gone from her silent rooms. She went
down on all fours to the feeding bowls, but could find no
trace of it there. Nevertheless she found the empty tin and
scraped the remains into it to be analysed, then she sat on
the bed and wept for a while. Afterwards she picked up the
fragments of Graham's notebook, but they were indecipher-
able. She remembered most of the details, she told herself,
not just the names, except that her head was aching too
badly at the moment for her to recall. Her nostrils felt

stuffed with rust. She went to bed so as to close her aching eyes.

When she managed to sleep she kept wakening convinced that the cats were near her. Remembering why they weren't made her feel hollow and frail. Once she dreamed that one of them was outside the window of the main room. She saw a thin lithe shape leap from a treetop and grasp the sash, dragging it down, and awoke with a cry that left her heart quaking.

In the morning she felt so empty that she ached. Why couldn't she have stayed at home last night instead of wasting time on her frustrating visit to Roger? Everything seemed meaningless, no longer worth her trouble, and that frightened her. On the underground she hugged the carrier bag that contained the tin of cat food and clenched her fist on the overhead strap.

The presenter of the consumer advice programme was Piers Falconer. On screen he wore a permanent concerned frown, but when she looked into his office his large round face was almost blandly welcoming. He frowned when he heard her story, and took the tin from her. 'I'll send it in today for analysis and let you know the outcome the moment I hear.'

She went upstairs and tried to interest herself in editing a tape shot at a football match, where spectators attacked the away team as they came on to the pitch. The people around her left her alone when she kept answering them monosyllabically, until Lezli came looking for her. 'Phone for you.'

'Sandra? We've been meaning to call you. How are you? Still enjoying your work?'

It was her father. His voice made her feel unexpectedly homesick for the house in Mossley Hill, the log fires he would light as soon as the winds off Liverpool Bay turned chilly, the long evenings when she had been able to discuss all her adolescent problems without holding anything back. Homesickness solved nothing – her parents didn't even live there now – and she didn't want him to know how upset she was when, at that distance, it would only make him feel helpless. 'Oh, pretty well,' she said.

'We heard that your friend died. We remembered how fond you said you were of him, how he helped get you known and so forth.'

She wasn't quite sure of his tone. 'Graham and I had a lot of respect for each other.'

'Well, there's nothing wrong with that. We tried to bring you up to appreciate all kinds of people, within certain limits.' He cleared his throat and made her think of the pipe he smoked, whose smell had made Bogart and Bacall restless when he and her mother had stayed overnight. 'A neighbour pointed out a comment in the paper to us just yesterday. The person searching for the film your friend claimed he found – that isn't you, is it?'

'Yes it is. Why?'

'For your mother's sake, Sandra, I hope you'll leave it alone.'

'Because of what the paper said about it, you mean? I've met the man who wrote that and he's harmless, don't worry.'

'But we do. Surely an old film isn't worth the fuss.'

'It might be, and Graham's reputation is. You wouldn't want me to let a friend down.'

'Time always confirms the reputations of the deserving. Think of Bach. Why risk your own good name? If the film was objectionable when it was made it may still be, if it even exists. Neither your mother nor I have heard of it, though it's the kind of thing we would have lapped up before the war changed all that. You'll give it up, won't you? Let it rest, and then your mother can.'

'Does Mother know you're phoning?'

'She won't even admit she's anxious, but I know her as well as I know you.'

'Then you know you brought me up to do what I thought was right even if you disagreed.'

'How can this be right – some trash with two old hams in it? What can be right about a horror film?' He sounded

65

desperate with realizing she'd outgrown him. 'Won't you promise?'

'Daddy, I'm sorry, but I already have.'

'God help you then,' he said heavily, and rang off.

She was staring at the speechless lump of plastic in her hand and feeling as if guilt were gathering as solidly inside her – guilt at leaving him anxious, at reminding him that she and her mother understood each other more than he often did, even at being almost as upset about her cats as she had been by Graham's death – when Lezli murmured, 'Boswell wants to see you.'

Emma Boswell was Deputy Programme Controller. 'I can do without being told how much use I am,' Sandy said.

'I don't know if that's what she wants. She sounded a bit guarded.'

'I wish I were,' Sandy said, and trudged to the lift, trying to think how to do better with the tape of the football match. When the doors let her out she walked automatically down the corridor to Boswell's outer office. Two newsmen were sitting at opposite ends of one of the unyielding couches, arguing about Enoch's Army. 'We need an interview with Enoch Hill before the story goes stale on us,' one said.

'We've tried, and not only us. He won't be filmed, don't ask me why, even to put his side of things.'

'We've committed too many resources to the documentary to kill it now. His father's a banker, isn't he? Has anyone gone after him?'

'Good God,' Sandy cried, 'can't anyone choose not to be filmed? Isn't there anything else to life?'

They stared at her as if she had betrayed them or herself, and Boswell's secretary told her, 'Ms Boswell will see you now.'

Sandy must have been audible through the secretary's intercom, and Boswell's plump yet delicate face was quizzical. She indicated a chair with a gesture like a conductor muting an orchestra, and leaned forward. 'Tea for two,' she said, and switched off the intercom. 'Some trouble outside?'

Sandy refused to talk to the top of her head or even to

the silver fingernails she was running through her greying hair. When Boswell looked up, Sandy responded, 'Just over invasion of privacy.'

'A difficult decision sometimes, but a decision professionals have to make. Is it your privacy you feel is being invaded?'

'Should it be?'

'Or did you actually talk to the newspaper?'

'I met the film reviewer once and we had an argument, that's all.'

'You seem prone to those currently. I'm sure you know what I'm really asking. Did you tell him you were hunting for this film on our behalf?'

'I didn't, no. He made that up. He obviously wants to make things difficult for me.'

'Why should he want to do that?' There was a hint of bedside manner in Boswell's voice. 'You do appreciate you mustn't claim to be doing research you aren't authorized to do, or we'll have the unions complaining. Let's say it slipped out in the heat of your argument with the reviewer and forget about it. I'm sure the world already has. In any case, it doesn't sound the kind of film we'd want to transmit.'

'Graham would have.'

'You miss him, don't you?'

'Especially when he can't defend himself.'

Boswell held up a hand as if to forestall any more answers she would rather not hear. 'I wonder if we've made enough allowance for your being there when he died. I shouldn't like it to affect your work. Ah, the tea.'

When her secretary had left the tray and closed the door, Boswell brought Sandy a cup. 'I wasn't implying your work has been suffering. I feel you haven't let yourself live through what you saw, you haven't let it get to you, which means it's still there inside you, waiting.'

Sandy felt almost suffocated by Boswell's need to comfort her. 'Maybe,' she mumbled, and sat back, away from the other woman, who went back to her desk as if nothing had been meant to happen. 'What do you think you could do with a couple of weeks off?' Boswell said.

'Try and clear Graham's name.'

Boswell sighed. 'On whose behalf?'

'His and mine, if nobody else cares.'

'I want you to understand that if there's even a suggestion that you're acting for us it will be viewed extremely seriously. I can't forbid what you do as a private individual. I trust it's what you need, that's all.'

She gazed at Sandy, who sipped her tea, telling herself that she wouldn't be forced to reply or even to drink faster. 'Thanks for being understanding,' Sandy said, and stood up. 'When shall I take the time off?'

'Start now, on full pay.' Sandy was at the door when Boswell added, 'I hope you liked the tea.'

'A lot,' Sandy said, and the newsmen stared at her. She let her face relax into a grin. She felt as if she'd just survived an interview with a headmistress and been given a holiday into the bargain – but it wouldn't be a holiday, she promised herself.

12

She told Piers Falconer and Lezli she was leaving, and then she ran across to the park and sat on a bench. A glinting knife crossed the whitish sky with a sound like a proposal of thunder. She dug an electricity bill out of her handbag and scribbled on the envelope all the names she could remember from Graham's notebook. Several brought names of towns with them, but those were as much as she could recall of the addresses. Perhaps more details would return to her once she stopped straining to retrieve them. A dog or a tramp was lying down behind a nearby clump of bushes, and kept distracting her. She went back to Metropolitan and downstairs to the switchboard room.

The switchboard clicked like restless claws while she leafed through various British telephone directories. She found all the names on her list, in some cases by remembering the full addresses once she saw them in the directory. She was tempted to make the first call at once, but she didn't want to antagonize Boswell. She called from a wine bar in Wigmore Street instead.

The only London number was for a Walter Trantom of Chiswick. She carried her glass of lager to an oaken alcove that enshrined a white telephone, and dialled the number. As soon as the ringing was answered, the shouts of the drinkers around her were joined by a huge blurred distant roar. Sandy pressed her free hand over her free ear. 'Is Mr Trantom there?'

'It's for Wally. A woman for Wally,' the man yelled, and he and several others chortled. What sounded like a giant door slid back and let out another male voice, this one high and stumbling higher. 'Er who, er who, er who's there?'

Sandy knew there must be smothered mirth behind him.

'Mr Trantom?' she said as gently as the hubbub would allow. 'Did you know Graham Nolan, by any chance?'

'Graham er, oh yes. Who?'

'I believe you may have been some help to him.'

'I hope,' Trantom said, and turned wary. 'I mean to say, I don't know. Who says?'

'I'm a friend of Graham's. Sandy Allan. He used to show me the films he found.'

'Did you see the horror film?'

His lurch into enthusiasm was as sudden as his wariness had been. 'No, but he told me about it,' Sandy said, 'and I'm looking for it now.'

'You're a friend of his from where he worked, aren't you?'

So Trantom had read about her. 'This has nothing to do with where we worked, this is for him and me.'

'So what's it got to do with me? I can't talk long, I've left a car up in the air.'

'I thought you might be able to give me a lead, but I take it – '

'No, wait. I should meet you, and there's someone else who'd want to. Can you tonight?'

'If you're free, I am.'

'I'm free all right,' he said with a nervous giggle, and gave her an address in Chiswick as one of his workmates whistled meaningfully. 'About eight,' Trantom said, and rang off.

Chiswick was on the same side of the river as her flat, but as distant as half of the Northern line added to half of the District. Driving tonight would give her more freedom and more control, and less time to be distracted. As she waited for the train at Marble Arch, she thought she saw a workman in the dark between the token lamps in the tunnel beyond the platform. It must be something else entirely, for even if any workman was that thin, he wouldn't keep so still.

The cats' grave was untouched. All the same, she didn't like to leave it so unprotected while she searched for the film. A broken flagstone from the garden path was leaning against the house. She dragged it to the flowerbed, where it landed with a moist thud which, she told herself quickly, didn't remind her of anything. It was like a horror film, she preferred to think, some film in which they laid weights on the earth to make sure the dead couldn't rise. 'Nobody can touch you,' she whispered.

She played a Billie Holliday album while she made herself coffee. When the music and the coffee were finished she sat in the window seat, the sunlit window warm against her back, and set about calling the numbers she'd listed. The first was for Harry Manners, less than an hour's drive away. His phone rang twice, and a voice boomed, 'Aye?'

'Harry Manners?'

'Present.'

'You're the actor?'

'So long as I'm out of my casket I am, and then I'll hope for a curtain call. To what do I owe the pleasure of hearing such a sweet young voice?'

'I'm trying to locate a film you appeared in,' Sandy said, and held her breath.

'Do you say so? Well, you brighten my day. I must be entitled to a few more performances as long as I'm still remembered. Are you here in Hatfield? Will you dine with me?'

'I'm busy in London tonight, I'm afraid.'

'Lunch tomorrow? Tell me which picture it is and I'll sort out whatever I have.'

'The one with Karloff and Lugosi.'

'Ah, those old troupers. What was the name of it? *Tower of Fear*? By all means come. I've something that will interest you.'

He gave her directions to where he lived and made her promise not to let him down. His eagerness was infectious, and she made two more calls that proved encouraging. An antique dealer in Newark said that his uncle had been a film cameraman before the second world war, and that though he was walking by the canal just now he would

71

probably be pleased to talk to her. The retirement home in Birmingham where the stunt man lived had had its phone repaired, and the receptionist expected that Leslie Tomlinson would talk. At last, Sandy thought, a day when things began to go right for her. Even the Toyota started first time, though she hadn't driven for weeks.

She drove with the windows down, to feel the breath of the reddening sky on her face, and came off the urban motorway near Gunnersbury Park. Walter Trantom lived in a box of flats on Chiswick High Road. Its dozens of identical rectangular panes appeared to be emitting the blurred roar she'd heard when she had spoken to him – the roar of the motorway beyond. As she locked the car, two youths with Dobermans strutted by, jerking their thighs at the air. A green light's worth of cars sped past in the direction of the airport, and their individual notes were swallowed by the monotonous roar of the landscape.

Sandy stepped over trodden chips and hamburger cartons in the entrance to the flats, and rang the bell for Trantom. The intercom mumbled at her, its words almost indistinguishable because of the remains of a cheeseburger that had been stuffed into the grille. 'Sandy Allan,' she said, having poked the answer button gingerly with one fingernail, and peered at the entrance hall through safety glass smeared with ketchup. The man who plodded down the unlit concrete stairs was almost at the glass before she saw his face.

Even allowing for the way telephones shrank voices, he hadn't sounded nearly so large. He was at least a head taller than Sandy, and twice as broad. He wore faded green check trousers and a frayed purple cardigan, spectacles poking out of the torn breast pocket. He opened a crack between the door and the frame and lowered his balding head towards it, blinking fiercely. 'Who, er who did you say?' he demanded.

She could see pimples under the stripes of mousy hair. 'Sandy Allan. We said eight o'clock.'

'It's only five to,' he said inaccurately, glancing at his wristwatch. It had string in place of a strap. He dragged his cuff down as if he'd exposed too much of himself to her, and widened his eyes to stop them blinking. 'How about some proof?'

When she turned her digital watch towards him, he snorted like a horse. 'Not the time. Who you are.'

She dug her credit card wallet out of her handbag and flourished it at him, staff identification card uppermost. 'All right,' he said with unexpected relish, and led her upstairs, trailing a smell of the motor oil that blackened his fingernails.

He lived one floor up. As he knocked on his door, a dull fat sound, a dog snarled and clawed at the inside of the door across the corridor. A woman with rubber bands dangling from her undecidedly coloured hair, and eyes bruised by lack of sleep, answered Trantom's knock. She gave Sandy a disinterested stare and trudged back into the kitchen, a cramped room which smelled saturated with Brussels sprouts. Despite her apathy, her presence seemed welcome when Sandy heard another woman screaming in the next room.

Trantom struggled along his corridor, past a bicycle and a coat-stand whose fractured upright was bandaged with insulating tape, and emitted a sound somewhere between a warning cough and a roar. The screams were drowned out by a disco beat, and a man said loudly, 'That disembowelling was a load of tripe.'

'This is good, look, where they gouge her eyes out,' a younger man said.

Trantom opened the door noisily and sidled around it, jerking his head to indicate that he wasn't by himself, not noticing that Sandy had already ventured after him. Two men were sitting in armchairs that looked carved of cork, facing a television and video recorder. The teenager wore jeans and a T-shirt printed with the slogan I WANT YOUR BODY (COS I'M A CANNIBAL); the man in his thirties might have been a businessman, dressed as he was in a dark suit and waistcoat, white shirt and black tie. 'It's all there,' he said to Trantom. 'Here's where the one with the big tits gets them chopped off.'

Trantom jerked his head again, and noticed Sandy as the others did. The teenager craned to see her, his T-shirt flapping about his undernourished torso. 'That's her, is it?' he said.

Trantom stepped forward as if her nearness were forcing him into the room, and she followed him. 'I'm Sandy Allan.'

'What do you reckon to this, then?' the man in the suit challenged her, pointing one gleaming shoe at the screen. All she could see was what looked like a tin of pale red paint that had just been opened to the accompaniment of the disco beat and screams: sharper details had been lost between transfers from a foreign tape. 'It does nothing for me,' she said.

'You'd censor it then, would you?'

'I can't imagine being given the option.'

'But if your lot bought it,' the teenager said, brandishing his knuckly face on its wiry neck at her and narrowing his bloodshot eyes, 'you'd cut it, no question.'

'No question that it would ever be bought.'

'If the films you buy aren't that bad, why the fuck cut them?'

Wearied by the way the conversation was progressing, Sandy turned to Trantom. 'May I sit down? Then you can introduce me to your friends.'

The floor was cluttered with piles of magazines and video cassettes. Soundtrack albums were strewn across a red two-seater couch. Trantom gathered up the records clumsily, splaying his fingers almost as wide as the breadth of the covers, and dumped then beneath a shelf of plastic monsters. As Sandy sat down he dropped himself beside her, seesawing the couch. 'They write for my magazine,' he said, his voice even higher with pride. 'That's John in the T-shirt that writes our video reviews, and this is Andrew Minihin. You must have heard of *him*.'

When she shook her head and smiled Minihin grunted, Trantom sniggered incredulously, John's thighs began to vibrate as if he were preparing to run laps of the cluttered room. 'You must've. A paper wanted all his books banned,' John insisted, and listed them: '*The Flaying. The Slobbering. It Crawls Up You. It Crawls Back Up You. Entrails* that they wouldn't let him call *Puke and Die*, that was the best yet.'

'I've seen them around.'

'Wondered how anyone could buy such crap, did you?' Minihin said.

The three men grinned at her as if they were watching a trap. She imagined them as three witches with Halloween hats, and felt more in control. 'Not that I remember.'

'I used to, because crap is what it is,' Minihin said with a klaxon laugh. 'It's what you have to write to compete with films like this one here. If millions of silly bastards want to read it I'd be even stupider than they are if I didn't give it to them. Maybe some of them will grow out of it. I'm getting fan mail from ten-year-old kids.'

'Watch out, you'll have her wanting to cut your books,' John said.

Sandy lost her temper just enough to give her voice an edge. 'Do you believe everything you read in the papers? Can't you see that Stilwell wrote that about me because I dared to suggest he was wrong about the film my friend was looking for? I don't cut films, I assemble them, and I'd be a born-again archivist as far as this film is concerned. Except if everyone I approach is going to believe what Stilwell said about me I may as well not bother. Would you like to turn that down? I'm not used to having to talk over someone screaming.'

Trantom groped down the side of the couch until he found the remote control. The zombie dentist on the screen continued his work in silence, and Trantom muttered, 'What do you think, boys?'

'The paper could be after her like the other one went after Andrew. They don't like anyone who stands for horror.'

Minihin shrugged as if the question mattered as little as anything else. 'All right,' Trantom said, 'we trust you. We'll help.'

'You'll tell me what you told Graham.'

'We didn't tell him anything. He'd heard of my magazine and thought we'd know collectors who might have a copy of the film. I mean we'll help you look.'

His enthusiasm was so great that it carried him past his stammering. 'That's kind of you, but I really only wanted to find out if you had a lead,' Sandy said.

'He keeps his wife on one. What's your problem?' Minihin demanded. 'Don't you want to be associated with us?'

'You haven't seen the magazine,' Trantom said, and grabbed one from a pile behind the couch.

It was a stapled bunch of duplicated typed pages called *Gorehound*. She thought someone had spilled coffee on it, until she realized that the stain was meant to illustrate the title. 'I should have thought the film I'm looking for wouldn't do much for you after the kind of thing you watch.'

'Some films were pretty good even then,' John disagreed. 'Lugosi bursts a blind man's eardrums in *Dark Eyes of London*, and that was before the war.'

'And before that, in *The Raven*, he cripples Karloff's face,' Trantom added eagerly, 'and locks him in a room full of mirrors.'

'And in *The Black Cat* he starts ripping his skin off,' Minihin offered.

'If your film was banned it must be good,' Trantom said. 'If it's horror we're interested. We can never get enough.'

'No fucker tells us what to do.'

Sandy wasn't sure if Minihin was talking about censorship or her. She found their enthusiasm more disturbing than their suspicion of her had been. It made the room seem smaller and hotter, and raw as the silenced carnage on the screen. 'So you can't tell me anything about the film itself.'

'It must've upset someone,' John suggested.

'Told them something they didn't want to know,' Minihin said.

It was clear that they were only speculating. 'If there's any way you can help I'll let you know,' Sandy said, and pushed herself off the couch. 'But the people I need to meet may be as wary as you were, and they'll also be considerably older.'

The men stared at her, red-eyed from the film, from its reflection or from the way it quickened their blood. All three were between her and the door. Someone exploded on the screen, and red splashed the walls and furniture and the faces of the men, which seemed to swell like sponges. 'Turn up the sound,' John said. 'They're pulling her tongue out.'

'Tongue my arse,' Minihin disagreed. 'That's her liver.'

John clasped his knees to stop them jerking and gasped, 'Turn it up, quick, turn it up.'

Trantom rummaged on the floor for the control, and Sandy sidled past him. She was almost at the door when Minihin sprang to his feet and came after her, one pudgy hand outstretched. He was reaching to turn out the light so that they could see the image more clearly. They and the furniture appeared to be leaping to catch spurts of red from the screen. As Sandy slipped past the coat-stand and the bicycle, the woman with the bruised eyes looked out of a bedroom next to the kitchen, a baby mouthing at her breast, which was covered with scratches. The television screamed, and the woman winked heavily at Sandy. 'If it wasn't her it might be us.'

Trantom blundered along the corridor, shouldering the coat-stand against the wall, as Sandy unchained the outer door. The dog in the flat opposite was snarling and whining. Someone must have hit it to make it sound so nervous. Sandy stepped on to linoleum the colour of mud between glistening tiled walls, and Trantom wobbled after her. 'What's that?' he stammered as if he had been about to ask her something else. 'Did you bring someone with you?'

Sandy peered along the corridor. She didn't think she'd glimpsed a shadow dodging out of sight around the bend of the bare grey stairs, but he made her feel as if she had. 'Of course not,' she said.

'Got to be careful.' He stepped back clumsily, almost

tripping over his ragged doormat. 'Never know who might come snooping around after my films.'

'If you were a gentleman you'd see me to my car,' she said, and gazed at him until it drew him into the open. He rushed at the stairs so recklessly she was afraid for him. He was stooping, butting the air as if to warn anyone who might get in his way. As she followed him, the smell of sweat and motor oil met her on the stairs.

He flung the street door open and blundered out, fists clenched. The street was deserted for hundreds of yards. Something that smelled of stale food scuttled behind him in the dark – a hamburger carton, which Sandy kicked aside as she made for her car. 'I'll let you know if I trace the film,' she said, and he took refuge in the building at once. As she turned the car she thought that he or one of his companions had darted out of the building to beckon to her. It must have been the shadow of a lamp post, a shadow that dropped to the ground as her headlights veered away. It had been too thin even for Trantom's undernourished friend.

13

When Sandy came off the urban motorway she found she was driving for the sake of driving, to give herself a chance to think. It didn't work. She stopped the car outside Regent's Park, by the zoo. Above the park the edges of clouds were raw, but the light wasn't sufficient to show her what kind of animal was prowling beyond the railings. She stared at the cover of *Gorehound*, and then she drove to a phone box. She needed to talk.

Roger answered halfway through the first ring. 'You're at your desk,' she guessed.

'Sure am. Is this Sandy Allan? How are you today?'

'I'm . . . various things, such as sorry if I interrupted you.'

'I'll be through with this paragraph in quarter of an hour. Why don't you come over? That is, if you've nothing – '

'Nothing I can think of.'

'God, I'm predictable, right? I'll try and make myself more random while I'm waiting. If I'm not here I'll be round the corner buying wine.'

'Yes, let's celebrate,' Sandy said as she got into her car. She felt light-headed with too many emotions all at once. She sat with the window down, breathing the night air that smelled of flowers and wild animals, for a few minutes before she drove off.

Crowds swarmed around the glow of the stations at Euston and St Pancras and King's Cross. The five-way intersection at the Angel was a tangled knot of street lamps and unlit side streets. Sandy sped through the knot into Upper Street, and parked outside the arch that led to Roger's. When she slammed the car door the sound scuttled over the cobblestones. She hurried through the arch to the door opposite the path darkened by shrubs. Before she could ring his doorbell, she was blinded.

Roger had glanced out between his curtains. The desk lamp was pointing straight at her face. His footsteps beyond the blur that had wiped out most of her vision sounded more distant than the stealthy restlessness behind her, which must be twigs scraping the edges of the path. As soon as she heard him open the door she walked blindly in. 'Sure, come in,' he said in her ear, and then, 'Sandy, what's wrong?'

She didn't know where to begin. Now that she was inside she was happy to wait for her sight to return, but staying mute seemed unreasonable. She heard the door shut, and he came closer. 'It's okay, don't talk if you need to be quiet,' he said, and put his arms around her.

It was her temporary sightlessness as much as her silence that made her feel she had found him at last, in a place beyond words. She hugged him and hung on as they walked leisurely down the hall. She felt surrounded by his warmth and awkward gentleness, by the smell of his skin and of a sweetish aftershave he must have dabbed on his face for her benefit. The walls beyond the patch of blindness opened out as he led her to the nearest armchair. When he placed her there and made to let go she held firmly on to him. 'This won't be very comfortable,' he murmured.

'Then let's go where it will be,' she said, and touched his tongue with hers. The contact blazed through her like sunlight, awakening her nerves. To her delight, he lifted her and carried her into the bedroom. However many films this might be like, she could tell he wasn't acting out any of them. Before they reached the bed she had unbuttoned his shirt, and their open mouths were pressed hungrily together.

His face came into focus as he lowered her on to the bed. She brushed his hair back from his forehead as he pushed up her blouse and freed her breasts for his mouth to excite. She raised her hips so that he could slip her panties down for her to kick away, then she unzipped him quickly and took hold of his rearing penis. She ran her fingertips along it until he moaned, and then she dug her

80

nails into his buttocks and pulled him into her. She felt herself widen, sucking him deeper, and thrust her tongue deeper into his mouth. His hands squeezed her breasts, passed lingeringly down her and lifted her thighs to stroke inside them. She came almost at once, and then again. The second time he cried out and came too, hugging her shoulders helplessly, throbbing inside her as if he might never stop.

She held on to him and kissed his eyes and lips while he dwindled inside her. Eventually he lay back and pulled the duvet over them. She rested her head on his arm and gazed at him. She felt drowsy, calm, remote from the rest of the day's events, completely at home. At last he said almost apologetically, 'I did get some wine, by the way.'

She smiled at his tone and kissed his cheek. 'You think we ought to celebrate, do you?'

'Sure. I mean, if you do.'

'Need you ask? Lead me to it. If I don't match you glass for glass, it's only because I'm driving.'

'You don't have to drive tonight if you don't want to.'

'Well, I don't suppose I do. And do you know, I don't suppose I will. I've nobody to go home to, after all.'

'Except your cats.'

'I'm afraid Bogart and Bacall have joined the great film show in the sky.'

'Sandy, I'm sorry. Is that what was wrong? When did it happen?'

'Last night. They were run over. It seems much longer ago.' That struck her as even sadder than their deaths, but she didn't realize she was weeping until he wiped away the tears. 'I think I might like some of that wine now,' she said indistinctly.

'I'll bring it,' he said, and swung his legs off the bed, penis wagging.

She dabbed at her eyes with the duvet and wrapped it around herself. When Roger came back with the bottle he was draped in a black robe edged with gold thread. He insisted on her wearing it, and tramped bare-buttocked to

81

the bathroom for a towelling robe for himself. Sandy poured the wine, and they touched glasses. 'Here's to beginnings,' she said.

'And many episodes.'

'With lots of action.'

'Leading to climaxes.'

'You needn't worry on that score. You made up for the rest of the day at the very least.'

'Shit, you mean it wasn't only your cats being killed?'

'Shall we say it's been a varied kind of a day? I've been given time off work whether or not I want it. So I started out to look for Graham's film, and met some people who made me wonder if I should. They write a magazine. I'll show you.'

She glanced through it before passing it to him. Trantom's misspelled editorial was addressed to 'all the psychos and sickos like us'. An article by John the Maniac described weeks of wandering around seedy video libraries in search of under-the-counter horrors. Andrew Minihin's page concluded: 'They're only special effects, and if you can't tell the difference you must be sick in the head, so fuck off to a nuthouse and let the rest of us enjoy them.' Sandy refilled the glasses while Roger scanned the pages. 'Somehow I doubt Graham would have had much time for them,' she said.

'I remember now, they presented him with a copy of their organ, gave him one of their organs as you might say. He thought the joke was on him. He was kind of relieved they weren't any help, because he would have felt obliged to invite them to his premiere. Imagine having to introduce these guys to royalty.'

'It isn't how squalid it is I mind so much as how meaningless.'

'Sure, the cinema disappearing up itself, or reverting to a kind of magic show. If you have to spend your time reminding yourself it's fake and that's the point, what *is* the point? Maybe it's a rite of passage for people who never grow up. But when audiences have had enough of being shocked they generally want something more subtle, and you might be helping to revive that by finding Graham's movie.'

'I suppose so.'

'Listen, don't let me bore you. Maybe you're thinking I'm like those guys, living in the movies because I'm scared of real life.'

'Why should I think that? Using your talent is part of real life, and you're using yours to make people see what you see, make them look again.'

He smiled rather wistfully at her. 'The best I can hope for is that we're both right. Movies were somewhere I could go and let my feelings out for a couple of hours, once I was old enough that my folks had to accept I could go out by myself. I guess I got into the habit of suppressing how I felt in case it made them anxious. I should tell you they had their reasons. I had a sister who died of meningitis when I was three years old and she was six.'

'Poor little thing. Do you remember her?'

'Sometimes I dream I see her face, but I don't remember it really. The one memory I have is of her coming into my room and standing at the end of the bed with the light from the doorway behind her. She looked as if she was drawn in light, turning into light, you know? My folks tell me that must have been her saying goodbye the night they had to take her to the hospital.'

Sandy licked a stray tear from his cheek. A hint of aftershave underlay the salty taste. 'I wouldn't say you were afraid of reality.'

'Maybe just of getting involved in case I lose someone else.' Then he grinned. 'That's Hollywood bullshit, don't you think? It doesn't work that way unless you've seen too many movies and let them do your thinking for you. Deep down most of us need someone. I do.'

'It's mutual,' Sandy said, feeling as if his former awkwardness had been transferred to her.

'I hope you don't just mean that the way Charles Dickens did.'

'Nothing so literary. I mean what I feel.'

'You feel good. I'd say we've something more to celebrate, but we've killed the wine.'

'I can think of a better way to celebrate.'

This time it was unhurried and inventive, and taught them more about each other. Afterwards they lay exhausted in each other's arms, and soon they were asleep. Whenever Sandy awoke, his closeness was a renewed surprise and a sleepy pleasure. Once she awoke convinced he had a dog which they'd forgotten to let in, and was halfway to the door until she realized her error. She was missing the cats, she told herself, but snuggling under the duvet with Roger was such a compensation that she slept again almost immediately.

In the morning he brought her breakfast in bed and then worked at his desk. She showered and hoped he might join her without being asked, but this was one shower scene he was shy of. She used his toothbrush and went out to find him, his hair dangling above the keyboard of his word processor. She held his shoulders and stooped to kiss his forehead. 'Such a lot can happen in one day,' she said.

He reached up and stroked her neck. 'So what's happening today?'

'I ought to go on my travels. I shouldn't let Graham down, or my lunch date.'

'I have to work on this book for at least the next couple of days, but maybe I could catch up with you after that if you want company.'

'I'd like that.'

He saved his file and slipped the disc out of the word processor. 'If you need to make any calls, go ahead while I take a bath.'

Calling so early in the day proved useful. She arranged two interviews that would lead her across the map from Hatfield without her needing to retrace her route. One was with Denzil Eames, who had written the film and who sounded querulously eager to be interviewed. By the time she'd finished, Roger was out of the bathroom, looking pinkly youthful in his towelling robe. She hugged him, but when his hands ran down her skirt and under it she murmured, 'I really ought to go home and pack. I'm supposed to be in Hatfield for lunch.'

'Sure,' he said, his hands springing away.

'Otherwise I'd stay, I hope you know. And I'd love to have you come after me when you can.'

'Don't count on much of a start,' he said, which made her want him so much that she hurried herself away to grab her handbag. At the door she kissed him, lingering even longer for the benefit of whoever she sensed watching. But when she let go of him at last, she could see nobody. How could anyone be thin enough to hide behind the shrubs in daylight? She gave Roger a last hug and ran across the cobbles to her car.

14

As Sandy drove off the motorway near Hatfield she met the autumn. Tips of leaves were yellowing on trees that seemed to wither against the glare of sunlight from moist fields. When she rolled her window down she felt the chill that the buildings of central London had kept at bay. She drew a long breath that tasted of mist and smoke. Whenever she left the city behind, her senses reached out for the countryside, and she realized how habitually she kept them in check.

She had to do so in order to drive into Hatfield. The outskirts of the town were a maze of roundabouts and of roads whose numbers had been changed. Mechanical diggers flung mud about, a British Aerospace playing field gleamed emptily, prefabricated flats for students at the poly-technic stood on thick stilts above mud. Sandy found herself driving back and forth between anonymous terraces and fields steeped in mist, and she was beginning to wonder if she'd come to the wrong Hatfield – there were at least two more in the AA guidebook – when, among the omnipresent signposts to the polytechnic, she caught sight of one for Old Hatfield. She had to drive twice around the roundabout before the traffic would let her off.

The Georgian streets of the old town climbed to St Ethelreda's church. On Fore Street the car began to labour until Sandy changed down two gears. She caught sight of the name of the side street she was looking for, nailed to a blaze of sunlight and whitewash, and braked to let two women wheeling baskets heaped with vegetables cross the junction. Halting gave her time to blink away the dazzle of sunlight, but as the car coasted into the side street, she blinked again. For a moment it seemed she had driven into

86

a film. The street was a set along which an actor was striding.

She'd seen him half a dozen times, but never in colour. He had been an innkeeper, a stallholder at a medieval fair, a pirate's first mate who had tired of killing and saved the heroine before dying on a sword himself. She was sure he'd had a tankard in his fist at some point in every film. She stopped the car and waited for him.

Harry Manners' jowls that used to shake with jollity were veined, she saw; his hair was grey and sparser. None of this lessened him: as he came closer his presence seemed more overwhelming, less contained, now that it was scaled down off the screen. He must be nearly eighty, but his eyes were keen enough. He stopped fifty yards short of the car and peered under his grey caterpillar eyebrows at her, a smile sending ripples through his jowls. 'It's you, isn't it?' he boomed, and strode towards her. 'My luncheon treat?'

She climbed out and stretched. 'How did you know?'

'I saw you hunting and hoped I was the lucky man.' He clasped her hand in both of his. 'Your voice was a melody, you are the symphony. I shall entrust myself to you. Ignore me if I cover my eyes occasionally.'

'You aren't fond of cars.'

'I wasn't even when they had to huff and puff to put on fifty miles an hour, especially after what happened to poor Giles Spence. As for how they drive outside town these days, is that what's meant by a white-knuckle ride? You'll excuse me if we don't go far. Will duck pie be to your taste?'

'Sounds tempting.'

'To the Crooked Billet, then,' he cried like several of his roles, and lowered himself into the passenger seat, tugging at his trouser legs that were as wide as thirty years ago. 'Back down the hill. Not *too* precipitately, if you'd be so kind.'

As she turned downhill his face looked as though he were trying to suppress the flatulence of panic. As soon as she glanced at him he smiled bravely. 'Please ask whatever you came to ask. Take my mind off my cravenness.'

This wasn't the moment to ask what had happened to Giles Spence. 'I get the feeling you'd be pleased if I found this film.'

'Pleased for you and for your friend, mourned by many, and for myself. Don't you dare let the scribbler in that excuse for a newspaper deter you. The film has survived worse than him.'

'Have you any idea who bought the copyright?'

'I don't think any of us had except the producers, and they were both killed in the war. They wouldn't even tell Spence's wife.'

'Did you ever wonder why it was suppressed?'

'I wonder all the time at a host of things. It keeps me breathing. At the time we thought someone had bought the film who could afford to hold it back until the public was hungry for horrors again, and later we assumed whoever owned the negative had let it deteriorate. You'll appreciate we had other things on our minds, especially during the war.'

'But now you think whoever owns the rights didn't want the film to be shown.'

'So your friend told me he had reason to believe, which angers me. Making the film was enough of a nightmare without its being to no avail. Left at the end here, I should tell you. And now perhaps I'd better concentrate on navigating.'

At the first of the roundabouts she wished he had continued reminiscing. 'Next,' he gasped, 'no, left after here, ah, best go round again.' He kept shading his eyes as if he were struggling not to cover them. She found the pub by accident, having strayed back into the confusion of mass-produced terraces. She parked on gravelly soil and gave Harry Manners her arm as he heaved himself out of the car, saying 'Thanks, thanks' to her or to whatever powers had kept him safe.

It was the kind of small old country pub she ordinarily loved, but it didn't seem ideal for interviewing the actor. Most of the drinkers crammed into the bar greeted him by name. 'You never said you had a daughter,' a woman complained.

'I've no reason to curse the manufacturers of prophylactics. This young lady's an admirer, if I may presume to say so.'

'You want to revive his yesterdays, do you?' the woman said, one gloved hand flourishing an unlit cigarette in a holder.

'And to encourage him to go on performing,' Sandy said sweetly, and ordered food and a black ale the actor recommended. She followed him out to a table on a lawn beside several henhouses that backed on to a field glowing with misty sunlight. 'Forgive me for not introducing you,' he said. 'I thought you mightn't want to spend the next hour hearing about when she had a singing voice.'

'So long as you don't mind what I said. *Are* you still acting?'

'Every waking moment and on the stage of my dreams, but you mean professionally. I still tread the boards where I'm invited. A television producer was in touch last week to see if I might accept very little money to appear in a play about the exploitation of pensioners. If we still breed the likes of Giles Spence, I fear they've fled to Hollywood.'

'You obviously admired him.'

'If there were any justice his name would come up whenever people mention English films. You've never seen his *Midsummer Night's Dream*, have you? Bought and suppressed by Hollywood so there was no competition. And his film about Boudicca wasn't preserved properly, so it's decayed beyond repair. That would never have happened if he had still been alive. God help anyone he thought was harming his work.'

'Was that why the film was a nightmare to make?'

'Him? No, we could all see the pressures he was under. Hostility in the press, for one thing. I brought you some of that to keep.'

He produced a rolled-up magazine from inside his jacket as a barmaid brought them a tray of food. The magazine

89

was called *Picture Pictorial*, and contained an interview with Karloff and Lugosi. 'We'd have chased the young pup out of the studio if we'd known what he planned to write,' Manners said. 'Still, he was the least of the intrusions we had to contend with.'

Sandy raised her voice as the hens grew loudly restless. 'Why, what else was there?'

'We thought it was the local children to begin with, getting in at night somehow, and then we thought it might be some of the citizens of Ruislip. Not everyone relished the presence of a film studio on their doorstep. Only Giles was having new sets built at night, and you might think nobody would have ventured in while there were chaps working in the studio until the early hours. Some of the craftsmen got quite nervous. One drove a nail through his hand, one fell off a ladder. One asked for his papers because he claimed he saw some kind of animal with something amiss with its eyes prowling about the sets, and before long we had reason to believe that he wasn't entirely mistaken. There must be a fox about,' he explained as the hens continued to flap and cluck.

Sandy could see nothing moving in the field. 'You had reason to believe him.'

'We came in one morning after the studio had been unattended overnight and found an entire set scattered to the winds. It must have taken hours of vandalism, yet nobody who lived nearby would admit to having heard anything. One chap insisted that the studio had been entirely dark. So Giles hired another night watchman and we tried to get on with the job and keep Giles' spirits up.'

'Things were getting to him?'

'Alas. He banned all visitors – a pity the long-nosed fellow whose interview you have there had already been and gone – but he still kept behaving as if there were intruders while he was shooting. More than once he called a cut halfway through a take because he was convinced someone had looked out of a window on camera. Perhaps the nervousness he infected us with added to the atmosphere of the film. Still, I was quite relieved when I'd finished my stint.'

'You weren't there for the whole film?'

'No, I left during the last week, before some unhappy incident involving a stunt man. And as thought all this weren't enough, the studios burnt down before another film could be commenced. After all that, I think justice demands that the film should be seen, though I hope you don't revive its devil's luck.'

'You don't believe in that, do you?'

'My child, every actor does. Why do you think we don't name the Scottish play? As for Giles' film, what with the director and producers dying shortly after it was completed, and the studios destroyed – well, you might even wonder what it had to do with your friend's death.'

'I might not.'

'The mouth, the mouth.' He slapped himself across the lips. 'I didn't mean to upset you, nor to deter you from your search. Please, if all this clucking isn't ruining your nerves, let me buy you another drink.'

Sandy sipped her ale while he downed several large Scotches. She drove him home, where he insisted on making her a coffee and showing her an enormous scrapbook of posters bearing his name. She hadn't the heart to rush away, though soon it would be the peak hour on the motorway to Cambridge, her next destination. She had to convince him that his remark about Graham hadn't upset her before he would let her leave. 'May the ghosts of the film help you search,' he said as she started the car.

By the time she reached the motorway, his comment about Graham no longer upset her so much as it angered her. Graham had died because he'd been chasing a thief and hadn't realized he was too exhausted to repeat the jump he had achieved once, she told herself. To suggest anything else demeaned his memory to the level of a cheap horror film. 'Bloody nonsense,' she growled, treading hard on the accelerator to overtake two lanes of lorries, and her anger made her face so hot she had to spit it out. 'I'd like to see anything that would have dared do that to him.'

The motorway ahead was clear. She swung into the middle lane and then into the inner, above a bank that sloped to a hedge bordering a cornfield. Then she braked and almost swerved, thinking that a crouching shape had darted away from the hedge and up the bank. She made herself regain speed for the sake of the traffic behind her, but as soon as she reached a service area she stopped for several cups of coffee. The ale at the Crooked Billet must have been stronger than she'd realized. She'd thought that before she had lost sight of it the shape beside the motorway had raced the length of the field, faster than her car.

15

Sandy booked into a hotel on the outskirts of Cambridge, only to discover that none of the bedrooms had phones. She couldn't face driving around Cambridge in the rush hour to find a hotel that was better equipped. She was hoping Denzil Eames wouldn't mind if she met him an hour or so later than they had agreed, to give herself time for a rest before dinner. She went down to the small russet lobby, where the receptionist was reading an Andrew Minihin novel with a gouged eye embossed on the cover, and stood under the porous helmet of the phone booth. She opened her handbag, and groaned and struck her forehead. She'd left the list of names in Roger's flat.

'Silly bitch,' she hissed at herself. She must have overlooked it in her haste to leave before the temptation to stay grew irresistible. At least Denzil Eames was listed in the directory beneath the phone. She growled at herself while his phone rang, and sucked her lips between her teeth as she heard the hasty clatter of a receiver. 'What is it now?' a voice shrilled. 'Who's there?'

It sounded sexless with age. He'd been querulous when she had called him from Roger's, but not like this. 'It's Sandy Allan, Mr Eames,' she said. 'I'm to visit you this evening.'

'Who? Oh, oh, to talk about that cursed film. Let it stay buried. I don't want to be reminded of it, I've decided. Nothing more to say.'

'But this morning you told me you were pleased with your work on it. Couldn't we at least –'

'Not tonight. I need my sleep. Call me tomorrow if you must, but don't be too hopeful,' he quavered, and cut her off.

'Well, there you go, if that's how you feel,' Sandy said.

Could Stilwell's comments in the *Daily Friend* have reached him since this morning and changed his mind? Might someone from *Gorehound* have traced his name and address and pestered him? More likely he was just acting his age. Frustration, mostly with herself, made her dig in her purse again for the cost of a long-distance call.

When Roger heard her voice he said, 'Your list. My fault for distracting you. I tried to call you at home as soon as I realized, but you must have been on the road.'

'I shouldn't have wanted to do without the distraction.'

'That's good to hear. Me neither. Did you get to Harry Manners at least?'

'He's a sweetie, but he hasn't got the film.'

'Shall I read you the whole list? It's been here by the phone just waiting for your call.'

'Hold on.' She found her pen and diary, and had to feed the phone again. 'Here I am.'

'Are there any you already have? Hang on, what's that?'

'I didn't say anything,' Sandy told him, but the sudden silence at the other end made her realize he hadn't meant her. The sharp quick rattling was the sound of curtain-rings on the rail above his desk, she thought, just as he said, 'It couldn't have been anything. I thought someone was tapping on the window.'

'I wish I were, right now. You needn't give me details for Newark or Birmingham, I've already put those in my diary.'

'Okay, let's see. Hungry little bugger, isn't it?' he said as the phone began to cry for more coins. When Sandy had fed it he said, 'Why don't I call you back?'

'Because I'm looking at a sign that says this phone does not accept incoming calls.'

'Well, how about this? Suppose you give yourself a break while I call some of these numbers and see if I can set up interviews for you? Your phone there doesn't sound too ideal. I can use the excuse to take time off from this chapter.'

'And I can phone you tomorrow from a better hotel, I hope.'

'Fine. You have a good evening and don't be too lonely.'

'Keep your fly zipped for me,' Sandy said, earning herself a shocked look from the receptionist.

Later, when she took her place among half a dozen sales representatives in the dining-room that smelled of plastic bouquets and surreptitious cigarettes, she saw the receptionist whispering about her to the waitress, who was trying to rub nicotine off her fingers with a serviette. Sandy chose the plainest course on the menu for safety, but something on the plate of fatty beef managed to taste of garlic from another course. 'This should curb my sex life,' she remarked to the waitress, who fled.

In the bar, where concealed lighting flared over paintings so that they appeared to sink into the shadows of their frames, the only unoccupied seat was at a table with two young salesmen, both of whom immediately bought her a drink. She chatted to them until it became abruptly clear that they both expected to join her in her room. 'I'm a one-man woman,' she said happily.

'Don't knock it till you've tried it,' said the salesman with gold teeth, and his plump pale friend, whose smile was growing wet and loose, told her, 'You only say that because you've never tried it from both ends at once.'

'I've never tried catching AIDS, either,' Sandy said into a pause in the Muzak. She left them staring after her and muttering blame at each other. The barmaid, who had overheard her, was scurrying up and down the bar like an animal in a trap, impatient to be out to tell her colleagues what she'd heard. 'I hope I get a discount for providing the entertainment,' Sandy said, and made the barmaid gape.

The lift was about the size of a large telephone box. It raised Sandy to the upper corridor, which was papered brown as the carpet. She glanced back from her door to confirm that nobody had followed her. At least the room had a bathroom attached, and she didn't need to venture further until tomorrow. She kicked off her shoes and up-ended the pillows against the headboard, then sat back on the brown quilt of the narrow bed and opened *Picture Pictorial*.

It fell open at a photograph of Karloff and Lugosi. They were sitting in canvas chairs and drinking tea from bell-shaped china cups. They looked oddly uncomfortable, taken unawares by the camera or by whatever might just have been said. In the background a tall man with a long oval face and a thin black moustache was frowning at the camera. The caption – 'The monsters take a break while their director clocks them' – didn't seem quite to fit the image. OUR MAN WITH THE NOTEBOOK SAYS 'BOO!' TO THE BOGEY-MEN was the title beneath the caption, and Sandy read on.

'When I find Boris Karloff and Bela Lugosi on the set of their first British film they are singing a duet. "D'ye ken John Peel?" they demand while Karloff murders a piano. I think this must be how monsters carry on between scenes, but it turns out it is part of the film. The bogey-men must want to prove there's more to them than scaring children. Readers, judge for yourselves.

'I am given lunch with the 'orrible pair. Karloff eats like the lorry-driver he used to be; Lugosi's portion looks red enough to put me off my food . . .'

Sandy groaned and wondered how much more of the article the writer had simply made up.

'I am meant to understand that the interview is a rare privilege, because "Mr Lugosi does not usually give inter-views". Perhaps that means whoever normally handles his publicity has enough sense to refuse on his behalf.

'Lugosi doesn't want to talk about horror or the way his films may warp the minds of the impressionable. When I ask about his film *The Island of Lost Souls*, which was so objectionable it was banned in Britain (and Mr H. G. Wells, who wrote the original novel, was in favour of the ban), all Lugosi does is wonder if Mr Wells' novel should have been banned too. He wants me to know how much he enjoyed watching a soccer match near the studio, but I hope no children were there. He tells me how sad he was to have to leave his dogs in quarantine when he came to England. He offers me an expensive cigar and asks if I have seen any of his comedies. In *International House* he keeps bumping

96

into W. C. Fields, and in *Hollywood on Parade* he leers over Betty Boop's throat and slavers, "Boop, you have booped your last boop." Screamingly funny, don't you think? "I vant to make ze ow-di-yence laugh," he rumbles as if he can frighten us into laughing. "I vish you had seen me play Rooh-meo," he says, but since that was on stage in Hungarian, I think Shakespeare may rest in peace.

'Karloff is proud to be monstrous. He calls Frankenstein "my monster". He got the monster role when the producer laughed at Lugosi's screen test, and I gather there is no love lost between the bogeys. Both fee-faw-fums seem to feel they are badly done to. Karloff thinks the monster should never have spoken (and parents of children may feel the same about Karloff); Lugosi complains that in the sequel to *Dracula* his part was played by a wax dummy. Perhaps he is upset that nobody noticed. He won't confirm that he resents being paid half Karloff's fee on *The Raven* (the film that has outraged so many millions of English parents) for doing more work, but his eyes answer for him. In his last film before he "went on relief", he even had to play a character called Boroff. He seems particularly put out that in their "Horror Boys from Hollywood" routine the Ritz Brothers burlesqued Laughton, Karloff and Lorre, and didn't even think of him. If he and Karloff spend so much time complaining when they are in Hollywood, it is no wonder they have to come here to find work, though I understand the Daughters of the American Revolution are also waiting there to deal with them.

'In this film Karloff plays a member of the English aristocracy whose land is haunted by his ancestors until Lugosi sees them off with some mumbo-jumbo. Hardly the kind of film a loyal Englishman would want to make, and would he need to import the 'orror boys if it was any good? I am reminded of the words of Mrs Lindsey, the respected American journalist, in *Log of the Good Ship Life*: "To take a child to see one of these Karloff and Bela Lugosi horrors is to outrage its nervous system and perhaps warp it for life. No child should ever be allowed to see one of them." If our censor should be so ill-advised as to grant this film the new Horrorific certificate, I think we English can be trusted to treat it with the contempt it deserves. Back to your lairs, bugbears! We English subsist on more wholesome fare.'

'You ought to meet the staff of *Gorehound*,' Sandy murmured. She hadn't realized that the outcry against horror films in the thirties had been so vicious. Karloff and Lugosi would be remembered long after the writer was forgotten, she thought, especially since he hadn't signed the article. She turned idly to the contents page, and felt her jaw drop. The writer's name was there in the table of contents, beneath the title of the article. His name was Leonard Stilwell.

16

In the night Sandy was awakened by the feeling that someone was outside her door. Perhaps it was one of the salesmen, she thought drowsily, or one of the staff trying to hear if Sandy had company. At least the door had a strong lock and chain. Sandy lay waiting for whoever was out there to make a sound, until sleep began to edit her awareness. Just as sleep took over, she thought she heard a sound as if a body had lain down in the corridor, settling against the lower panels of the door.

It must have been a dream, she told herself next morning, but it felt as if it was still beyond the door. She eased back the bolt, inched the door open as far as the length of the chain and peered around the edge. One of the salesmen who had accosted her was emerging from his room on the opposite side of the corridor. He stared at her and sniffed disapprovingly, so hard that his upper lip pouted. Apart from him and a smell of greasy breakfasts, the corridor was empty. A staleness about the smell made Sandy inclined to skip breakfast, except that avoiding the staff and the other guests would seem an admission of guilt. She closed the door and had a bath.

The stale smell must have been in the corridor outside her room, but the breakfast was greasy enough. Gristly bacon was embedded in the white of the lukewarm egg. A sliced loaf of Staff o' Life bread was the most wholesome item on the table. She made do with bread and jam, and left the crowded watchful smoky room as soon as she had gulped two cups of instant coffee.

She ducked under the telephone's helmet, and had hardly dialled when the receiver was snatched up. 'Who's there?' demanded a voice almost as shrill as the pips.

It sounded anything but promising, but at least she would have tried. 'Mr Eames?'

'Is this the woman who called me last evening?'

'I'm afraid so,' Sandy mouthed, and said, 'Yes, it is.'

'All right, let's get it over with. I've a lecture to prepare. How long will you be?'

'I'll come now,' Sandy said, so surprised that she wondered if he had mistaken her for someone else. 'I can be there in half an hour.'

'That's as long as I can see you for, and less if you're late,' he snapped, and rang off.

The receptionist looked away quickly from watching. 'Yes, it's another man,' Sandy said, and went upstairs to pack. She noticed that the lower panels on the outside of her door looked scratched, which seemed typical of the shabbiness of the hotel. By the time she was out of the building, having waited for a remark that never quite escaped the receptionist's lips, she had forgotten the marks on the door.

Cambridge was crowded. Students and gowned dons spilled off the thick pavements or queued outside coffee shops. Cyclists came flocking out of Jesus Lane, and Sandy missed her exit from the one-way system. She had to creep past Great St Mary's Church, outside which the striped awnings of a market had sprung up. This time around she was able to find Christ's Pieces, where tennis players darted and leapt in cages of wire netting. She parked opposite the green and climbed out of the car, kneading the back of her neck.

A breeze wandered across Christ's Pieces, strewing a jingle of bicycle bells. The taut metronomic beat of tennis balls on rackets stumbled and regained its rhythm. Beyond the trees on the green the town looked petrified in the act of stretching spiny yellow pinnacles towards the sun that had scoured the sky. A clock began to chime, and then another, and they sent her running to the nearby side street where Eames lived.

At first she thought he was the proprietor of a second-hand bookshop, who sidled swiftly out between two shelves of folios to ask what he could do for her. When she mentioned Eames he fluttered his long fingers at her and jerked his head at the dim ceiling, flourishing the tassel on the cap he wore. 'Up there. Door next to my window. If he's gone out don't bother telling me. I've had all the rows with him I'm having over taking messages for him.'

She'd walked past Eames' door, whose grimy number was almost indistinguishable from the wood. She rang the bell and heard a distant rattle that made her think of a worn-out clockwork toy. After a minute or so she leaned on the button in case Eames was hard of hearing, and a window slammed open above her. 'Just rein yourself back,' Eames cried. 'Shall I break my neck for you? Is that your idea of an interview?'

The window slammed so hard that Sandy expected glass to splinter, and then there was a prolonged silence. She hadn't heard him on the stairs when the door wavered open, and he peered up at her. His head, which was almost bald and spotted with age, didn't reach her shoulder. His face made her think of a fruit squeezed colourless and dry; his white lips were puckered into an O that seemed disapproving. 'Come up if you've anything to say,' he snapped. 'I won't be canvassed on my doorstep.'

The edges of the carpet on the narrow stairs were turned up against the walls. Eames hoisted himself upwards using the banister, planting both slippered feet on each step. At the top he beckoned her with a gesture that looked as if he were trying to dislodge an object stuck to his skinny forefinger. As soon as she stepped through the skewed doorway he said like a challenge, 'Well, here I am.'

She wondered if he also meant the low room, the two worn armchairs draped with clothes, the window that overlooked a similar window across the street, the vintage typewriter exhibiting a page on which a single I was typed, the neat pile of typescripts beside it on the stout oaken desk. Sandy pointed to the typescripts. 'Is one of those your script for Giles Spence's last film?'

'That film, that film! Do you think that twaddle is the only thing I ever wrote?'

'No, of course not,' Sandy said and trailed off, at a loss.

'But it's all you know of me, isn't it? You should do a bit of homework before you start using up my time.' He sucked in his wrinkled cheeks and sounded grudgingly forgiving. 'I suppose when I was your age there were several great writers whose work I didn't know. The older I become, the more I regret having penned that last scenario for Spence.'

'Did you ever see the film?'

'I did not, and I know nobody who did. I'm surprised so many of you are after it now.'

'How many?'

'You and before you, your friend whose trail you said you were following. How many should I mean?'

'Just the two of us, I'm sure,' Sandy said, now that she was. 'But there's quite a lot of interest in the film. Weren't you at all proud of your work on it at the time?'

'At that age? Far too much so. I congratulated myself on my professionalism. Perhaps you don't know that Spence originally wanted me to write about a tower that was so high it brought the dead back down from heaven like a kind of aerial? Then he hired that Hungarian and I had to change the script to explain his accent, and then Spence went away somewhere halfway through the film and decided that there should be more of a conflict between the two stars. He became quite impassioned about rendering the aristocrat more unsympathetic, I remember. And after all that, not only was the film taken out of circulation but I've borne the stigma ever since. Nobody would hire me to write anything but horrors, nobody would stage my plays, and now it turns out that your generation ignores everything else I wrote.'

'Have you any idea who took possession of the film?'

'Someone with a lot of money and a grudge against us, I imagine. What does it matter now?'

'If I could find out who, it might be worth my trying to persuade them to release the film.'

'I'd stay well clear of anyone who has the power to make

something they don't like disappear.' Unexpectedly he laughed, a bird-like chattering. 'Still, I've almost been wiped from the face of the earth, haven't I? If you find your film then at least the public will be able to judge, and perhaps I may be invited to talk about it and my body of work.'

'I'll do my best to see you are,' she said, hearing the appeal he was too proud to acknowledge. She indicated the typescripts, intending to cheer him up further. 'Have any of these been published?'

'Haven't been and aren't likely to be.'

'Oh dear.' She suppressed a giggle at herself for getting her approach so wrong. 'What would you want the public to appreciate about your work? Did Spence ask you to make any other changes?'

He turned away so abruptly that she was afraid he found her singlemindedness insulting. He brushed past her to the desk and sat down with his back to her. He grabbed the edge of the desk with one hand to keep his balance while he groped in his hip pocket and produced a key with which he unlocked the desk drawer.

'You can sift these for yourself.'

When he didn't reach in the drawer, Sandy stepped forward. Lying at the bottom of the drawer were a few brownish pages torn raggedly from a notebook. In the shadow of the drawer the pencilled scribble on the topmost page looked too faded to decipher. 'Take them if you want them,' Eames urged her. 'They're the notes Spence gave me. They won't bite.'

He hadn't opened the drawer very wide. As Sandy reached in, she had the irrational notion that he meant to close the drawer on her wrist like a trap. She touched something cold and small that made her think of uneven teeth until she realized they were paper-clips. She lifted the pages out by one corner. 'Will you help me read them?'

'Didn't I begin by telling you I'm busy?' He flapped his hand at the pages. 'Take them with you. You can read them if you put your mind to it. I had to.'

Sandy shaded her eyes and leaned close to the grey writing. 'Does this say "biblical parallels"?'

'I believe it does,' Eames said with another of his unexpected laughs. 'You'll have less trouble with them than I had. He had too many ideas too late, it seems to me. Some of this stuff I didn't even try to incorporate.'

'You'd have liked to stay closer to the story the film was based on.'

'No, just to know at the outset what was expected of me. That story was nothing special. Have you not read it? I found the book for tenpence recently, below in the shop.' He fumbled under the suit draped over a chair and produced a book. 'My sometime friend downstairs seemed glad to be rid of it. You may have it.'

The pages hung out of the binding, which was so shabby that she couldn't make out the title or even what colour the boards had once been. 'It's very kind of you,' Sandy said. 'Did you show this to Graham Nolan?'

'I hadn't found it then, nor the notes. Don't forget those.'

Sandy picked up the ragged pages and thought she heard the doorbell stir. The restless clatter must have been a bird on the roof, for Eames didn't respond to it. She slipped the pages inside the book and realized that he was smiling at her. 'Do you know,' he said, 'I'm quite glad I changed my mind and let you come. It must have been a relief for me to talk. I certainly feel better.'

'I hope it helps you with your lecture.'

'I'm sure it will. I'll be more encouraging. These aren't mine, you should know,' he said, patting the pile of manuscripts. 'They're from the writers' group I have to lecture to, thanks to the bookman downstairs. Who knows, there may just be one among them I can guide into the career I should have had.'

He watched her make room for the book in her handbag and snap the clasp. 'Are you bound for the coast now?' he said.

'Not that I'm aware of. Should I be?'

'Didn't you say you aimed to talk to anyone connected

with the film? Tommy Hoddle is in Cromer, in a show at the end of the pier. I heard him being interviewed on their local station on the wireless.'

'Tommy Hoddle . . .' She remembered the name from Graham's list.

'The comic relief. He and Billy Bingo used to play two timorous policemen. I quite enjoyed writing their scenes. Billy died some years ago, but Tommy's still performing a solo version of their stage routine. It must be the only life he knows.'

'You wouldn't know if Graham met him?'

'I believe he already had when he came to see me.'

In that case she ought to meet him, however unlikely he sounded as the owner of a copy of the film. She could drive east to Cromer now and still be in time for her next appointment, in Birmingham tomorrow. 'Thanks for all your help,' she said to Eames. 'I'll be thinking what I can do to keep your name alive.'

He grinned down at her, his false teeth glinting in the dimness at the top of the stairs, as she closed the outer door. She was pleased that she'd cheered him up. The sunlight felt like a smile on her face as she hurried to her car. She thought she might have some fun at the end of the pier.

17

Two hours later she was in the midst of Norfolk, and reminding herself never to rely on the map. A road drawn almost taut on the page seemed in practice never to run straight for more than a few hundred yards. She ought to be in Cromer in plenty of time to catch Tommy Hoddle before the evening show, but she thought she had better do without lunch. When she found herself at the tail end of yet another cortège unwilling to overtake a slow-moving car, she shifted down a gear as soon as she saw an uncurved stretch of road ahead, and was past the four cars before any of them had started indicating.

In her mirror she saw them trundle into a side turning, and then she was alone on the road. A doughy cloud half the size of the sky lowered itself over the horizon until the sky was clear above the fields. Although the landscape was flat she could never see far ahead, because of the hedges that bordered the devious roads. Sometimes the roads named on signposts at junctions weren't the roads the map would have her believe they were. Once she reached Cromer she would make time to relax, she promised herself.

She braked at curves, gathered speed, braked again. Fields of grain stirred beyond her open window. She glanced at the mirror in case the movement she'd glimpsed back at the last curve meant that someone intended to pass her, but the road was deserted, shivering with dust and heat beneath the glaring sky. She swung around another curve and looked to see what was coming up fast behind her. It must have been a trick of perspective, a shrub of the hedge appearing to leap on to the tarmac as the curve shrank in the mirror before disappearing from view.

The hedge nearer the car was growing taller, throwing the noise of the engine back at her. The noise seemed so like a choked growling in the hedge that she braked in case the engine had developed a fault. She was glad when the hedge and the noise sank, and she was able to hear that nothing was wrong with the car. A breeze rushed through a swathe of the grass of the field she was speeding past – either a breeze or an animal. The airstream of the car might be causing the restlessness in the grass: surely no wild animal would stay so close to a moving vehicle. She trod hard on the accelerator as the road continued straight. It must be the car that was disturbing the field, for the movements were still pacing her. She reached a long gradual curve along which the hedge reared high, and didn't brake at first. She came in sight of the next straight stretch, and jerked her foot off the accelerator. Where the road curved again, a police car was waiting.

'Exactly what I needed,' Sandy sighed. 'Thanks so much.' She would have more to say to her imagination if it had brought her trouble with the police. She was a hundred yards from the police car when it flashed its lights to halt her.

As she pulled on to the verge, the driver climbed out and shut his door with a chunk like the stroke of an axe. His shoulders were so wide that they made her think of American football. She wondered if walking slowly was part of police training, intended to give their quarry a chance to quake. He pushed his peaked cap higher on his ruddy forehead that looked dwarfed by his shoulders, and glanced up from her number plate. 'May I ask where you're going to?'

'Cromer.'

He nodded as if he was weighing her answer. 'Where from?'

'Cambridge.'

'You're a bit lost then, aren't you?'

'I shouldn't be surprised, the way you signpost your roads.'

She didn't mean him personally or even the police force,

but his face drooped like a hound's. 'Actually,' she said, 'I'm sure this will take me to Cromer.'

He tramped around her car and took hold of her door, resting the ball of his thumb on the groove into which her window had sunk. 'I'd like to see your driving licence.'

She imagined him playing hockey instead of football, in a gym-slip, and felt somewhat better as she opened her handbag. 'I believe you'll find that's in order,' she said, flicking through the transparent plastic pockets until she found the one that held her licence.

He scrutinized both sides of it, and made to hand the wallet back to her. As he did so, her staff identity card flipped up. He stared at it with such distaste that she had the absurd notion that the ubiquitous Stilwell had even managed to prejudice him. 'I'd watch out if I were you,' he said.

She would have asked what for if she had thought he would tell her. He went back to his vehicle, walking slowly in the middle of the road, as if warning her not to overtake him. He'd made her so tense that when she passed the junction he must have been watching she neglected to read the sign. It was a minor road, surely no use to her, and besides, there was a signposted crossroads a few hundred yards ahead.

A dull sound of engines had begun to weigh down the air. She thought it must be farm machinery, though she could see none in the fields. Now she could read the signpost, which confirmed that she was on a road to Cromer. Lights across the field that met one angle of the junction caught her eye, and she braked. Whatever was rumbling towards her from the south-west, it had a police escort.

She stopped at the junction to watch for a minute. It was Enoch's Army, still roving England in search of a hospitable county. The decrepit vans and caravans and mobile homes crawled across the landscape as slowly as a funeral, boxed in by police cars with blue lights throbbing on their roofs. Despite the police escort, the convoy seemed for a moment old as the land, a nomadic tribe without a time or place to call its own. Its time had been the sixties, Sandy thought, and watching it wouldn't get her to Cromer. She started the car and shot across the junction, which was clear for hundreds of yards. She was just past the crossroads when a boy of about seven ran out of the long grass to her right and into the road, straight in front of her car.

She slammed on the brakes. The car skidded across the tarmac, almost into the ditch the child had jumped over. As Sandy turned into the skid a woman in a kaftan ran out of the grass after the child. She made to leap the ditch, stumbled backward as she saw the car, slipped on the muddy verge and fell awkwardly at the edge of the field. When she tried to rise and then lay wincing, one hand on her ankle, Sandy parked the car on the opposite verge and went to her.

She hadn't reached the woman when the boy flew at her, brandishing a jaggedly pointed stone he had picked up. Sandy was already shaking with the effects of the near miss, and the way the boy clearly felt he needed to defend his mother from her turned her cold all over. 'I'm not going to hurt her,' she assured him. 'I want to help.'

The woman raised her face, which looked scrubbed thin and pink. Though her uneven hair was greying, she was about thirty years old. 'Are you not from round here?' she said in a broad Lancashire accent.

'No more than you are,' Sandy said. 'Would that matter?'

'People don't like us going near their homes or their land.'

'Pretty unavoidable, I'd say.'

When the woman smiled gratefully at her, the boy dropped his stone in the ditch with a splash. Sandy helped the woman to her feet. She took two steps and moaned through clenched lips, and tottered against Sandy. 'We ought to get you to a hospital,' Sandy said.

'No hospitals. They make us wait until they've dealt with anyone who's got a home address. We've herbs and a healer in the convoy.'

'Do you want to wait here for them, or shall I drive you back?'

'I want to go back,' the boy pleaded, and slapped the roof of Sandy's car. When Sandy supported his mother to the vehicle and let him into the back she saw he had left earthy handprints on the roof. He was the first small boy she'd met who smelled as grubby as he looked, and his mother seemed to have no use for deodorants either. Sandy turned the car and said, 'What was he running away from?'

'Arcturus? All he wanted was to go in a hedge because we've no toilet in the van, and the farmer let two dogs chase him.'

'What did the police do?'

The boy hissed at the mention of the police, and the woman laughed curtly. 'Looked the other way. They don't want to know about us except to try and destroy us because we might make people see there are other ways of living besides theirs. Enoch says anyone who wears a pointed hat must be a dunce or a clown. One lot of police down south smashed all Arcturus' toys while they were pretending to search the van for drugs. They remind me of his father. *He* used to like to smash our things until we left him and joined Enoch.'

'Enoch's our daddy now,' Arcturus said.

Sandy felt light-headed with so much unexpected information. 'The dogs didn't hurt you, I hope.'

'No, Enoch chased them off, but Arcturus didn't realize. And do you know, the farmer started shouting, "Don't you hurt my dogs"? Enoch says that people caring more for animals than humans shows how we've lost touch with the old ways but can't do without them. Society wants us all to dress in hides and skins now, but it used to be the priests who put on skins so they could communicate with the animals they shared the land with.'

'Hmm,' Sandy responded, playing safe. She was on the side road now, and the foremost police car flashed its headlights at her. As she pulled half off the tarmac and felt her left-hand wheels sink into the verge, she saw Enoch Hill

110

marching at the head of the convoy, behind the police. She hadn't realized he was so big: six and a half feet tall at least, with a black beard that hung on to his chest, and hair that streamed as low on his back. He wore a waistcoat and trousers that appeared to be woven of rope. Sandy found the sight of him so fascinating that at first she didn't notice that the police were gesturing her to make a U-turn. 'I've brought an injured woman back to her van,' she called. 'She fell on the road.'

'I'll take her,' Enoch said. His voice was so big that it crowded out any trace of where he came from. He strode around the police escort and waited, breathing like a bull. Sandy helped her passenger out of the car, and he lifted the woman in his arms. 'Vaggie's driving your van. She can drive while Merl sees to your leg.'

'I'll walk with you in case there are any dogs about, shall I?' Sandy said to the boy, and his mother gave her a grateful look.

The van was at the rear of the parade of some forty vehicles, which were still moving, herded by the police. Men with piratical earrings stared out, and children with straw braided in their hair. Sandy had to trot so as to keep up with Enoch. She felt as if she were being borne along by his energy and presence, the smell of sweat and rope, the veins that stood out on his leathery arms, his hair and beard gleaming like wire. 'Thanks for looking after these two,' he said. 'Sorry to be pushing you, but this isn't the place for a stroll.'

'Absolutely,' Sandy panted. 'Have you far to go?'

He turned his huge weathered head and stared keenly at her without breaking his stride. 'As far as we have to until we find somewhere that needs to be fed and that won't make us its slaves.'

The woman in his arms nodded vigorously. 'Feed the land and it will feed you.'

'Our way is to move on when the land wants to rest and dream, but the mass of men won't leave it alone. Man and the land used to respect each other, but now man pollutes the land, or he stakes his claim on it and then neglects it, or he cultivates it for food that will never feed anyone. There'll come a day when the earth demands more of man than it ever did when man knew what it wanted.'

Some of this made sense to Sandy, despite the phrasing. 'Do you have somewhere in mind for yourselves?'

'We found a place last week, but the people around it rose up against us,' Enoch said. 'Territory breeds violence.'

They had reached the woman's vehicle, a van painted with sunbursts around the headlamps, clouds on the sides. Immediately the woman who was driving halted to let her and the child climb in, the police car that was following began to blare its horn.

'Lo and behold,' Enoch said. 'Everywhere is someone's territory where we aren't welcome.'

'There must be people who have some sympathy for you.'

'Find me them,' Enoch challenged, and strode back alongside the convoy. 'People hate us for showing them what's wrong with their lives, like being made to live where the state decrees, and living too close together, and being scared someone else will steal what they've got, and having their family come apart around them but not daring to work out a different kind of family life.'

Sandy wondered if the whole convoy used his words as the woman had. 'Man is as savage as he ever was,' Enoch was saying. 'Violence used to be necessary, it used to be part of the relationship between man and the earth. Now it has lost its meaning it can only get worse.'

'It surely can't be that simple.'

'How can it mean anything when we know the bomb can destroy the land and every one of us? What do you do?'

He was asking what her profession was, she gathered – presumably to demonstrate that she couldn't refute his ideas. 'I'm a film editor.'

He frowned at her, his hairy nostrils flaring. His frown felt like a change in the weather. 'Then you're adding to the violence,' he said sadly. 'Making images of it doesn't take it out of people, when you put it up in front of them

112

in the dark like a god. That's just feeding the images and making them feed on themselves, and that gives them power. Soon they'll have nothing to do with humanity, they'll just be another power that gobbles up meaning and feeds people the opposite.'

'Come on, all films aren't violent.'

'All fiction is an act of violence.' His words had almost the rhythm of a marching song. 'It's all an act of revenge on the world by people who don't like it but haven't the strength to change it. It's a way of putting your own prejudices into other people's heads. Me and my folk, we've been made into a fiction, a scapegoat people think will carry away everything they hate if they can only get rid of us.'

'If you let yourself be interviewed,' Sandy said, more to give herself a breathing space between his arguments than to persuade him, 'mightn't that let the country see you as you are?'

Enoch grunted and ducked his head bull-like towards her. 'All they'd see is what they want to see. I've never watched films or television since I was old enough to walk away from them. They're both addictive drugs, and we've none of those here. We tell stories at night in the old way, stories the land and our dreams tell us. Anyone can add to the story and tell it again, and it belongs to us all. That's what films and the rest of those industries stole, the old stories we're rediscovering. They stole them and spoiled them so the tellers could pretend they were the property of just a few. Man can't resume his old relationship with the earth until we remember the tales that told the truth. We had a blueprint for living, and civilization tore it up.'

'I'd like to hear you tell those stories,' Sandy said as a friendly farewell. He had led her to the front of the convoy, which had almost reached the crossroads. She gave him an apologetic smile to go with her remark, and turned to leave. Then she drew a breath that stung her nostrils. Beyond the relentless repetitive glare of the police car, a van from Metropolitan Television was waiting on the Cromer road.

Directing the cameraman was one of the newsmen with whom she'd had the disagreement outside Boswell's office.

He made to wave to Sandy, then tried to take the gesture back. Enoch had already noticed. He didn't even frown at her, he ignored her, which was as good as saying he'd known all the time she had meant to trick him. 'I didn't even know they were here,' Sandy protested. 'I wasn't trying to soften you up.'

'None of my folk will talk to them,' he muttered like thunder. 'We won't be made into images for you to put in people's heads.'

She left him striding behind the police car, and stalked across the junction, past the television van. The newsman pretended not to know her until she came abreast of him. 'Well done, Sandy,' he murmured. 'What have you got for us?'

'My self-respect, and I'll keep it, thank you. I'm on leave, in case you didn't know. They don't want you to film them, and they're allowed to refuse, aren't they, even if you think it's for their own good?' By now she was at her car, and shouting. She climbed in and slammed the door and breathed hard until her rage subsided, and then she drove towards Cromer without looking back.

18

Two hours later she drove out of a forest and up a long slope past a derelict zoo, and there was the sea beyond Cromer. A shoal of sunlight played on it, all the way to the sharp horizon. A breeze that felt like a memory of sand and cold salt water made her face tingle. The openness was such a relief after the crooked roads that she drank in the view for a minute or so before heading down into the narrow streets.

The crowds in the town were so brightly dressed and so variously sunned that they looked almost cartoonish. Families nudged one another off the pavements outside shops dangling red-cheeked postcards and sprouting bunches of plastic buckets, inflated ducks, wrinkled pink lifebelts. Side streets were flagged with signs: Fish 'n' Chips, Tea and Staff o' Life, Hotel de Paris . . . She thought it best to head for the esplanade, where tall slender hotels overlooked bathing chalets and the pier. The first hotel she walked into had a vacant room.

She checked in and went on to the pier, where the pavilion was advertising *Valentine the Vampire: a Show for All the Family*. Tommy Hoddle's name had been forced almost to the bottom of the posters by photographs of a comedian and of the male and female leads, none of whom meant much to Sandy. He wasn't in the theatre, the girl in the box office told her, and wouldn't be until his make-up call. The best the manager could offer was a ticket for the evening performance and the possibility of interviewing Tommy Hoddle afterwards. Sandy thanked him and wondered where the actor might be now. 'He always walks as far as he can and be sure of getting back on time,' the manager said. 'He might be on the cliffs or on the beach.'

'Do you happen to know what he's wearing?'

The manager shrugged. 'The usual sort of thing.'

Sandy had an incongruous vision of him wearing a policeman's uniform, which Hoddle and Bingo had always worn in films – a vision of him wandering the beach like a sad clown searching for his mate. She stood on the pier and scrutinized the coast in case she might recognize him. Children marked out territories with sandcastles near their supine parents; a dog that looked starved went scrabbling up the cliff near her hotel. She could see nobody by himself on the beach or the cliff. She returned to the hotel, to use the phone in her room.

Roger didn't answer for a while, and then he said only, 'Yeah, hold on.' His preoccupation deserted him as soon as he heard her voice. 'Hi, Sandy! Where have you got to?'

'I'm taking the sea air in the jewel of the Norfolk coast,' she said, quoting the sign she'd passed on the road into the town. 'I've tracked down half of the comic relief in the film and I hope to meet him later. How are things with you?'

'The book's growing, coming along fine, I think, despite whichever of my neighbours can't keep their pets under control. Listen, I've some news you'll want to hear. Stilwell is going to have to eat his words. I've got part of the movie he said never existed.'

'Where did you find it? How much have you got?'

'Well, ah, just a couple of frames. But they're consecutive shots, Karloff on a tower and Lugosi looking up. I'll stake my reputation that they're not from any other movie. I only wish I had more footage, say a complete scene. It would prove to the world that Graham was right all along. Toby found these frames at the flat, and there was a witness to confirm he did.'

'What made him go back?'

'He was moving out the bed now that he's got a new place of his own. I guess he wanted a memento he'd shared with Graham. The guy who was helping him noticed something caught under the door near the hinges. Toby says he's not surprised the cops overlooked it, it must have had to work itself loose before anyone could see it. I guess these

116

frames are from the end of a reel. Whoever stole the film from Graham must have caught the end in the door and ripped this piece loose, the way it's chewed up. Hell of a way for anyone who's supposed to care about movies to behave, even a thief.'

'It is, isn't it?' Sandy was trying to find words for the uneasiness it made her feel when Roger said, 'Toby tried to contact you at Metropolitan before he called me, and he says someone there wants to talk to you.'

No doubt a rebuke for her behaviour at the crossroads was awaiting her. It could wait, she thought, and said, 'Do you want to read Graham's list to me while I've some time to spare? I promise to guard it with my life.'

'Sure, so long as having it doesn't stop you calling.' He dictated the list to her. 'You're in Birmingham tomorrow, right? I made you an appointment the day after, in Wordsworth country, near Keswick. Charlie Miles, the set designer. Graham didn't trace him, but I managed to. Sounds crotchety but talkative.'

'Well done, armchair hunter.'

'The day after that I can probably meet you if you want me to, if you let me know where you'll be.'

'I will. Here's something for you to ponder until we meet again. Harry Manners and Denzil Eames both gave me material relating to the film, including a film magazine called *Picture Pictorial*, and do you know who was attacking the film before it was even completed? None other than our friend Leonard Stilwell.'

'Jesus, that's strange. What's behind all this, do you think? I'll see what I can find out here.'

'Don't go getting yourself badly reviewed.'

'You wouldn't deny me a taste of the thrill of the chase.'

'I'll have to remember that turns you on.'

She might have said more, but she felt inexplicably constrained, as if their conversation were being overheard. She copied down the details of her appointment in Keswick, and said goodbye to Roger with a kiss that felt clammy in the mouthpiece. She tried to call several addresses further north, with so little success that she began to think she was misdialling: perhaps she needed to unwind after her journey. Shouldering her handbag, she strolled down to the promenade and sat on a bench to examine what Denzil Eames had given her.

After glancing through F. X. Faversham's book, she dropped it back in her handbag. The ornate Victorian style of writing seemed too much like hard work just now, and besides, Eames had said that the film had little to do with the original story. Instead she unfolded Spence's notes.

The large wry handwriting proved easy to decipher once she identified several of the letters, but all it seemed to let her know was that the notes were random ideas rather than the products of research. 'Man killed while building tower . . . his accidental death dedicates it to some pagan god . . . biblical parallels (Babel; others?) . . . demands sacrifice . . .' Much of the notes concerned Lord Belvedere, apparently the Karloff character: '. . . haughty, strutting, vainglorious, impervious to argument, chauvinistic, unyielding . . .' After more of this, written at such speed that some of the letters had torn the paper, Spence had tried his hand at dialogue:

'Belvedere: You are trespassing in what you say. Never dare to question an Englishman's title to his land. Do not judge my country by the savagery of yours.

'Gregor: Can't you see that your denial lets it grow stronger? Truth is our only weapon against that which has been buried but not destroyed. While you deny the blood your ancestors caused to be shed, it will have blood.'

A breeze prowled through the grass on the cliff, and a shiver took Sandy by surprise. She wondered if Eames had paraphrased the dialogue or hadn't bothered to incorporate it in the film. There seemed to be an insight lurking behind her thoughts, but it wouldn't emerge into the light of her mind. She took out the musty book and glanced at 'The Lofty Place'. Yes, the character was called Lord Belvedere; Gregor had been added to expand the tale to feature length, of course. She closed the book and gazed out at the leisurely unravelling of the waves. That helped her relax, but she was still feeling dissatisfied and thick when it was time to return to the hotel.

She ate Cromer crab at a table set for one in the dining-room that overlooked the beach, which was almost deserted now. Before long she had to stop herself trying to creep up on the idea that was staying stubbornly out of reach. She kept thinking the waves looked like a shape that reared up and crouched, slithered on its belly along the glistening sand, reared up again closer to her. She was tempted to order another half bottle of Chablis, but decided that the show at the end of the pier might be what her nerves needed. She drank a token cup of coffee and strolled out of the hotel.

The evening was reawakening. Couples promenaded arm-in-arm above the beach, wheelchairs squeaked. Close to the pier a back street jangled with pinballs and tenpenny rides. In the twilight the inflated beach toys that hung in bunches outside shops looked like huge strange vegetables. Families were hurrying down the zigzag ramp that descended from the esplanade. She joined the queue as it began to clatter on to the pier.

The manager was standing in the doorway of the pavilion, rocking on his heels and bowing to the audience as they filed in. He saw Sandy, and slapped his brilliantined scalp. 'Tommy Hoddle. I forgot to mention you to him. I'll have a word with him before the final curtain.'

The auditorium was almost full, of at least as many children as adults. Sandy's seat was on the aisle, close to the exit. In the row ahead of her a small boy was licking a green ice lolly whose wrapper showed a vampire with his hair slicked back. Nearer the stage, a little girl was clutching a grey doll with a boxy head and bolts protruding from either side of its neck. As Sandy noticed those, the lights went out.

The curtain rose to reveal two headscarved women chattering over a garden fence, complaining about newcomers to their village. Only that morning the man with the pizza wagon had offered one of them a bite of his big salami (hoots of shocked mirth from a party of old ladies), and what about the family who'd bought the old house on the hill and who never came out in the daytime? They even sent their little boy to night school. 'It'd drive me bats to live like that,' one woman crowed, to a few knowing groans from the audience.

The women carried on in that vein for a few minutes, the dialogue not merely begging for laughs but cocking its leg as well, and then the spotlight beam which denoted the sun dropped like a stone. Children in the audience began to murmur and stir. 'It's all right, they're friendly vampires,' a mother behind Sandy whispered. 'The little boy saves everyone when there's a flood at the end. He turns into a bat and flies to get help.'

The women at the fence peered into the wings and fled as the family appeared, a cloaked man who intoned 'Good evening' in a deep indeterminately foreign voice, a hooded woman wheeling a pram shaped like a coffin and shaking a rattle made of bloodshot eyes, and finally a diminutive comedian wearing a cloak and short trousers, who was greeted with applause and cheers. They sang a song, 'Flittery Flappery Floo', and then complained of a smell of garlic and retreated offstage to make way for the pizza wagon, whose proprietor sang, 'You can't-a have-a da pizza without-a you gotta da garlic,' while Sandy considered walking on the beach until the curtain. What she thought might be the world's oldest young couple sang a tepid love duet, until the simpering fiancée pushed her beau away. 'Behave yourself, here comes my father,' she said as the band struck up the theme from a television series about the police. It could only be announcing Tommy Hoddle, and Sandy sat forward to watch.

He backed on to the stage, stooped over as though the lantern in his hand were bending him. His policeman's helmet was too large, his jacket and trousers were absurdly small, exposing his bony wrists and ankles. The jump he gave as he pretended to notice the audience made her think of a grandfather trying to entertain youngsters. He pushed up his helmet, which had slipped even lower, and goggled at them.

His downturned mouth was so wide it might almost have been painted on. His eyes seemed larger and more prominent than they had in the one film of his and his fat partner's that she'd seen. He cupped his ear until someone in the front row shouted 'Boo', and then he nearly fell over backwards. 'He's just pretending,' the mother whispered behind Sandy, for his panic was so convincing it was barely funny. Even the reappearance of the two gossips came as a relief.

He had to go up to the house on the hill, they cried, and find out what them foreigners were up to. They scattered as the diminutive vampire came onstage to sing, 'I'm just a little bats today'. A blackout made him vanish, a rubber bat swooped across the stage, and the lights came up for the first interval.

The next act began with Tommy Hoddle in front of the curtain, dressed as a scoutmaster and singing 'With me little peg and hammer in me hand' in a high occasionally shaky voice. No doubt the tent-pegs were meant to come in handy later on as stakes. An owl hooted onstage, and he took refuge in the wings while the curtain rose to display the vampires' front room, mirrors turned to the wall, a coffin by the fireplace, false fangs in a glass on the mantelpiece, the midget vampire playing with a tarantula doll. 'Don't let him go on there or you'll wake Granny,' his mother said, indicating the coffin, and glided away to answer the doorbell. She came back followed timidly by Tommy Hoddle, and offered him a drink. 'See if you can dig up your father, wherever he is,' she said to her boy, and they left Hoddle alone.

He didn't notice the coffin at first. Sandy felt her lungs tightening as she waited for his leap of panic. He peered up the chimney, he picked up the glass in which the teeth bobbed and opened his mouth to take a gulp without looking. Several old ladies shrieked with mirth and shock, a reaction that seemed to disconcert him more than it should, for the glass rattled sharply against the wooden mantelpiece as he put it back. He paced to the footlights and stared over them, eyes bulging. 'What's to do?' he inquired, just as the lid of the coffin began to rise.

Children squealed and pointed, and he leaned forward and cupped his ear. 'Behind you,' a little girl called uneasily, but he pretended not to hear. When other children took up the cry, he only stared harder – not at Sandy, of course, though he was looking in her direction. 'Remind me of what?' he said in an odd flat voice, as if he had performed the script so often that he was repeating it automatically. 'Behind you!' the audience shouted, and he seemed to freeze.

He wasn't staring at Sandy, his eyes widening until a little boy near her covered his own, gasping, 'They're going to pop.' He was staring past her at the exit. 'Behind you!' the audience yelled, laughing loudly at last, and she found herself joining in. The shouts didn't move him, but only Sandy turned to look where he was staring.

Just beyond the glass doors, where it had grown almost dark, a man was standing. She couldn't see his face or any other details, except that his silhouette seemed exceptionally thin, yet she had the immediate impression that he was waiting there for one of the performers in the show. He must be carrying a bouquet to present to someone, she thought: that was why she could see a glimmer of flowers about his face. The audience laughed louder still, and she turned to see Tommy Hoddle race offstage, so clumsily he almost toppled across the footlights.

The laughter died down, and there was silence. In the midst of the laughter Sandy thought she heard a clank and thump backstage, as if a door had been flung open. The vampire mother and her son appeared from the wings, and were so obviously bewildered to find nobody for her to give the glass of red liquid to that the audience roared approval. The small comedian made several puns and jokes before saying rather desperately, 'Let's go and see what's keeping my dad.' They hurried into the wings, and the stage stayed deserted for so long that the audience grew restless. Their murmurs invoked a figure in black, not a vampire but the manager. 'I'm very much afraid to have to announce that Tommy Hoddle will not be able to continue,' he said.

19

The audience seemed not to miss him, nor did the plot of the show. During the interval Sandy looked for the manager to ask what was wrong, but couldn't find him or the thin man with the flowers. She squirmed throughout the third act, and thought the cast would never finish singing 'Flittery Flappery Floo' at the end. She willed Tommy Hoddle to appear at the curtain call, but there was still no sign of him when the audience left amid an upheaval of folding seats.

The manager was waiting by the doors to apologize for the hiatus. Sandy hung back until she would be able to talk uninterrupted. As she approached he brushed his fingertips hard across his forehead, pulling his eyebrows momentarily awry. 'I'm sorry I didn't come back to you,' he said, 'but you'll have realized we had problems.'

'I couldn't have thrown him by just being here, could I?'

'Did he know you?'

'No.'

'Then no, you couldn't have, because he wasn't aware you were after him. I didn't get a chance to tell him.'

All the same, she felt somehow responsible. 'Do you think I might be able to talk to him now, at least say hello to him?'

The manager gazed unreadably at her. 'I'm afraid that's impossible,' he said, and showed her out and locked the door behind her.

She was still on the pier when the lights at the front of the pavilion went out, extinguishing her path. The night seemed to take a step forward. For a moment she thought she saw the man with the flowers leaning towards her from the cliff, but it must be a scrawny bush. A breeze crept behind her, bearing an unidentifiable smell that made her think something had died nearby. She hurried to the top of the concrete zigzag and back to the hotel.

Because she felt in need of company, not so much to talk as just to be with, she went into the bar and carried a gin and tonic to a seat by the window. The dark waves appeared to have found a piece of wood: a long thin object lay at the water's edge, glistening as it fidgeted like a dreaming dog. Sandy tried unsuccessfully to distinguish its shape, then glanced around as a couple entered the bar. They were two of the cast from the show: the vampires.

As soon as they sat down, Sandy went over to them. The man's hair was still combed back in a V from his high forehead; there was a trace of stage make-up in the woman's reddish eyebrows. She looked up first, her wide face tired and wary. 'May I sit down?' Sandy said. 'I was just at your show.'

The man blinked at her over his shoulder. Without make-up his round face looked porous as a sponge. 'How were we?'

'Good for the children.'

'But not so good for you, eh?'

'Perhaps I wasn't in the mood.'

'Thank God for a spoonful of honesty. Sometimes meeting one's audience feels like being lowered slowly into treacle. Sit down by all means,' he said, and sat back expansively. 'Better days are on their way. This winter will see Hattie here in an Agatha Christie, and I'll be making merry with Robin Hood.'

'At least we're working here, Stephen, when it seems half the country is resting,' Hattie rebuked him.

'Resting is more of a task than working,' he agreed, and said deadpan to Sandy, 'The worst part is not having somebody telling one what to say and do.'

'Though there are lines it's a nightmare to have to repeat at every performance.'

'I heard a few tonight, did I?' Sandy suggested.

Hattie gave her a sharp look. 'I was hoping the strain didn't show.'

'Not on you, but what about the unofficial interval?'

The actor and actress exchanged glances like a secret

sign. 'Maybe Tommy's act got the better of him,' Stephen said.

'How do you mean?'

'Maybe he'd done it so often he forgot he was only pretending to be panicked. Some nights he's been so damned convincing that the producer's had to tell him to tone it down for the sake of the younger members of the audience. That's what one calls living one's role, I suppose.'

'Is he better now?'

'We trust so. Any particular reason why you ask?'

'I was hoping to speak to him.'

'Ah, that *is* who you are. The manager mentioned you'd approached him. Speak about what?'

'I'm researching a film in which he and his partner appeared.'

The actor gazed at his colleague, who showed him her empty hands. 'I don't know when you'll have a chance to speak to him, if at all,' the actor said. 'None of us knows where he is.'

A wind tried the window and then blundered away into the night. On the beach a piece of the dark stirred and settled itself. 'He didn't just run off the stage, he ran off the pier, and nobody saw him stop running,' Stephen said. 'As we came over here the theatre was alerting the police.'

It wasn't her fault, Sandy thought: it couldn't be. She imagined Tommy Hoddle out there in the night, still running, eyes and lungs bursting. 'It may just have been stage fright. That never really goes away,' Hattie said. 'Which film are you researching?'

'The one he made with Karloff and Lugosi.'

The actress opened her mouth, and then she fed herself a sip of whisky before speaking. 'Did he know that was what you were after?'

'He couldn't have.'

'We can't blame you for chasing him away, then.' All the same, the actress fixed Sandy with a gaze that would have reached the back of a theatre. 'If you're feeling kind-hearted, you might leave him alone when he does come back.'

'If you think that's advisable.'

'You aren't offended, are you? Meeting you would buck him up, I'm sure it would, if you were wanting to ask him about anything except that film. Chances are it was partly to blame for how he acted tonight.'

'How could it be?'

'You'd be surprised. He's often said his nerves were never the same since, and he thinks it's what gave his partner a bad heart, doesn't he, Stephen?'

'Billy did drink,' Stephen said.

'Did he before they made that film?'

'Maybe not as much.'

'Then don't make me out to be a liar.' She gazed at Sandy with a fierceness that seemed both weary and habitual, and said, 'We may as well tell her what he told us. At least then she won't need to go bothering him.'

'Tell her about the film?' When the actress nodded impatiently he said to Sandy, 'He told us about it in here one night, over quite a few drinks. As a matter of fact, he was sitting where you're sitting now.'

Sandy suppressed an irrational urge to look behind her, at the stretch of the window that was out of her sight. 'But when we asked him about it the other day,' Hattie interrupted, 'he seemed to wish he'd never brought it up.'

'Which is to say, what happened to his partner.' Stephen closed his eyes, and Sandy couldn't tell if he was collecting his thoughts or using an actor's trick to build suspense. 'We gathered that for most of them the film was simply a job to be done well, but in his way Billy took it as seriously as the director Giles Spence did. Billy had thought it was going to be one of those thrillers where the ghosts are explained away at the end. He said he was afraid that his and Tommy's audience would resent not being told at the end not to worry, but he turned out to be afraid of something else.'

'What was that?' Sandy said, trying to ignore the restlessness on the dark beach.

'He must have been superstitious, not just in the way of all of us theatricals. The more progress they made on the film the more nervous he became, apparently, until he began to get on Tommy's nerves as well. They'd always shared a room wherever they were working, but now he would hardly allow Tommy to go to the lavatory by himself. Tommy says the worst of it was that Billy refused to admit he didn't want to be left on his own.'

'Tell her what's supposed to have happened on the film.'

'I was about to,' he said, and paused to display the rebuke. 'Billy was convinced there were people on the set who shouldn't be, for one thing – we assume he meant people. He ruined more than one take because he said someone made a face at him round the scenery, and he got more nervous when the director asked what kind of face. Then there was something about a smell when they were in the last week of filming. They couldn't trace it, they thought it had to do with some plumbing nearby, and so they did their best to forget it, all except Billy. He kept insisting it was something dead.'

'Something someone had hidden in the studio to spoil the film, he meant,' Hattie said.

'I'm not sure if he did or not. Anyway, two incidents nearly finished him. Whether they drove him to drink or vice versa you must judge for yourself, young lady. One day he was checking his make-up in the mirror and he thought he saw Tommy come into the room behind him, only he wasn't sure if it was Tommy because he couldn't see the face. Then he knew it wasn't Tommy or anyone else who ought to have been there, because of what was covering the face, and that was all he'd say. I imagine Tommy didn't try very hard to get more out of him.'

'Two incidents, you said.'

'The other was on almost the last day of filming. They were shooting a scene where Tommy and Billy had to run off in opposite directions, on to other sets, you understand, which weren't lit particularly well just then because they weren't in use. So Tommy and Billy ran off, and the director shouted cut and print or whatever one shouts in those circumstances, and then Billy ran back trying to scream. It wasn't until weeks later that Tommy managed to get him to say what he thought he'd seen. All he would say was that he'd run into something he'd thought was propping up the scenery, because nobody could fit into a corner like that, only it had started to come after him.'

'Tommy says he was never the same after making that film, and it wasn't even released.'

'Does he know why?' Sandy asked.

'If he does, he isn't telling. He did say to us that once the director died, everyone Tommy knew who'd worked on it was quite glad to see it quietly buried.'

'In Tommy's case that may have been because he hoped it would help Billy sort himself out,' Hattie said. 'They stayed together for the sake of their act, but off stage Billy nearly drove him crazy, Tommy says. Billy didn't just not leave him on his own, he kept on at him to put on more weight, can you imagine? When Billy had drunk too much he would always start to sing some kind of a song. "Bony and thin, bony and thin," he'd sing. And drunk or sober, he would nearly have a fit if Tommy ever stood behind him. Whenever they were walking he'd step back to make sure Tommy stayed in front, especially if they were casting shadows. Tommy got so desperate he suggested they should build it into their act, but Billy wouldn't admit he was doing it. Tommy thought he mightn't even have realized he was.'

'How did he die?' Sandy said, though she wasn't sure that she wanted to hear.

'They were going out to entertain the troops during the war,' Stephen said. 'Tommy decided he absolutely had to get away on his own for half an hour before they left – told Billy he'd bring him a bottle of Scotch. So Tommy came back in half an hour and there was Billy at the dressing-table, with the doily he'd pulled off it draped over his knee and all the jars of cream smashed around him on the carpet, and him dead and staring back over his shoulder with his eyes nearly springing out of his head.'

'Tommy went out with the troops anyway. At least he had that to keep him going.'

'Nothing like hard work to take your mind off things.'

'Until tonight, in his case,' Sandy said.

'He'll be back. You can't keep an old dog down in this business,' Stephen assured her. 'Young lady, we must be going before our landlady locks up, but don't you let your sleep be troubled by anything we've said. I've heard stranger tales in a lifetime of treading the boards.'

Sandy didn't quite see why that should be reassuring. When they'd left, Hattie favouring her with a regal wave, she stared out at the wakeful night and then sent herself to her room. To her surprise, she drifted off to sleep almost as soon as she crawled into bed.

The dawn roused her, spreading golden furrows across the sea. She made herself coffee with the kit provided in her room and went out on the balcony to taste the last of the mist. She wouldn't trouble Tommy Hoddle, she promised herself, though perhaps she might call him on her way back south. She put down her cup and leaned over the balcony, and saw that one name on the poster for the show at the end of the pier had been pasted over.

She showered and dressed hurriedly, and headed for the pavilion. Only a cleaner was there so early, but she told Sandy all that she needed to know, in a booming monotonous voice. The police had found Tommy Hoddle late last night. He couldn't have been looking where he was going. He'd run off the edge of the cliff and was dead of a broken neck.

20

All she could do was drive to Birmingham. She drove south-
west across the flat land, past King's Lynn where the market
was served by the sea, past the orchards of Wisbech, where
apples were glazed with a lingering dew. Soon the sky grew
smudged, first with the burning of peat on the Fens and
then with the smoke of factories that had ganged up on the
cathedral at Peterborough. Further on, amid pastures and
spires that gleamed through trees, the steel town of Corby
was rusting, as though the ancient landscape were
reclaiming its elements. The road began to flourish old
names – Marston Trussell, Husbands Bosworth – until it
reached the motorway, where the race of cars sent her
speeding past Coventry towards Birmingham.

Her drive had been prolix, but at least it wasn't confusing
until she reached Birmingham. She followed the ring road
in search of the hotel she'd called from Cromer, until she
felt as if she would never stop driving: the road was like a
race track with her playing the mechanical hare. At last
she checked into a hotel opposite the railway station, and
cancelled her other reservation as soon as she was in her
room; then she went out for a stroll before lunch.

It proved to be almost as easy to lose one's way on
foot as it had been while driving. Subways led under the
pavements outside department stores and emerged in front
of gloomy offices or at the edge of razed ground where
yellow excavators gnawed the earth. When she'd had
enough of the snarling of machinery she made for the
nearest subway, which seemed bound to lead back towards
the shops she could see but was unable to reach because
of the traffic.

She might have chosen a more appealing route. All the
overhead lamps except one were smashed, their multi-

coloured entrails dangling, and the one that still worked was buzzing and fluttering helplessly. Once she had walked beneath the lamp, the half of the subway ahead seemed much darker. The glimmering tiles of the walls were blackened with graffiti like tangles of exposed roots. She trod on scattered fish-and-chip papers and almost lost her footing. She wondered if an excavator was digging close to the subway, for the smell of stale food was mixed with a smell of earth: indeed, she thought she heard a trickling of soil and a faint sound of clawing. She hurried to the end of the subway and glanced back out of the daylight. It must be litter which lay where the tunnel was darkest and which stirred as if it were about to leap from crouching. She made herself walk slowly up the ramp, into the sudden lunchtime crowd.

She ate lunch in a bar in the basement of the hotel. A blind man sitting at a nearby table had draped his coat over his guide dog, whether for warmth or concealment she couldn't tell. Every so often the coat would rear up as the dog's head emerged, its grey tongue lolling. Sandy patted the animal as she headed for the multi-storey car park.

She couldn't locate the muffled scraping that she heard among the ranks of empty vehicles until it was beside her, and a figure slithered out from beneath a parked car, his hands glistening with oil. She was so angry with herself for flinching that the poor man must have thought she was swearing at him, not herself. She gave him an apologetic grin and took refuge in her car.

At least there were plenty of signs beside the tangled streets to guide her out to the route north. The retirement home where the stunt man lived was close to an exit from the motorway. Sandy thought the location might be inappropriately noisy, but though she saw the sign for The Dell almost as soon as she left the motorway, the land had already cut off the rumble of traffic. She swung the car between the globed gateposts and coasted up the wide drive.

The Dell was an extensive three-storey house, sporting a weathercock on an ornamental tower. Nurses dressed in blue and white uniforms patrolled the gravel paths that wound about the lawns. Some were wheeling patients, one was shaking her finger at an old man in a wheelchair who had been surreptitiously feeding birds behind a tree. As Sandy parked on a rectangle of gravel she noticed a play area, swings and slides and a seesaw. They must be provided for visiting grandchildren, she thought, not for inmates who had entered their second childhoods.

A receptionist was reading a hospital romance behind a desk in the hall, at the foot of a wide staircase. She placed the book open on the desk and broke its spine with the heel of her hand as she said, 'May I help you?'

'I called earlier this week about speaking to Leslie Tomlinson.'

'Oh yes. Would you like to wait a moment? I'll fetch Nurse.'

Sandy sat on a leather couch with rolled arms opposite the desk, where the hospital romance was trying feebly to raise itself. Upstairs an old woman was crooning, 'Tooraloooraloora tuppence a bag,' while in the ground-floor lounge several old people were watching a war film; a man wearing a beret waved his stick every time the enemy were hit. Soon the receptionist came back with two nurses, whose blue and white uniforms had begun to make Sandy think of fast-food waitresses. 'Just see to Mr Hunter. We don't want him wearing his hat indoors, do we?' the older nurse said to her colleague, and sat by Sandy on the couch. 'You wanted to visit Mr Tomlinson?'

'Please.'

'You're not a relative?'

'Just a researcher,' Sandy said, displaying her staff card. 'I wanted to ask him about one of his films.'

'Have you come far?'

'From London.'

'A fair way.' The nurse brushed a speck, so minute Sandy couldn't see it, off her knee. 'We certainly didn't anticipate problems when we discussed your visit with you. Mr

Tomlinson was most responsive. But shortly before our lunch period today he took a turn for the worse.'

'Because I was coming, you mean?'

'No, I'm sure that's not the case. He wasn't just over-excited. Something upset him rather badly, and we haven't been able to persuade him to say what. To be frank with you, he won't open his mouth.'

'I'm sorry,' Sandy said, and stood up. 'I won't keep you any longer. I hope he gets better soon.'

'I was thinking you might be able to help.'

'If I can,' Sandy said, feeling as if she should first have asked how.

'He never talked much about his career, and none of us knew enough about it to get him talking. You may be able to remind him of something that will start him off.'

'I only really know about the film I'm researching, and I believe he injured himself making that one. Would it be wise to remind him of that just now?'

'It doesn't have to be a pleasant memory,' the nurse said as if Sandy were questioning her professional judgement, 'so long as it brings him back to us.' She clapped her hands at the old man in the television lounge, who was clutching his stick with one hand and pressing the beret to his scalp with the other. 'Look, we've a visitor. What must she think of you? Behave yourself, now, or there'll be no outing for you tomorrow,' she called, and marched upstairs.

Sandy hesitated long enough to make it clear that she was choosing to follow. The nurse padded briskly to the end of a corridor on the middle floor, where a window overlooked the play area. 'We think Mr Tomlinson may have seen someone climbing on the children's frame. One of the staff thought she saw someone running away. You'd wonder what they've got between their ears, someone who won't even leave our old folk in peace.' She pushed open the last door in the corridor and motioned Sandy forward. 'Here's someone to see you, Mr Tomlinson,' she pronounced in a slow clear hearty voice.

Sunlight was streaming into the room beyond the door,

through pink curtains drawn back towards wallpaper printed with baskets of flowers. In the midst of the brightness, which all the white bedroom furniture appeared to be directing at him, an old man lay in bed, smiling at the sky. The flowered quilt was pulled up to his plump mottled chin. His hands lay slack on the quilt, and between them were several childish paintings of the sun above yellow fields. 'Were his grandchildren here recently?' Sandy whispered.

The nurse looked puzzled for a moment. 'Oh, you mean the pictures? He painted those.'

Whatever made him happy, Sandy thought – but it didn't seem as if she had much chance of communicating with him. She was disconcerted to see that though he had performed stunts for both Karloff and Lugosi in the film, he didn't resemble either of them. Still, his face had puffed up with age, and the weight of it had dragged it and his vague smile slightly askew.

The nurse strode over to the bed as if she meant to heave him out of it. 'Now then, Mr Tomlinson, aren't we going to say hallo to our visitor? We'll have her thinking we've forgotten our manners. She wants to talk about one of the films we made.'

Even her casting herself in the film didn't startle him into awareness. His hands moved on the quilt, but only as they might while he was asleep. His gaze seemed as empty as the sky. The nurse gestured Sandy to step closer. 'Look, here she is,' the nurse wheedled, and directed Sandy to stand where he was gazing.

As she moved into his gaze Sandy felt uncomfortable, tongue-tied, out of place. She felt compelled to speak, to counteract the absence in his eyes, the meaningless brightness of the room. 'I'm Sandy Allan, Mr Tomlinson. I'm a friend of Graham Nolan's.'

'You remember Mr Nolan. Mr Nolan,' the nurse repeated as if he were deaf. 'The nice gentleman who's seen all your films.'

The names, his own included, seemed to fall unrecognized past him. 'You remember,' the nurse said almost accusingly. 'He was interested in the film Miss Allan wants to talk to you about, the one where you hurt your back.'

Though he appeared not to react, Sandy felt resentful that he should be reminded of his accident while he was gazing at her. She turned deliberately and followed his gaze. 'It's a lovely view,' she said, though the climbing frame out there made her unexpectedly nervous – she thought that if an adult stood on the top rung, their face would be level with Leslie Tomlinson's window. She had just realized that when a voice, composed as much of indrawn breaths as exhalations, bayed behind her. 'Made me fall,' it said.

Sandy swung round. The stunt man was still gazing as if there were nothing between him and the sky, but his mouth had fallen open, its corners sagging. 'Who made you fall, Mr Tomlinson?' the nurse demanded. 'When did they?'

Sandy's impatience with the nurse overcame her determination not to trouble him. 'While you were making the film, do you mean?' she said. 'While you were standing in for Boris Karloff?'

To her surprise and rather to her dismay, the name made his eyes gleam and then roll in their sockets. He glanced around him at the flowered walls and the flowered quilt, as if he were searching for somewhere he could bear to rest his gaze, then he looked beseechingly at her. 'It looked through the window,' he said, never closing his mouth.

Was he someone else who'd been distracted by intruders on the set of the film, or at least by the director's paranoia? 'I was Mr Karloff,' he said loosely. 'I fell off the tower.'

She had to go on, even if it disturbed him. 'What did you see at the window?'

His gaze began to rove again, so desperately she wished she hadn't asked. He stared at the walls and the quilt, and his hands began to pluck at the latter as if he wanted to tear the images of flowers off the cover. He stared past her, and she glanced nervously out of the window. The only figure in sight would be out of his, an old woman on a lawn chair, reading a book printed so large that Sandy could read it at that distance if she strained her eyes. When she turned to the stunt man, his gaze had quietened and was back in the sky. 'The dogs,' he mumbled like a last trace of an answer.

'What about dogs, Mr Tomlinson?'

'Mr Lugosi. He was worried about the dogs.'

'Oh, his pets,' Sandy remembered. 'He couldn't bring them to England because of the quarantine regulations.'

For the first and only time, Tomlinson looked directly at her. His face quivered with strain, whether to call a memory to mind or to fend it off she couldn't tell. The quivering spread to his lips, which fell open. By the time he finished speaking, his gaze had drifted back to the sky, and neither Sandy nor the nurse was able to provoke any further response. 'Not his dogs,' he said windily. 'The dogs he saw and I did. The dogs with a man's face, and things growing in their eyes.'

21

Only her sense of the absurd let Sandy approach the reception desk at the hotel. She'd already cancelled one booking today, and now she was going to cancel another. She told the receptionist that unexpectedly she had to visit her parents. It wasn't quite a lie, more a way of making herself seem less unreliable. She'd meant to visit them soon anyway, she told herself. They lived less than an hour away from her route to the Lakes. She wanted to make her peace with them if she could, but wouldn't she also welcome the chance to be safe with her family while she tried to think over the last few weeks? Once she admitted that to herself, she was so uncertain of her motives that she didn't call her parents before she set out from Birmingham.

She drove out of a bunch of lorries on the motorway and sped north for an hour. As soon as she grew used to the speed, a song began to run through her head: 'D'ye ken John Peel in his coat so gray?' She'd left Tomlinson singing that line over and over almost tunelessly as he smiled at the sky and feebly tweaked the quilt. The song was part of the score of the film, but knowing that didn't help her dislodge it from her brain. It had been too bloodthirsty for her taste when she was a child, and now the tune dredged up lines which she was perhaps remembering inaccurately but which still made her uncomfortable: '. . . from the chase to a view, from a view to a death in the morning . . .' '. . . and the cry of his hounds would awaken the dead . . .' and one she had never understood: 'D'ye ken that bitch whose tongue is death?' Sounds like another case of blaming the female, she thought, but the thought didn't help much. When she reached the division of the motorways, she followed the route to Liverpool.

She cruised through the town for a few minutes. Many

of the buildings she remembered from her childhood had been ousted by anonymous shopping precincts, and she felt so disoriented that she headed for the tunnel at once, though driving under the river made her claustrophobic. Midway she glimpsed a figure emerging from the subterranean wall on to the walkway alongside the road. He must have been a workman, and of course he wasn't chasing her; he must have gone down on all fours to examine something. She was glad to be back on the motorway beyond the tollbooths and racing, however briefly, before she turned off towards the sea.

Beyond Hoylake the houses and their grounds grew larger, more aloof. At West Kirby the peninsula rose to show a panorama of the Irish Sea beyond an obelisk. A tanker gleamed on the horizon and eased itself down over the edge of the world. Sandy took the road opposite the obelisk, towards the farms and the common. Her parents lived just out of sight of the sea. She parked outside the small detached white house, and was opening her door when her mother ran to her along the garden path.

She hugged Sandy and kissed her and called past her, almost deafening her: 'See, I told you it was Sandra's car. Didn't I tell you this morning I could feel we were going to have a visitor?' She touched Sandy's ear and grimaced apologetically, the wrinkles around her large brown eyes and at the corners of her wide dry lips multiplying, before another smile fluttered across her broad face. 'I knew it was going to be you,' she whispered, 'but there's no use trying to persuade your father.'

He came to the front door and peered over his reading glasses, and ducked his head to his hand as always to remove the glasses. Because Sandy remembered him as reading throughout her childhood, to himself or to her, his top-heavy face with its pale blue eyes blinking at the low sun looked unprotected; his small ears seemed to have nothing to do now that the heavy earpieces weren't hooked over them. He screwed up his eyes and limped forward, and gave her a hug that smelled of tweed and pipe tobacco and a hint of rosin. 'This is a treat. We were hoping to hear from you. You'll be staying, won't you? As long as you like.'

'I thought overnight, if it isn't too much trouble,' Sandy told her mother.

'How could you ever be too much trouble? You know your room is only the guest room when you aren't here. Where will you be off tomorrow?'

'Up to the Lakes.'

'The good old Lakes. Your father and I stayed there once for a dirty weekend,' Sandy's mother cried, and glanced about in case the neighbours had heard.

'We hadn't realized you were due for a holiday,' Sandy's father said, 'or is this work?'

'They've given me time off to recover.'

'We discovered just the other week that two of your father's quartet were gay,' her mother said before the silence could grow awkward. 'They told us halfway through a Mozart recital. We were flattered they felt they could tell us.'

Her father gave Sandy another squeeze and stepped back. 'Carry your bags, miss.'

'You settle yourself in, Sandra, and then we'll have a drink and a chat before we go out for dinner.'

Her father dropped her cases at the foot of the bed and waited until Sandy said, 'I'll be down in a few minutes.' She kicked off her shoes and stretched out on the counterpane she and her mother had made together one Christmas. The room still felt like hers, with the furniture and floral wallpaper and curtains that she'd chosen as a teenager, and being in it still felt like taking a breather. Today her parents were more emotionally overwhelming than ever, though perhaps by displaying their broadmindedness they were trying to convey obliquely that they were prepared to forget last week's disagreement. She seemed hardly to have lain on the bed when her father called, 'What drink will you have?' She sighed and shouted her preference, and soon she went downstairs.

Her mother was waiting to show her the work she was

doing in the botanical gardens at Ness, sketches of rare plants in all their seasons. Sandy sat on a Queen Anne chair in the front room, which was moderately full of elegantly carved furniture whose lines seemed to be developed by the silvery oriental patterns of the wallpaper, and sipped her gin while she admired the sketchbook. 'That one was a little swine,' her mother said as Sandy reached the last drawing. 'I just hope your London shops won't think the book is too provincial when it's done at last.'

'I'll make sure every one of them stocks it. I'm looking forward to being able to say it's by my mother.'

'Yes,' her mother said, so tentatively that Sandy wondered what she wasn't saying.

'Here's to it,' her father said, elevating his Martini.

The three of them clinked glasses. 'And to the Liverpool Philharmonic,' Sandy said.

'Long may they let me saw,' her father said. 'Which reminds me, I must buy some rosin.'

'Colophony prevents cacophony,' Sandy said for him.

'How old were you when you learned that? Too young to stay up for a concert, I remember. Lord, how many things we bury in our memories to be revived to brighten our declining years.'

'If you two are declining, the rest of the country may as well bury itself.'

'I suppose there's some life in us yet, right enough. Here's to yours.'

'Amen,' her mother cried, and paused. 'Someone in your line of business was asking to be remembered to you, Sandra.'

'Who was that?'

'An old boyfriend of yours. Can't you guess? Why, Ian whatever his name was, who escorted you to one of your father's concerts. I should have thought you would know he's in television now.'

'Quite a few people are, you know. He wasn't really what I'd call a boyfriend. I never realized someone wearing so much aftershave could be so unshaven. I bore the scars for weeks.'

'He seemed quite polite and musical to me. Anyway, he's grown a beard now, and he's working for the BBC. He'll be moving back to Liverpool now that they've opened their dockland studio.'

'Good luck to him.'

'I wish you were staying long enough for us to show you round dockland. It's a real little village now, you know. Lovely shops and restaurants, and independent television have a studio there too.'

'We'll go next time, but I hope you won't be disappointed if it doesn't tempt me back from London.'

'If you've made your mind up in advance there's no point in showing you at all.'

She was angry with herself for being scrutable rather than with Sandy, and so her tone was only faintly injured when she asked Sandy her news. The conversation had become equable by the time the family went out for dinner. They drove along the peninsula to Parkgate and ate at Mr Chau's, where coloured lights swam in a fountain in the middle of the restaurant and vegetables were shaped like dragons. Halfway through the main courses Sandy's father said, 'How are Tracy and Hepburn?'

Her mother chewed furiously, and said 'Bogart and Bacall' as soon as she could.

'They're feeding the weeds, I'm afraid. They were run over last week.'

Her mother reached for her hand. 'No wonder you don't know what to do with yourself with all this death around you.'

'I do, honestly. Don't fret.'

'Well, perhaps you do. I can understand your wanting to go up somewhere by yourself. You can see all the way to Wales if you go up on the common, you know, if it's only solitude you're going to the Lakes for.'

'I want to do a bit of research as well.'

'For what?'

Lying wouldn't be fair to herself or to them. 'About the film Graham Nolan was going to revive.'

'You do what you think is right,' her mother said, so heavily that all her remarks during the rest of the meal felt like the same veiled accusation.

As soon as Sandy was home she escaped upstairs, pleading a headache, and lay on her bed, hearing her father's placatory murmur in the living-room. It seemed that coming home wouldn't let her ponder after all, but surely the truth was that she didn't need to: Tommy Hoddle's nerves had got the better of him, and Leslie Tomlinson was senile; both encounters had disturbed her, but what was the point of looking for connections where none could exist? What she needed before she continued her search was a good night's rest. She awoke once, remembering her mother's suggestion that she was surrounded by death. She blinked at the walls and the curtains, between which a gap glimmered. She wasn't surrounded by death but by flowers, she thought drowsily, and went back to sleep.

In the morning she awoke to see her mother tiptoeing out of her room after setting down a mug of coffee on the bedside table. The sight of her mother in her dressing-gown, her grey hair trailing over the collar, made Sandy long to stay at least until they had reached a better under-standing. She glanced at the clock, and saw that it was already later than she had planned to leave. She struggled out of bed and stumbled with her coffee to the bathroom, and was in the shower when her mother rapped on the door. 'I'm making your breakfast,' she called.

In that case, Sandy knew, she would be at least thirty minutes. Sandy was downstairs in half that time. 'May I use the phone?'

'Of course,' her parents said in unison, so amiably that she felt a twinge of guilt for using it to carry on her search. All the same, she should try to set up an interview for tomorrow, since the composer who had scored the film lived just across the Scottish border. She dialled and heard the ringing cease. 'Neville Vine?'

143

Her father gave the name a wry glance that stopped short of recognition. A voice that sounded shivery with age demanded, 'Who wants him?'

'My name's Sandy Allan. I'm from Metropolitan Television. I wanted to ask Mr Vine about one of his scores.'

'Television? I want nothing to do with them,' he declared, more shakily than ever, 'nor with anyone who has.'

'You did talk to a friend of mine, I believe. Graham Nolan.'

'Never heard of him.'

'It might have been a year ago or more. He would have asked you about a film you wrote the music for, *Tower of Fear*.'

'I can't help you.'

Vine's voice had grown so shrill that she was afraid he was about to cut her off. 'Would you be prepared to talk to someone else who was asking me for information about the film? He isn't connected with television, he's writing a book.'

'No use. I don't know anything about the picture.'

'But you did write the score for it, didn't you? Surely you could – '

'I've told you, I don't remember,' he screamed, and replaced the receiver so clumsily that she heard its clatter for seconds before it was cut off.

Sandy's mother waited for her to meet her eyes. 'No luck?'

'He denied Graham ever spoke to him.'

'Didn't we tell you your friend was mistaken? Perhaps now you'll let him and his film rest.' The next moment she slapped her own face and walked rapidly to Sandy. 'Don't listen to my doddering,' she mumbled into Sandy's shoulder, 'you trust your instincts as you always have,' and then she gazed moistly at her. 'Just don't you dare put yourself at any risk,' she said.

22

Less than two hours later, when a downpour met her on the motorway, Sandy remembered her mother's warning. The grey clouds nesting on the Lakeland mountains surged forward and began to lash the traffic, and the mountains above the road dissolved into cloud, the vehicles around her were reduced to drowning headlamps and the weeping wounds of tail-lights. Even when she dropped her speed to thirty miles an hour she didn't feel safe, but there was nowhere to pull over, no slip road for miles. At least the other drivers were keeping their distance. For a while she was virtually alone except for distant struggling lights and a dark shape that seemed to dance between her and the lights, until she began to suffer an unpleasant notion that if she didn't increase her speed the blurred shape would launch itself at her rear window. Instead she slowed down even more to let the lights creep closer, reminding her of eyes, unable to blink. 'Shut up,' she told her imagination, and stared ahead at the wall of rain, which thinned and parted at last and let her accelerate over the flushed concrete under a bleary sun.

Charlie Miles, the set designer Roger had called on her behalf, lived on a minor road above Derwentwater. By the time Sandy left the motorway the clouds were sailing like ghosts of mountains into the sky, unveiling slopes of granite and heather and gorse crystalline with rain, and rushing streams above roads that blazed silver. Sandy felt her senses flowering, feasting on the refreshed landscape.

She had to assume that the unsignposted road on to which she eventually turned led to the set designer's house. As her route wound higher it gave her views of the lake, a giant section cut from a darker sky to fit the elaborately curving shore among the mountains. Sheep swerved away from her car and up the grassy slope, and then she met a coach full of pensioners. Rather than reverse almost a mile, she backed on to the soggy verge as a wizened little man with a large balding head and hands that seemed all knuckles emerged from a cottage beside the road and leaned on his gate to watch.

While the coach struggled to manoeuvre past her he took out a pipe and puffed at it until it was lit to his satisfaction, then he strolled over to the coach and began to direct the proceedings. 'Come on, come on, hey up, come on, hey up, hey up, come on . . .' The coach groaned by at last, and the oldster trotted over to Sandy, looking ferociously helpful. 'Thanks,' she said hastily, 'I can manage.'

As soon as she restarted the car, the old man slouched along his path and slammed the cottage door. Feeling rather mean for having disappointed him, Sandy eased the vehicle on to the road. She came abreast of the cottage, and glanced at the gate, where a name was all but engulfed by moss. She had to brake and lean out of the window before she could be sure that the name was Miles.

She turned the car, inching back and forth across the road six times, and parked beside the wall of the plot in front of the cottage, a garden planted with vegetables whose shoots glowed against the wet earth. She walked along the cracked path and knocked on the faded door. He made her wait before he jerked the door open and confronted her, his knuckly fingers drumming on his hips. 'I thought you didn't need any help.'

'I didn't realize who you were.'

'That's supposed to make a difference, is it?'

'It certainly does to me. I'm Sandy Allan. I was coming to interview you.'

He stared past her, wrinkling his nose, as if he were wondering if she'd hidden an accomplice somewhere near, then he stepped back so abruptly she thought he was going to shut the door in her face. 'Let's be hearing from you, then,' he said, and as soon as she opened her mouth: 'Give a man a chance to sit down.'

146

The front room was small and bare. A chair stood by a folding table spread with an embroidered tablecloth, on which lay a sketchbook with a pencil threaded through its spiral binding. Two easy chairs faced the window, which overlooked the lake. Several brown oval photographs of an unsmiling couple Sandy took to be his parents stood on the rough mantelpiece. Open doors let her see into a stone-floored kitchen and a bedroom that looked fit for a monk. She only glanced towards them as she took the unoccupied chair, but Miles shook his head at her. 'Trust a woman, hardly in the house before she's seeing what she would change.'

'I was just missing anything to do with films.'

'Then you're the only one here who is, because I want nothing to do with them.'

Could Graham have known better than to interview him, or was she in the wrong house? 'You used to have, didn't you?' she said.

'Long before you were born. Back when there were films to take a pride in.'

'So you're proud of the work you did.'

'Did you hear me say that? Is that anything like what I said? Your generation's fed on so much television and films that you've no time for words. Before we know it we'll be back where the pagans were, not wanting to write.'

'I take it you weren't satisfied with the films you were involved in.'

'Chuck me in the lake if I said that either.' He took pity on her then, which was just as infuriating. 'I was pleased with the Boadicea picture. I once read a Yankee magazine that praised my work on that. Only those were the days when a credit for set design meant something.'

'I think it still does.'

'Then it shouldn't,' he cried in what sounded like triumph. 'Some of my students took me to a film in Keswick last year and woke me up just in time for the end titles. It's a wonder if you can even find the set designer among the mob who get their names put up.'

147

'I suppose they feel their work deserves a credit too.'

'More like the unions would close the studios down otherwise, and no loss either if you ask me. Deserves a credit! My God, the carpet fitter got a mention, and the caterer, and the banker. It's a wonder they didn't have a credit for whoever bought the paper for the lavatory. If someone in the film fiddled with a radio there'd be a credit for the music they didn't even listen to, to make up a soundtrack record for all the damn fools in the audience to buy. That's assuming they can read.'

'Some of us still can.'

'Watch out you don't get hunted down for knowing too much, then. There was a newspaper in this film where the headline had nothing to do with what was under it, and don't tell me they would have put that in if they thought anyone had the brains to notice.'

'I've seen newspapers like that in films from fifty years ago.'

'Exactly. That's when folk started being robbed of their intelligence,' he said, and beamed at her. 'I enjoyed that argument. You'll have to come again.'

He cocked his head towards the window, and she wondered if she'd sat through all this only to leave herself no time to question him. 'Are you expecting someone?'

'Should I be?'

'I thought maybe your students.'

'Not today, and never here. One of them runs me into town to teach. I can still teach art, even with these hands.' He displayed his swollen knuckles and then hid his hands between his thighs. 'Your turn to talk. Tell me what you came all this way for.'

'To ask you about the last film you designed for Giles Spence.'

'That damned thing? It was more bloody trouble than it was worth. It's a wonder it was made at all. What do you know about it?'

'As you say, it was dogged with problems.'

'As I say?' He seemed about to lecture her again, but

instead he went on: 'Half the problems were of Giles' own making, if you ask me. I sometimes think he was behind the things that were supposed to have happened at the studio – trying to get his cast in the proper mood.'

'Then from what I've heard he went too far.'

'If you know so much about it I don't know what you expect *me* to tell you. I wasn't even there for most of the production.'

'Might you have kept any sketches you made?'

'For that film? No chance, as my students say. I was glad to get out of the studio the last time, after Giles called me back. I've never liked that kind of film since.'

Surely this gave the lie to his scepticism. 'What was it about the film you didn't like?'

'I'd rather not discuss it, thank you very much. The whole damned lot of them, Spence and everyone he'd implicated, were close to wetting themselves the last time I was there. Nobody should be that nervous just over making a film.'

Sandy felt she was getting nowhere. 'You said Spence called you back.'

'That's what I said,' he agreed impatiently, and then his grimace relaxed. 'Come to think, I do remember something I can show you, if it's of any interest to you. Pass me that pad.'

Sandy went to the table and gave him the sketchbook. When he flipped it open, she saw that it was blank. He tugged the pencil out of the binding and began to sketch, wincing at his arthritic clumsiness or the pain of sketching, glancing up at the window so often that she thought the light must be troubling him: whatever he was drawing, it certainly wasn't the view. Without warning he heaved himself to his feet, almost dropping the sketchbook, and clung to the edge of the table. 'Don't let me see you,' he warned.

Sandy pressed her hands over her racing heart. 'What's wrong?'

'Some damned animal getting in my vegetables. A sheep, it must have been. Didn't you see it look in the window?'

149

Sandy had been intent on trying to make out what he was attempting to sketch. 'No,' she said.

He stared at her as if she had called him a liar. 'Well, there it is,' he said, flinging the sketchbook on the table. 'That's the best I can do for you.'

Sandy glanced out of the window, beyond which she could see nothing intruding on the view of lake and grassy slopes except her car, and then she examined the sketch. She hadn't realized he had finished it. Was it meant to show a mass of vegetation in the shape of a face? If so, what kind of face? All she could identify was the tongue that bulged thirstily from the jagged mouth, unless the tongue was a swollen root, and the stalks that curled upward from the eyes to form horns above the low forehead. She couldn't bring herself to ask what the sketch was meant to represent when the drawing of it had caused him so much pain, but she thought of a question that sounded less cruel. 'Can you tell me the significance of this?'

'It's the last thing Giles asked me to design for his film. It was supposed to be the Karloff character's coat of arms.'

Sandy remembered something Denzil Eames had told her. 'That would be after Spence had done some last-minute research.'

Miles laughed brusquely. 'Is that what you call it?'

'Wouldn't you?'

'Giles would have. He wouldn't have wanted any of us to know where he'd been or what he might be dragging us into.' Miles turned towards the window. Sandy wondered nervously if he'd heard movement in his garden, but he seemed to be gazing at his memories. 'I only heard about it later from his wife, after he ran his car into a tree up at Toonderfield. I'd known her for years. I designed the sets for a play she was in, and she introduced me to Giles when he started making pictures.'

'You were saying about his research,' Sandy prompted.

Miles glanced at her so resentfully she wished she hadn't broken in on him. He thumped the sketch with the tip of one forefinger. 'Seen enough of this?'

'I think so.'

'Good riddance to it, then.' Before she could protest, he tore the sheet from the pad, ripped it up and threw the crumpled pieces into a wastebasket. 'You may as well know I've never forgiven him for that.'

'For what? I don't understand.'

'For making me put that in his film just so he could get his own back. Believe me, if we'd known what he was up to, he'd have been left without a cast or crew.'

'But what *was* he up to?'

'Haven't I just said? Getting his own back.'

She was afraid Miles' impatience would cut her off from the truth, and then she realized it wasn't impatience that was making him less than forthcoming. 'Keep this under your hat,' he muttered. 'I can't have the word getting round that I was a party to it, not at my age, even if I didn't know what I was doing. I won't have the life I've made here spoiled now. I'm naming no names, and I wouldn't tell you this much if I thought there was any chance of the film ever coming to light.' He glanced out of the window as a wind crept away through the grass, and put one hand over his mouth while he said, 'When Giles took time off he went to see the fellow who'd attacked the film in the House of Lords before we'd even started filming. And when he came back he wanted me to add what I just showed you to the set, and you'll have to find out why for yourself.'

23

The library in Keswick was closed for the day. In any case, it looked too small to stock reports of the proceedings of the Houses of Parliament. Sandy drove through the narrow streets, past houses fat and grey as pigeons, until she found a parking space by a telephone box. Ramblers wearing their holiday homes on their backs tramped by as she tried to make her calls. It was hardly surprising that she felt overheard.

There was no reply at Roger's. In any case, it would be quicker for her to track down the information herself. The nearest library she was able to locate that held copies of Hansard, as she phoned towns that appeared promising on the map, was in Manchester, at least three hours' drive away. 'Someone owes me a stiff drink when all this is over,' she told herself, and went back to the car.

In half an hour she was back on the motorway, and beginning to feel as though her interviews and her nights in hotels were nothing more than breaks from the race of juggernauts and coaches. As the mountains sank, a cloudy twilight advanced over the glum fields. By the time she reached Manchester, cars were switching on their lights. She had to drive twice through the gloomy Gothic one-way streets in search of somewhere to park. A line of meters opposite a bookshop from which police were bearing armfuls of confiscated horror magazines proved to be unusable after four o'clock. The second time she passed the library, a car was backing out of a space, and Sandy slipped in with a groan of relief.

The dome of the library loomed above the street lamps like a fallen lump of the sky. She climbed the wide steps beyond the columns of a portico and hurried into the lobby, which sent the echoes of her footsteps chasing her. An attendant directed her to the Social Sciences desk, where a man with a soft thick Lancashire accent found her an armful of bound volumes and carried them to a table for her.

The index of debates during 1938 included no entry for Censorship or Horror, but there were several entries under Cinematograph. The most substantial dealt with the Cinematograph Bill, and she turned to that debate. The Bill was moved by the Secretary of State for Air, and was meant to ensure that a fixed quota of British films would be shown in British cinemas. In an attempt to do away with quota quickies, cheap films produced in the knowledge that British cinemas would have to show them, the Bill set the minimum budget of a feature film at fifteen thousand pounds. The Archbishop of Canterbury expressed disappointment that there was to be no statutory test of quality. 'Day by day and night by night, the films are for weal or woe moulding the habits, the outlook and the way of life of the community . . .' Lord Moyne regretted 'the common type of imported film which gives a false picture of life', and the Bishop of Winchester thought it 'a most serious matter that 75% of the time in cinemas is occupied with foreign films'. The speakers seemed to be presenting such a united front that you could hardly call it a debate, Sandy thought, scanning another column and then another. She turned to the last pages and found that there was only one more speaker, Lord Redfield. She gazed at the name, her thoughts beginning to race, before she read his speech.

Lord REDFIELD: My Lords, I have listened with great interest to the discussion of the Bill the noble Viscount has moved. I am happy to be assured of the general health of our film industry and of any industry that we may call our own. Nevertheless I should like to sound a note of warning. The right reverend Prelate has reminded us of the moral basis of this Bill, which bids to counteract the colonization of our picture-houses and the minds of our picturegoers by alien influences. Yet your Lordships are aware how much more dangerous an enemy within may be, and I feel obliged to draw the attention of the House to an unhealthy aspect of our film industry – that is, the germ of the British horrific film.

I apologize to any of your Lordships who deplore the invasion of our fair language by this ugliest of words, but it appears that the content of this breed of film is such that no existing word can adequately describe it. In speaking of these films the noble Lord, Lord Tyrrell, said that the power of the cinema, improperly used, might bring civilization to an end. The noble Lord also issued a stern warning against the production of films dealing with religion or politics, since this could contravene the exhibitors' licence not to show films that might lead to disorder. I ask your Lordships to appreciate the greater threat posed by horrific films to the civilization of which we may consider ourselves guardians. He is not a true Englishman who will not shed blood in defence of the land – I speak as one who lost many tenants to the trenches during the Great War – but righteous violence is altogether separate from the lust for blood which these films stir up. In some of our counties – though not, your Lordships may rest assured, on any land that bears the Redfield name – libertarianism apparently demands that parents be allowed to subject their children to the influence of these films. It is heartening to observe that our nation recognizes the snares of libertarianism for what they are, and that there have been public outcries against the exhibition of such films. I am relieved to learn that a certification is shortly to be introduced that will bar children from viewing films that are judged to be too mild in their gruesomeness to be banned outright from our shores, and I think your Lordships may be proud to hear that our national aversion to the horrific has caused Hollywood producers to turn their energies to the creation of more wholesome fare. But, my Lords, all those advances may be rendered fruitless if British producers are allowed to exploit these savage appetites.

I understand that only one such film is presently being produced here, and it is my belief that an example should be made of it in order to check this poisonous growth. The story of the film need not concern us here – it is drawn from an undistinguished piece of gruesome fiction on which time has already passed judgement and which no civilized taste would wish to see revived – but it is of such offensiveness that the producer has been forced to import actors sufficiently degraded, or sufficiently desperate, to accept the work. One, who plays the role of an English lord, was in fact born an Englishman, but emigrated to America and adopted a Russian name, the better to portray thugs and monsters. I gather he was once a lorry-driver, and your Lordships may agree that the world would be healthier if he had remained industrious and unknown. His partner has played both Jesus Christ and the vampire Dracula. Your Lordships may wonder that any nation which is not steeped in heathenism refrains from casting out such a blasphemer. In his native Hungary he was a revolutionary, and was almost slain by the just wrath of the patriotic crew of a vessel on which he fled. His American audiences have been led to believe that his father was a baron when in fact the father was a baker, a trade which an Englishman would surely have thought cause enough for pride. I am informed that the mere appearance in public of this actor has been known to lead to panic, and I wonder if the laws barring undesirables from our shores may not apply in his case.

I hope your Lordships will not feel I have devoted more time to my theme than is justified. The noble Lord, Lord Moyne, warned your Lordships of imported films that present a false picture of life; how much more vile is a film such as this, which presents a false picture of England! Is our land to be represented abroad by such trash? Is the world to be led to believe that the English have a taste for savagery, a thirst for blood? There are horrors enough in Germany and elsewhere overseas

155

without worse being stirred up in the name of entertainment. The day may dawn when we as a nation will need to bare our teeth at the Hun. Until then, let England enjoy the peace which it has earned and which is its right and its nature, and let all those who seek to undermine that peace be hunted down and subjected to the full force of the law.

Lord Strabolgi, the next speaker, thanked him for his eloquent plea for vigilance and expressed the hope that any appropriate action would be taken, and returned to the subject of the Cinematograph Bill with what Sandy suspected might be relief. She wondered if any of the listeners had been struck by the most suggestive aspect of Lord Redfield's speech: how knowledgeable he was about Karloff and Lugosi, about details so obscure that she was certain he must have gone to some trouble to learn them. She scanned the little that remained of the debate, then leafed through the volumes in search of other speeches by Lord Redfield, without success. A librarian announced that the library was closing shortly, and Sandy carried the pile of volumes to the desk. She had one more lead to follow. The librarian found her *Willings' Press Guide*, and in a minute she confirmed what she had thought the moment she'd seen Lord Redfield's name. The Redfield family owned the *Daily Friend*.

24

Sandy booked into the Midland, a four-star hotel opposite the library, and imagined how next month's bill from her credit card was growing: another forty pounds to manure it by the time she checked out tomorrow. In the lobby she caught sight of a poster for the Corner House, which was showing the version of *Alice* Graham had restored. She jogged to the cinema to give herself another look at the film. The auditorium was full of children enjoying Laurel and Hardy in the roles of the Walrus and the Carpenter. Perhaps some small children at the back were restless, for the exit doors that gave onto a subterranean foyer crept open more than once. Sandy was certain Graham would have been delighted to see a new generation enjoying a film that might have been lost except for him.

After the film an upsurge of children carried her out of the cinema and left her beneath a street lamp. She thought for a moment that the coach had left a child behind, until the low shadow dodged into an alley. She bought a Greek sandwich to eat as she strolled back to the hotel, feeling optimistic but bemused. She was almost sure she knew who had bought the rights to Spence's film in order to suppress it, but why had they? Before she reached her room, the exhaustion of driving overtook her. She lay awake in bed for a few minutes, wondering drowsily why someone was padding up and down the corridor, and then she was asleep.

In the morning she went out before breakfast for a copy of the *Daily Friend*. LAY-BYS AREN'T FOR LAYABOUTS SAY LORRY-DRIVERS, a headline declared. Enoch's Army had attempted to park for the night in several lay-bys on a road fifty miles or so west of where she had encountered them – she wondered where they'd been wandering meanwhile – and lorry-drivers were complaining that they had nowhere to pull off the road for a break. 'Someone's liable to get killed.' a lorry-driver had apparently said in bold type. Sandy leafed through the paper at the breakfast table, and was about to discard it when a full-page Staff o' Life advertisement caught her eye. 'Hold on,' she murmured, her memory brightening.

She went over to the library as soon as it was open, and consulted a business directory. Staff o' Life was both owned by the Redfield family and based in the town of Redfield. She copied down the phone number of the factory at Redfield, and hurried back to the hotel through a procession of businessmen and early shoppers, barely noticing them as she homed in on the telephone in her room. She felt lithe with clarity, cool with anger. Smoothing her skirt as she sat on the bed and then picked up the receiver and dialled all felt like a single movement that was reaching down the line and finding her quarry at last.

The phone rang twice and released a woman's voice that was completing a remark. The voice came closer. 'Staff o' Life?'

It sounded welcoming, almost intimate, and sufficiently Northumbrian to turn the first word into 'stuff'. 'I'd like to speak to Lord Redfield,' Sandy said.

'May I ask what this is in connection with?'

'His family history.'

'One moment, please. Connecting you with the press office.'

'Wait, it isn't something – ' Sandy protested, but the voice had already been replaced by a recorded jingle, a music-box version of a song she remembered from childhood:

> Pat-a-cake, pat-a-cake, baker's man,
> Bake me a cake as fast as you can.
> Pat it and prick it and mark it –

Sex and violence gets everywhere, Sandy thought wryly, trying to ignore her sense of being listened to. A voice interrupted her thoughts and the jingle. 'Press office. Mary speaking.'

'I've been put through to the wrong extension. Can you transfer this call to Lord Redfield?'

'What would this be relating to?'

'It's a private matter.'

'I'll put you back to the switchboard.'

'Before you do you might tell me –' Sandy said, and held her breath. The press officer was saying, 'Can you switch this caller to Lord Redfield? She says it's private.'

There was a pause that made Sandy's head swim. It was apparently meant as a rebuke to Mary in the press office, for at last the operator said, 'Putting you through to Lord Redfield's press secretary.'

'. . . And put in the oven for baby and me,' the jingle resumed, having omitted the notes where the song would have indicated what the cake was to be marked with. 'Pat-a-cake, pat-a-cake,' it repeated, and a woman hummed the next bar. 'Annabel Worthington, Lord Redfield's press secretary,' she said.

'I keep being wrongly connected,' Sandy said with all the impatience she could muster. 'I'm trying to reach Lord Redfield about a family matter.'

'Whose family?'

'His.'

'If you'd like to leave a message I'll make sure it's passed on.'

'I don't think Lord Redfield would want me to. I think he would want to speak to me personally.'

'Does he know you?'

'I believe so.'

'But you haven't the number of his direct line?'

'Not with me, no.'

'If you'll leave your name and a number where he can reach you I'll see the information is with him as soon as he's free.'

At the moment this seemed to be the best Sandy could hope for, and certainly preferable to another round of extensions and pat-a-cake. She gave Annabel Worthington her name and the number of the hotel, and added impulsively, 'Tell him it's about his grandfather.'

The press secretary cut her off with an efficient click. Sandy replaced the receiver and set about packing, and began to regret having left the message. At the very least she'd trapped herself into waiting for a call that, now she thought about it, she had no earthly reason to expect; the nobility weren't so easily summoned. She ought to have driven straight to Redfield instead of announcing herself and her suspicions. No wonder she felt more spied on than ever, and caged by the anonymous room. She'd finish packing, she decided, and then call the press secretary to say she had to move on. That way surprise might still be on her side when she arrived at Redfield.

She was snapping the clasps shut on her case when the phone rang. It was the hotel receptionist, she guessed, and took her time about picking up the receiver. 'Yes?'

'Miss Allan?'

'I'm just leaving.'

'Can you wait? I have Lord Redfield for you.'

It was a voice from Staff o' Life, not from the hotel. Sandy swallowed and straightened her back. 'I'm here,' she said.

If they played pat-a-cake with her now, she thought she might scream. She was steeling herself against the jingle when a man's voice breathed in her ear. 'Miss Allan.'

'Yes.'

'I believe you have been after me.'

The voice was light, controlled, gracefully modulated, effortlessly sure of itself. 'That's right,' Sandy said.

'I'm sorry you've had so much trouble.'

Whatever he was apologizing for, the apology threw her. 'Well, yes, I did,' she said awkwardly.

'I'm told that you spoke of my grandfather.'

A hint of regret in his voice seemed to suggest it was her turn to apologize. 'That was the message,' she said, feeling churlish.

'I should like to clear up any misunderstanding. Will you come here?'

'Where's that?'

'To my town,' he said as if he were too polite to sound amused by her question. 'Once you arrive, ask anyone for me.'

'When would you like me to come?'

'Why, the sooner the better, I think you will agree.'

'Today?'

'Ideal. I shall look forward to dealing with you face to face.'

'Me too,' Sandy said, to say something, and held onto the receiver when he had vacated it. She snorted at herself to jar herself out of her reverie, and poked the receiver rest to clear the line of static that sounded like thin breathing. When the line buzzed at her to dial, she did.

The second ring brought her a preoccupied response. 'Mmh?'

'Roger?'

'Sandy! I was wondering where you'd got to.'

'I didn't want to call you until I knew where I'd be next.'

'Before you head off anywhere, you ought to know what I've found out. This may be the break you've been waiting for.'

'I'm pricking up my ears.'

'The magazine one of the guys you met gave you, *Picture Pictorial*? It was owned by the same family that owns the *Daily Friend*.'

'Redfield.'

'Oh, you know?'

He sounded so crestfallen that she wished he were close enough to hug. 'I didn't know that, and it's one more reason for me to go where I'm going. It was the Redfield family that tried to stop Giles Spence making his film.'

'Do you want me to be there when you talk to them?'

'How soon could you be? Redfield must be five or six hours' drive from London.'

161

'I'll be on the road as soon as I finish this chapter. If I can't be there tonight I'd expect to be tomorrow morning.'

'I really ought to go there now. I've been invited. I'll be fine, don't worry,' she said to reassure both of them. 'And then I'll wait until you get there, if you like. Call Staff o' Life when you arrive. I'll leave a message with the switchboard to say where I am.'

'I'd really like to go with you,' he complained, 'but another book has started to germinate as well.'

'Got a title?'

'Disney's Noses.'

'I can't wait,' she said, and added, 'to see you.' She wasn't sure if he heard; he was saying, 'See you there.' He broke the connection, leaving her alone with the static that sounded more than ever like laborious breathing close to her ear, or like a wind rattling in and out through a gap between sticks. 'See you there,' she echoed Roger, and made her way out of the hotel.

25

More motorway. It swooped east through the Pennines, where factories sprouted red-brick chimneys in valleys among crags. Headlights in a drizzle turned the motorway into a river of diamonds, spilling over the horizon and winding in wide curves down the slopes. Further into the mountains, a mile-long procession of lorries was hauling itself upwards, laboriously as wagons in a mine. As she sped past and left the drizzle behind, she felt she wasn't so much driving as being driven. She'd covered so many miles on Graham's behalf that she had lost count of the days she had been travelling.

Beyond the Pennines the land grew flat, then flatter still. Sandy left the motorway at the exit which she judged to be closest to her destination, though Redfield wasn't marked on the signboard that announced the exit, nor on the sign at the intersection to which the slip road led. The widest road from the intersection, heading more or less east, appeared to be her route.

It was unfenced. Only ditches separated it from fields of grain and cabbages and grass beneath a pale bare sky out of which the sun had been cut, a round spyhole into a white-hot furnace. Sandy wouldn't have thought it possible for the landscape to grow flatter, but it had. The occasional line of trees at the limit of her vision was grey not with mist but with distance. Here and there a piece of farm machinery picked at a field. Mud tracked onto the road spattered her windscreen so often she began to worry that she might run out of washer fluid before she could reach a garage. Once, as she cleared the windscreen yet again, she almost ran over a pheasant in the middle of the road.

The route sloped down through a copse, then climbed until it reached a humpbacked bridge, and stayed slightly higher than the landscape it wound through. The whole of the land was yellow with the widest fields of wheat she had ever seen. There was no movement except for the nodding of stalks and the occasional scarecrow. When she rolled down her window she heard the landscape rustling. The sound and the unrelieved yellow that appeared to stain the border of the sky made her feel oppressed, and so did her body. She'd started her period a day early, just as she'd reached the copse. She was more in need of a garage, or somewhere else with a toilet, than ever. When she caught sight of a thatched roof beside the road ahead she drove faster, willing the building to be a pub.

Soon the pub sign came into view, swaying on a forked pole above a car park so meagre it looked in danger of being reclaimed by the fields. The pub was called the Ear of Wheat. She parked under the sign, whose faint repetitive squeal she took at first to be the sound of a fault in her car engine. It was swaying in the incessant wind, the irregular breath of the land, a breath that smelled of soil and decay and growth. The wind, or the effect of so much driving, or her period made her shiver. She steadied herself with one hand on the muddy car and hobbled, dragging her suitcase, towards the pub.

It wore its thatch pulled low above its small windows. Though she could see lights within, hers was the only car. She lifted the latch and sidled into the porch, the wind chasing her as she shoved the door shut, bills announcing dances and amateur productions fluttering on the glass of the porch. She turned the shaky knob of the inner door and stepped over the stone threshold.

Black oak beams stood out from the walls and the low ceiling of the only room. A paunchy man with a pencil perched behind one ear was fitting an inverted bottle of whisky in front of the mirror behind the bar, a squarish woman with her red hair in pigtails and wearing slippers in the shape of a cartoon tiger's feet was dealing ashtrays onto the oak tables that were scattered about the room. The only door besides the one to the porch was unmarked. 'Excuse me,' Sandy said, 'is there a loo?'

'Aye, we've a pair of those for customers.' The landlord glowered at her in the mirror as if she had accused him of being unduly primitive. 'What can I get you?'

'Leave the lass now, Alan. You don't want him hindering you, hen, we girls know how it is. Come through here.'

The woman ushered Sandy through the door next to the bar and closed it behind her, leaving her in a short passage narrowed by a bare stone staircase. Sandy jerked the stiff latch of the Ladies', a stone cell with barely enough room for her to open her suitcase. At least she'd had the foresight to buy tampons in Manchester. Even in here she felt spied upon, presumably because the landlord must know what she was doing. She yanked her skirt down and stalked into the bar to buy a drink.

She carried her half of beer that smelled of grain to a corner table, and was sitting down when the woman sat on the stool opposite. 'Bound anywhere special, are you, dear?'

'Redfield. Is it far?'

The landlord looked up from polishing a tankard and said unwelcomingly, 'You're there.'

'The town, I meant.'

'Straight on. There's no missing it. Nowhere else to go.' A frown tweaked his eyes. 'Not looking for work, are you?'

'Just visiting.'

He grunted and recommenced polishing. 'Never mind him,' the woman said, 'it's his way with strangers. Living all your life where you were born makes some of us like that. Me, I like a new face now and then.'

'Do you see much passing trade?'

'No more than we need to,' the landlord said, and muttered an addendum: Sandy was almost sure she heard, 'And that's bloody little.'

'I expect you're crowded when they're working in the fields,' Sandy said. 'I don't suppose Lord Redfield ever comes in for a drink.'

The landlord raised his head like an animal disturbed while feeding. 'He knows our place.'

His quiet pride sounded like a warning to her to be careful what she said. She emptied her glass and lifted her suitcase. 'You just carry on the way you're going,' the woman said, opening the porch door for her, 'and you'll see Redfield before you know.'

Sandy made herself as comfortable as possible in the driver's seat and eased the car onto the road. A wind shook the dormant windscreen wipers; the fields surged at her like a wheaten sea. Ripples hundreds of yards long came through the fields to meet her as she drove. For a while she thought they were confusing her sense of perspective, making her unable to determine how far ahead a lonely tree stump was. Then the town appeared, thatched roofs like clumps of mushrooms, and she realized that the stump was beyond the town. It was a tower, a grey watchtower so tall that it seemed to command the town and the yellow landscape. For a moment she felt dwarfed by being watched, tiny as an insect ready to disappear into the earth.

The road sloped gradually upward to the town, and brought the tower rearing higher. As she reached the outskirts of the town she thought she saw a figure at the top of the tower, but it must be growing there: the colours were wrong for a face. She slowed at the town sign, which stood quivering slightly on the trim verge, its four legs planted in the soil.

REDFIELD
HOME OF STAFF O' LIFE
DRIVE CAREFULLY

Beyond it a man was mowing the verge, and turned to watch Sandy as she passed. The ragged tongue that stuck out of his face and swayed in front of it was a stalk he was chewing.

A few hundred yards past the sign, the town began. Terraces of small newish Tudor cottages gave way to thatched houses on both sides of the road. The front gardens

166

looked as if they were competing for an award for neatness. Much of the western side of the town consisted of the Staff o' Life factory, and she headed towards it through the town square, in which women leaned on pushchairs full of children and groceries and gossiped beside a war memorial. The square gave Sandy a view of the tower beyond a thoroughfare, and as far as she could see, the top was deserted.

A road of piebald cottages and thatched houses the colour of stubble led straight to the factory gates, which were open and unattended. A wide drive curved past a sprinkler flinging rainbows at a lawn. A few cars were parked in the shadow of the long Victorian façade. Sandy tidied her hair in the driving mirror, but a wind that smelled of baking tousled her hair as soon as she climbed out of the car.

A ring on the bellpush by a waist-high sliding panel in the wall just inside the entrance produced a bust of a young woman with heavy bluish eyelids. 'Welcome to Staffolife,' she said as if the name were a single word.

'Thanks so much. I'm Sandy Allan, looking for Lord Redfield.'

'Yes, of course. Go to the hotel and there'll be a message,' the young woman said with a horsey smile so bright it seemed to linger after the panel was back in place.

Sandy assumed there was only one hotel. She drove back to the square and turned along the main road. The building two storeys higher than the shops was a hotel, the Wheatsheaf. An arch that looked mortared with moss led into the hotel car park. She hauled her suitcase up the steps into the lobby, where chandeliers dangled fragments of light above carved oak banisters, settees like unwound leather scrolls, a reception counter inlaid with a rectangle green as a marsh. A plump pale girl with white hair was typing a menu behind the counter, and stood up to greet Sandy. 'You may have a message for me,' Sandy said, 'but first can I have a room?'

'What would your name be?'

'Sandy Allan.'

'Your room's ready, Miss Allan.'

'Really?' Sandy swallowed her surprise and picked up the key the girl laid on the counter. 'Shall I register?'

'No need, Miss Allan. Your bill's taken care of. You're to let us know if there's anything else we can do for you.'

That sounded more like a command than Sandy cared for. 'Is there a message?'

'Wasn't that it?' When Sandy said she presumed not the girl promised, 'I'll call you the moment I hear.'

Sandy lugged her suitcase to the next floor up and stumbled along the corridor, past lamps budding in carved leaves that sprouted from the walls, to her room. A print of a harvesting scene hung above the bed. The patchwork quilt and padded curtains and ornate Victorian washstand made the room feel more like a guest room in a cottage than a hotel bedroom. Sandy dumped her case beside the bed, and was sinking back on the quilt when the phone rang.

It was the hotel receptionist, stuttering with eagerness to deliver herself of the message. 'Lord Redfield will see you this afternoon. You're to have lunch first if you've not already fed.'

'I've eaten, thanks,' Sandy lied, feeling that an hour's rest would be more useful. 'Where will he be?'

'At the big house, of course.'

'And where's that?'

'Why, you can't miss it. Just go out of town and there it is.' The girl took pity on her ignorance, and added a landmark. 'Head for the tower,' she said.

26

Sandy went next door to the bathroom she shared with whoever else had a room in the corridor, and ran herself a bath. She lay in the water until she felt relaxed. Once the door rattled, and she called 'Someone's in here' before she realized that it must have been a draught from the fire exit at the far end of the corridor, since she could see nobody beyond the frosted glass that formed the upper panel of the bathroom door. She scrubbed herself and climbed out feeling refreshed. As she towelled herself, a trickle of blood was sucked into the unplugged whirlpool.

She dressed in a suit and pinned her grandmother's pearl brooch to the collar of her blouse, and strolled out of the hotel. She stood beneath the stained-glass awning for a few minutes, enjoying the freedom from driving, watching children skipping home from school with sunny paintings clutched in their hands, and then she made for the edge of the town.

The shops that clustered near the hotel became infrequent as the terraces stepped back to make room for gardens. Children gazed at her from the houses, one group even turning away from a television to run to the window. Sandy flashed them a smile and wondered if everyone in Redfield knew she was a stranger. That must be why she felt watched.

As soon as she stepped into the open she had a clear view of the building which the receptionist had called the big house. It was a Tudor palace on a broad strip of grass-land which led through the fields of wheat to the tower. In the afternoon light the brick façade of the palace glowed like red clay freshly dug. Ranks of nine windows in the roof-high bays caught facets of the light. Chimneys spiralled up from the steep roofs, and in the midst of the long frontage the towers of a gatehouse rose above turrets and gables. There was no wall between the palace and the town.

The road forked, one branch leading north to the tower, the other east to the palace. As Sandy walked eastward, the wind played around her legs and tugged at her skirt. Now and then it touched her face, bringing her the smell of sunlit grass. She would have been more alive to the walk if she hadn't kept sensing the tower at her back. Having once looked over her shoulder to see that there was nobody in sight, she ignored the tower as best she could.

It took her twenty minutes to walk from the edge of the town to the palace. As the palace bulked above her, her shadow rose like smoke up the red brick. She pressed the bellpush, the cold white pupil of a gleaming brass eye. Whatever sound it made was held fast within the massive walls. She thought she might have heard dogs bark, but now there was only the prowling of the wind. She was about to press the button again when the carved oak door swung open.

A butler in livery stood there, his long smooth pinkish face politely neutral. 'Madam?'

'Sandy Allan for Lord Redfield.'

'If madam will follow me,' he murmured, and closing the door tight behind her, led her beneath a stone-ribbed vault into a great room panelled in oak that reached almost to the exposed beams. Family portraits interrupted by paintings of hunting and harvesting were stationed on the panels. Logs blazed, a token fire, in the centre of a huge arched fireplace. A carpet patterned with sheaves stretched from wall to wall. Here and there about the room, half a dozen sofas spread their arms. The butler indicated the sofa closest to the fire. 'If madam will make herself comfortable.'

Once he withdrew, Sandy stood up and began to roam. She felt unreal, as if she were in a film: she couldn't help imagining the room in black and white. Some of the portraits were so old and dark that the Redfield faces seemed to be rising out of earth, large flat faces with eyes set so wide that they made the foreheads appear lower than they were, long

170

broad noses linked to either side of their thin lips by deep grooves in the flesh.

There was no portrait above the fireplace, only a carving of the Redfield coat of arms. Sandy glanced at that and passed on, then went back for a closer look. The shield was bordered by braids of wheat that curved up to form elaborate horns. She was trying to remember what they reminded her of, trying so hard that she ceased to hear the crackling of the fire, when a voice said, 'Miss Allan.'

As she turned, her body seemed to flare up, prickling; she thought for a moment that the fire had. His face was the face of the portraits made fleshier, faint purple veins beginning to claim his cheeks like a sketch for a beard. He was about fifty years old, and a head taller than she was. He wore a suit so unobtrusively elegant it had to be expensive, with the cousin of his dark green tie peeping out of his breast pocket. His eyes were dark and calm, almost dreamy, but watchful. The grooves between his nose and the limits of his mouth deepened as he gave her a formal smile and unfolded one hand towards the sofa by the fireplace. 'Please,' he said.

She wasn't sure if she felt hot or cold now, only unsteady. When she was seated, Redfield sat on a sofa diagonally opposite hers, pinching the knees of his trousers as he lowered himself. 'Will you have a drink?' he said.

'I'd love some tea.'

'Name your quencher.'

'Earl Grey?'

'What else.' He rang for the butler and ordered a pot, and detained him with a gesture so small it was practically invisible. 'Have you dined,' he said to Sandy, 'or will you try a sandwich?'

'That would fill a hole, if it's no trouble.'

'None at all.' He sat back and crossed his legs as the butler departed. 'Tell me then, how have you found it?'

'I'm not sure what you mean.'

'Why, our town. Our way of life.'

'It seems very . . .' Sandy said, and began again, determined not to be overawed by him. 'It seems very orderly.'

'I believe so. Did you mean that as a criticism?'

'Should I have?'

'Surely you aren't electing me to tell you what you should do,' he said, smiling slightly. 'I was forgetting that you've only just arrived. Take your time and see if you can find any of our people who are unhappy with their estate.'

'I haven't thanked you for the accommodation,' Sandy said. 'Thank you.'

'My pleasure.' His momentary frown made her feel she had committed a gaffe. 'I want you to have time to see whatever you wish to see. The town and its history are yours. I wonder if you know how the town earned its name.'

'I don't,' Sandy said, leaving her questions to bide their time. 'Please tell me.'

'This was once the site of a battle which you may have learned about at school. You'll recall that after the Battle of Hastings, the north of the country rebelled against William of Normandy. The lord of this land offered aid to the north, and an army led by one of William's nobles marched on him here and took him unprepared.'

'It does sound familiar.'

'In a single day they slew the lord and his men, and every woman and child. The fields beyond the battlefield were laid waste, and every house and farm was put to the torch. Even the graves in the graveyard were dug up and their contents burned. I fear my ancestor suffered from an excess of zeal.'

'Sounds that way to me.'

'William made my ancestor the lord of all that he had laid waste and gave him the name that described what he'd made of the land. All that remained was the manor that stood where this house is now, and his men were billeted there while they worked the land and built homes for themselves. Perhaps William intended them to turn against my ancestor and join William's army as it marched north, and yet my ancestor had only been demonstrating his loyalty to his king. By our standards those were savage days, you know. I believe this land gave him and his men their just reward and redeemed them by allowing them to feed the populace. The soil made us its own, and we have been here ever since.'

Could hereditary guilt about the battle have made the family hostile to Giles Spence and his film? 'The way you said "the soil . . ."'

'The Redfield soil. The marvel of pedologists. They've studied it over the centuries, but they never agree on the source of its fertility. We need only to know that we can trust it to produce the finest wheat in the country year in, year out, no matter how poor the crops are elsewhere.'

'Won't your wheat grow anywhere else?'

'It was developed to be ideal for this soil. I think we have never forgotten the self-sufficiency we had to learn in the early days of Redfield. Not only wheat grows proudly here, all produce does, and the vigour of our people soon became a watchword. Our men hauled stone for many miles so as to build a tower to watch for danger to the kingdom.'

He glanced up at the darkest portrait, which hung closest to the coat of arms. 'Sometimes I wish he could have foreseen how his land made our name. My grandfather used to delight in showing us an agricultural encyclopedia from more than a hundred years ago, which listed eighty-five different varieties of wheat and ignored Redfield out of pique. A variety called Squareheads Master was the leader then, but who has even heard of it today? Still, envy can't hurt us. Now you may have a taste of what we're envied for.'

The butler was approaching with a silver tray. He arranged the tea service and a plateful of cucumber sandwiches on a table beside Sandy, and went away. Redfield watched as Sandy poured herself tea and took a bite of a sandwich. 'Lovely,' she said.

'Worth preserving?'

'Definitely.' The bread tasted like a summer afternoon, she thought: at least, the taste was so rich and strong and lingering that it made you glad there were English summer afternoons to encourage you to take all the time you needed to savour it. 'I've always liked your bread,' she told him, 'but here it seems even better.'

'I rather think it is. What you have there is the true Redfield taste, the bread that nowadays is baked only for our town and our guests.'

Sandy swallowed, but a faint flavour of iron stayed in her mouth. 'You don't grow enough grain to make bread for the nation.'

'Not even Redfield is so fertile. When the cities began to demand our bread we bought grain to mix with our own, and so Staff o' Life was born. We never sell our grain to be mixed elsewhere. It may surprise you to hear that there has never been a strike or any kind of industrial dispute at Redfield, and we have the lowest incidence of crimes of violence in the country. Sadly, today's media have no room for that kind of story. They are too hungry for savagery and despair to see what is worth preserving, I sometimes think.'

'I've had some trouble with the media myself.'

'Yes.' There was a glimmer of regret in his eyes. 'I did say when we spoke earlier that I wanted there to be no misunderstanding. You should understand that I exert no editorial control over the newspaper.'

'I find that hard to believe.'

'You have my word.' He gazed at her until she nodded, then he said, 'I did feel that the columnist who pilloried you behaved improperly. I spoke to the editor, and you may have seen that later editions of that issue omitted the paragraph. I hope it caused you no undue distress.'

'I got off lightly compared with Enoch Hill. Your paper has been stirring up hatred against him and his followers all summer.'

'Not simply expressing an honest English view?'

'If you value peace as much as you say, you ought to leave others in peace.'

'Perhaps we needn't be so economical with our peace as

174

with our grain. I remind you, though, that the newspaper isn't my voice.'

'But doesn't it employ writers who agree with you? Leonard Stilwell, for instance?'

'My grandfather rewarded him for loyalty. Would you say that was the same thing?' When she didn't answer he went on: 'Stilwell undertook some research on my grandfather's behalf while he was writing for a magazine of ours. The magazine was a casualty of the war, and since Stilwell was medically unfit to fight, my grandfather arranged for him to have the job he holds now.'

'Stilwell researched the background of the film your grandfather attacked in the House of Lords.'

'Precisely.'

'The film your family bought the rights to and suppressed.'

'The same.'

Her question was intended to take him off guard, but instead it was his response that did so to her. 'You admit it?'

'Why should I not?'

His impregnable poise was infuriating. 'Then maybe you can tell me what your grandfather said to Giles Spence,' she blurted.

'My family would have had no desire to speak to him.'

Had his voice stiffened, just a little? 'But one of them did,' Sandy said.

'You're mistaken.'

'Spence certainly came here while he was making the film. I've seen proof of that,' Sandy said, praying that he wouldn't call her bluff. 'He may even have been on his way here again when he died.'

'Do you think so?'

'He died on the road after making the film, I know that. Somewhere on the way north.'

Redfield raised the fingers of one hand like a lid and pressed them against his lips while he appeared to ponder. 'I do remember something,' he murmured.

He reached into an iron basket on the hearth and dropped a log on the fire, and sat back. 'Perhaps I do remember Mr Spence, though I was scarcely toddling. He came here to the house and caused a scene under the impression that our family was trying to sabotage his film. Even as a child I knew that was untrue. This family has no need to hire saboteurs. I rather think that whatever befell Mr Spence's film was brought upon it by Mr Spence.'

'What happened to it finally? What happened to the negative?'

'A choice word for it and its intentions, I must say. My father destroyed it. I'm sorry that dismays you, but I rather wonder why this film should mean so much to you.'

'I've never seen it,' Sandy said, breathing hard to control her anger, 'but I know people who believe it deserves a place in history.'

'It's a curious notion of history that wants to preserve a film which tells so many lies about England and the English. You and I and anyone else of intelligence might be able to see it for what it was, but there's grave danger in assuming everyone to be like ourselves.'

'You're saying that was the only reason why your family destroyed a man's work?'

'Did I imply that? I didn't mean to. No, the truth is simply that when Mr Spence failed to receive whatever satisfaction he demanded here, he attempted to lampoon us in the film. More specifically, he inserted into the film a parody of our coat of arms.'

Sandy glanced at the shield carved above the fireplace, and saw what she had been trying to remember. The braids of wheat were very like the horns in the design Charlie Miles had sketched for her, and his arthritis would explain why the rest of the design had looked so odd. 'I wonder if your research tells you whether his collaborators on the film knew what he had smuggled into it,' Redfield said.

'I don't think any of them did.'

'Does that suggest to you that Mr Spence was not a very admirable person? Not only did he continue filming when he must have known that the nature of the film was likely to lead to its being banned or at the very least to severe restrictions on its distribution, he made his cast and crew unknowing accomplices to slander. They might have lost more than the time he made them waste if my family hadn't been content just to suppress the film.'

He interwove his fingers as if he were about to pray, then turned his palms upwards. 'I do sympathize with your motives. Your friend's scholarship ought not to have been disputed in the newspaper. But the country will have forgotten the slur on his name, whereas to revive the film would reopen old wounds. Would you expect me to be less loyal to my family than you are to the memory of your friend?'

'While I'm here,' Sandy said, trying to sound casual, 'do you think I could speak to your father?'

'Out of the question, I'm afraid. He's old and frail and easily upset, precisely why I cannot allow the film to be revived, even if an illegal copy were to come to light.' He gazed at her with a mildness born of total confidence. 'I ought to say that if anything I've told you were to find its way into the media I should feel bound to take strong action to protect our name, and I rather think my son would too.' He looked past her and beckoned. 'Miss Allan, my son Daniel.'

She hadn't heard anyone come in, but he must have been close behind her, because he was in front of her before she could turn. He was in his twenties, wearing expensive casual clothes. His face was a chubbier version of his father's, and more humorous. He'd inherited his father's economy of gesture. As he bowed slightly to her a faint smile brightened his eyes, and she couldn't help feeling favoured. 'Excuse me, father, I didn't realize you were in conference,' he said.

'I'm glad Miss Allan could meet you.' When Daniel had gone Lord Redfield murmured, 'I hope there will be no need for him to learn what we have been discussing.'

She didn't feel menaced, nor did she think he intended her to. She sensed how proud he was of his son. The

Redfield bread lay in her stomach like sunlight and lazy contentment, and she felt as if she had done all she could. She took a last sip of Earl Grey and was pushing herself to her feet when he said, 'I shouldn't like you to think you are simply doing my family a favour. Regard yourself as helping to preserve a little of the best of England and Englishness.'

He smiled almost wistfully, his gaze sinking inwards. 'My father said that to me, just as his father said it to him. We are the guardians of this portion of old England, and should we ever fail it or abandon it, our good fortune will abandon us. We're as much a product of this land as our crops are. This soil is in our blood. This land is rooted in our souls, and every one of us has his place in the chapel.'

He gave a barking laugh. 'Now you've heard me being pompous,' he said, and escorted her to the gatehouse. 'I hope that will be the least happy impression you take away from Redfield.'

She thought it might be. She walked back to the hotel, past fields of wheat that the lowering sun was turning to gold. Between the stalks the soil glowed redder than the Redfield palace. She felt as if the warmth of the landscape were focused in her stomach and spreading through her, making her steps springy and light and relaxed. She felt the memories of Graham must be as peaceful as she was.

In her room she phoned Roger, but there was no reply. She would have told him to wait while she drove back to London. Apart from pleasure and waiting for him, she could see no reason to linger in Redfield: at least, none that she could identify. She lay on the bed until a gong announced dinner, and went downstairs slowly, preoccupied. Her sense of wellbeing wasn't quite enough to hush the notion that while interviewing Redfield she had somehow missed the point – that there was still a crucial issue to be raised.

27

That night she slept more soundly than she had for weeks. She dreamed of a tower that was a single stalk of wheat, swaying so widely that its ear touched the horizon, first north, then south, then east, then west... At each touch the landscape brightened, until it was white and scaly as chalk. The brightness must have been a translation of the morning sunlight, which eventually wakened her by finding the gap between the curtains and settling on her face.

Children were singing, playing a game in a schoolyard. It must be close to nine o'clock. Sandy stretched and yawned and resisted the temptation to turn over and go back to sleep. No doubt she had missed breakfast, but she ought to get up to meet Roger. He might already be in Redfield, he might even be waiting downstairs if she had slept through a call from the receptionist. She glanced at her watch, and was wide awake. The children weren't playing before school, they were enjoying their mid-morning recess.

She had a quick bath and dressed in jeans and a T-shirt, and went down to the desk. The white-haired receptionist smiled plumply at her. 'You go straight in and she'll get you your breakfast.'

'Aren't I too late? I don't want to be any trouble. Won't the other guests have breakfasted by now?'

'Just now you're our only guest.'

'Oh, I thought – ' Last night she'd assumed the other guests had dined after she had trudged sleepily upstairs to bed. Realizing that the hotel was operating solely for her was as disconcerting as having slept so late. 'I think I'll skip breakfast, thanks. Could you tell me if there's a message?'

'I gave it to you,' the girl said, with a bluffness that seemed anxiously defensive. 'You remember, yesterday, to go up to the big house.'

'Since then, I mean, and not from Lord Redfield.'

'No, nothing else at all.'

Sandy was turning away when the receptionist detained her. 'Will you be having the lunch?'

'Possibly. I'm not sure.'

'But you'll be here for the dinner?'

'I don't expect to be,' Sandy said, and hurried upstairs to phone Roger in case his writing had delayed him and she could head him off. His phone rang and rang until she terminated the call and tried Staff o' Life. He hadn't called or shown up there either. He must be on his way, she thought, and went out for a walk.

Under the high sun the town looked newly swept. Token shadows stuck out from beneath the buildings. Tudor cottages gleamed at one another across streets, brown houses sunned their smooth thatched scalps. As Sandy strolled, glancing in shop windows at glass-topped jars of striped sweets sticky as bees, hats like mauve and pink and emerald trophies on poles, elaborately braided loaves, knitting patterns and empty rompers, she heard children chanting answers in a classroom.

She passed a church, a Sunday school, a graveyard that reached out of the town alongside the factory, towards the fields. Several overalled youths were tending the graves and the grass. She thought idly of Redfield's challenge that she should try to find someone discontented, but everyone she met looked well-fed, comfortable, satisfied. All of them bid her good day, many of them asked how she liked the town. As she completed her perambulation of Redfield and strolled back to a pub that looked out on the central green, she realized what she had missed seeing. On all the shops and houses, there hadn't been a single For Sale sign.

The pub was called the Reaper. She bought a pint of murky beer, and cheese rolls made of the Redfield special, and sat at a table outside. For a while she lazed and ate and drank, feeling as if she were slowing from the rhythm of the click of bowls on the ditched section of the green to the pace of the sundial shadows of chimneys. She took another drink and then another bite, the tastes of beer and bread combining into a warm dark earthy flavour, and remembered that she was still carrying the book by F. X. Faversham in her handbag.

It had been in there when she'd met Lord Redfield. Of course, that was what she had been trying to call to mind about her interview with him, that was the point she had missed. His grandfather hadn't seen the film when he'd attacked it in the House of Lords, but he'd known it was a version of this story. Perhaps whatever had disturbed him had been with her all the time.

She opened her handbag and glanced about. Two old ladies in slacks were playing bowls, and she was visible from all the houses bordering the green, but why should that bother her when everyone was so welcoming? The Redfield tower commanded the roofs, but Lord Redfield had explained its purpose to her and so drained it of any menace. If she was being watched, so what? 'So watch,' she said conversationally, and pulled out the book and read the first line of 'The Lofty Place'.

'There was once a man who presumed to build the highest tower in Christendom.'

Well, there it was. No wonder the Redfields had felt libelled – though why should they have, unless the story grew more specific? She read on. 'Long before the edifice was raised, the workmen set to cursing it and one another in a Babel of old tongues . . .' So Faversham had had the Old Testament in mind, not Redfield? 'At the instant when the last stone of the parapet was cemented, the architect commenced to run up the countless thousand steps. Time's heartbeat ceased until he burst out upon the parapet. The outflung fields spun in a dizzy dance to greet him, the hub of the world's whirling . . .'

Soon the story turned moral, as the architect lost patience with the way a church blocked his view of a distant lake. He climbed on to the parapet to see beyond the spire. 'A wind like the rage of the heavens caught him up and cast him, as he were a shot bird, to the harsh earth.'

His son appeared in the next paragraph, and grew up in a subordinate clause. As he neared the age at which his father had died he became fascinated with the tower. At fifty years old, just like his father, he craned to see beyond the church, and fell, leaving Sandy wondering why he hadn't simply walked over to the lake. Would his son, whose birth had several intertwining clauses all to itself, repeat the pattern? His mother's family had him educated abroad, and he distinguished himself in the tropics until 'a wasting fever' brought him home to England and his father's dilapidated property. 'There he bethought himself of his father's last day on the earth, when his father had borne him shoulder-high upon the tower and he had glimpsed the promise of the water which the church had cloaked.' He struggled up the tower and clambered on to the parapet, and managed to stand upright. 'For the space of a guttering heartbeat he saw the water clear, and the uprush of air into his eyes could not snatch that vision from him as he fell. The spectres of his ancestors sprouted from the earth that their blood had sown, to bear him to that place of which his eyes had glimpsed the merest symbols.'

That was all, and it left Sandy scratching her head. She shouldn't be surprised that the tale had so little to do with her impression of the film – that was nothing new in her experience of the cinema – but what was there in the story to trouble any of the Redfields? She finished her lunch and walked back to the Wheatsheaf, hoping she could discuss the problem with Roger.

He still hadn't arrived. When the receptionist asked her again if she would be having the dinner, Sandy was politely noncommittal. She thought of resting upstairs, and then she strode out of the hotel. She could walk off her lunch while she was waiting for Roger, and perhaps she might learn what she was disregarding in 'The Lofty Place'. She would go up the tower.

28

Clouds were bustling across the sun as Sandy walked out of the town. Whenever the sun cleared, the colours of wheat and rusty soil blazed up, a silent leap all around her. The shadow of the tower welled up through the grass, sank muddily into the earth, reached out again towards the road along which she was walking. The voices of the children at the school shrank and were swept away by the rustle of the landscape, and then that was the only sound except for the small dull sounds of her shoes on the tarmac. When she stepped off the road on to the broad strip of mown grass that led from the tower to the palace, her tread was muffled by the earth.

The sun bloomed through a gap in the clouds, and the shadow of the tower seemed to swerve towards her. She walked along the shadow to the doorway. There was no door, just a frame with a thick lintel, a shape that made her think of standing stones. As she glanced up the rough grey shaft whose only features were glassless windows as thin as her waist, the tower stooped towards her out of the rushing sky. She closed her eyes for a moment to steady herself, and then paced into the tower.

The stone tube closed around her, chill and grey as fog. She zipped her jacket and started up the steps, each of which was uncomfortably tall. She kept grasping her right knee to help herself climb, and running her left hand over the outer wall to make sure that she didn't lose her footing. She climbed one complete turn of the spiral and could barely see her way; another turn, and the wall began to glimmer with the light from the first window-slit; another, and she was level with the window, overlooking a pinched vista of the fields. The light fell behind as she clambered upwards; dimness filled the next turn of the spiral and made her eyes feel swollen until she came in sight of a further horizon beyond the next window. She stopped at the fifth window to rest her aching legs, and at the seventh and ninth, wishing she had counted the slits so that she knew how much higher she had to climb. She rubbed her legs hard, and then she climbed beyond the light of the ninth window, into a dimness that seemed to be thickening and lasting for more than a turn of the spiral, more than two turns, no longer dimness but darkness that smelled faintly rotten. She pressed her hand against the wall and made herself step up, her legs trembling and aching dully, and something cold touched her scalp.

She flinched and peered upwards, and saw a line of daylight narrow as a knife-edge. It was the outline of a trapdoor, from which hung the iron ring that had touched her. She shoved at the trapdoor with her left hand, then with both hands, until her neck felt as if a weight were threatening to sprain it and her body was a mass of prickling. The trapdoor didn't even creak.

She braced herself on the next higher step, legs wide apart, and tried to throw her whole weight upwards. The trapdoor stirred, rose, tottered and fell open with a hollow thud beneath the sky, and Sandy heaved herself on to the crown of the tower, on to stone that felt unexpectedly warm. She sat there, eyes closed, to recover from her climb and her struggle with the trapdoor. After a while she crawled to the parapet and used it to help herself to her feet.

The landscape rose with her, flexing its fields of wheat. She grasped the parapet with both hands, feeling as if the sky might sweep her from her perch. If the wind hadn't already snatched her breath, the view would have. Fields that the afternoon had polished yellow as honey stretched to the rim of the world, where the land and the sky turned pale. At the eastern limit she saw the sea, the edge of an enormous scythe-blade. A flight of birds swooped glittering from above the bunched town on her right towards the palace on her left. There was a chapel beyond it, she saw, a squat grey building that looked older than the palace, old as the tower. The birds flew up from the chapel like scraps of a fire and wheeled towards the distant sea, but Sandy's attention was still on the chapel. Redfield had said that every one of his forefathers had a place there, and he'd told her to go wherever she liked. She could see nothing about the tower to suggest why the Redfields had objected to the story she'd read earlier, but there might be some explanation at the chapel.

She gripped the parapet and walked around the tower for a last view. She felt as if her senses were raising the top of her head to let it all in. Clouds poured by above the tower, and she sensed the turning of the world; for a dizzy moment she felt herself clinging to the tip of the tower protruding from the world, racing through the sky. The thought of climbing higher made her throat tighten. She let go of the parapet and crossed to the trapdoor.

A faint stale smell rose to meet her. Rain must have seeped around the trapdoor and watered some growth on the steps. If she didn't close the trap behind her on her way down, the steps wouldn't be safe for anyone who came up after her. She climbed down as far as the dark, to see if there were any patches of vegetation she would need to avoid. Having found none, she went back to shut the trapdoor.

She closed both hands around the scaly ring and hauled at it. When the door ignored her, she took a step down and threw all her weight backwards. The ring shifted in its socket, and she lost her footing and swung into space. Her weight on the ring heaved the door up. She had barely time to duck, pressing her chin against her collarbone so hard she couldn't breathe, when the door crashed into place, blotting out the light like a fall of earth.

Her feet scrabbled at the dark that smelled of rot, her wrists aching from the slam of the trapdoor. At last she found a foothold. She let herself down on to the step and crouched there trembling and hugging her knees, cursing the Redfields for building their tower exclusively for men, with a trapdoor no woman could manage without endangering herself. The steps were male too. She gathered herself, breathing as deeply as she could bear with the stale smell, and stood up.

This section of the steps would be the longest stretch of darkness before she reached a window. She pressed her hands against the cold close walls and stretched one leg out, groping downwards. She stepped down, steadied herself, groped again. Perhaps it wouldn't be such a task; her body was establishing a rhythm. But she had climbed down fewer than ten steps when she faltered and held her breath.

She had to go down, there was no other way. The sound like hollow irregular breathing below her must be wind through the first of the slits in the wall, a wind that was intensifying the stale smell. All the time she had been at the top she had seen nobody within a mile of the tower. She mustn't imagine that someone was waiting for her just beyond the turn. She thrust her hands against the walls as if the stone might lend her a little of its strength, and made herself go down.

Ten steps, eleven, twelve. Each one felt like the absence of a step just before she found her footing. It didn't feel as if someone unseen were waiting below her to grab her foot and jerk her off balance, she told herself fiercely. Another step, and her eyes began to flicker with glimpses of the curve of the outer wall. She hopped down, almost losing her hold on the walls. The steps ahead were deserted. She climbed down into the light, as far as the highest window.

She rested and peered out of the tower. She would have liked to see someone in the fields, not to call out to them but simply to know they were near. She mustn't linger, or she might lose the will to keep descending. She pushed herself away from the window, and was stepping into her own shadow when she froze. She'd heard a rattle of metal above her. It was the iron ring.

The trapdoor hadn't been quite closed, she reassured herself. It must have fallen belatedly into place. There couldn't be anyone above her, but just the idea of it brought the darkness below her alive as well. A stale sour taste of fear grew in her mouth. She felt sick, and then furious. She thumped the walls and let herself down on to the next step.

When she could no longer see where she was going, she began to kick out before stepping downwards. The thin irregular breaths of the wind, only the wind, were both above her and below her now, and the rotten smell seemed to be. She would have dug the whistle out of her handbag, but then she wouldn't be able to hold on to the wall. She controlled the urge to lash out with her feet, for fear of overbalancing, but she was climbing down so determinedly that more than once she almost fell.

She made herself climb past the next window without stopping, so as not to be dazzled, nor to be tempted to stay in the light. There were only another six windows to go, almost twenty turns of the spiral which led into darkness that felt poised to leap or just to let her walk into its arms. Each stretch seemed a little darker than the last, and in each the hollow windy sounds above her seemed to be strengthening. Wouldn't they, since there were more and more windows above her? The steps felt as if they were growing taller, especially where it was dark, but that simply meant her legs were tiring. By the time she had counted five more windows her palms were throbbing from the roughness of the walls, her legs felt scarcely capable of holding her up.

She stumbled past one more window. She groped down through darkness that felt as if it were turning sluggishly and sneaking the steps away from her reaching feet. Something was wrong; the light from the doorway should be visible by now. The breathing darkness seemed to lurch towards her. She floundered downward and saw light, too faint, too narrow. Even the sight of the window that was its source wasn't reassuring. She had miscounted, she told herself: this had to be the last one, she couldn't go on labouring downward past window after window; that could happen only in a nightmare. She scraped her palms on the walls as she ventured down towards the darkness that seemed suddenly to be holding its· breath. When she saw the edge of the daylight that lay within the doorway, her relief was so great that she almost missed the next step.

Once she reached the bottom of the steps she sat on them, ignoring the darkness at her back, and gazed at the sky until her legs ceased shivering. At last she pushed herself to her feet and limped outside. The road was still empty, and so were the fields as far as she could see, except for a scarecrow in the wheat near the grass. Its ragged head was a dark blotch against the sunlight that glowed through holes in its torso and gleamed dully through the bunches, which looked disconcertingly sharp, at the ends of its arms.

She was halfway to the town before it occurred to her how odd it was to place a scarecrow so near the edge of a field. She had to assume that someone inexpert had put it there, for when she glanced over her shoulder it was no longer to be seen. It must have fallen and be lying low in the wheat. She headed for the houses as fast as she could limp, not looking back.

29

'Will you be – '

'I'm still not sure,' Sandy said. 'Are you quite certain there's no message?'

'I've been here ever since you went out, Miss Allan,' the receptionist said with a hint of testiness.

'And nobody new has come in?'

'They couldn't have, or I'd have seen them.'

'Thanks anyway,' Sandy said, and made for the bar to check, in case there was another entrance. There wasn't, and in any case the bar was locked. She hurried upstairs, feeling as if she were dodging another repetition of the question about dinner. Dodging it infuriated her, and so did the receptionist's maternal interest in her welfare, if only because it made Sandy feel childish – childish enough to have panicked in the tower. Her behaviour there enraged her most of all. It was one reason why she wished Roger were here, so that he could scoff at her.

She slammed her bedroom door and phoned Staff o' Life. Nobody had been looking for her there or left a message for her. She called Roger's flat, and cut off the ringing when she'd had enough. His book must have delayed him, but why couldn't it have delayed him long enough for her to reach him now? At least his absence gave her time to visit the Redfield chapel.

She made herself comfortable and went out of the hotel, half-expecting to see Roger or to hear him call to her. The children were quiet now, home from school. The next crowd would be of workers from Staff o' Life. As Sandy walked she heard the scrape of a spade in a garden, the rising shriek of a kettle, the voice of a presenter of children's television, proposing a game with unctuous heartiness.

The tower stepped back like a master of ceremonies,

189

opening the fields to her. There was no sign of the scare-crow, no movements higher than the swaying wheat. Several hundred yards short of the palace she moved on to the grass, towards the shadow of wheat that lay like a seepage of mud along the border of the fields. She thought of skirting the palace widely, but why need she be surreptitious? She walked straight to the chapel.

Curtains that looked too heavy to shift blinded the multiple eyes of the bays that swelled out from the palace, and she told herself that it was only her imagination that made her feel watched, a lone figure in the midst of the flat landscape. She resisted the urge to place the chapel between herself and the palace, and strolled to the entrance.

The chapel was an early Norman building, squat and grey. The windows in the thick walls were narrow and arched, the door of stout oak studded and hinged with iron was set in an arch bulging with rough pillars. She reached out to push the door, and glanced up at the palace. A naked woman with her legs spread wide and her fingers digging deep into herself was staring down from the corner of the chapel with eyes gouged out of the stone.

She'd seen similar figures, apparently intended to rob the faithful of any pleasure in sex, on other Norman churches. She went to the corner and surveyed the corbel, where there were several other figures: a man with a chipped erection and a mouth stuffed with wheat, a face with hands pulling its lips wide to let out a grotesquely long tongue, a woman holding what Sandy hoped were two fruits in front of her chest to feed a pair of fleshless canine figures, which were biting and clawing at them. Sandy turned away, and a voice above her said conversationally, 'Miss Allan.'

Lord Redfield was leaning out of an upper window of the palace, his large flat face almost bored, his eyebrows slightly raised, creasing his forehead. 'Still getting the lie of the land?' he said.

'You did say I could go where I liked. I saw your chapel from the tower and thought you wouldn't mind.'

'Nor do I. Steep yourself in our history by all means. You've done the tower, have you? I'm impressed.'

'It took something out of me, I'll admit. I wouldn't call it your main tourist attraction.'

'It was never meant to be. It was strictly for those with sufficient of our strength. I hope you will excuse me now if I leave you to your delving,' he said, and closed the window.

Sandy strolled back to the door of the chapel. There was no handle, only a rusty keyhole. One push told her that the door was locked. She supposed she could ask for the key, except that it seemed clear Redfield would have offered it to her or had the door opened for her. It was the family chapel, after all, hardly a public place. Perhaps he wouldn't mind if she looked in the windows, but she went round to the side of the chapel away from the palace, just in case.

Beyond the first window, over which a man squatted with his penis in his mouth, she saw dark pews stained by the afternoon light and standing on a rough stone floor. Through the next window, beneath a figure which appeared to be splitting itself open from anus to chin, she could see more pews and a corner of the altar. Between this window and the one nearest the altar, mossy steps led down under the chapel.

If she wasn't meant to enter the chapel, she could scarcely expect to go into the vault. She went to the top of the steps and shaded her eyes. The nine steps led down to an iron gate, so elaborate that she could see nothing beyond it. She listened for a moment in case anyone was nearby, then she picked her way down the softened slippery green steps.

Gripping both uprights of the pockmarked arch, she ducked close to the iron tracery of the gate. Apart from the stirring of her own blurred shadow in the dimness beyond it, she could see nothing she could put a name to. She ventured forward another inch, and her foot skidded off the lowest step.

She flung up a hand to protect her face, and inadvertently elbowed the gate. It groaned and swung inward. She hadn't thought to search for the bolt, taking it for granted that the

191

gate was locked. Now she saw that part of the tracery was in fact the bolt, pulled back just short of the socket in the wall. She glanced up the steps, past the top where blades of grass trembled, and cupped her ear. The field was as quiet as the clouds sailing by. She stooped under the arch, feeling as if she was being made to bow to all the Redfields, and stood waiting for her eyesight to catch up with her.

Now that the gate was open, the vault was less dark. Beyond the fat grey pillars that supported the ceiling, which was so low she thought the present Redfield might have to duck if he ever went in there, she could see memorial plaques set in the greenish walls. She began to read the plaques to her left, starting with the first that didn't look too overgrown to decipher, inscribed to the memory of a fifteenth-century Redfield. She read four plaques before she admitted to herself she had been mistaken to suspect what she had half suspected. There was no pattern to the dates of death – nothing like the regularity of which 'The Lofty Place' had made so much.

She read one more plaque, to be absolutely certain. There was no need for her to venture into the darker reaches of the vault, which must extend beyond the chapel, towards the fields of wheat. The faint stale smell must be the smell of moss or something else that had grown in the dark, and the muffled hollow rustling had to be the wind in the grass at the top of the steps.

She was on her way out when she noticed that a shift in the light had made another plaque visible, close to the gate. It was so old that it had cracked from corner to corner. She crossed the floor, the stones of which felt swollen, and squinted at the inscription. The plaque was so overgrown that most of the carved letters were stuffed with moss, which she thought must be one source of the smell of stale growth. She'd assumed that a shadow was making the diagonal crack appear wider than it was, but in fact it was wide enough to slip her fingers through. Strings of moss glistened between its lips. She moved aside a little so as not to block the light that was reflected from the nearest pillar, and squatted down to bring her face closer to the plaque. Eventually she managed to distinguish the date of death, which suggested no more of a pattern than the other carved dates had. 'Sorry to bother you,' she murmured, and grasped her knees to push herself to her feet, her dangling handbag nudging her like an old dog. Cramp in her thighs arrested her in a curtsy halfway to standing, and so she had time to see what she hadn't realized she had already glimpsed through the crack.

It was only a hole, a large hole that seemed to extend back farther than would have been necessary to house a coffin. Presumably there had been a coffin which had rotted away at some time in the past. No doubt the far end of the niche had collapsed with age too, Sandy thought, trying to massage the cramp from her thighs so that she could move away. The object she could just make out beyond the crack must be a tangle of roots, and of course it wasn't really stirring. Roots must have broken through the collapsed wall of the niche, another proof of how fertile the soil was, and over the years they'd formed a scrawny shape that looked crouched, about to leap. Though her thighs were still aching, she had unlocked her muscles sufficiently to be able to stagger to her feet – but she staggered so badly that she needed to support herself, and the only support within reach was the plaque.

She felt it give way. Perhaps the moss hid other cracks in the stone. The plaque was about to fall to pieces, opening the niche. She wavered backwards, bumping into the pillar, before she realized that she hadn't felt stone giving way, only its pelt of moss. She rubbed her forehead with the back of her hand, roughly enough to steady herself, and then she marched herself towards the steps. A face loomed out of the darkness above her, inside the arch.

Her legs jerked together, bruising her knees, and she almost fell headlong. She retreated a few inches and saw that the face was a carving. 'Panicky bitch,' she snarled. It looked at least as old as anything in the vault, probably older. It was so eroded that she couldn't tell if it was meant to be a hungry face composed of wheat, or overgrown by it, or turning into woven stalks. It looked dismayingly threatening and primitive, and far more like the sketch Charlie Miles had made for her than the coat of arms carved above the Redfield mantelpiece had.

She hurried to the steps and closed the gate behind her, and saw its vague shadow flood across the stone floor like an upsurge of soil. She scrambled to ground level, wondering why the rustle of vegetation had seemed louder in the vault than in the open. Just now she was more concerned that Lord Redfield might think she had been out of sight for too long. Once she was past the chapel she could see nobody watching, but that didn't make her feel less watched.

She walked quickly back to the town, through the teatime streets and into the hotel. Roger must have arrived; the receptionist was opening her mouth to say so. 'Cook was wanting to know –'

'Has anyone been asking for me?'

'Cook has, to know if you'll be –'

'You know what I mean. Has anyone been here looking for me or left a message?'

'I'd have said if they had,' the receptionist said huffily. 'But I need to let Cook know –'

'I expect I'll be having dinner,' Sandy said, and trudged up to her room. Could the girl have been instructed to withhold any messages to her or even to tell callers that Sandy wasn't staying at the hotel? Could Roger have already been and gone, having been told she'd left or had never been there? She mustn't grow paranoid, it was only her period thinking for her. Most likely Roger had been delayed and had failed to let her know, or perhaps the receptionist at Staff o' Life wasn't prepared to accept messages for her. Now Sandy thought about it, it had been somewhat cheeky of her to assume that anybody there would.

She dialled Roger's number and listened to the ringing until her head began to throb. She considered driving back to London, leaving a message at the hotel in case he was on his way, but even if she set out now she would have to drive most of the way in the dark. She went downstairs to apologize to the hotel receptionist for having been brusque with her, and couldn't bring herself to say she had changed her mind about dinner.

Dinner ended with bread pudding that tasted strongly of the Redfield special, and after that she felt too heavy even to dream of driving home. She went out to walk off her meal. The night had closed down like a lid, and the streets were illuminated by lamps of a kind she hadn't seen since early childhood, bolts protruding from both sides of their necks. The Staff o' Life complex was lit and rumbling. In the pubs, and in some of the houses, she heard snatches of folksong above the tuneless continuo of the wind. The light from a bedside lamp hovered on the ceiling of a child's bedroom, and a woman was humming a lullaby. In another house Sandy heard a shot, a scream, the Vaughan Williams melody of a Staff o' Life commercial. Out beyond the northern edge of town, where the tower soaked up the night, the fields were pale and restless.

Back at the Wheatsheaf she stood under the awning and gazed along the main road, hoping dreamily to see head-lights that would prove to herald Roger's arrival. She felt too sleepy to be discontented. She didn't know how long she had been standing there when the receptionist approached her. 'I'll be locking up when you're ready, Miss Allan. Nobody's come for you or called.'

'Well, that's men for you,' Sandy said as they went into the hotel.

The girl gave her a look so placid it was beyond interpretation. 'What does your man do?'

'Writes.'

'And you too?'

'No, I'm from television,' Sandy said, disconcerted to realize how long she had had to be wary of saying so. She thought she could be open here, but she changed the subject anyway. 'He'd have to come along that road from London, wouldn't he?'

The girl locked the front doors and withdrew the key

with a loud rattle. 'Aye, that's the only way, the Toonderfield road.'

Sandy faltered, her mouth tasting suddenly stale. 'Which road did you say?'

'The road through Toonderfield.'

'Where's that?'

'Toonderfield? Why, you came through there yesterday. It's the edge of Redfield, past the Ear of Wheat as far as the wee wood.' The girl stared at her, the iceberg of a countrywoman's contempt for urban ignorance just visible in her eyes, and snapped the keyring on to the belt of her uniform. 'You'll see it when you leave,' she said.

30

So Giles Spence had died on Redfield land. That needn't seem sinister or even very surprising, Sandy told herself as she brushed her teeth. Lampooning the Redfields hadn't helped his film, and so he'd come back. It seemed clear that Lord Redfield had waited to be sure that she wasn't aware of it before he would discuss Spence's first visit, but after all, Redfield had been protecting his family from suspicion. Or perhaps she was being too suspicious, and he genuinely didn't know where Spence had died, given that he himself had been barely out of his cradle at the time. As for Spence, if he'd driven off in a rage after having failed a second time to shake the Redfield poise, the copse beyond the humpbacked bridge was a likely spot for him to have lost control of his car.

She unbolted the bathroom door and padded to her room. The wall lamp by her door had died; the glass bud among the wooden leaves was grey as a parched seed. The other lamps illuminated sheaves that were printed on the wallpaper, all the way along the uninhabited corridor to the empty stage of the landing. She wondered where the staff of the hotel slept; wherever it was, she couldn't hear them. They wouldn't be able to hear her, but why should that worry her? She let herself into her room and locked the door.

Toonderfield might be a contraction of Two Hundred Acre Field, she thought as she brushed her hair. The insight made her feel sleepily contented, not least because it seemed self-contained, a bit of information that was already tidying itself away at the back of her mind. She stood up from the stool in front of the dressing-table and stretched and yawned, and was ambling to the bed when she heard a sound beyond the window.

She parted the thick curtains and opened the window wide, and leaned out to see what the regular sound might be that made her think of pacing claws. The street lamps sprouted from their plots of light, but otherwise the street was deserted. Of course, the hotel sign was making the sound, ticking as it swayed in the wind.

She closed the window and the curtains, and climbed into bed, catching hold of the light-cord to let herself down into the dark and sleep. She must have been exhausted last night not to have heard the restless sign, the wind blustering at the window. The weight of tonight's dessert sank her into sleep.

Silence wakened her. The wind had dropped. At some point, she realized, she'd heard the rumbling of lorries from Staff o' Life. Lying under the quilt in the midst of the silence, she felt peaceful and warm and safe. She listened to the muffled noises of the hotel sign, which sounded even more like the pacing of an animal now that there was no wind to blur them – but if there was no wind, the sign shouldn't be making a noise.

The thought stiffened her body, held her still and breathless, straining to hear that there was a wind after all. She was wide awake now, her nerves buzzing. She lifted her head from the pillow, wishing that she hadn't drawn the curtains so closely that no light could reach the room, and then her neck grew rigid as she realized what she was hearing. The sound of pacing wasn't beneath her window, it was in the corridor outside her room.

She kicked off the quilt, grabbed the light-cord and hauled at it so fiercely she thought it would snap. The small cosy room sprang into view, and it felt like a cell. Some part of her mind had hoped that the light would drive away the sound, but it was still there beyond her door, a rapid clicking like claws on the linoleum. 'So now you know I'm in here,' Sandy cried, 'let's see what you look like,' and flung herself off the bed, ran to the door, grappled with the lock and snapped the bolt back. Seizing the doorknob with both hands, she threw the door open and stalked into the corridor.

It was deserted. A moment before she had looked out she'd heard the pacing just outside, but the corridor was deserted. The doors of the empty rooms paraded away to the stairs, reminding her how alone she was up here. Nobody could have got to the nearest room, let alone the fire exit that led to the car park, in the time it had taken Sandy to look; an animal, which was what the noises had suggested to her was prowling the corridor, couldn't even have opened a door. She tried to think that the staff quarters were on the floor above, that the noise had been coming from there, but the trouble was that the corridor wasn't quite empty, after all. A faint stale smell lingered in it – a smell she fancied she had met before.

She stared along the corridor and thought of heading for the stairs, but then where would she go? She backed into her room and secured the door. She could ring the switchboard and raise the staff from wherever they were sleeping, but what would she tell them? Deep down she was nervous of calling unless she absolutely had to, in case nobody responded. She leaned her cheek against the door and listened, and eventually crept to the bed and pulled the quilt over herself. She couldn't quite bring herself to turn off the light; why should it matter if the light showed where she was? As she closed her eyes she had the unpleasant notion that she would be just as easy to find in the dark, if not easier. It took her some time to doze off, even when she had managed to suppress that idea. Not only was she listening nervously, but she was trying not to recall while it was still dark where she had first encountered the faint decaying smell.

31

In the morning it was gone. A smell of toast drifted upstairs. Sandy found she had slept late again, and ran to the bathroom with hardly a glance along the corridor. She'd meant to call Roger as soon as she awoke, so early that if he hadn't left London he was bound to be in his flat, assuming that he wasn't sleeping somewhere else. She went back to her room and dialled, and galloped her fingers on the bedside table while she listened to the ringing, ringing, ringing. At last she dropped the receiver daintily into its cradle. Whatever he was playing at, she wasn't prepared to wait any longer. Today would be her last day in Redfield, she promised herself.

She dressed in a T-shirt and denim overalls, and went downstairs. The receptionist greeted her warmly, if slowly. 'The breakfast's ready when you are.' she said, and Sandy hadn't the heart to leave without eating, since they would be cooking it only for her. It would have done for two people: the slabs of fried bread under the bacon and eggs were as thick as the slices of toast in the rack. Since this would be her last taste of the Redfield special, she indulged herself, and almost gave in when the waitress asked if she wanted more toast. 'Do you all sleep in the hotel?' she said instead.

'Aye, downstairs.'

Perhaps the noises had been coming from down there or even somewhere else entirely. Perhaps they'd been caused by a fault in the plumbing; that would explain the smell. They hardly mattered, since Sandy was leaving, though not straight away. When she plodded upstairs to brush her teeth she felt too full to begin driving at once. She needed a walk, especially since she would be spending most of the day in the car.

She couldn't move fast enough to elude the receptionist, asking the question the waitress had already asked. 'Will you be having the lunch?'

'I shouldn't think so,' Sandy said, and received a look of polite scepticism as she left the hotel. All right, yesterday she'd said she wouldn't be here for dinner, but today was the end. 'You'll see,' she muttered, low enough not to be heard by the women who were gossiping outside the nearest shop. 'Good morning,' they said as if they were inviting her to join them. She couldn't imagine being content just to gossip and shop.

She walked to Staff o' Life and called the receptionist there to her window. 'Nobody's asked for you, Miss Allan,' the young woman with the horsey smile said. Half of the waiting was her own fault, Sandy thought, for assuming she meant more to Roger than in fact she did. Serve her right for making so much of a one-night stand – for not realizing she needed to. At least she was learning a few truths about herself.

The walk had made her feel lighter, if not exactly energetic. She came out of the visitors' entrance and saw the graveyard, reaching alongside the factory towards the fields. It ought to be a good place for a last stroll and for her to be alone with her thoughts. She walked out of the factory grounds and around to the churchyard gate.

The church was early English: austere walls, windows full of tracery that led up to pointed arches. Given the extent of the graveyard, she concluded that the church must have been raised on the site of an older building. Feeling nostalgic, she strolled among the graves.

The youths she'd seen working here yesterday had gone, having finished what appeared to be a thorough job. The grass was neat, the plots were weeded. There were no trees, only shrubs whose shadows the sunlight was tucking under them. Flowers in vases decorated mounds, wreaths that looked freshly plucked lay against headstones. As Sandy followed the gravel paths she read inscriptions: 'Dust to dust', 'Called home', 'As ye sow so shall ye reap'. Many of the epitaphs referred to harvesting, predictably enough. Most of the graves were family plots, but she saw very few inscriptions for children or young people: another tribute to the local diet, she supposed.

She was in the eighteenth century now, and nowhere near the limit of the churchyard. She stepped off the path to glance at stones that weren't readily visible. There were more images of harvesting; the tops of some of the headstones were carved into sheaves. 'Thou hast made us like sheep for slaughter,' an epitaph said.

Towards the field the blackened stones grew greener. Weeds spilled over the rim of a cracked urn on a pillar; an angel so weathered it was almost faceless had lumps of moss for eyes. Beyond the angel the graves were marked by horizontal slabs. Sandy strolled among them, musing over the inscription carved on the angel's pedestal: 'Nor shall the beasts of the land devour them.' She was treading on the seventeenth century, where some of the inscriptions were decidely savage. 'He slashes open my kidneys and does not spare', for heaven's sake! Admittedly this would have been in the time of the bubonic plague; perhaps the inscription, or the treatment it referred to, had been intended as a deterrent to the townsfolk, though she couldn't quite see how. She stepped over several mossy decades. 'A wild beast has devoured him,' said a stone she almost trod on. The angel hadn't helped him, then, but of course the angel had been erected later – most of three hundred years later, she assumed. She stooped to the date, which was more overgrown than the epitaph. Fifteen-something: 1588, comfortingly distant. A couple of strides took her back another few decades, to an inscription that made her shiver: 'He led me off my way and tore me to pieces.' She wasn't even nearly at the hedge that enclosed the far side of the graveyard. There must be markers as old as any she had ever seen, but she wasn't sure that she would bother exploring that far, especially when another epitaph caught her eye: 'One who goes out of them shall be torn in pieces.' She could just distinguish that it dated from the fifteenth century,

1483, to be precise. The date wasn't as reassuring as she felt it should be; the past no longer seemed quite dead enough. She turned towards the church, the town, her car, and then stopped short. She peered fiercely at the slab, and bit her lip. The final digit had been partly obscured. The date wasn't 1483 but 1488 – exactly one hundred years before the last date she had deciphered.

The inscriptions were disturbingly similar, but couldn't that be a coincidence? She hurried towards the path, and saw another epitaph. It was for a woman, yet the text read: 'And his nails were like birds' claws.' Its blurred date might be 1433, except that the last two digits weren't quite the same: the final one was incomplete. Beyond it another slab proclaimed: 'Their land shall be soaked with blood.' The thought of going any further made Sandy's mouth taste stale and sour. She picked her way back over the slabs, looking for the ones she'd read, praying that she would be proved wrong.

She snapped a twig off a shrub and poked the moss out of the date beneath 'He led me off my way', and sucked in a shaky breath. The year of the inscription was 1538. She stumbled to her feet and went from grave to grave, willing there to be a date that didn't fit, that would show her she was imagining a pattern where none existed. But she already knew that 'A wild beast has devoured him' referred to 1588, and now she remembered the date of the inscription about kidneys: 1688. The gap between those wasn't even slightly comforting; after all, there were many stones she hadn't read. The last date on the angel's pedestal was 1888, and 'Thou hast made us like sheep for slaughter' was dated 1838. Worse than any of this was the thought that Giles Spence had died violently at Redfield in 1938 – fifty years ago.

She mustn't think about that now, mustn't make herself nervous when she was about to drive, to escape. There would be time for reflection when she was well on her way. She hurried past the church, forcing herself to breathe slowly and regularly, and then she faltered. Three women were waiting for her just outside the churchyard gate.

32

She should have been able to find them absurd. They reminded her of rose-growers converging on a judge who had given someone else the prizes they coveted, or diners cornering a waiter to complain about afternoon tea, or members of a townswomen's guild confronting a civic blight. All three wore hats like garish lacy coral, pinned with imitation pearls. One carried a basket of vegetables, one held a long loaf under her arm like a club; the third, whose hands were even larger and stronger than those of her companions, carried nothing. 'Had enough?' she said.

Taken singly none of them would seem threatening, Sandy told herself, and the three of them seemed so only because they were between her and her car. 'Enough of what?' she said as calmly as she could.

'Of us. Of our town.'

How could they know she was leaving? She saw their broad unsmiling faces, their stout bodies blocking her way; she felt the graveyard at her back. 'Why do you say that?'

'Why do we say that?' The woman turned to her companions. 'Why do we say it, she says, when we saw her running through the churchyard like a hare with the hounds on her tail.'

'Like a scared rabbit,' the woman with the basket said.

'A scalded cat,' said the one with the loaf.

Their deliberateness felt like thunder, like a threat of violence underlying the docility of the town. The way they blocked the gate like three sacks of potatoes made Sandy want to lash out at them. Her impatience quickened her mind instead, and gave a cold edge to her voice. 'I dropped something, that's all. It blew away.'

'A notebook, was it?' the empty-handed woman said.

'All the notes she's been writing about us,' said the woman with the vegetables.

'A handkerchief.'

The three women stared at Sandy as if she had spoken out of turn. 'She'll be telling us next she was having a weep,' the woman with the loaf said. 'She'll be saying she's got someone buried there.'

'Of course I haven't,' Sandy said, and told herself she wouldn't shiver, even though the women had started to smirk as if she had betrayed herself. 'What's the problem?' she demanded.

'She wants to know – ' the woman with the vegetables began, but the empty-handed woman interrupted her. 'We haven't much time for reporters,' she said.

The third woman tucked the loaf more snugly under her arm, so hard that the crust crunched like a bone. 'There was one came looking for trouble the other year.'

'Aye, came looking for folk who wanted to be in a union,' the vegetable woman said. 'And when he couldn't find any he made up stories to put in his paper. Made out we were afraid to say we weren't content because he couldn't believe what he saw. And you know what? He did us a kindness. Kept outsiders from coming sniffing round for jobs.'

'We've a paper of our own,' the empty-handed woman said. 'We don't need his kind.'

The woman with the loaf stared hard at Sandy. 'We don't need strangers poking round, trying to stir things up.'

'I believe Lord Redfield invited him to look for discontent,' Sandy said, and realized what she ought to have told the women in the first place. 'It was Lord Redfield who invited me here.'

The three faces grew sullen, almost accusing. 'We'd like to be sure he's glad he did,' the empty-handed woman said.

Sandy might have told them she wasn't a reporter – the hotel receptionist must have let them know she was from television – except that saying so might raise more dangerous questions. 'I don't lie,' she said, holding her voice steady. 'Excuse me now, please.'

They didn't budge, but her interrogator rubbed her hands together with a soft dry hollow sound. 'Where are you going?'

'If you want any further information, please ask Lord Redfield. He told me I could go wherever I liked.'

That didn't move them; if anything, they seemed to grow more monolithic. 'Should have asked for some guidance,' said the woman with the truncheon of bread.

'Can't say you've seen a town until you've met the people.'

'Can't get the flavour of it if you leave out the salt of the earth.'

If they were hostile to her only because she hadn't interviewed any of the townsfolk, how did they know she hadn't? She felt as if the empty-handed woman could read her thoughts, for she smirked and stepped back a pace. 'Let her come out or we'll have her thinking there's somewhere she can't go.'

The others moved just enough to let Sandy sidle by. She took a deep breath that she would release slowly once she was past them, and the vegetable woman said, 'Why, look at the time. She can come with us.'

The empty-handed woman displayed a wrist thick and knobby as a branch as she consulted her watch. 'Aye, it's time.'

There wasn't quite enough room for Sandy to squeeze past them after all. She was about to demand what they were talking about when the woman with the loaf told her. 'We'll take you for lunch. Give you time to get to know us.'

Lunch would include more of the Redfield special, Sandy realized – more of that heavy contentment which had delayed her. For the second time that day her mouth tasted stale, the rusty Redfield flavour rising into her throat. 'I can't, I'm sorry,' she said. 'Thanks anyway, but you'll have to excuse me. I'm already late.'

The women stared grim-faced at her, their broad shoulders almost touching. 'You'll learn nothing sitting by yourself,' the vegetable woman said.

How did they know she would be? Having to lie to them,

being nervous of telling the truth without quite knowing why, made Sandy hot with suppressed anger, but she would say anything now to shift them. 'I have to get back to the hotel. I'm expecting a call,' she said, uncertain whether that was a lie or a desperate hope.

'Fine,' said the woman with the loaf. 'We'll walk with you and when you've had your call we'll give you your meal.'

'Then let's walk,' Sandy said edgily, afraid they might guess what she was planning. 'It's very kind of you,' she added. 'Thanks so much.'

They moved apart at last, and stepped back. The sight of an escape route was so tempting that she had to restrain herself from dashing for her car. She imagined herself fleeing three stout women with hatpinned hats as the townsfolk watched, imagined discovering that breakfast had left her too weighed down to outdistance the women, and felt absurd and irrational, barely capable of pretending that nothing was wrong. She made herself smile confidently as she passed the gate.

The women closed around her, the vegetable woman on her left and the woman with the loaf on her right, the empty-handed woman so close behind her that Sandy expected the large dull black shoes to tread on her heels. A group of gossiping shoppers bade the women good morning but ignored Sandy, which made her feel even more like a prisoner. So did the question the woman tramping at her heels asked almost casually. 'Let's hear about it, then. What have you been seeing?'

She didn't mean the graveyard, Sandy thought, wishing she could watch the woman's face. 'I had afternoon tea with Lord Redfield, and I've been up the tower, and all round the town. Oh, and I've been to the factory a couple of times.'

The women greeted that with silence, in which the tramping of feet beside her seemed oppressively loud. Ought she to have mentioned the Redfield chapel? Could they know of her visit to it and be wondering what she had to hide? She was about to mention it when the empty-handed woman spoke, so loud that Sandy felt the breath in her hair. 'Nobody we know saw you in the factory.'

'And we've got cousins there,' the vegetable woman said.

'I said I went to it, I didn't say I went in. Lord Redfield sent me there.'

'Well then,' the woman at her heels said triumphantly, 'that's where we'll take you after lunch.'

'That's where you'll meet the folk you should meet.'

'That's where you'll see the lifeblood of Redfield.'

They had reached the hotel. They were passing the entrance to the car park. Sandy could see her car, its misted windows dim, its wheels stained with reddish mud. She made herself stride onward, up the steps into the lobby, the women on both sides of her shoving the doors back. The receptionist smiled slowly at the four of them, and Sandy told herself that the girl was just glad Sandy was meeting the townsfolk. Then the girl's mouth straightened. 'Sorry, Miss Allan. No calls.'

For once Sandy was grateful to hear it. She turned towards the stairs, and the woman with no shopping moved into her path, holding up her palms, which looked hard and raw. 'She'll tell you when your call comes. You can sit down here and talk.'

Sandy felt as if a shovelful of hot ash had been flung at her. She changed her panic into rage, let it glare out of her eyes and chill her voice. 'Please wait here for me. I'm having my period and I need to go upstairs.'

The woman stared doggedly at her. Sandy wondered if she was about to ask one of her friends for a tampon and usher Sandy to the toilet near the reception desk. 'Talk to the receptionist about lunch,' she suggested, and pushing past the woman with the reddened hands, marched upstairs without looking back.

As soon as she was out of sight beyond the landing she halted and held her breath, though it throbbed in her windpipe and threatened to make her teeth chatter. The women weren't following. She hurried to her room, snatching the key out of her handbag, and slammed the door behind her. With the sound still thudding in her ears, she grabbed her suitcase and threw it on the bed, snapped the clasps back, swept everything she'd laid out on the dressing-table into the case and pulled open the wardrobe door. The jangle of unclothed coathangers made her catch her breath. She lifted her clothes out of the wardrobe as swiftly as she could without rattling any more hangers and slung them into the case, cursing the women for making her crumple them. 'I ought to send you the bill,' she said through her teeth, and gave the room a last glance as she locked the case. She ran to the door and easing it open, leaned her head into the corridor.

The women were downstairs. She could hear them murmuring dully, one after the other, in what might almost have been a chant. She seized her case and walked loudly across the corridor, opened the bathroom door and closed it with as much noise as she could, and then she tiptoed rapidly to the end of the corridor, to the door that opened on to the fire escape.

She took hold of the bar across the door with both hands and pushed it gently, shoved it harder, bore down heavily on it. It didn't shift. She leaned backwards, listening breathlessly for anyone coming upstairs, then let herself fall on to the bar. The only response was sweat that sprang out of her palms, making the bar feel colder and spiky, undermining her grip. She shut her eyes so tight that her vision blazed red, and flung her whole weight at the bar. As she felt it jerk away from her she restrained it, and it emitted only a muffled clank as the door inched open. She fumbled her keys out of her handbag and almost dropped both bag and keys. She clenched her slippery fist on the handle of her suitcase, and stepped on to the fire escape.

Should she close the door? Mightn't someone in the lobby notice the draught? She set down her case on the iron mesh of the fire escape in order to shut the door quietly, and all at once she felt grotesquely ridiculous. How could she sneak away like this without saying goodbye to Lord Redfield or thanking him for his hospitality? What was she afraid of – three women in silly hats? Embarrassment and guilt were massing in her stomach, an aching weight that needed to be assuaged.

Suddenly it wasn't the women or even the dates in the graveyard that frightened her, but her own growing inertia that felt like a hunger to stay in Redfield. She grabbed the handrail so hard it shook the iron stairs beneath her, and clutched the handle of her suitcase. Though a staleness that might be a taste or a smell was threatening to make her dizzy, she tiptoed quickly down the fire escape.

Her car was cold: the misted windows showed that. The engine wouldn't start at once, and how much time would she have to start it before the women noticed her? Hers was the only vehicle in the car park. If she began anticipating the worst she wouldn't be able to go down. She forced herself to think of nothing but reaching the foot of the fire escape, crossing the mossy car park, slipping the key swiftly and easily into the lock of her car, as she did.

She opened the door wide and heaved her suitcase on to the back seat. There would be time to move the case into the boot once she was out of Redfield. She climbed into the driver's seat and closed the door gently but firmly, holding her breath. She pushed the key into the ignition and rubbed condensation off the inside of the windscreen with her forearm, and risked one sweep of the wipers. They left two arcs like monochrome rainbows of mud, but she could see ahead. She could see the hotel receptionist, less than twenty feet away from her beyond the window behind the girl's desk.

Sandy pulled the choke out as far as it would go, and gripped the key until the tips of her thumb and forefinger ached. 'Start first time,' she whispered, halfway between a command and a plea, it didn't matter which so long as it worked. She poised her foot ready to tread on the accelerator, and the receptionist stood up.

She wasn't coming to the window, she was going to the counter. Sandy let a shiver pass through her and opened her fists to release it, and grasped the key again, just as the three women appeared at the counter. If they glanced past the receptionist they would be looking straight at Sandy. 'Try and stop me,' Sandy mouthed at them, and twisted the key, held it as the engine roared. She let go of the key, shoved the lever into first gear, trod on the accelerator. The engine made a clogged sound, and died.

The receptionist had already turned towards the noise, and now she came to the window. As she caught sight of Sandy, her face grew sullenly determined. Behind her Sandy glimpsed the garish hats bobbing as the women craned over the counter to see her. She twisted the key again, and the hats disappeared. The women were coming for her.

The engine coughed, revved, belched fumes that filled the driving mirror. The car sprang forward so abruptly that the wheels skidded on the mossy stone, and the left-hand headlight barely missed the edge of the entrance arch. The car lurched out of the car park, but she had to brake at the street to let a delivery van coast by. The women piled out of the hotel and ran down the steps like a grim chorus line, each of them with one hand on her hat, the other outstretched towards Sandy. 'Hoi!' cried the woman with the reddened hands, and the engine stalled.

It wouldn't start when Sandy twisted the key. The women sprinted the few yards between the hotel steps and the gap in the pavement. They meant to block her way, and they could. With the clarity of desperation, she realized she'd forgotten that she had to switch off the ignition before she could restart the engine. She turned the key back, then forward, and the engine caught. The car swerved past the women on to the road.

She swung it round the delivery van, shifted into second gear to pick up speed. In the mirror she saw the three women on the pavement, performing a kind of impromptu dance of rage, hands on their hats and their fists in the air, and then the van blocked her view. People outside shops and in front gardens glanced at her as she drove past, but nobody else moved to detain her. The last houses dwindled behind her, the planted Redfield sign shrank. The road sloped down into the sea of wheat, which flooded around her beneath a pale sky. She shoved in the choke and trod hard on the accelerator, and began to hum to herself, a wordless song of escape – from what, she wasn't sure. But she was still in sight of the tower of Redfield when she stamped on the brake.

33

The road was higher than the fields now. Both the road and the fields were deserted apart from the scarecrows in the wheat. Had there been as many scarecrows when she had last driven along this route? Ahead of her was the Ear of Wheat, and beyond it, where the haze began, the tops of trees in the copse past the bridge at Toonderfield. Beyond the copse there was a choice of roads, and that was why she was hesitating. Once the roads divided, she couldn't be certain of meeting Roger if he happened to be on his way to meet her.

He wouldn't be coming so belatedly, she told herself, but suppose he was? This wasn't much more than a day later than he had said he would join her. Perhaps he had become so engrossed in his work that he had forgotten to call her, or perhaps he'd assumed she would call him if she was moving on, or perhaps his phone was out of order. She knew she wasn't thinking logically, but she seemed unable to do so while her fears were so vague. What did she imagine would happen to him if he went to Redfield, for heaven's sake? He would head for Staff o' Life and be referred to the Wheatsheaf, where he would learn that she had already left: what else? But the fear she had been suppressing since she'd encountered the three women at the churchyard gate was finding its voice, chanting 'fifty years, fifty years' in her head. If Roger's phone had been out of order, surely it would have been repaired by now, and if he had simply forgotten to call her, she mustn't let it matter. She would feel considerably happier if she could speak to him before she reached the division of the roads. She peered hard at the driving mirror to reassure herself that she wasn't being followed, and then she drove to the Ear of Wheat.

The fields swayed around her, and she had the disconcerting impression that some of the scarecrows were rearing up. She swung the car off the road and parked beneath the pub sign. A wind made the sign cry out, made the car shudder. She locked her suitcase in the boot and strode to the porch.

The wind rattled the latch before she lifted it, and slammed the door behind her. A draught that smelled of earth followed her through the porch and roused the posters on the inside of the glass, set them reaching towards her as she opened the inner door and stepped into the oak-beamed room. The paunchy landlord was behind the bar, his red-headed wife was padding about in her tigerish slippers and wiping tables. 'Here she is,' the landlord said without looking up.

He must have seen Sandy crossing the car park – surely they hadn't been told to expect her. The woman stooped to examine the table she was wiping. 'Will you be having lunch?'

'Just a drink,' Sandy said, 'and may I use your phone?'

The woman hadn't sounded especially welcoming, and now her voice grew brusque. 'Ask him.'

The landlord was watching Sandy as he polished the beer-pumps. His expression seemed just short of hostility, and didn't change as she met his eyes. 'May I?' she said.

'You've not said what you'll have to drink.'

'A half of lager, please,' Sandy said, and went to the phone on the wall at the end of the bar. Perhaps he and his wife had had an argument about Sandy after her first visit, and that was why the woman had grown as curt as he was. From her place by the phone Sandy could see the road to Toonderfield through a window between two prints of hunting scenes. She dug in her purse and found she had almost no coins. 'Could you give me some fifty-pence pieces?'

The landlord stared discouragingly at her ten-pound note, and then at her. 'Long distance, is it?'

'I'm afraid so,' Sandy said, telling herself that he didn't intend to sound menacing.

He took the note from her, set down her glass of lager, rang the till open. He peered into the drawer and slapped a five-pound note on the counter, and then four pound coins, which the phone wouldn't accept, and the change from a pound. She was about to argue when he took back a pound and replaced it with two fifty-pence coins. 'That's all I can do for you.'

'If it is, then thank you,' Sandy said, and dialled Roger's number. She knew it by heart, and the sound of his phone ringing, deceptively close to her. She gazed out at the empty road beyond the prints of English countryside and imminent bloodshed, and the ringing ceased. 'Hello, yes?'

She'd become so used to receiving no reply that she almost dropped the coin. She shoved it into the slot and waited until she heard it drop. 'Guess who this is,' she said, 'and guess where I am.'

'I'm sorry, I don't know. Who is this?'

'You don't know? Well, that's wonderful. Thanks so much.'

She was tempted to cut him off without even warning him to stay away from Redfield. 'You've forgotten my voice already, have you? It's a good thing I remember yours.'

'Excuse me, I think you're making – '

'Damn right I've made a mistake. I made it a few nights ago, twice if you remember, or has that slipped your mind too? Who helped you forget, Roger?'

'I told you you were mistaken, miss. This isn't Roger.'

'Oh, you aren't Roger?' Sandy cried, and sensed the landlord and his wife listening behind her. 'You just happen to be in his flat and sound exactly like him, do you?'

'We would sound alike. I'm his father.'

Sandy opened her mouth and shut it again as her face blazed. The pips began, and she thrust in the second coin, grateful for the interruption. 'God, I'm so sorry. I'm a friend of Roger's. We were planning to meet, but of course he

216

wasn't expecting you to visit. I see that must have put our arrangement out of his mind.'

'Well, no, it isn't quite like that, Miss . . . ?'

'Sandy, Sandy Allan.' She was suddenly breathless, his voice had turned so grave. 'What is it?'

'Roger is in the hospital. That's why I flew over. He's been in there since the day before yesterday. He hasn't been able to say much.' Roger's father coughed and said, 'All I know so far is he was attacked by someone wearing a mask or with something wrong with their face.'

34

Sandy wrote down the name of the hospital and apologized again for her tirade. 'Let it go,' Roger's father said. 'He wanted me to make a call, but I couldn't get the name he was saying. Now I've heard yours I'm sure it was you.' He promised to tell Roger she was on her way, and wished her a safe journey, and then the phone began to chirp, hungry for change. Before she could say any more to him he'd gone, presumably assuming she had been cut off.

She held on to the receiver for a few moments, though it felt like a handle that had come off in her hands. She mustn't start blaming herself for having suspected Roger when in fact he was lying in hospital. She mustn't start wondering how badly hurt he was. His inability to speak or to make himself understood might be the effect of painkillers, but then how much pain would he be suffering otherwise? She couldn't help him by brooding. She hooked the receiver onto its rest and fished her keys out of her handbag. Snapping the bag shut, she turned towards the door to the porch.

She saw the red-haired woman exchange glances with the landlord and step into her path. They had been biding their time, she thought numbly: they must have been instructed not to allow her to leave. Then the woman pointed beyond Sandy, her face heavy with regret. 'You're not leaving your drink?'

'I'll have to. I only bought it to get change,' Sandy said, and was so afraid she would burst out laughing at her panic and appear unforgivably rude that she was almost running by the time she reached the porch.

She sat in her car and laughed at herself until she had to gasp for breath and wipe her eyes, and then she set off. As she drove onto the road, the tower rose in her driving mirror. Scarecrows flapped and swayed on both sides of the road. One seemed to stoop beneath the wheat as she passed, but she wouldn't let that or the tower distract her. The tower would be out of sight as soon as she was past the bridge at Toonderfield.

The tower seemed not to be shrinking as quickly as it should. 'Freud knows why,' she scoffed at herself, but it made her feel as if the car wasn't moving as fast as the speedometer claimed. She mustn't let her fears tempt her to drive faster, or she might go off the road as Giles Spence had. At last the yellow distance between her and the bridge telescoped, the canal gleamed like teeth in a thin mouth She sprayed her windscreen with almost the last of the washer fluid, and the wipers scraped an arc relatively clear of mud as she braked at the narrow bridge and accelerated down into the copse.

Trees leaned over her, nodding their dense heads of leaves. A greenish tinge crept into the mud that coated the windscreen beyond the sweep of the wipers, as if moss had grown there, unnoticed until now. Trees linked branches above her as the road began to curve. She didn't remember the copse as being so extensive or so dim, but on her way into Redfield she'd had no reason to notice. At least she was past Toonderfield, she thought, and immediately wondered if she was. If Spence had run his car into a tree, it had to be down here. Toonderfield must end on the far side of the copse.

The road zigzagged, and she braked reluctantly. She was about to see the sky beyond the copse, she promised herself. What did it matter to her if Spence had died here all that time ago – just fifty years ago? At least she was out of sight of the tower. There had been nothing about the tower in the graveyard, she thought: only about the land – the land that 'shall be soaked with blood'. She couldn't help peering through the dimness and the mud that framed her windscreen at the trees, to see if she could identify which one had been marked by Spence's crash. But it wasn't the sight of any tree that made her foot jerk on the accelerator, nearly stalling the car.

It was only a scarecrow. Someone must have dumped it among the trees rather than cart it away when it ceased to be of use. It must have been abandoned quite some time ago for its head to have grown into such a mess, though admittedly more than one of the scarecrows she'd glanced at as she passed the fields hadn't had much of a face. A wind scuttled through the undergrowth, and the scarecrow swayed out from the tree in whose shadow it was propped. The looming of the fattened greenish blob that might be more like a face that she cared to see made her press the accelerator hard, slewing the car across the curve. The road turned sharply back on itself, and she saw the sky a few hundred yards ahead, at the end of the next straight run. She was so dazzled by the daylight, and by the relief it made her feel, that she almost didn't notice the scarecrow.

The copse must have been used as a dumping ground for the figures. It couldn't be the same one, since it was behind a different tree, between her and the open road. This tree, a stout oak, looked as if it had been damaged at some time in the past; perhaps it was the tree she had been searching for earlier. She'd no time and no wish to look closely at it, nor at the ragged famished shape that was silhouetted behind it, poking its spiky greenish head forwards. She came abreast of the tree, and as it blocked her view of the figure she felt compelled to accelerate. The oak tree passed out of her vision and reappeared in her side mirror, and she saw the scarecrow lurch after her and vanish on all fours in the heaving undergrowth.

She cried out, grappled with the wheel as her hands jerked nervously, fought the urge to look over her shoulder. She was almost out of the copse, out of Toonderfield. The wind had overbalanced the scarecrow, that was all. What looked like a blotchy face darting after her through the ferns and grass must be the shadows of leaves.

She sped between the last trees. A sudden panicky notion that she hadn't made it after all felt like a hook in her stomach. Then the sky opened overhead, and she raced into the wide landscape. The copse shrank in the mirror as if it were returning to its seeds, and then there was nothing around her but fields, nothing behind her and ahead of her except the road. Soon the landscape would calm her, she tried to reassure herself. Soon she wouldn't feel as if she was still being followed and watched.

35

When she reached the motorway it was a relief to have to concentrate on driving. All she could see following her was the occasional car rushing up the outer lane, determined to scare anything slower out of its way; all she could see watching her were lorry-drivers, gazing down at her legs from their cabs. In Nottinghamshire a vanload of miners whistled at her, in Warwickshire a truckful of muddy bare-kneed men sang her a rugby song. Homing planes gleamed in the sky over Luton. The passengers must be able to see London, she thought, and felt as if she was finally home.

She came off the motorway during the rush hour. If she headed straight for the hospital, she might well find nowhere to park. She swung towards the North Circular, through the roaring tangle of flyovers, and made for Highgate station. She'd forgotten there were so many traffic lights, nearly all of which turned red when they saw her coming. At last she was able to edge out of the shuffling procession and drive down the slope to the station car park.

Less than five minutes later she was on the train. At Warren Street she dashed across the zebra carpet of a crossing to the hospital. The tiled lobby made her think of a cave carved out of an iceberg, except for its mugginess. She knew which ward to head for, and the nurse who was regulating visits let her in.

She had a view of all the beds in the ward as soon as she was past the double doors. Dressed heads chatted from their pillows, wrapped plastered arms with gloves of bandages were stretched out on sheets, but she couldn't see Roger. If he'd been moved out of the ward, shouldn't that mean he was recovering? Surely the occupant of the farthest bed, a man wearing a Balaclava of bandages and with one leg hoisted in the air, couldn't be Roger. His bandaged arm stirred on the sheet, and the man sitting at the bedside turned to her.

His large dark eyes needn't mean he was Roger's father, but he stood up and held out his hands as if he were apologizing for what she was about to see. At once all the anxiety she had been suppressing in order to drive came at her like a wave, and for a moment she thought she was going to faint with the mugginess of the hospital. The sight of Roger, almost unrecognizable with bandages, made her realize how much worse his injuries might have been, and how unbearable it would have been for her to lose him. Just the thought of doing so felt like the threat of a wound not much smaller than her life.

She hurried forward between the beds, trying to swallow, and Roger's father met her halfway. Beneath his lined forehead and greying eyebrows his face looked tired and sad. 'You're Miss Allan,' he said, in a voice that didn't sound nearly as much like Roger's as it had over the phone.

'Please call me Sandy, won't you?'

'Be glad to. Since I spoke to you I've been hearing from Roger how much you mean to him. From the way you talked at first I guess the feeling is reciprocated.' He'd taken her hands and was holding them firmly; his plea made his eyes waver. 'I mean,' he added hastily, 'when I have to go back I can tell his mother that our boy's being looked after.'

'I think you can.'

'Well, that's good. That's fine. And when he's better I hope that you, well, ah . . .' His directness had deserted him now that it had achieved its aim. He let go of her hands and rubbed his forehead with his knuckles. 'Time for me to step aside. Do you mind if I hang around, or would you rather be alone?'

She was touched by his concern. 'Whichever you'd rather.'

He went quickly to the bed and leaned on Roger's pillow. 'Can you see who's here, son? Someone you were asking for. Can you see?'

'Sure, Dad,' Roger said, and gave him a determined

smile. 'Nothing wrong with my eyes. They're some of the bits of myself I missed injuring.'

Sandy gazed at him from the foot of the bed, and winced. Both his arms were bandaged, and most of his torso. He smiled at her with a wryness which she could tell was caused partly by the pain of smiling, and glanced meaningfully at his hoisted leg in plaster. 'Hardboiled eggs and nuts,' he intoned.

His father unbent, massaging the base of his spine. 'I'm forgetting my manners. Please, Sandy, have this seat here.'

She went round to the head of the bed. She wanted to hold Roger, but she was afraid that if she even laid a finger on him it would hurt him. At least his face was unmarked; in the bandages it looked like an unshaven nun's face. She knelt and kissed him, and the tip of his tongue met hers. Sensing that his father was discreetly averting his eyes, she sat on the chair and slipped her hand beneath Roger's fingers. 'Well, this is a fine mess.'

'Ouch.'

She couldn't keep up the bantering. 'What sort of animal did this to you?'

'Don't work yourself up on my account, Sandy. I near as damn it did it to myself.'

'Your father said – '

'He wasn't so clear then,' his father interrupted. 'They had him pretty well doped up. It's good they already feel they can reduce the medication, isn't it?'

'Sure,' Roger said, just as Sandy said, 'Of course.' His fingers stroked her palm, a secret thanks. 'So all right, how did you get yourself into this state?' she demanded.

'Not looking where I was going.'

'You forgot which side of the road we drive on.'

'No, I stepped into a hole in the road, just round the corner from me. I guess some kids must have thought it would be a good gag to dump the warning sign in there, and the fence that should have been around the hole. Still, I'm the only damn fool I know of who found out how far it was to fall and how much stuff there was to fall on.'

224

Sandy felt queasy, furious, helplessly affectionate. 'But what's all this got to do with someone wearing a mask?'

'Oh, my father told you about that,' Roger said, a rebuke that was obviously aimed more at himself. 'That's the most foolish part. I don't even remember it too well. I saw this guy who must have been on his way to a masquerade coming after me. It was getting dark, and that must have made him look worse than he really could have, I guess. Anyway, he was why I didn't look where I was going, and you see where I ended up.'

'Can't you remember what he looked like?'

Roger grimaced. 'Does it matter?'

Not that much just now, she thought: not if it made him feel worse. 'Let's talk about something more interesting,' he said, 'like how you fared.'

His father cleared his throat. 'If neither of you needs me for anything I'll head back to the flat and sleep off some of my jet lag. But call me any time, Sandy, if you need to. I'll see you tomorrow, son, and make sure you've been mending.'

He lingered at the doors for an anxious backward glance, and left the doors swinging, trying to meet. 'You're glad he came, aren't you?' Sandy said.

'Sure. Not everyone would have flown across. But I'm gladder to see you.' His fingers moved in her loose grasp. 'I'm sorry if I kept you waiting where we were supposed to meet. Until he told me that you'd phoned I couldn't think how to let you know. They'd closed my brain down for the day.'

His apology made her want to thump him. 'You,' she said, and had to apologize for squeezing his hand too hard.

'So tell me what's been happening and let me rest my jaw.'

'You haven't broken that too?'

'No, I just want to hear how you wouldn't have needed me anyway.'

'Seriously? I think I did.' She held his hand gently in both of hers, feeling his warmth through the linen. 'Redfield's a

225

strange place, so perfect you feel it just has to be suppressing something. I think I imagined some things I wouldn't have imagined if I hadn't been alone, but don't you dare start blaming yourself, because that wasn't all. Every fifty years there's been some kind of violent death.'

'Exactly every fifty years?'

'That's what it looked like,' she said, hearing scepticism where perhaps there wasn't any. 'At least, I found half a dozen inscriptions in the graveyard that were dated either 'thirty-eight or 'eighty-eight, and all of them had to do with being savaged by some sort of beast.'

'There weren't inscriptions like that for any other dates?'

'I don't know. Not that I saw.'

'Mightn't there have been wildcats or some such dangerous creatures roaming that part of the country if you go back, say, a hundred and fifty years? All I'm saying is that kind of death mightn't have been so unusual.'

'I suppose not.'

'But you found there'd been that kind of death every fifty years for what, three hundred?'

'Not every fifty. There were some gaps.' She was taken aback by how annoyed she felt, not so much with Roger, lying there like a bedridden detective, as by how all that had seemed mysterious and frightening was being explained away. 'If it was all a coincidence,' she protested, 'I can't see why the Redfields objected to the film in the first place.'

'Did you meet them?'

'I met the man whose grandfather objected to the film. As we suspected, it was the family that bought the rights. They destroyed the negative.'

'Bloody vandals,' Roger said, and winced at having breathed too hard. 'You're right, they must have had a reason to go that far.'

'I found out the reason. Spence included part of their coat of arms in one of the set designs to get his own back for the way they were making things difficult for him.' She remembered feeling she would never be out of the copse at Toonderfield, and wished she could hold Roger's hand tighter. 'Apparently that didn't satisfy him. He went up to Redfield as soon as he'd completed the film, because he thought the Redfields were somehow responsible for problems he'd been having on the set, and his car went off the road. He died on Redfield land, in 1938.'

'Which you think means . . . ?'

'Lord knows,' she said, suddenly tired of herself and of speculating. 'Less than it seemed to while I was there.'

'Well, okay. So will you go on looking?'

'For the film.'

'Right. Give me something to get out of bed for,' he said, and pushed his lower lip forward in a grimace at himself. 'Besides you, I mean.'

'Out of this bed and into another, you mean.'

He grinned, then moaned. 'You just reminded me of another bruise.'

'Oh no. Think of Karloff and Lugosi if that doesn't turn you on,' she said, thinking how the film seemed unimportant, almost irrelevant to her now. 'I'll go on looking when I can, if only for Graham's sake, but I have to go back to work.'

'I'll take up the search as soon as they let me out of my wrappings.'

He'd already helped her search, and this was where it had brought him. The idea was so fleeting and irrational that she ignored it. 'Whatever it takes to get you up,' she said, and was rewarded with a wink and a wince.

She stayed after the bell, until a nurse tapped her on the shoulder. At the station she waited fifteen minutes on the platform, listening to distant trains that sounded like breaths and restlessness deep in the mossy dark. At Highgate she bought a pizza to slip in the microwave, and drove home. When she opened the door of her flat she couldn't help bracing herself, though there were no cats to leap out of the darkness, only a pack of bills to greet her. She opened windows to let out a faint stale smell. While she ate the pizza she thought of nothing in particular; being home and pleasantly tired was enough for now. She went to bed, leaving the bedroom window ajar. There must be a breeze, even though it didn't stir the curtains, for the stealthy creaking of the tree outside the window lulled her to sleep.

36

In the morning she called Boswell. 'I'm back.'

'Improved?'

'I hope so.'

'As you used to be will do. Your friend Lezli has been impressing everyone she's worked with, but you're missed.'

Her absence had done Lezli some good, then. 'While you were gone I had a word with the appropriate people,' Boswell said. 'You'll be getting sick pay for this time off and still be entitled to a holiday.'

'That's really kind. I appreciate it. When do you want me back?'

'Any chance of right now?'

'I'm on my way,' Sandy said.

Five minutes later she was at the flowerbed where the cats were buried. The earth around the flagstone hadn't been disturbed, except by the green shoot of some flower, a sight she found heartening. It stayed with her as she made her way through the park. Once she thought someone wanted to catch up with her, but she could see nobody behind her on the paths.

She had to stand all the way to Marble Arch, faces looming over both her shoulders. She ran across the lobby at Metropolitan, into a lift that was closing. She poked the button to hold the doors open, but nobody was following her after all. As she walked into the editing room she was greeted by cheers, and Lezli gave her a hug. Footage of a train crash was just coming in, so much of it that it took her and Lezli all their time to have it in shape for the one o'clock news. Sandy had almost forgotten how much she enjoyed the challenge of editing.

She had lunch with Lezli in the pub around the corner, and heard about Lezli's new boyfriend, who was playing

Doctor Seward in the new stage musical of *Dracula*. Eventually Sandy remembered something that had slipped her mind. 'Were you trying to get in touch with me while I was away?'

'No, why?'

'Toby said someone from Metro was.' It might have been Boswell, wanting to tell her about her sick leave – and then she realized who she hadn't contacted. 'Of course, Piers Falconer.'

After lunch she found him in his office. His on-screen frown of concern appeared on his bland face as he saw her. 'I tried to let you know about your cat food,' he said.

'I've been running about so much I forgot to call you back.'

'I wanted to put your mind at rest. I had the food you gave me tested, and it came out clean.'

'I don't understand,' Sandy said.

'No poison, nothing that shouldn't have been there. Whatever made your cats run away, it didn't come out of that tin.'

She wondered why he should expect that to ease her mind: presumably because she needn't blame herself for having fed them the cause. Might the food have contained some additive against which they'd reacted? Why hadn't the allergy shown up before? She put the problem out of her mind in order to concentrate on editing, but it returned to bother her as she walked to the hospital. It made her feel pursued by something she couldn't quite define or didn't want to.

Roger was able to hold her hand, indeed anxious to demonstrate his grip. When his father, who looked better for a night's sleep, made to leave them alone, Sandy insisted that he stay and left early herself, so as to ponder issues she didn't want to trouble Roger with while he was hospitalized. She ought to look into the history of Redfield, though she wasn't sure what she would prefer to find: a pattern, or none? She ought to find out whether the circumstances of Giles Spence's death had been reported anywhere in detail.

The question of what could have sent the cats fleeing made her rooms feel colder and lonelier and more like a series of hiding-places than she liked. 'Get well soon, Roger,' she wished, and repeated it inside her head as she lay waiting for sleep.

Near dawn she drifted awake. She rolled sleepily on to her back and let her arms stretch out on either side of her, inviting the soft weight of the cats to land on the bed. 'Come on if you're coming,' she murmured blurrily, and then she wakened enough to remember that they never would. No doubt her conversation with Piers Falconer had brought them prowling into her dreams – but she still felt as if something was roaming beyond the foot of the bed and about to leap on to the quilt.

She shoved herself back and up, the headboard scraping her shoulders, and tugged the light-cord. Only the room sprang at her, jerked by the light. She couldn't tell if there was a stale smell in the room; perhaps it was the taste of panic in her mouth. It had gone by the time she returned to bed, having searched the rooms to prove they were deserted.

She showered, and ate breakfast as the sun came up. She found she couldn't eat much; the bread tasted so flat she checked that it was the loaf she'd bought yesterday, not one left over from before her travels in search for the film. At least she had plenty of time for a stroll through the wood.

The sunlight hadn't reached the paths yet; it was cold and dim beneath the trees. The activity on both sides of the paths, the shadows dodging between the trunks and through the undergrowth, must be of birds, but she wished they would identify themselves by singing.

Commuters ran after her down to the Highgate platform. She managed to find a seat on the train, where faces nodded above her. At Metropolitan the lift opened on the way to her floor, though there was nobody in sight beyond the doors. She worked all day in the editing room to keep herself occupied, and made do with a sandwich for lunch. That bread tasted stale too. Now and then she was left alone in the room, and kept thinking that someone had come in behind her to watch. Once she thought a dog had managed to stray upstairs.

She had a drink with Lezli after work to help herself relax, then she walked to visit Roger. They had lowered his leg and unbandaged his head and arms, and he was sitting up. 'They're showing me the door tomorrow,' he said.

She felt brighter and clearer at once. 'You're that much better?'

'Better than whoever needs this bed, I guess. And it's cheaper for your health service to lend me crutches.'

'Are you going to be able to write?'

'I would if I had anything ready,' he said, wriggling his fingers to show they didn't make him flinch. 'Maybe I can hobble into the British Museum and get some use out of my reader's card while I'm waiting for the ideas to come back, if there's any research you need me to do.'

'The history of Redfield and any report of Giles Spence's death.'

'Sure, why not? No need to look as if you're asking me to break my other leg. I want to get something definite as much as you do.'

'And when you're more mobile we'll go looking for Spence's film, shall we?'

'You bet. While I've been lying here it occurred to me that the Redfields may not have sewn up the American rights. If they can't stop me showing it over there you can blame me for resurrecting it if you like.'

'So you're planning on going back to America.'

'Not for a while,' he said, and squeezed her hand, held on as they saw his father approaching. The conversation became more general, but his grasp stayed with her, even when she left the hospital. It felt like a companion in the sparsely populated streets and in the underground, where someone unseen was pacing, heels clicking clawlike. It felt like a promise that she wouldn't be spending many more nights by herself.

She walked home around the outside of the wood, eating fish and chips out of a copy of the *Daily Friend*: no danger of putting on weight today. She must phone a few friends to let them know she was back in town and to introduce Roger. She let herself into the house and tramped upstairs. She switched on the lights in her flat and made herself a drink of Horlicks, sipped and then downed it as she watched the end of a comedy show on television. She undressed, washed, brushed her teeth. By the time she'd finished brushing her hair she felt pleasantly tired. She wandered into the bedroom, switched on the bedside lamp, and went to the window. She grasped the curtains and was about to draw them when a movement in the wood made her look down. Her body jerked, almost dragging the curtains off the rail. Propped against the railings at the end of the garden, its vague blotchy greenish face upturned towards the window, was a scarecrow.

37

She felt as if she might stand there until the sun came up, stand there afraid to loosen her grip on the curtains and step back, afraid to let the scrawny figure at the railings out of her sight for even a moment, afraid to think why. All she seemed able to think was that scarecrows didn't have hands, and so the scarecrow couldn't be holding on to the railings with whatever was at the ends of its arms, however it looked. If she switched on the main light in her bedroom it would illuminate the edge of the wood where the figure was. The light from the bedside lamp stopped at the window and obscured more down there than it showed, but the little she could see was keeping her at the window, unable to run to the light-cord.

The figure at the end of the garden was rocking slightly back and forth under the swaying trees as though it was preparing to leap. Something like hair streamed back from its overgrown face. Perhaps the figure was dancing in the wind as if celebrating Sandy's helplessness, and wasn't part of its bunched face moving, writhing? She was struggling to open her hands, willing them to shove her away from the window and let her reach the cord, when the phone rang.

She cried out, flung the curtains away from her, sprawled across the bed. The phone was on the bedside table. She seized the cordless receiver and pressed it to her cheek. 'Hello?' she gasped.

'Miss Allan.'

It was a man's voice, one she felt she ought to know. In diving for the phone she'd knocked the light-cord out of reach. She grabbed at it as it swung back, missed, caught it at last and tugged. 'Yes, of course it is,' she said wildly. 'Who'm I speaking to?'

'We spoke recently, you may recall.'

234

He sounded offended that she hadn't recognized him. For a moment she thought he was Lord Redfield, and found that her instincts were framing a plea to him: 'Call it off.' That was several kinds of irrational, she thought, pushing herself away from the bed: it wasn't Redfield, and even if it had been, how did she imagine he could help? 'Spoke about what?' she demanded.

'About my father,' the voice said, and paused before adding resentfully, 'My father, Norman Ross.'

'Norman Ross, oh yes.' He'd been the assistant editor on Spence's film, the first of the names from Graham's notebook she had succeeded in contacting, except that she had spoken to his irritable son then too. These thoughts seemed distant, for she had reached the window and was peering down, peering harder. There was no scarecrow at the railings, nothing at all. 'You wouldn't let me talk to him,' she said, hardly aware of speaking.

'I told you why at the time. I didn't want him troubled more than he already was.'

Whatever she'd seen at the railings, it couldn't be on its way into the house. It must have been a large stray dog, she told herself. It had looked as much like that as like a scarecrow, not that she had been able to see it at all clearly. No wonder she was seeing things when she needed to catch up on her sleep, but she had to concentrate on the phone call. 'I'll be able to talk to your father now, will I?' she said.

'I'm very much afraid not. He died several days ago.'

'Oh dear,' she said, feeling inadequate and also bitter that she had been denied the interview. She was still peering down into the wood, where she could see no movements that might not be of trees or undergrowth. 'My condolences,' she said, wondering why the son had bothered to phone her at all.

'I won't apologize for standing in your way. My father's nerves were bad enough. You may as well know it was those and his heart and his imagination that killed him.'

'I'm sorry to hear it, but why are you telling me?'

'I'm trying to suggest that I may have been wrong to

prevent you from obtaining what seems to have obsessed both of you. Perhaps if I hadn't, my father might still be alive. Shortly before he died he asked me to contact you, and so I have.'

Sandy scanned the wood once more, then backed away from the spectacle of so much dark restlessness to sit on the bed. 'I'm sorry, I'm not clear why.'

'Because he had the film you're so anxious to find.'

She closed her eyes and took a breath. 'Had?'

'In his strongbox at the bank. You understand I had no reason to suspect this.'

She clenched her fist and punched the mattress hard. 'And where is it now?'

'Why, still at the bank. Under the circumstances I hope you will collect it as speedily as possible.'

'Forgive me, I've forgotten whereabouts you are.'

'Near Lincoln.'

'I remember.' Not too far from Redfield, she thought, and suppressed the thought that it wasn't as far as she would have liked. 'Let me write down the details,' she said, and when she had: 'I may not be able to get off work until the weekend. Will Saturday be all right?'

'Presumably it will have to be if you can't make it sooner. The bank closes at twelve.'

'I'll be early.' She hoped she wasn't about to sound impolite; he clearly still resented having to talk to her. 'Do you mind if I ask whether anyone else knows you have the film?'

'I haven't got it. The bank has. I want nothing to do with it, I assure you,' he said, and even more peevishly, 'My father asked that only you should be informed, and I've respected his wish, obviously.'

'I'm very grateful. I'll look forward to seeing you on Saturday.'

'Yes,' he said with an attempt at warmth, and left it at that. When he'd rung off, Sandy gazed at the phone in delight at his message, and threw herself back on the bed, her arms and legs splayed wide. She wished Roger were

236

already home so that she could tell him the news. She lay for a while, relaxing, then strolled to the curtains and drew them tight. She was feeling so pleased with herself that she didn't even bother to glance down into the dark.

38

She slept dreamlessly, and wakened when the curtains began to glow. She stumbled to them, pulled them apart and looked down. Long shadows of branches were dancing slowly and haphazardly in the undergrowth, but the railings were deserted. She had known they would be, she needn't even have bothered to look. Having looked made her feel spied upon, until she ignored the impression. Nobody except Norman Ross' son and possibly his family could be aware that she knew where the film was, and they wouldn't be telling anyone.

Before she left for work she called the hospital and asked for Roger. 'Can he hop to the phone?'

He was there unexpectedly quickly. 'I was just heaving myself up and down the ward to try out my extra legs. I'm being let loose in an hour or so.'

'Don't fall over yourself, but here's another reason to get well. It's a secret between us, all right? I know where to find the film.'

'You're sure? Gee, that's – Hold on, I'm dropping this.'

She heard a clatter as he attempted to hang on to the receiver while keeping himself propped on his crutches. Eventually he said, 'I guess you could hear how bowled over I was. That's great news. Don't tell me over the phone where it is, but you're sure it's safe?'

His warning annoyed her, because it revived her sense of being overheard. 'Absolutely. It's locked away in a bank.'

'Will you be able to get it today?'

'It's not that close, and I can't take the day off,' she said, smiling at his boyish eagerness. 'It'll have to stay locked up until the weekend.'

'If I weren't in this state I'd pick it up for you.' He

sounded furious with himself. 'Maybe I'll be fit to travel with you.'

'Fine, if you are. So where will you be today?'

'I'll take my leg where the rest of the mummies are, and use my reader's card. If you want to meet me in the lobby when you finish work we could load me into a cab and go for dinner.'

She edited deftly and satisfyingly all day, with a token break for lunch, and didn't once look behind her. She wanted to be sure of finishing work on time, so as not to leave him standing in the lobby of the museum. But someone had provided him with a folding chair, on which he sat just inside the entrance, his plastered leg stretched out like a primitive version of a visitors' book, awaiting signatures. 'You look as if you've donated yourself to the museum,' she said.

'I wouldn't be the first, if the company I had today was anything to go by. I'll swear the librarians must go round after hours and dust some of them off.'

'You had a quiet day then at least.'

'Quiet? If a mime had gone in there the readers would have started shushing him. This leg didn't meet with much approval, I can tell you. I opened a book too loud and I thought I was going to be marched out, the stares I got.'

He was levering himself to his feet. 'Seems like there are different rules for the staff,' he said. 'Some guy who works in the museum kept wandering back and forth where I couldn't see him properly. He must have been something to do with masks, he kept going past with one in front of his face. I guess you get used to him. He didn't seem to bother anyone but me.'

'Let's get you out of here and then you can thump along as much as you like,' Sandy said, and helped him down the steps outside. 'Would you rather we went to a restaurant or back to your place? I'd take you to mine, except we'd never maneouvre you up the stairs.'

'Let's go to mine so I don't trip up any waiters, and I'll

buy us a take-away. Just you and me,' he said. 'My father went back home.'

She propped Roger by the gates of the museum while she hailed a taxi, and helped him flounder on to the seat. 'So did you find out much today?' she said as the taxi sped off.

'Nothing too important, and nothing too pleasant.'

She had to be content with that, for the taxi-driver began a monologue about broken limbs, injuries in sports, horses injured during races, horses injured by hunt saboteurs, people meddling with traditions they didn't understand, trying to destroy everything English ... The taxi reached Roger's at last, and Sandy went ahead with the key and switched on the lights so that he could make straight for the sofa and sit like a victim of gout. He phoned through their order for dinner while she poured wine and then sat next to him. 'Let's hear the gory details, then,' she said.

'There are more of those than you may like, particularly when we're about to eat. I don't know if you even need to hear them.'

'You might let me decide.'

'Okay,' he said reluctantly. 'The librarian did find a report of Spence's death. He crashed into a tree at the edge of Redfield and must have gone through his windshield. According to the paper he crawled maybe a mile toward Redfield before he died.'

Spence would have been heading for the Ear of Wheat, for help. He would have bled across a mile of Redfield land. His wounds must have resembled those suggested by the inscriptions in the Redfield graveyard. She managed not to shudder. 'Well, I can cope with that. What else?'

'Nothing to confirm what you were saying about Redfield.'

'What are you saying I was saying?'

'Why, that the place needed some kind of regular blood-shed, weren't you?'

She didn't think she had said that, but it had undoubtedly

been at the back of her mind. 'I've heard of people acting on that kind of belief,' she said.

'Me too. You're thinking of the Aztecs and their cereal gods, are you? And in India some tribes reared people just to be sacrificed to the fields, until the British stopped them. And way back in Ireland they used to sacrifice children to make the land fertile, and not too long ago the Pawnee Indians would sacrifice a girl to Morning Star for the good of the fields, but I'd rather not go into that before dinner. Let's just say I read about various rituals like those today, and one thing they had in common was they were supposed to be practised every year. There wasn't one that happened only every fifty years.'

'But you're talking about rituals that were consciously practised,' Sandy said, and trailed off: what other kind did she imagine had been repeated so often at Redfield? 'Suppose there was a ritual that was forgotten over the centuries but still subconsciously remembered, and somehow that lessened its frequency,' she said, just as fingers tapped on the window behind her.

She smelled the food before she parted the curtains. The figure she glimpsed heading for the front door was delivering the take-away meal, of course. She opened the door and took the carton piled with foil containers, and he came after her, since Roger was announcing loudly that he would pay but couldn't stand up. When she saw him out she thought for a moment that a companion or a pet was waiting for him, but it must have been his shadow that dodged into the gloom between the shrubs.

She served herself and Roger, and discovered that she was ravenous. It must only be bread that didn't taste so satisfying since she had come back from Redfield. Roger was obviously enjoying food that didn't savour of the hospital, and they let conversation lapse for a while. Eventually she said, 'So did you have time to read up on Redfield?'

'Plenty of time, but not much to read. You'd almost think it was being kept out of the history books – in fact, the librarian seemed kind of outraged that it wasn't in something called the *Victoria County History*. There's hardly even any references to the battle that gave the place its name.' He dabbed at his mouth with a paper handkerchief and reached in his pocket. 'I did copy something about that part of the country. There's no reason to suppose it was Redfield, I only wrote it down because it sounded like the kind of thing you were looking for. I'll read it to you, you'd take all night deciphering my scrawl. I didn't like to ask the librarian to photocopy it after he'd brought me so many books.'

He leafed through his notebook and squinted at a page. 'I should have noted where I got this from. Some translation from Latin, some kind of study of the Roman invasion. It talks about how civilized the folk in Kent were supposed to be, then it goes on: "Of the indigenous tribes, the most savage were reputed to be the northerners. The Britons themselves illustrated this by telling of a tribe which farmed a fertile tract of land to the north of Lincoln. Each year a human victim would be hunted through the fields and cut countless times in order that his blood (so it was believed) would strengthen the crops. This tribe was eventually slaughtered by a tribe that envied the fertility of their soil. Not satisfied with killing every man, woman and child, the victorious northerners exhumed all the dead of that district. Having dismembered the corpses, they made a pyre of them, so high that the smoke was seen for many miles. This they did, it was reputed, so that their dead alone would feed the land . . ." What's wrong?'

'That's Redfield.'

'You can't be certain of that, Sandy.'

'I *am* certain. That's exactly what the first Redfields did to the people they took the land from.'

'Huh. Well.' He seemed to feel responsible for having taken her aback. 'Maybe they wanted to show this tribe what it felt like to have it done to them, even if it was generations later.'

'Maybe,' she said doubtfully. 'Except what does it mean about their dead feeding the land?'

'Becoming part of it, I guess. Fertilizing it, if you like.

Hell, I don't know. That's what it said in English, anyway. I can't read Latin.'

'I shouldn't think that would make any difference,' she said, but she could tell he still felt inadequate. She cleared away the empty containers and washed the plates. 'In your condition I'm sure I wouldn't have done half so well,' she told him, and snuggled against him on the sofa, walked her fingers down his stomach until he winced. 'Still painful where it hurts most?'

'Afraid so.'

'Let me know when I can take a hand in the healing process.'

'Sure, I'll tell you as soon as I'm ready for a physical.'

'Or an oral examination.'

'Right now all I can take is suggestion therapy.'

Being married must feel something like this, Sandy thought, this swapping of amiable innuendoes, this sleepy contentment that made it unnecessary to put them into practice. 'I guess I may take my leg to bed,' Roger said eventually, and when she had pulled the quilt over him: 'Stay if you want to, just as you like.'

She undressed and slipped under the quilt with him, intending only to spend a peaceful hour. She told him about her travels, about meeting people from the film and her encounter with Enoch Hill, then she dozed and thought about Redfield. Once every fifty years was less than once a generation: a generation was reckoned to be thirty-three years, the length of Christ's life. Suppose the fifty-year cycle was some kind of token ritual that kept the tradition of bloodshed alive? If so, who was performing the ritual? 'There he is now,' Roger muttered in his sleep, and for a moment she thought the man with the carton had returned and was outside the window; she even thought she smelled stale food, or food mixed with earth. She made herself waken, and the impression faded. Giles Spence's death might have been a coincidence, she told herself, but if it hadn't been, what could she do? Prickly dissatisfaction weighed on her, and she seemed unable to crawl out from beneath it, able only to escape from it into sleep.

She got up before dawn, and left Roger a note. The streets were deserted and silent except for a noise like wind through a dry field, which she identified as the sound of a truck brushing the kerbsides. She caught a train home, where she bathed and changed her clothes, and went to work.

She had grown so impatient with feeling she was being followed that she almost closed the doors on a news producer, one of those she'd argued with outside Boswell's office. He stared at her for the first two floors as if to ascertain from her expression if she had meant to shut him out, and then he said sarcastically, 'I see your camera-shy friends have found someone else to defend them.'

'That restores my faith in humanity,' she said as another floor murmured by. 'Who?'

'Some landowner up north who says they can camp on his property while they work out where they're heading, assuming they've enough brain cells left between them.'

The lift had reached his floor. Sandy had to restrain herself from grabbing his arm to stay him. 'Do you happen to know what he's called?'

'His lordship? He's called the same as his land. Your friends had better hope it doesn't live up to its name.' The doors closed behind him, trapping her with his answer. 'The name is Redfield.'

39

The lift soared up, blinking its numbers, and Sandy's thoughts sped faster. Enoch's Army mustn't go to Redfield. She had barely tasted the hostility that lay in wait there for strangers, but if anything was capable of releasing the violence that drowsed beneath the contentment of Redfield, it would be the convoy of scapegoats. Fifty years, her mind intoned like a refrain, and she wondered if the scale of the violence she foresaw could be what the land and its token bloodlettings had been waiting for. She strode out of the lift and down the corridor, into the editing room.

Lezli was running the image of a politician's face back and forth, making him rant in the voice of a cartoon mouse. 'Lezli,' Sandy said, 'would you feel too much under pressure if I had to go away for another few days?'

'I'd miss you, but I quite like the pressure. Helps me grow.'

'I'm pleased for you. Don't tell anyone I asked you this, but are we still following Enoch's Army?'

'No, we gave up on trying for an interview. We're taking film from the local networks. I believe one of the landed gentry is offering Enoch's lot a breathing space.'

'Do you happen to know when they'll get there?'

'I can find out. I'll say it's me who wants to know.' She phoned down to a newsman and told Sandy, 'Looks like it should be late tomorrow afternoon.'

'So can you hold the fort here for the rest of the week?'

'If you need me to I will. Tell me what I've been helping you with when you can, all right? You can buy the drinks.'

Sandy went up to the top floor and sat on a hard couch. Ten minutes later Emma Boswell's secretary sent her in. Boswell's nails were golden today, and flashed as Boswell flourished her hands on both sides of her face in a welcoming gesture. 'Settling back in?'

'Certainly am, though I feel I hardly need to, the way Lezli has been coming on.'

'I hear she's good, and I'm pleased you feel able to say so. Was that it?'

'No, I wanted to ask – ' Sandy made herself relax so that she wouldn't sound too eager. 'I wouldn't ask if Lezli weren't doing so well, but I wonder if I could take a few days of my holidays.'

'You haven't settled into work as well as you were claiming, then.'

'It isn't that. A friend of mine was in an accident and can't get about by himself. There's a journey up north that has to be made.'

'Can't anyone else undertake it?'

'There's only me.'

'You must be close,' Boswell said, and sighed. 'When are we talking about your leaving and returning?'

'Ideally I should go today, now, if possible, and I might be away for the rest of the week.'

'Nothing in life is ideal.' Boswell gazed at her for what seemed to Sandy an unnecessarily long time. 'You'd better have a word with news. If they don't object to your going I don't suppose I can either, but I shouldn't like to find that you've caused any problems.'

Problems were fine so long as they could be filmed for broadcasting, Sandy amended, but they weren't the kind she intended to cause. When she told the newsroom that she needed to leave on an errand of mercy, nobody objected. She said goodbye to Lezli and hurried away.

A placard for the *Daily Friend* stood against the railings of Hyde Park. ENOCH'S ARMY OFFERED RESTING PLACE, it said. Beyond it a tramp was gripping the railings and staring out at her side of the road. A trick of the sunlight as it flickered behind a rush of clouds made him seem impossibly thin, framed by altogether too few railings, and his face looked more like a lump of the park. She shivered as a shadow rushed at her, and ran into the underground.

Instead of going straight home she caught the train to Roger's. He'd managed to position himself at his desk, his plastered leg poking out to one side, and was leafing desultorily through a print-out of a chapter. 'You're back early,' he said.

'Just to see how you are and give you this.' She kissed him and eventually stood up. 'I've got to go back up north.'

'Only for the film, I hope.'

'I expect I'll take the chance to bring it back, but I don't know what you'll think of my reason for going.' She filled a glass with water from the kitchen tap and gulped it to ease her throat, which was suddenly dry. 'Enoch Hill and his tribe are on their way to Redfield at Lord Redfield's invitation.'

He crossed out a phrase and sprawled the pages face down on his desk. 'You don't think they'll be welcomed.'

'Not in a way they would want to be.'

'You're saying Lord Redfield is luring them into some kind of trap?'

'I don't know if he means to. The sort of violence I'm afraid he may provoke wouldn't do much for the Redfield image. Maybe he thinks he can control his town, but this is one situation where I'm sure he can't. Maybe he genuinely doesn't realize what he's doing, but he should, for heaven's sake. Ignorance isn't supposed to be an excuse, especially when you've as much power as he has.' She swallowed some of her harshness and said, 'The bugger of it is, I feel partly responsible. I took him to task about the way his newspaper had kept after Enoch's Army, and he may even be trying to make amends.'

Roger heaved himself round in his swivel chair, his leg bumping in an arc. 'But are you really saying this is happening because these fifty years are up?'

'Roger, I don't know,' she said, wishing he hadn't asked, and glanced at her watch. 'I should be on my way. Let me just make a call to find out where to head for.'

The AA told her that the convoy was in the Fens, moving slowly north. With luck, though she was loath to consider how much of that she might need, she would be able to turn Enoch away from Redfield and then go on to Lincoln to retrieve the film. 'I ought to thank you for helping when you didn't even know you were,' she said to Roger. 'I said I had to chauffeur you about, to get the time off work.'

'Sounds like what the doctor ordered. Where's the car?'

'At my place. Wait, though, I didn't mean –'

'But I do, Sandy. You could fit me in, couldn't you? Maybe you'd like to have some company on the road. Maybe I might even turn out to be some use.'

'You already are, and a whole lot more than that,' Sandy said, and held his hands and squeezed them harder than she meant to. When he didn't wince she smiled into his eyes. 'I'll go home and get the car,' she said impulsively. She needn't feel selfish for letting him come with her, not when his book was at such a low ebb. Whatever the reason, she had just realized that she would rather not be alone on the road.

40

They started out well. Roger loaded himself into the passenger seat and patted his outstretched leg as if it were a dog that he was pacifying. When Sandy found that the act of shifting gears rapped her knuckles on the plaster, he picked up his bundle of leg and swung it over a few inches. His crutches lay diagonally across the back seat with his coat draped over them to stop them rattling. 'Here goes the last leg of the journey,' Sandy said with a grin at his plaster. 'We hope.'

She was on the Great North Road before the lunchtime traffic began to bunch where trucks were parked. As she drove past signs for Elstree and Borehamwood, Roger gave an appreciative laugh as if he had seen a small joke in a film. Soon the car was on the motorway, and then among the roundabouts of Hatfield. She remembered Harry Manners, and realized that he was the only person she had interviewed about the film who hadn't been nervous during the interview – unless his heartiness had been meant to conceal that he was.

She followed the Roman road towards the pastures around the Ouse. Roger kept pronouncing names of passing villages and towns like a litany of Englishness: 'Biggleswade, Potton, Duck's Cross . . . Hail Weston, Diddington, Alconbury Weston . . .' The land was growing older; lonely villages across the fields of grass looked as if they had absorbed time rather than let it change them. She could never have imagined she would shiver at the sight of thatched roofs, and they were still hundreds of miles from Redfield.

'Pidley, Pode Hole, Dunsby, Dowsby, Horbling . . .' Roger seemed to be trying to distract himself while he shifted about in search of comfort. They were in the Fens now, fields of wheat interrupted by windmills, houses with Dutch gables, dykes, here and there an airstrip where dusty weeds danced, as if the land were expressing its victory over the concrete. The fields had had to be reclaimed from marshland, Sandy reminded herself: the land wasn't as old as Redfield, and so it surely couldn't be soaked in any similar tradition. All the same, the sight of miles of wheat flexing themselves as her car approached made her anxious to head off Enoch and his followers long before they were in sight of Redfield.

An hour further north along the winding road she saw them on the horizon to her left. Even at that distance the motley parade of vehicles looked more worn out than ever. At either end of the slow procession, police cars winked as if lapis lazuli were set into their roofs, catching the light of the bare sky in repeated lingering glares. To Sandy it looked unpleasantly ritualistic, as though the convoy were being ushered to the slaughter by a ceremonial guard.

Roger hoisted himself up in his seat, to see better or to relieve his discomfort. The minor road along which the convoy was being conducted disappeared over the horizon, and Sandy accelerated while Roger traced the roads on the map with his forefinger. 'You're planning to head them off,' he said.

'It seems the best idea.'

'I believe I've a better one. I see where you should be able to join the road they're on in a few minutes, before they can see us.'

'And then what?'

'Be honest with yourself, Sandy. Are you really expecting them to listen to you when they identify you with television? The way you told it to me, Enoch Hill is liable to feel you already tricked him once.'

'But some of his people may listen. The woman I helped after I nearly ran her over,' Sandy suggested, her voice sharp with hope. 'I've got to try. If I don't stop them, who else will?'

Roger knocked on his plastered leg. 'Behold the knight in armour.'

'More like a knight who's fallen off his horse.'

'Well, I guess that'll make me seem less threatening and give me more of a chance. You drop me once we get to their road and then you can go on to meet them, okay?'

She gave his arm an affectionate squeeze. 'What are you thinking of? Using your leg as a roadblock?'

He hitched himself round in his seat, uncomfortably, to face her. 'Don't you want us to do everything we can to stop what you're afraid of? If they won't listen to you they might listen to me. I recall enough of how I used to feel to sympathize with them. I dropped out for a while myself, until I got lazy and wanted to be comfortable.'

She felt touched and yet angry with him. 'Roger, how could I ask someone in your condition –'

'You're not asking. I'm saying what I'll do. These guys aren't violent, I'll be in no danger. Look, there's the road they're on. Turn left here.'

She had been turning the wrong way at the junction, she was so distracted by the argument her thoughts were having. Roger was determined to prove he was of use, but need that mean he wouldn't be? How could she abandon him in the middle of nowhere when he wasn't even able to run? If she did, wouldn't that force her to try harder to stop Enoch so that Roger wouldn't need to? Perhaps she was angry because Roger seemed not to realize the demands he was making on her. 'This is it,' he said suddenly, urgently. 'Drop me now or they'll see what we're doing.'

Her foot faltered on the accelerator, and then she braked. As soon as the car was stationary she dragged at the hand-brake, which made a harsh toothed sound, and held on to his arm with both hands. 'Roger, I truly don't think you should do this. You've been more help than you realize.'

He opened the passenger door and leaned over to kiss her. 'Then let's see what more I'm capable of,' he said, and heaved himself out of the car, turning his wince into an expression of relief at being able to stretch. 'Hand me my crutches, would you?' he said, his voice muffled by the roof. 'Better be quick.'

The metal shafts of the crutches were as cold as the wind that was creeping out of the fields and through the open door. She wanted to refuse, but she thrust the crutches at him and wedged the rests beneath his armpits. As he stepped back, she heard the muddy verge smack its lips. He ducked in order to grin at her. 'Don't wait around or you'll ruin my chances. Look at me now, how could these guys not take pity on me? Never mind worrying about me, you take care of yourself.'

'You make sure you do,' she said fiercely, the wind flattening her voice.

As she started the car he waved, wobbling so much he had to clap the hand to his prop. He was having a good time, she thought as he grinned, so why should she worry about him? In the mirror she saw him standing like a bemused sculpture, the tips of his crutches sunk in the verge, his plaster heel touching the grass. He tossed his head to flip back an unruly curl, and the field at his back quivered towards him. It was the motion of the car that swept him away, not the landscape that was carrying him off, but she twinged her neck for a last sight of him, lonely and immobilized and too unaware of how he looked.

She resisted the temptation to lift her foot from the accelerator. Now he was out of sight, at least a mile back, but there was no sign of Enoch's folk. She could have talked to Roger at more length, she might have been able to persuade him to stay in the car. Her hands clenched on the wheel, her head ached with indecision, and then, above a dip in the road ahead, she saw a roadside oak grow momentarily blue with the light on the roof of the foremost police car.

She braked and veered the car across the road, backed almost into the ditch, swung the car on to the yielding verge on the nearside of the convoy. As the blue lamp glared beneath the oak, she climbed out of the car and leaned against the door. The police car rose from the dip, and then

Enoch did, as if the police were drawing him along behind the vehicle, a captured warrior. The driver stared hard at Sandy, and she did her best to look like a casual spectator, though her throat felt blocked by her pulse. 'Stay there until all this is past,' the driver called out to her, and drove on as soon as she nodded, hardly hearing him, bracing herself to meet Enoch's scrutiny.

He frowned at her over the police car, then he stared straight ahead. He hadn't recognized her. Perhaps he was too exhausted, if he had led the procession on foot ever since she had last seen him. Dust from the roads had dulled the glint of his wiry hair and beard, had turned the ropes of which his waistcoat and trousers were woven the colour of dry earth. The veins of his weathered arms were more prominent than ever. The veins made her want to shout a warning to him or stand in his way, except that the police would intervene.

An ancient estate car fumed by, the amiable moon-faces that were painted on its sides sinking into layers of dried mud. A hearse sprayed with rainbows passed, and then she saw the van embellished with clouds and sunbursts. The order of the vehicles had changed. The woman she'd helped was driving the van, and her son was beside her. 'There's that lady,' he shouted.

His mother craned across the wheel to peer through the sunlit grime of the windscreen, her thin pink face unpromisingly blank. Her son looked delighted, and slid back the door as the van reached Sandy, who jumped on to the running-board. 'Hello,' she said. 'Can I ride with you a little way?'

'I told you not to open that door when we're moving, Arcturus,' the woman muttered as he made room for Sandy on the seat, 'and you know what Enoch said.'

The boy gave Sandy a glum look. 'About me?' Sandy suggested, sliding the door shut.

'He won't answer you,' the woman cautioned him.

'But you needn't be afraid to. Couldn't Enoch be wrong?'

'You would say that.'

'Not necessarily. I'm on your side, remember. I helped you when you fell.'

'Enoch says you did that so your crew could film us. Maybe you made me fall so you could help me, he says. I don't think you made me fall, but I don't like being used by anyone.'

Pots and pans were jangling in the van's brightly painted interior, where a stove and two sleeping-bags took up most of the floor space, and the noise wasn't helping Sandy's nerves. 'There you are, you're agreeing he was wrong,' she said, and heard herself sounding even more suspect. 'I'm not saying he's wrong in his beliefs. It's partly because of things he said to me and things you said that I'm here now.'

The woman looked both incredulous and uninterested. 'Don't say you want to join us.'

'No, I want to warn you about where you're heading. I've just come back from there. I'm sure Enoch wouldn't lead you there if he knew what it was like.'

The woman gave Sandy an ominous smile. 'Well, now you can tell him,' she said, and the door beside Sandy slammed open.

She had been so intent on her task that she hadn't noticed Enoch waiting for the van. His bristling face was almost level with hers, his smell of sweat and rope was overwhelming. 'I didn't realize it was you. I didn't expect we'd see you again,' he said, so grimly that she thought he was about to heave her out of the van.

'I only came back because of what you told me. You said that land can grow hungry because people have forgotten what it wants.'

'I did?'

'Something like it, anyway,' Sandy insisted, desperate to stop the progress of the vehicles and Enoch's inexorable march before they came in sight of Roger, never mind Redfield. 'The point is, the place you've been invited to is like that. They used to make human sacrifices to the land, and the bloodshed hasn't stopped. It's happened every fifty years, up to fifty years ago.'

She sounded grotesque to herself. She was suddenly unconvinced, but did that matter? Surely it was the kind of thing Enoch believed. The woman driving the van was visibly troubled. 'You mean you think we've been invited so that –'

'She doesn't think that at all,' Enoch rumbled. 'She's acting, can't you tell? She thinks she's in one of her films, some horror film she made.'

'I don't *make* films,' Sandy said, and saw that she was undermining her credibility even further. 'I'm not suggesting you've been invited so you can be harmed. I've met the man who invited you, and I think he may not even realize what will happen, but doesn't that confirm what you were saying about how we've lost touch with the land?'

Enoch growled in his throat. 'Stop the van,' he said.

As soon as the woman braked he leaned towards Sandy, his shoulders almost filling the doorway. 'I don't believe you want to help us. I think you're still looking for something to film.'

'I never have been. I wasn't when I met you,' Sandy protested, hating her voice for trembling. 'I'm telling you I've been to Redfield, and they don't like strangers. I only just got away safely myself.'

'Sounds like you're not popular anywhere. You're beginning to know what it feels like, are you?' He took hold of her wrist with a gentleness that felt like a threat of crushing her bones. 'Get down. We've no more time to waste.'

She appealed to the woman. 'Please listen to me, for your own sake and Arcturus'.'

The great hot rough hand tightened on her wrist. 'I know what she wants,' Enoch said. 'To keep us on the road so they can film us. To cause us more trouble that their audience want to watch in their homes while they eat their dinner.'

'You're right, that must be why they sent her,' the woman cried. 'This is my home, you bitch. You fuck off out of it right now.'

Did the hysterical edge to her voice mean that Sandy had

reached her? Sandy could only hope. She climbed down on to the verge and waited for Enoch to let go of her. She wouldn't plead or cry out because he was squeezing her wrist; he wouldn't dare to injure her, the police were too near. 'Leave us alone,' he growled, and released her. 'Don't try to speak to any of my folk. I won't let you spoil this chance for us.'

The procession was moving again. She peered beyond the repetitive glare of the police car, but couldn't see Roger. Enoch watched her as she began to hurry to her car, half a mile back. She rubbed her bruised wrist when she was sure he couldn't see what she was doing, and ran past the vehicles, slipping on the verge. She would never get to Roger ahead of the convoy if she went on foot. She had to stop him, for wouldn't Enoch know that Roger was connected with her as soon as he began to warn them as she had?

But the police who were following the convoy refused to let her drive past. When she tried to overtake, the driver gestured her back, looking ready to arrest her if she continued trying. The convoy wouldn't pick up Roger, she reassured herself. Surely he would appear too suspicious, stuck in the middle of nowhere with no indication of how he had got there. Then her heart sank, for she could see the junction where she had joined this road. She must already have passed the spot where she had abandoned Roger, and there had been no sign of him.

She followed the convoy for miles, hoping to see him put down at the roadside again, until the police car stopped in front of her. The driver tramped back to her, his face red, his lips thin. 'If you don't leave off following,' he said, 'I'll declare you and your car unfit for the road.'

41

So she had to go to Redfield after all. If necessary, she would have to block the road where it descended into the copse. She felt spiky with anger and frustration, but all the same, she had to be grateful to the police: at least Roger ought to be in no danger while they were near. Surely he was in no danger anyway; surely if he was suspected he would have been dropped by now. He must have realized that he needed to avoid sounding like her. She turned the car and drove south, feeling more watched than ever, even when the police were well over the horizon. At least she would be able to tell Roger when they next met that she had Giles Spence's film.

She found a phone box in a village so small it could barely have freckled the map, and called Norman Ross' son. 'I'm in your part of the country earlier than I expected. I'm sorry it's such short notice, but I wondered . . .'

'I assure you, the sooner you relieve us of this legacy the happier I'll be. When had you in mind?'

'Would today be inconvenient?'

'Not unbearably. If you can be here at least half an hour before the bank closes, that will be appreciated.'

'I'll do my best.'

'Then that must suffice.' As soon as he had told her how to find him he broke the connection, presumably to start her on her way. The weeks-old comments in the *Daily Friend* must have made him nervous about the film, she thought, but there was no longer any reason for them to trouble her.

She drove north-west to Lincoln. The cathedral rose over the horizon like a stone crown for the fields of wheat. Soon she saw a ruined Norman castle above steep streets the colour of the fields. There were Roman ruins too, and the sight of them beyond the wheat reminded her uncomfortably of the Roman account of the history of Redfield. She would be there ahead of Roger, she vowed, and just now she was here on his behalf as much as on her own.

She drove across a bridge above clattering trains and turned towards the river. A side street almost choked with students slowed her down. The river flashed in her mirror, and ahead of her she saw the insurance broker's she was looking for. As she parked, her tyres bumping the kerb, a tall pot-bellied man with a long face whose mouth drooped towards his pointed chin darted out of the broker's. 'You mustn't park there,' he announced.

'I'm picking someone up from your office.'

'Miss Allan? In that case, ignore the line.' He called, 'I'll be an hour or less,' to a colleague, and sidled into the passenger seat. 'Please, drive. I'll tell you where.'

He directed her through Lincoln, past cobbled streets of houses that looked as old as the Redfield chapel. 'I was sorry to hear about your father,' Sandy said.

'Ah, well. He'd about run his course. He still had his imagination, but not the use of his hands. The industry had put him out to pasture in favour of younger technicians such as yourself. I haven't inherited his imagination, and I won't pretend I wish I had.'

'That's obvious.'

'Turn left here. I wouldn't care to die as he did.'

Another cobbled street drifted by like a steep shadow full of houses carved with symbols secretive with age. 'How was that?' Sandy said, wishing that he wouldn't make her ask while she was driving.

'Of his nerves. I can only conclude he felt guilty about possessing this film but couldn't bring himself to destroy what might be the sole surviving copy. Once he'd gone I considered destroying it myself. I would have if it hadn't been for his express wish that you should be told.'

'I'm sorry I couldn't have taken the film away sooner.'

'So am I,' he said, so coldly he seemed to be blaming

258

her rather than himself. 'He spent his last days in a panic, convinced he was being watched. Here, park here.'

Sandy drove into the car park and backed into a space, her hands nervous on the wheel. 'Watched by whom, do you know?'

'By his own doubts, I imagine. Possibly by his memories. He claimed he'd felt spied on while he was helping edit the film, though I don't know how much credence that warrants. My wife had to ask him to keep his fears to himself, because he was upsetting our small daughter. Towards the end he wouldn't have her pet dog anywhere near him. We had to stop the child from going in his room, because he started saying that a dog or some such thing came into the room at night and watched him, stood at the foot of the bed all night with its paws on the rail. I'm afraid his imagination was quite out of control. During the last week, for some reason, he wouldn't even have flowers in the room. This is the bank.'

The interior of the building was so much newer than the exterior that it felt intrusive and unreal. Ross marched to an inquiry window and thumbed a button while Sandy followed him, trailing questions which she could hardly ask him in the bank and which made her uneasy about framing them at all. An official came to the window and recognized Ross and the key in his hand. When the official opened a security door Sandy started forward, but Ross frowned curtly at her. 'We won't be long.'

Sandy sat on a straight chair at a table with a blotter, on which someone had doodled a rudimentary face almost buried in a tangle of scribbling. A queue shuffled forward as tellers lit up their signs, a typewriter clacked like impatient claws. Sooner than she expected, Ross appeared beyond the thick glass door, his arms laden with a cardboard carton. As she stood up, his companion glanced towards her. For a moment she thought he was looking behind her, or at something she had dropped under the table, but all she could see there was a deep rectangular shadow. She hurried forward as the door buzzed open. 'We'll go straight to your car,' Ross muttered.

He mustn't want to be seen with the film. His secretiveness made her peer warily about the car park. He trudged to the rear of the car and waited truculently for her to unlock the boot. As soon as he'd dumped the carton into it he wiped his hands on a handkerchief. His palms must be damp with exertion, of course.

Sandy gazed at the squat square carton sealed with heavy tape. It was big enough to contain two cans of film, but she had a sudden grotesque thought: what if after all her searching the carton proved to be empty, or full of something else entirely? She would have opened it there and then if Ross hadn't been drumming one heel nervously on the concrete. She slammed the lid of the boot and climbed into her seat and eased the car forward, anxious not to run over the stray animal which had just dodged behind the vehicles next to hers. 'I'll drop you at your office, shall I?' she said.

'I thought you might want to make sure this film is what it's claimed to be.'

He sounded resentful. 'I will as soon as I can,' Sandy assured him.

'Then assuming you've nothing better to do, it may as well be now. A friend of my late father's is renovating a cinema and used to let him watch films there. I spoke to him after you called. He'll put on the film for you.'

'I thought nobody outside your family knew about it except me.'

'Apparently my late father let him into the secret, and he's been hungry for a viewing ever since. Of course he was sworn to secrecy, but I made him renew the vow, on your behalf, you understand. I shan't be watching. Cross the bridge.'

His directions grew more irritable as he manoeuvred her towards the far edge of the town, where the architecture entered the twentieth century, and she sensed that his nervousness was increasing. Without warning he fumbled at his safety-belt and sent it fleeing into the body of the car. 'Slow down. We're here.'

The cinema formed the rounded corner of two streets. With its strip of cataracted windows above the wrap-around marquee, the building made her think of a helmet too old to see out of. Beneath the marquee, at the top of three tiled steps, were three glass doors obscured by torn posters for circuses, concerts, some kind of festival. Ross knocked on the festival poster, in a rhythm that seemed to want to sound like a secret code.

An old clown with dusty hair and an ordinary mouth opened the door into the unlit foyer. 'This is Miss Allan,' Ross said, already retreating. 'I must get back to the office.'

The clown rubbed his hands on his baggy suit, through which the elbows of his shirt gleamed like bone, and came out quickly, closing the door on sounds of scraping and dragging. 'He didn't tell me you would be this early. I've some work being done just at the moment. I'll turf them out as soon as I decently can. Would you like to sit in the office if I can get the kettle going?'

'Do you mind if I bring the film in with me?'

'I'd rather they didn't know about it, in case – well, in case.'

His cautiousness was understandable, but his vagueness was as disconcerting as the sight of him had been, even though she could see that he was clownish with plaster dust that emphasized the wrinkles of his face. 'I'd better stay in the car, then,' she said.

She sat in it for a while and tried to listen to the radio, but some kind of interference made the broadcast voices decay, sink into a mass of static and then lurch at her. She spent half an hour leaning on the boot lid and watching the street as idly as she could, seeing the first children race out of a nearby school like hares started by the bell before the rest of the pupils crowded after them. Eventually she lost patience. Nothing could happen to the film so long as she kept the car in sight, she told herself. She dug in her handbag for Toby's new number, which he'd left at Metropolitan for her, and called him from a phone box outside a pet shop where a puppy kept leaping up inside the window. 'How are you doing?' she said.

'Getting on with life and being loved.' He sounded drowsy, as if she'd just wakened him, but happy. 'And yourself?'

'Both of those, I think, and something I wanted you to know but to keep to yourself until I make it public. I've found Graham's film.'

'Good for you, Sandy. I knew you would if anyone could. Thanks, love, and I mean that from Graham too.'

When her change ran out she paced back and forth past houses and neighbourhood shops, several hundred yards each way, feeling as though she were on a leash or in a cage. People were coming home from work and taking dogs for walks. She began to regret having lingered, though surely she would prefer not to arrive at Redfield too far in advance of the convoy. As muddy shadows oozed from under the buildings and spread, two whitened men peered out of the gloom beyond the glass doors of the cinema. They stood on the steps, dusting themselves and gossiping, until a third livid man emerged from the gloom. All three drove away in a builder's van, and the man who had opened the door to Ross came out to find her.

He'd washed himself as best he could but had overlooked a line of dust at his temples, which made him appear to be wearing a wig. A few traces of plaster had lodged in cracks of his jovial face, which looked as if it had once been even plumper. 'I didn't introduce myself,' he said, giving her hand a soft loose shake. 'I'm Bill Barclay, which sounds like something you'd say to a bank, doesn't it? Welcome to the Coliseum.'

'Shall I bring the film in now?'

'Oh, please do, yes. The projectors are all set. So have I been, for weeks. I won't pretend conditions are luxurious, but I hope you'll be reasonably comfortable. I've a few seats I cleaned up for friends until I can open to the public.'

'I'll be on my own, won't I?'

'Heavens yes, never fear. This is just our secret, as it was poor Norman's.' He stood close to her while she unlocked the boot, and lifted the carton before she could. As he hurried stumbling towards the glass doors he said rather plaintively, 'I hope you'll come and see my picture-house again when it's done up.'

He bumped a door open and leaned on it to let her in. Dusk was spreading down the steps beneath the marquee. She was able to see the foyer almost as soon as she smelled it, plaster dust and the turned-earth smell of old brick. Plaster had been hacked off a yard-high strip of the walls, obviously in preparation for injecting a damp course. A mound of broken plaster lay on the bare floorboards near the walls, surrounding a paybox so dusty she couldn't see through the glass. The mound was interrupted by the double doors that led to the auditorium and by a corridor along which an open door poked a wedge of harsh light. 'Come in here for a tick,' Barclay said.

The open door led to his office, where an unshaded bulb glared above a desk on to which he lowered the carton, puffing and smearing his forehead with the back of his hand. He picked up a flashlight from the top of a rusty filing cabinet, and shook it hard. 'That should do it,' he said. 'I'll show you to your seat whenever you're ready.'

He was already in the corridor, beckoning her with a haste that stopped just short of rudeness. Either he was anxious to see the film or not to leave it unattended, or both. He chased his shadow into the foyer and eased the double doors open. Fallen plaster gnashed beneath them. As Sandy followed him, he swept the flashlight beam around the auditorium.

A red carpet that looked muddily sodden had been rolled back from the walls, and was heaped against the outer ends of the rows of seats. Between the carpet and the exposed bricks of the walls lay another long mound of plaster. Beneath the screen, which was flanked by two pale giants, it formed a dim border to the flashlight beam as Barclay ushered her along the central aisle to a row of seats covered with a whitish plastic sheet, which he folded back for her. He stamped on the carpet and grunted. 'Didn't think the dust would reach this far, but I wasn't taking any chances. Stay here and light my way back, would you? Enjoy the film.'

She spread a carpet of dimness for him as he ran up the slope to the foyer. He was eager to start the film, of course, not afraid the light would fail. The double doors clapped together clumsily, leaving her alone with a trail of greyish footprints, and she swung the flashlight beam around her. Shadows darted from behind the rolled carpet and slithered over the heap of plaster. When Barclay had shone the beam into the auditorium she'd thought at first that he intended to scare away some animal, but surely he would have told her if there were rats.

She sat back in the folding seat, which smelled of metal and dusty cloth, and sent the beam wavering over the walls that framed the blotchy screen. At that distance the light barely diluted the darkness, but she was able to distinguish that the figures on either side of the screen were flourishing sheaves of grain, which must have appealed to the architect as sufficiently Roman to go with the name of the cinema. They made Sandy uneasy – uneasy enough to glance behind her to see who was watching her. Of course it was Barclay, at the projectionist's window. He gave her a thumbs-up sign, and stepped back. He was about to start the film.

42

So she was to see the film at last. Her mouth went dry, and she found she was unexpectedly close to tears. She wished Roger and especially Graham could be here to share the film with her. The projector came to life with a whir whose echoes seemed to leap behind the mound of plaster, and Sandy switched off the flashlight and placed it between her feet. As she looked up from making sure that she knew where it was, the screen blazed. The Romanesque statues flexed themselves and raised their sheaves, but that was only the play of the light. For a few seconds the screen remained blank except for stains, and then an image wobbled into focus. It was a painting of a tower.

Though it didn't look much like the Redfield tower, the sight of it made her heart beat uncomfortably fast. Terse credits solidified out of the mist that loitered in front of the tower:

A BRITISH INTERNATIONAL PRODUCTION
KARLOFF and LUGOSI
in
TOWER OF FEAR

She could scarcely believe she was reading this after so much searching. She was dry-mouthed again, breathless. The names of some of the people she had interviewed appeared beneath Giles Spence's, and without further ado, to the strains of a studio orchestra's version of a Rachmaninov *Dies Irae*, the film began.

It was the scene Toby had described to her, Karloff gazing emotionlessly from the high tower at a man fleeing across a moonlit field. The man's flight cut a swathe of darkness through the field, and so did whatever was pursuing him, converging on him. He dodged into the tower and fled up the steps; each window showed his white face staring down in panic. No doubt it was the same set of a window each time, Sandy thought, surprised that she needed to reassure herself that way, though Toby had said he too found the scene disturbing. Even admiring the skill with which the film was edited didn't let her distance herself from it as the fugitive staggered on to the top of the tower and stretched his hands beseechingly towards Karloff, who shook his head and folded his arms. The man stared in terror down the steps, backed towards the parapet and toppled over, his cry fading.

She knew what it was like to panic in a tower, she thought, and that must be why her palms were sweating. Now here was Lugosi in a coat like Sherlock Holmes', stepping down from a train at a lonely station. A taciturn coachman with a left eye white as the moon drove him through the whispering fields to a mansion whose asymmetry made it look half-ruined in the moonlight. Karloff opened the massive front door to him, and the two actors set about upstaging each other, Karloff sinisterly unctuous, Lugosi resoundingly polite. Before long they were at the piano and singing 'John Peel', surprisingly musically. 'It takes more than a critic to shut them up, Leonard Stilwell,' Sandy declared, and wished that saying so had made her feel less nervous.

In the village Lugosi found that nobody, not even Harry Manners between wiping tankards and drinking out of them, would discuss his brother-in-law's death except to say, like Karloff and almost in the same words, that it had been an unfortunate accident. Hoddle and Bingo, the village bobbies, reacted to him as if he were Dracula, muttering oo-er and how they hadn't oughter look at his eyes in case he got up to some sort of foreign tricks. It was his gaze that made them tell him all about the look on his brother-in-law's face and the evidence of pursuit that had ended at the tower. Sandy knew she was meant to laugh, but the sight of Tommy Hoddle's eyes frozen wide by hypnosis was too

266

reminiscent of his last stage performance. She remembered that not all the terror in the film was faked.

Graham would have been delighted to know that here was one old film she didn't feel distanced from, but she would rather not have found that out in the middle of an empty cinema, where whenever a close-up on the screen brightened the auditorium, shadows seemed to crouch beyond the heaps of plaster. She glared at the debris and looked up as the scene changed. Karloff was alone, prowling a baronial hall she hadn't seen before. His face filled the screen, staring out with sudden unease as if he had seen something behind her. 'You silly bitch,' she scoffed at herself, and looked over her shoulder. The screen dimmed, shadows ducked behind the dozen or more rows of seats between her and the doors, and she turned back to the film. She wasn't quite in time to see the details of the carving above the mantelpiece in the baronial hall, but she thought she had seen it before.

The muddy blotches on the screen seemed to swell, wiping out the film, and then the second reel sharpened into focus. If the film was half over, why should that feel like a promise of relief? Nothing she had seen was a reason to feel there was someone behind her – but there was, and he was well on his way down the aisle to her before she heard the doors thump.

The mask that loomed at her shoulder, jerking closer as the light of a close-up seized it, was Bill Barclay's face, of course. 'The film's a bit longer than I bargained for. I'll have to nip round the corner for a loaf for the missus when it looks as if nothing's going to happen. I should be back before the end, but if not, just wait for me in the office.'

He scurried up the aisle, and she thought of calling him back. If he didn't need to be in the projection room throughout the showing, he could sit with her and watch – but why should she be so anxious to have company? In any case, he seemed to be lingering at the back of the auditorium to watch the next scene, in which Lugosi discovered that someone had fallen from the tower in very similar circumstances fifty years ago. She shivered, and was glad that she wasn't alone in the auditorium, except that when she glanced back she found that she was, so far as she could see past the projector beam. 'Poor little thing,' she mocked herself, and trapped the flashlight between her feet as she made herself turn to the film.

Lugosi was returning through the village to the mansion. Whenever he looked behind him he saw only shadows, but weren't they becoming increasingly solid, assuming shapes that would be better left in the dark? Graham would have admired this scene, Sandy told herself while shadows raised themselves around her as if they were peering at the film over the heap of plaster which had begun to remind her of an upheaved mound of earth. Here came Hoddle and Bingo, dodging after Lugosi like rabbits trying to be blood-hounds, until they discovered they weren't only pursuing but also pursued. They fled in opposite directions, and she remembered how Bingo was supposed to have run into something offscreen, something that had come after him.

Lugosi was leafing through a history of the tower and of the Belvedere family. It couldn't be long to the end now, she thought, and the stale smell of earth was really the smell of exposed brick. She would feel disloyal to Graham if she didn't see the film through. Lugosi shut the book and strode to find Karloff.

He found him in the baronial hall. In came Lugosi's sister and her new protector to be present at the final confrontation. Her husband had been no coward, Lugosi told her, but this man – Karloff – was doubly one for having sacrificed him in his stead, knowing that someone must die on the tower. Building a tower so high had made it a focus of occult forces 'that would climb to heaven', forces that demanded a sacrifice. Once it had been from every generation of the family. Only the death of the surviving member of this generation could lift the curse.

Not much of this made sense to Sandy, perhaps because her attention was held by the image carved above the mantelpiece behind Karloff. She must have known it would be there ever since she had seen it in the Redfield vault and recognized what Charlie Eames had tried to sketch for her: the face overgrown with wheat, or turning into wheat, or composed of it; the hungry face from whose eyes sprouted braids of wheat shaped like the horns of a satyr. It was the reason the Redfields had suppressed the film, but why was it making her so nervous? Every time the film showed it the shadows beyond the mound of plaster seemed to crouch forward. She glanced back, but there was no sign of Barclay in the projection box. She was alone with the film – with the image that had scarcely been seen outside the Redfield vault.

'Take the strangers who threaten this house,' Karloff cried, his exhortations growing wilder as the shadows came not for Lugosi or the others but for him. He fled to the tower, his unseen pursuers tracking darkness through the field, and climbed to the parapet. With a glance down the stairway and a groan of despair, he fell – or rather, Sandy thought, Leslie Tomlinson did, injuring himself because of something that had disturbed him. The tower itself crumbled as Lugosi and the others watched.

The next shot found Lugosi on the train, wishing his sister and her beau good luck, and it felt to Sandy as if Spence had wanted to get the film over with, though that left various issues still restless. Had he been as nervous as she was now? The train steamed away, merging with the blotches of the screen as the shot faded out. The film rattled clear of the gate of the projector. The screen glared dirty white, a pack of shadows raised their heads around her, and at once the screen went dark.

Bill Barclay hadn't switched off the projector. Nobody was in the projection room, crouched down where she couldn't see them through the small windows. The projector must have switched itself off to protect the film. She grasped the flashlight with both hands and turned towards the window, the glare from which served only to dazzle her. She pressed the button, and then she shook the flashlight as hard as she could. It still didn't work.

She shouldn't have wasted her time with it, she was making herself feel as though something she'd relied on had left her alone in the dark. Even if she couldn't see the exit doors, she knew they were there, to the left of the lit windows. She had only to ignore the smell of earth that was actually the smell of brick, the shapes beyond the heap of plaster that was just visible as a low greyness near the dim walls. In fact, since the screen was dark, it couldn't be creating shadows, and so the shapes she thought she was glimpsing couldn't be there at all, couldn't be peering over the grey mound, ready to pounce if she moved. The restlessness on both sides of her was only an effect of the way her eyes couldn't grasp the dimness. The creaking she could hear behind her and around her as she made herself let go of the back of the seat and tiptoe up the aisle, over carpet which felt threadbare enough to trip her up, was nothing but vibration she was causing, evidence that she wasn't moving as softly as she would like. She mustn't be tempted to go faster, she might fall headlong. She felt as if the dark around her were waiting for her to break, to run for the doors so that it could leap on her. The lit windows blinded her left eye, the dark gathered itself on her right; plaster dust settled on her, making her feel as if she were being stealthily buried. She stuck out her hands and the dead flashlight, and shoved at the doors.

The left-hand door baulked as if someone were holding it closed from outside, and then she felt the chunk of plaster that had lodged beneath it give way. She heard a sound like teeth grinding together. She flung the doors open and hurried into the foyer, past the paybox like an upended casket, its window coated with earth. The doors thumped behind her, so irregularly that she peered through the dimness to reassure herself that nothing had followed her between them.

The projection room was at the far end of the corridor, past the deserted office. As she reached the room, she heard a sound like claws on metal. It was the cooling of one of a pair of projectors that occupied much of the space in the room. She smelled hot metal, and told herself hastily that it smelled nothing like blood. She hurried to the carton Barclay had brought in. She clattered open the round can that lay uppermost in it, lifted the spool off the projector, lowered it carefully into the can. She fitted the lid on to the can and closed the cardboard flaps, and straightened up, her arms laden with the carton. A blurred face rose up in the auditorium and peered at her through a window.

It was her own face, reflected in the glass. She clutched the carton to herself and stumbled into the corridor, feeling as if her burden were dragging her forward, forcing her almost to run so as not to drop it. The dark foyer swallowed her shadow, and she staggered past the double doors, one of which was propped ajar by a fragment of plaster. She leaned on the paybox sill for a moment while she took a firmer grip on the carton, and then she launched herself towards the glass doors. A shadow half as tall again as she was came to meet her, towering among the shredded posters stuck to the outside of the doors.

It shrank to fit its head and hands around the face and hands that pressed themselves against the glass. 'I can't open the door,' Sandy called.

Barclay opened it for her and insisted on carrying the film to her car. 'I didn't mean you to have to deal with this all by yourself. The shop was shut and I had to go further. Was it good? Did I miss much?'

'Nothing you should regret missing.'

He frowned rather wistfully at her; he must think she was trying to cheer him up. 'Will you keep me in mind when it's going to surface? Maybe an invite?' he suggested, miming writing, and looked disappointed by her noncommittal murmur. As she drove away she saw him on the steps of his cinema, waving tentatively, and she was taken aback to find herself envying him. She was beginning to realize that managing to make her way safely out of the darkened cinema didn't feel at all like an escape.

43

She was driving around the outskirts of Lincoln, and debating whether to head back into the town for dinner, when she switched on the radio in search of company. Among the interchangeable rock stations, whose drums always emerged from the static ahead of any melody, she found a Lincolnshire voice reading the news. Seamen were on strike, and a lorry had overturned on Erskine Street, the Roman road north out of Lincoln. Enoch's Army would be travelling all night and would arrive at Redfield early tomorrow morning.

Sandy had expected them to rest somewhere overnight, and her informant at the AA must have. Either the police were keeping them on the move or Enoch and his folk were anxious to arrive where they believed they would be welcome. Did that mean Roger had failed to convince them of the danger? He still had more than half the night, he could be biding his time. All Sandy knew was that she had to be at Toonderfield before dawn.

She wouldn't be much use unless she ate. The first two pubs she passed on the increasingly lonely road had stopped serving dinner, but several miles further on she found one that hadn't quite, the Poacher. She ate jugged hare and gazed at polished oak and brasses. A hunting horn shone dully on a beam above her head. The strong beer she was drinking, and the respite from driving, loosened her thoughts and let them wander, but not far. Had there ever been poachers at Redfield? Once upon a time, wouldn't they have been shot on sight? That kind of bloodshed used to be taken for granted. If it had happened at Redfield during one of those fiftieth years, would it have satisfied the land?

She made her pint of beer last until shortly before closing

time, and was on her way out through an ungainly passage of fat bricks when she noticed that the worn stone stairs beside her led to guest rooms. The idea of resting on a bed in a warm room for a few hours was almost irresistible, but in order to be certain of reaching Toonderfield ahead of the convoy she would need to be up earlier than the staff of the pub. Besides, how could she even dream of taking a room when Roger was out there on her behalf? She marched herself out of the pub and breathed in the chill of the night, as if its sting would keep her more awake.

Other cars were departing, fanning out across the landscape. One followed her north-eastwards for a few miles, then its lights turned aside into a dip where they were extinguished so quickly that she thought there had been a crash until they reappeared in her mirror. They shrank like a spent match, and then there was nothing behind her except darkness and the cans of film.

The beams of her headlights nudged the dark, touching hedges, signs striped with arrows where the road curved, infrequent trees. Very occasionally she passed a handful of cottages, always unlit. At first she could hardly distinguish the flat land from the sky, except for the faint blur of mist where they met. Close to midnight a lopsided moon edged above the mist. It looked like a flaw appearing in a sky of black ice that weighed down the landscape. It turned the fields into a monochrome patchwork that made her feel surrounded by the black and white of the film. Her headlights seemed almost as valuable now for the glimpses of colour they snatched from the dimness as for lighting her way. She would have preferred the road behind her to be completely dark; she wasn't enjoying the way trees and hedges in her mirror were barely visible. Too often they looked as if part of them was threatening to reveal another shape.

She trod on the brake, and a hedge flared red behind her. 'There's nothing there, all right?' she cried in a rage, and flung herself out of the car to stare about. The silent empty land seemed paralysed by the weight of the sky, except for the part of the hedge which the brake lights had stained, the shrub which had then appeared to sneak aside into the dark. She couldn't identify which thin shrub it was; she might almost have thought it was no longer there. She slammed her door defiantly loud and wound the windows as tight as they would go before she drove off. 'Don't you dare start looking in the mirror,' she snarled at herself.

However much she concentrated on the road, it left her alone with her thoughts. Now and then a bump in the tarmac rattled the cans of film. They were safest with her, she told herself, and where else could she have hidden them? Even if she had arranged for them to be locked away at her bank she would have had to take them there personally. She wouldn't have had time. Nobody who was likely to betray her knew she had them, and the boot of her car was the last place the Redfields would think of looking for them. Why did that thought make her feel suddenly more vulnerable? She felt as if she might prefer not to know until she was somewhere less lonely, less dark.

The horizon was rising. There must be a main road to the uplands, but she had missed it somehow. The road she was on wound back and forth as if it didn't want to arrive where it was heading. At least she had plenty of fuel, and several hours in which to drive to Redfield. She still had several hours out here before the dawn.

At last the road looped upwards, so gradually that she was hardly aware of climbing. The land spread out below her in the moonlight like an icebound sea, patchily misted as if areas were melting. There wasn't a headlight other than hers in the entire landscape. From a crest of the uplands she saw an even wider loneliness, and found she was shivering. Of course it would be cold up here, and the smell of earth came from the fields or from the ditches that bordered the road. She couldn't close the windows any tighter to keep the smell out of the car.

A bump in the road shook the cans of film. The sound made her glance in the mirror. The road glistened emptily in the wake of the car. There was nothing behind her to be afraid of, nothing but the film. Even if it had disturbed her while she was watching it, it was locked away. It was nothing but two spools of celluloid packed into cans, it was just a series of images deadened by the dark. Without light and machinery to give them life, they were no threat at all.

But she couldn't help reflecting that the image she had seen in the Redfield vault was locked in the boot of her car – the only faithful reproduction of that image which had ever been seen outside Redfield. If the carving had been incorporated into the vault, did that matter? It might be as old as it looked, centuries older than the vault; it might have been carved in the days when the land was first fed with blood, but why should that make her nervous of the cans of film?

The road dipped, putting out the moon. The cans rattled as though the sudden shadow had wakened them, though of course it was the fault of the irregular surface of the road. Spence must have entered the vault in search of secrets he could use against the Redfields, or to find names to include in his film as a petty revenge. He'd seen the carving and had had Charlie Eames design an extra set in which it figured – and after that, more fear had attended the filming than could be accounted for.

Later Spence had been killed at Redfield, by natural causes or otherwise. Natural causes could scarcely account for all the violence she had read about in the graveyard; those responsible for the inscriptions clearly hadn't thought so. That wasn't to say that over the centuries there wouldn't have been bloodshed in the ordinary course of things, and some of this might well have coincided with the cycle she'd identified. Perhaps it was only in those years when human nature didn't feed it that the Redfield land sent out its servants to shed blood.

She wished she hadn't thought that now. It made her feel hunted – more hunted than she had been trying not to admit to herself she already felt. If she imagined that the land was able to send something to hunt victims on its behalf, she might wonder if the inclusion of the image in the film had brought the guardians of Redfield past the boundaries of the land, to ensure that the secret of Redfield wasn't betrayed. She might imagine that whoever saw the image in the film was in danger, or even anyone who helped revive the film. Suppose Graham had fallen because he was fleeing in terror from what he'd found he had chased? Suppose it hadn't been her cats that had torn up his notes?

'Shut up, don't be so stupid!' The night was thinking for her, she tried to tell herself. These were the kinds of thoughts you had when you wakened at the low point of the night and couldn't get back to sleep, but being unable to stop thinking them out here was worse. The more they raced the more convincing they seemed. The dark on either side of the lit patch of road and of the wake of her tail-lights was so thick that she could imagine parts of it were solid, pacing her on both sides of the road.

The road dipped towards the flat lands, and she let out a shaky sigh. A few hundred yards ahead it curved out of the oppressive shadow of the higher ground. If she couldn't hold her breath until she reached the sloping field of moonlight, surely she could hold her thoughts still. She pressed the accelerator, wishing that she didn't feel as if she were trying to outrun the dark.

She shivered as a smell of earth and staleness seeped into the car. The dark that flanked the vehicle was restless; she glimpsed movement at both edges of her vision. There must be a chill wind that was forcing the smell into the car. The moonlight was less than two hundred yards ahead. She sucked in a breath which she vowed she wouldn't release until she was in the light. How faint it was, and yet how reassuring it promised to be! She trod harder on the pedal as her breath built up in her throat; she felt as if she couldn't swallow. Here was the fringe of the light, and now it spilled like diluted milk over the bonnet of the car. The vehicle raced out into the moonlight, and so did the two figures that had been pacing it in the dark.

Though they were on all fours, they weren't animals. That much she saw as her hands wrenched at the wheel, as her leg jerked and shoved the acclerator to the floor. Their heads looked swollen, too large for their naked scarecrow bodies. Greyish manes that might be hair or vegetation streamed back over their stick-like necks, over their ribs where gaps were encrusted with shadows or earth. As she floored the pedal the two figures raced past the car, their muscles flexing like windblown branches, and turned their faces to her as they ran. She saw how their greyish manes grew out of ragged eye-sockets, from one of which a clenched flower dangled as if it had been gouged. The sight made her forget to breathe, shrank her mind around her panic, shrank it too small for thoughts. When a long curved sign appeared at the limit of her headlights, she didn't immediately recognize the danger.

She stamped on the brake as the beams of her headlights plunged over the drop beyond the sharp bend. The car skidded, its rear wheels screeching towards the drop, and zigzagged out of control along the winding road. Somehow she managed to keep the wheels out of the ditch. She must have cried out in rage and terror, for she was breathing again. The car juddered to a standstill before she thought to change gears. She gripped the steering wheel and pressed herself back in her seat, her body shaking, her breaths huge and helpless. She was struggling to regain enough control of herself to be able to drive when a figure padded in front of the car and reared up in the glare of the headlights.

Its mottled limbs looked both lithe and horribly thin. Its torso had shrunk around its ribs, its greenish penis had withered like a dead root. Almost worse than all this, she recognized the face. Perhaps she was recognizing that the eyes, when it had had eyes, had been set so wide as to make the forehead seem lower than it was, but the vegetation that patched the skull had grown into a misshapen parody of the face that had once been there – the Redfield face.

A movement in the mirror dragged her gaze away. The other figure was behind the car; its Redfield mask with the dangling eye looked raw in the glow of the tail-lights. She was trapped. If she tried to run them down they would

277

easily dodge the car, and she already knew that she couldn't drive faster than they could run. They must be capable of anything their land needed them to do. She could feel her body preparing to get it over with, to step into the cold and the darkness so that they could finish her off with their long jagged nails. At least, unlike Graham, she would know why she was dying. Like him, she would be dying for the film.

The overgrown faces lifted blindly towards her, as if they sensed her despair, and she let out a hiss of rage that made her teeth ache. She hadn't come so far to die alone out here. What would she be allowing to happen at Redfield, to Roger and the others, if she didn't go on? 'Fuck you,' she cried at the weedy faces, 'and fuck your film!' Shaking with fury and terror, weeping at the thought of giving up all that she had achieved on Graham's behalf, she groped under the dashboard for the boot release. If she gave them what they had come for, mightn't they leave her alone?

She tugged the handle, and the lid of the boot sprang up. The figure in the headlight beams poked its patchy face at her and crouched forward as if it meant to leap, and the car shook as something struck it from behind. She heard the cans of film begin to rattle violently, but the lid of the boot blocked her view. She reached stealthily for the ignition key, praying that however they were able to sense her they couldn't hear her thoughts.

Suddenly the cans of film were flung on to the road behind the car. The echoing crash made her draw a painful breath which she seemed unable to expel while the scare-crow figure blocked her way, its head turning slightly from side to side, its grassy mane waving in the wind, greenish blotches trembling on its cheeks and in one eye. It leapt, and she shrank back, even when she realized it was darting past the car.

As she clutched the ignition key she saw the figures begin to worry the cans of film, scrabbling at the lids with their claws, nudging them with their swollen faces. One lid clattered away into the ditch, and the two figures converged on the opened can as if it were a plate of dog food. Sandy thought they might be about to fight doglike over it, and giggled uncontrollably. She twisted the key in the ignition, and the faces lifted towards her from the can of film.

The engine spluttered, caught, coughed fumes at the two figures, obscuring her view of them. The fumes drifted away as the car jerked forward. The figures were still at the can. As the glow of the tail-lights gave them back to the dark she saw them clawing the film on to the tarmac and beginning to tear it to shreds.

The other can would delay them for a few minutes, but then would they follow her? They mightn't hunt her down just for knowing the secret of Redfield, but wouldn't they for seeking to prevent bloodshed there? She drove down on to the flat land, trying to keep her mind blank in case it betrayed her, forcing herself to concentrate on the route. More than once she missed her way on the lonely roads. She felt like a puppet able only to drive, capable of flying apart in panic if she let her thoughts even momentarily loose. She was afraid to glance in the mirror or out of the windows beside her, a fear that seemed to grip her tighter and tighter by the scruff of the neck.

The edges of the landscape turned greyer as the approach of dawn raised mist from the fields. The dawn itself was muffled, but at least it allowed her to dare to glance around her. As far as she could see, she wasn't being followed, though there was no telling with the fields of wheat around her. Her head throbbed with reaction to all that she'd been through, a throbbing that spread through her body, threatening worse if she relaxed. She couldn't, she hadn't time. The sun rose through the mist, turning the fields red, and she was nearly in sight of Toonderfield, surely she was. She prayed that the convoy was approaching on another road, still safe over the horizon behind her. Then the road she was following sloped up to a crest that showed her Toonderfield, among fields that looked bathed in blood, and she saw that she was too late.

44

The convoy was halted at Toonderfield. The line of vehicles wound back out of the small wood to the police car, the caution on the tail. She could see no vehicles on the far side of the trees. The sight of the convoy, lying still as a snake whose head had been cut off, made her desperate to find out what had happened. Perhaps it didn't resemble a beheaded reptile so much as a creature whose skull had been supplanted by the copse, a new green head that was too large. She managed to take slow regular breaths which just about kept her calm, and drove along the deserted open road as fast as she dared, towards the green clump that was darkened by the reddening of the landscape.

She braked hard at the last curve, before she came in sight of the police car. She mustn't risk being detained for speeding. She swung the car on to the verge and climbed out on to the slippery grass. By now she was so anxious she almost neglected to lock the door. She ran down the sloping curve, and saw that the police car and the vehicles ahead of it were unattended.

The sight of so much desertion made her heartbeat falter. She ran past the police car, past muddied sunbursts, painted smiles that looked as if someone had hurled mud at them. The vehicles seemed to smell of exhaustion. By the time she reached the outer edge of Toonderfield she was panting and half suffocated. She didn't want to lean on any of those trees; she gripped her knees to steady herself while she caught her breath, and then sent herself forward. There had to be people not far ahead, close enough to reassure her. She mustn't be afraid of the wood.

A greenish twilight that smelled of oil and worn-out metal closed around her as she ran under the trees. A cramp gripped her stomach as if she were about to start her period weeks early. The convoy blocked her view of the left-hand side of the copse, but that needn't mean that anything was lurking there, waiting for her to come abreast of one of the gaps between the vehicles, any more than the trees to her right concealed something. Every upright shape that wasn't immediately identifiable as a tree trunk reminded her of the scarecrow figures she'd seen in the copse. Once she thought she heard whispering above her, as if things perched in the trees were planning to leap down at her, but it must have been a wind among the leaves.

At last she saw daylight ahead, past the leading police car. A fifty-yard sprint under the trees, and she was able to see Enoch's people. They were crowded together just beyond the police car, and gazing towards Redfield. She ran faster, her body trembling with the effort and with panicky anticipation. She was nearly at the head of the convoy when she saw Roger.

He was in the passenger seat of the second vehicle, a van painted with green clouds. In the wing mirror his face looked bemused, dissatisfied, rather helpless. She was abreast of the van before he blinked at the mirror and caught sight of her. She saw him gasp and smile and feel immediately guilty, as if he'd failed her. He leaned stiffly towards the window and rolled it down, and murmured to her while he gazed ahead. 'It's several kinds of great to see you,' he said.

He let his hand stray down the side of the door, and she covered it with hers. 'Same here, and I'm so glad you're safe.'

'Oh, I'm safe enough. Why wouldn't I be? I looked so forlorn these guys had to take pity on me, and I've spent the night finding out how much we have in common. They trusted me enough to leave me in their van,' he said with unexpected bitterness. 'Only I guess they did a better job persuading me than I did on them, since you'll have noticed I didn't convince them they should stay away from here.'

He levered himself up to stare ahead more sharply. 'Another few hours and I might have, but I didn't realize

281

we were so close. I think Enoch was beginning to take notice. I figured I had to go slow or he might realize I was coming from you.'

'I know you had to,' she said, and pressed his hand. 'What's happening out front?'

'He's scouting the land.'

He sounded as nervous as that made her feel. 'I'd better go and see,' she said, and stopped him when he made to open the door. 'You stay here. We may still need them not to realize we're together.'

She sprinted up the last of the slope. The police from both cars were keeping Enoch's followers grouped at the edge of the wood. As Sandy ran out of the shadow of the trees, several people turned to her. All of them looked anxious, especially the women; perhaps they were feeling the thirst of the land in their guts, as she was. Nobody seemed to recognize her. Arcturus and his mother were on the far side of the gathering, and didn't notice when she went as unobtrusively as possible to the front, to see what everyone was watching. As soon as she was able to see along the road to Redfield, her throat grew tight and dry.

Enoch was several hundred yards down the road, marching towards the Ear of Wheat as if he was almost exhausted, swinging his arms like lead weights. His bristling head was thrown back; he might have been sniffing the air. A few minutes' walk ahead of him, lined up on both sides of the road past the Ear of Wheat all the way to Redfield, the townsfolk were silently waiting.

Perhaps they only meant to make the convoy feel unwelcome. Perhaps that was how the police interpreted the situation, and so they were keeping Enoch's people back rather than escort him, but couldn't they feel the threat of violence in the air? Both they and Enoch might be assuming that Lord Redfield could control his people, but if one of the townsfolk so much as stepped in front of Enoch, Sandy could see that his people would surge to protect him. It would take many more than four policemen to hold them

282

back, let alone to prevent the bloodshed whose imminence seemed to have stilled the wind, making the land breathless.

The sun had risen above the mists. The fields brightened as if the wheat were eagerly awakening. Again Sandy had the sense of watching a ritual, Enoch the victim marching towards the gauntlet that was to carry out the sacrifice, the townsfolk stiffer than scarecrows, figures erected to carry out the will of the landscape. Her feeling that everyone in sight was subservient to an invisible power filled her with sudden furious panic. She hardly realized she had started forward, opening her mouth to scream at Enoch to come back, until a policeman grasped her arm, not ungently. Presumably he realized she wasn't with the convoy. 'You'll have to wait until this is over and done with,' he said.

There was movement and a whisper in the crowd. Arcturus and his mother had recognized her. Sandy tried to look as if she were irrelevant to what was happening ahead, and cursed herself for distracting attention from Enoch's plight: how could that prevent the violence whose approach seemed to parch the air and the eager fields?

She heard Enoch's folk murmur uneasily. They were staring past her, uncertain how to take what they were seeing. Whatever it was, it made the policeman let go of her arm. She sent out a prayer for Enoch, too swift to be composed of words or even to have a specific destination, and made herself turn and look.

Enoch had halted about a hundred yards short of the first of the townsfolk, raising his head further, as if he smelled something. Several townsfolk swung watchfully towards him. The landscape brightened around him, the watching faces seemed to take on the colour of wheat, and Sandy felt Enoch's people growing tense. If the nearest of the townsfolk even made a move towards him, the police would be swept aside. She could see that his people were concluding that they should never have let him go so far on their behalf.

Then he took a step forward. He held up his hands and addressed the men on either side of the road. He must be trying to placate them, but had he forgotten how unwelcome the convoy was everywhere? They stared at him for so long that Sandy lost count of her racing heartbeats, and then they called out to their neighbours in the line. Their voices were carried away by a wind from the restless fields. By now her heartbeats were so loud that she could have thought they were the sound of the landscape.

Enoch moved again, and she gnawed her knuckles. He turned his back on the townsfolk and began to trudge towards the copse. He cupped his hands to his mouth and shouted, loud as a town crier. In the midst of the unquiet fields under the huge sky, even such a voice seemed small. 'We won't go here,' he shouted. 'This land wants us too much.'

Perhaps Roger had convinced him after all, but had Enoch sensed the nature of Redfield too late? The townsfolk were still watching him, they could still come after him if the sight of his retreat enraged them or otherwise tempted them to attack. His people seemed bewildered, which could mean dangerous. Then he gestured at them, pushing with his hands as if the air were thickening in front of him. 'Go back to the vehicles,' he shouted. 'This isn't the place for us. We aren't safe here. I've thought of somewhere else.'

Something in his voice told Sandy that he hadn't, that he was so anxious to take them out of Redfield that he was lying. If she could hear that, wouldn't they? But though they were muttering, some of them complaining, they were straggling disappointedly towards the trees. Far more reassuringly, the townsfolk were moving towards Redfield.

She was suddenly afraid that the police would oppose the change of plan, but they seemed ready enough to escort the convoy out of their jurisdiction. Reassured, she turned to watch Enoch. Someone ought to see him safe along the road and let him know that he wasn't alone, though she thought it best not to allow him to recognize her. As his people retreated towards the vehicles, she stepped into the shadow of the trees, from where she could see him more clearly than he could see her.

284

And that was why she alone saw the scrawny form that rushed out of the wheat and tore at Enoch's throat.

45

Her shock seemed to freeze the moment, brightly displaying what she was helpless to prevent. She saw Enoch recoil as the figure reared up, a scarecrow all the colours of a decayed tree. Its ragged head was level with his; he must be staring straight into whatever it had for a face. It must be that sight which paralysed him, made him stand like a resigned victim while the nails through which the sunlight gleamed slashed at his neck.

Enoch roared in pain and horror. His hands flailed at the attacker and tore away part of its head, and then he tried either to grapple with the figure or hurl it away from him. To Sandy it looked grotesquely as though the two of them were dancing a couple of steps of a forgotten dance. The scarecrow figure lurched away, a flap of its head wagging, and Enoch either fell or lunged at the figure, grabbing one of its legs as he sprawled on the tarmac. She heard a crack, which at that distance sounded like a trodden twig, before his grasp must have slackened. Dragging its broken limb, the fleshless shape scuttled three-legged into the wheat.

Enoch's yell had brought the nearest of his people running out of the copse, but they weren't even level with Sandy when the track through the wheat disappeared. Enoch lumbered to his feet and marched unsteadily towards the trees, one hand clutching his throat. The hand looked like a red flower, blooming. As Sandy ran to him the watchers began to murmur, and a woman screamed. 'Stay back,' one policeman said loudly. 'There was nobody anywhere near him. He must have done that to himself.'

'He didn't,' Arcturus cried. 'I saw. It was a dog.'

The policeman was trying to prevent further violence, Sandy realized, but couldn't he have said something less contentious? At least the citizens of Redfield hadn't halted their retreat towards the town. The landscape seemed to heave up with the motion of her running, as if Enoch's wound were wakening the fields. She thought she saw a trail of his blood on the road. Did it count if it fell on the tarmac? Mustn't it reach the soil? The fields rustled like locusts, the air grew parched around her; she stared about wildly in search of figures in the wheat. The fields surrounding Enoch were still brightening, bristling in anticipation of his blood. She felt sick, almost out of breath. She thought she tasted the rusty flavour of the special Redfield bread.

Roger shouted behind her. She twisted round and saw someone fling a glinting object at him. She thought it was a knife until the van jerked forward, and then she realized he'd been thrown a bunch of keys. He must have struggled across to the driver's seat when he had seen Enoch fall.

Enoch's followers dodged out of the road, taking the police with them, as the van lurched out of the trees. Roger was crouched awkwardly over the wheel, his face squashed together by determination. He slowed when he came abreast of Sandy, and she slid the passenger door open. He was slewed round in the driver's seat, his plastered leg wedged against the accelerator; he had to swing his whole body whenever he needed to work the other pedals. He looked more incongruous than he had when she'd left him by the road; he looked like a grubby knight who'd found his way into a modern vehicle by mistake. The sight of him was so comic and heartening that she wanted to weep. She would have changed seats with him, except that would waste time. As soon as she climbed into the passenger seat he thrust his cast down on the accelerator.

Enoch had halted in the middle of the road and was covering his throat with both red hands. As the van sped towards him he staggered aside. 'Don't,' Sandy cried, suddenly afraid that he would step into the field behind him. Roger must have thought she was talking to him, for he leaned so hard on the brake that she was nearly flung out of the vehicle as the door slid open. As she jumped down and ran to Enoch, Roger was already turning the van.

The cords of Enoch's waistcoat were beginning to turn red. His eyes looked in danger of glazing over, glistening with his struggle to stay in them. Though she had hoped before that he wouldn't recognize her, she was dismayed now that he seemed unable to do so. She grabbed him by the elbow and felt him trying not to collapse on to her. 'I've got you,' she said as firmly as she could. 'We'll take you back. There's a healer travelling with you, isn't there?'

He drew a breath so painful she thought he was choking. At last he managed to get out one word, in a shrunken laborious voice. 'Hospital.'

His hands let go of his throat as if to allow him to speak, and she saw how much he needed a hospital, saw the raw shredded streaming flesh he was attempting to hold toge-ther. Faintness brought the landscape dancing at her, but she forced herself to support him as far as the van, which Roger had succeeded in turning. Roger clambered down and helped hoist Enoch into the back, where there was a lumpy double mattress for him to lie on. 'Can you drive now?' Roger said to her. 'It might be quicker.'

It would also help her overcome her faintness. She scram-bled behind the wheel and started the vehicle as Roger slammed the rear doors from inside. In the mirror she saw his face as he propped himself at Enoch's head, murmuring to him, looking so encouraging that she knew he must be battling not to react to what he saw.

She'd scarcely gathered speed towards the trees when she had to brake. Both the police and the owners of the van, a long-haired middle-aged couple, were blocking the road. 'He's badly hurt. We need to get him to a hospital as fast as we can. Will you escort me?' she called down to the police, and threw down her keys to the long-haired couple. 'It'll be quickest if you take my car. It's just past all your vehicles.'

What sounded like authority was half panic, the sound of her determination to drive straight on if anyone opposed

288

her. The driver of the leading police car scrutinized her face, then turned quickly. 'Follow us.'

As he swung the police car around, its siren howling, a muscular woman with a crew-cut and the whitest teeth Sandy had ever seen jumped into the van and wriggled over the passenger seat into the back. 'I'm Merl. I'll look after him,' she said, and then with much less certainty: 'Oh Jesus. *Was* it a dog?'

'Whatever it was,' Sandy said, to fend off the subject, 'he didn't let it get away in one piece.'

'You should have seen what it was, you were there. If I'd been there I would have killed it myself.' She tore a strip off the hem of her loose ankle-length dress and wrapped it around Enoch's neck, and her voice became maternal. 'Rest now, rest and be strong. What is it? What are you trying to say?'

Enoch sucked in a choked breath. 'Don't let me die here,' he said indistinctly.

'We won't let you die at all,' Sandy cried, following the police car. Enoch's plea had made her fear of Redfield more immediate and more specific. All the victims of the land hadn't just spilled their blood within its boundaries, they had died there. The flashing light of the police car made shadows leap between the trees, and she was afraid that one or other of the thin vague shapes would spring into the van to finish Enoch off. When some of his folk stared resentfully at the police car and didn't clear the road immediately, she heard herself moaning between her clenched teeth.

The trees parted ahead, beyond the curve that led into the open, and all at once the copse smelled to her as if the earth were heaving up beneath the undergrowth. She had to restrain herself from ramming her fist into the wheel to sound the horn; it wouldn't make the police drive any faster, it was more likely to pull them up. The last branches sailed by overhead, and their shadows reached beyond the copse for the van. Then the vehicle was out under the sky, and she had to swallow before she was able to ask, 'How is he?'

The woman was singing Enoch a song, too low for Sandy to hear the words. It might have been a lullaby or a soft dirge. When she didn't interrupt it to respond to Sandy's question, Roger peered at Enoch. 'Alive,' he said.

At the most Sandy would have uttered a secret whisper of relief, but even that was premature. Half the convoy was still on Redfield land. As she raced after the police car she glanced constantly into the mirrors, seeing the trees close around the head of the convoy, the line of vehicles shrivelling with distance as though Toonderfield were consuming it. Fumes rose through the trees and drifted across the fields as the vehicles turned, and Sandy willed the drivers to be quick, get out, don't be distracted by any movements in the shadows, stay together . . . Perhaps there was safety in numbers, for as Toonderfield sank below the horizon to bide its time she saw the convoy following the second police car. She gripped the wheel so hard she bruised her fingers, to carry herself past feeling so weak with relief that she wouldn't be able to drive.

It took the police half an hour to conduct her to a hospital, and the cropped woman sang to Enoch all the way, wrapping more strips of her dress around his neck. Once he tried to say something about a dog, which Sandy thought was either a question or a denial. As Sandy parked the van in front of the emergency wing, one of the policemen came running out ahead of a doctor and two orderlies with a stretcher. Enoch was loaded on to the stretcher, and Sandy heard him speak. Later she agreed with Roger that he'd muttered, 'Can't be helped.' She hoped that meant he was resigned to what came, for less than five minutes later he was dead.

46

The police were ready to believe Arcturus, since he alone claimed to have seen what had happened to Enoch. Merl the healer said that Enoch had tried to tell her about a dog, and Sandy made herself keep quiet: this wasn't the place or the time to say what she knew. The police called in a warning about a savage stray dog and made to herd the convoy away, until Sandy managed to persuade the hospital to let Enoch's people pay their last respects.

Not all of them wanted to see Enoch. A group led by Merl knelt in the car park and chanted as a large bright cloud that made Sandy think of an unfurling sail glided slowly from above the hospital towards the distant sea. Most of those who went in to view Enoch shed a tear for him, but they seemed stunned by his death. He lay in an anonymous side room whose function was unclear, a sheet over his face until one of the men uncovered it and snarled at an orderly who started to protest. Sandy stood outside the room in case she needed to mediate, but that was the only skirmish. The sight of Enoch's huge head in repose, his beard wiry on the white sheet, seemed to impress even the hospital staff who passed along the corridor. As Sandy watched his followers trudging silently in and out of the room, she thought that despite the starkness of the setting he looked exactly like an ancient chieftain lying in state.

The last to visit were Arcturus and his mother. The boy held her hand and gazed at the dead face as if he were trying to understand. 'Where's he gone?' he said.

The woman didn't speak until she was out of the room and staring hard at Sandy. 'Somewhere better than we're going, but we'll be there too some day.'

Sandy thought she was meant to feel guilty, a feeling easily invoked in her just now, until she realized the woman only expected her to respond. All she could think of to say was, 'Where *will* you go?'

'We'll find an island,' the woman said, with a fierceness that sounded bitter rather than convincing.

'Maybe there's a country that'll like us,' Arcturus said in a dazed voice.

'Or one so big we won't be noticed, any road.'

Outside the hospital the police were making sure that everyone returned to the vehicles and prepared to drive on. The healer, who appeared to have taken over some of Enoch's leadership, was murmuring comfort to them as they left the building. 'Where are we,' Arcturus' mother began and was interrupted by an angry sob, 'supposed to go now?'

'As far north as we have to, we've decided.'

Not everyone seemed to agree. At least one couple were already arguing between themselves. If Enoch's death caused the convoy to split up, Sandy wondered whether that might be for the best. She watched the convoy meander away, following the beacon of one police car and trailed by the other, until it was out of sight on the road that led to Scotland. Some of the convoy would stay with the healer, she imagined, and there would be room enough for them in the harsh thinly populated highlands, but would they be able to survive there? Sending a wish after them, she went back into the hospital.

Roger was in another wing, having his cast removed. He would be expecting her to drive back to London once he was free, but she couldn't when the closeness of Redfield reminded her that nothing had changed, that the year wasn't over. A surge of the nervous energy that had kept her driving hustled her to the nearest pay phone, her hands digging change out of her purse.

The receptionist sounded efficiently warm as ever. 'Staff o' Life?'

'I need to speak to Lord Redfield. Not the press office, not his secretary. Lord Redfield himself.'

'I'm afraid he's accepting no calls.'

The swiftness of the answer told Sandy that it wasn't just

a standard response. 'Tell him Sandy Allan wants to speak to him. Tell him I saw what happened this morning at Toonderfield. I saw exactly what happened, and he needs to know.'

She felt uncomfortably like a blackmailer – indeed, one who was contradicting what she had told the police – but what else could she do? If she wasn't able to speak to him over the phone she would have to venture back to Redfield. All she wanted at this point was to arrange to meet him somewhere beyond the boundaries of his land, but the receptionist said, 'I'm sorry, Lord Redfield is in conference.'

That was a stock response if Sandy had ever heard one. 'What do you mean, in conference?'

'He's left instructions that he's not to be disturbed.'

'He's going to have to be. He'll want to know how a man came to be killed on his land.'

'Miss Allan, I'm not authorized – '

'Didn't you know that had happened this morning? He'll want to speak to me, I promise you. And no, I haven't got the number of his private line. If you'd seen what I saw earlier I think even you might be a bit disorganized.'

After a pause the receptionist said 'Please hold on' discouragingly, and made way for the Staff o' Life jingle. There should be children singing it, Sandy thought, not the sterile tones of a synthesizer. She leaned her forehead against the inside of the sketchy booth, and felt exhaustion lowering itself on to her shoulders. She blinked her eyes hard and stretched them wide several times, and then she was jarred awake. The second repetition of the jingle had been cut short, leaving her mind to sing 'mark it' where the jingle would have reached that phrase, and Lord Redfield broke the hollow silence. 'Well, Miss Allan.'

Either she was hearing what she wanted to hear or he wasn't as calm as he was trying to sound: his voice was a little too precise and high. 'I was at Toonderfield this morning,' she said.

'Many people were.'

'Yes, but one of them died, even though I got him to hospital. He died of being injured on your land.'

A sound like a shudder in the earpiece made her take the receiver away from her face, and she heard the last of that sigh in his voice. 'I was afraid of something of the kind after what I saw myself.'

Rage, the more uncontrollable because she felt it was to some extent unreasonable, shook her voice. 'You were there and yet you didn't do anything? I didn't see you.'

'I wasn't there. My grandfather was. Perhaps you saw him.'

'If he was, why didn't he – ' she demanded, and then what he was implying caught up with her. The heat and noises of the hospital seemed to retreat, leaving her alone and cold and yet closer to him, united in understanding. At last she said, 'How do you know?'

'I heard him coming back and I followed him down. I take it the victim put up a fight.'

'He tried to.'

'He broke my grandfather's leg, if I can call that my grandfather. I must, of course, since I am to be allowed no illusions. It nearly hid from me in its lair but wasn't quite swift enough. I wonder if you have the least idea what I'm talking about, not that it matters.'

'I'm afraid I have.'

'You have? You must have had sharp eyes while you were here. I wish you had tried to convince me of what I should have known. Once when I was very young and my grandfather was very old he told me the story his grandfather told him, but even he thought he was too modern to believe in that sort of thing. God help him, he must now. I quite see that was really just a way of letting ourselves take it for granted. The man you mentioned didn't die on our land, you say?'

Sandy felt Redfield was only intermittently remembering that he was talking to her rather than to himself. 'That's right.'

'Ah well,' he said in what might have been regret or

resignation, and then his voice strengthened briefly. 'I'm glad to have had another chance to speak to you. If you should find your film, please show it. There will be nobody here to object.'

'I don't – ' Sandy began, and was talking to the dialling tone. The last of her change clattered into the slot to be retrieved. She was suddenly anxious for him, all the more so when she realized she had insufficient change to place another call. She ran to the hospital shop, bought a *Daily Friend* and left it on the counter, dashed back to the phone, praying that it wouldn't be in use. Nobody had ousted her. As soon as the receptionist said 'Staff – ' Sandy interrupted her. 'I was talking to Lord Redfield. Sandy Allan. We were cut off.'

'Lord Redfield asks me to apologize, Miss Allan, but I'm not to accept any further calls from you.'

'Wait, don't cut me off, just listen,' Sandy cried, but the phone was buzzing emptily. She grabbed her change as it came rattling back, and ran to find Roger. He was hobbling across a lawn beside the car park, wearing someone else's old trousers and trying out his rediscovered leg. 'Is that your top speed?' Sandy panted.

'Let's say you shouldn't enter me in any marathons this month.'

'Head for the car. I'll meet you.' She sprinted to it, grimaced at how low the fuel level was, drove round two ranks of cars and pulled up beside him, narrowly missing him with the door as she opened it. 'Be as quick as you can that isn't painful.'

He snapped his seat-belt into place and stretched his legs luxuriously. 'Want to tell me what the hurry is? I've missed you too, a whole lot.'

'We'll celebrate, but not yet. Roger, I hope you won't give me a hard time about this, but I've got to go back to Redfield.'

He stared at her and gripped her knee. 'I don't know what happened there today, I don't know what I saw, but I really don't think you should do this. You've already done more than many people would.'

'Not people I'd want to know. Roger, I've just spoken to Lord Redfield. I think he's planning to harm himself when there may be no need. He's made sure my calls won't get through.'

He held on to her and then patted her knee as if to indicate he'd done all he could to dissuade her. 'Looks like you need to find a filling station fast,' he said.

She'd passed one as she drove the van to the hospital. She willed it to appear on the horizon ahead as the car raced back across the flat land under the declining sun. It came in sight just as the engine ran dry and died, leaving her feeling for an unpleasant moment that control of the vehicle had been snatched away from her. She ran the car on to the verge and tugged the boot release, and Roger swung himself out of the car and lifted the plastic canteen from the boot. 'This what you need?'

'It's all I've got. I never thought I'd have to use it.'

As she locked the car, he was already running. Before long he began to limp, and she caught up with him. 'Maybe – ' he said apologetically, and she stopped his mouth with a quick kiss and grabbed the canteen as if they were running a relay race. She ran to the pumps – twenty minutes of the canteen thumping her on one side, her handbag on the other – and had to pay before the slow proprietor would let her fill the canteen. Running back to the car, through the flat landscape which seemed designed expressly to display how far she had still to go, took her almost half an hour. She fell into the driver's seat, a stitch nagging at her side, and managed to catch her breath while Roger emptied the canteen into the tank, and then she drove to the pumps to fill the tank.

The car sped away from the forecourt, and Roger let out a sigh so loud it sounded as if he were emitting it on her behalf, to save her breath. After that he was silent for a while, but she sensed that he wanted to speak. At last he said, 'Did you pick up the movie?'

'Yes, but I haven't got it now.'

'I noticed. It's safe, though,' he said, not so much a query as a plea.

'It isn't, Roger. It no longer exists.'

He seemed to have half expected her answer. 'I guess you had to let that happen,' he said.

'It was either me or the film.'

'In that case there's no contest.' Some time later he said, so gently and casually that she wanted to hug him, 'Did you watch the movie? Was it any good?'

'In parts.'

'Maybe you can describe it to me some time so I can write it up for my book.'

'I will,' she promised. There seemed to be no need to say anything further, now that they'd agreed they had a future. The car raced across the flatness, and they were in sight of Toonderfield before Roger spoke again. 'What's that?'

He might mean the distant wail of sirens or the smudge of black smoke on the horizon towards Redfield. Sandy braked as the car reached the edge of the copse, and tried to analyse her sensations. She didn't feel threatened or seized by her guts. All the same, she closed her window tight and told Roger to close his before she drove beneath the trees.

She could see nothing between the trunks except green dimness and shadows. The drive through the wood seemed considerably briefer than last time. The car sped towards the Ear of Wheat, and before she reached the pub she could see that the smoke came from a building on fire. From the direction of the smoke she judged that the building was beyond the town.

The woman from the Ear of Wheat stood outside the porch of the pub, staring towards the smoke and wiping her hands nervously on her apron. Sandy veered on to the concrete and got out of the car. 'What's happening, do you know?'

The woman gazed at her as if it didn't matter who knew.

'It's Lord Redfield's chapel. They heard him smashing stones down there while the son wasn't at the house to stop him, and then he set fire to it and wouldn't come up out of it, God save him.'

She was talking about the family vault, whether or not she realized. He must have smashed all the plaques to make sure the fire reached in. 'Couldn't anyone reach him?' Sandy said, though she thought she already knew more than the woman could tell.

'His father went down after him, then the son tried to rescue the both of them. Nobody else could get near for the fire, and Lord Redfield wouldn't let them. The whole family were in there, and nobody could save them.'

And that was the end of Redfield, Sandy thought, and found a tear creeping down her cheek. Had he planned that his father and son should die too? Remembering his last words to her, she wasn't sure that she wanted to know. She felt almost as stunned as the woman looked, but the woman seemed also to feel robbed of meaning. Sandy wondered how the townsfolk must feel – how they would fare now that the spell of the land had been broken. 'Don't despair,' she said awkwardly, and was glad of Roger's hand on her arm as they turned back to the car.

She thought of driving to Redfield to make certain it was all over, but she would be even more unwelcome in the town now. As she swung the car towards Toonderfield she saw the smoke drift across the tower, which looked abandoned, a symbol rendered meaningless. It always had been, she thought, and it had taken her so long to realize.

She drove over the humpbacked bridge, and the tower seemed to collapse into the smoke. As the car passed under the trees, a leaf fluttered across the windscreen, and then another. When she ducked her head to look up through the foliage, she was sure she could see more of the sky than she had been able to see that morning. Autumn was already here, she thought, but would spring come to Redfield? Her throat grew unexpectedly dry, and she steered with one hand while she held Roger's with the other. He smiled at hèr, but she didn't think he was sharing her awareness. All the way to the edge of Toonderfield, until the car sped up into daylight that felt like a return to life, she sensed the land dying.

Bestselling SF/Horror

☐ Forge of God	Greg Bear	£3.99
☐ Eon	Greg Bear	£3.50
☐ The Hungry Moon	Ramsey Campbell	£3.50
☐ The Influence	Ramsey Campbell	£3.50
☐ Seventh Son	Orson Scott Card	£3.50
☐ Bones of the Moon	Jonathan Carroll	£2.50
☐ Nighthunter: The Hexing & The Labyrinth	Robert Faulcon	£3.50
☐ Pin	Andrew Neiderman	£1.50
☐ The Island	Guy N. Smith	£2.50
☐ Malleus Maleficarum	Montague Summers	£4.50

Prices and other details are liable to change

A Selection of Legend Titles

☐ Eon	Greg Bear	£3.50
☐ Forge of God	Greg Bear	£3.99
☐ Falcons of Narabedla	Marion Zimmer Bradley	£2.50
☐ The Influence	Ramsey Campbell	£3.50
☐ Wyrms	Orson Scott Card	£3.50
☐ Speaker for the Dead	Orson Scott Card	£2.95
☐ Seventh Son	Orson Scott Card	£3.50
☐ Wolf in Shadow	David Gemmell	£3.50
☐ Last Sword of Power	David Gemmell	£3.50
☐ This is the Way the World Ends	James Morrow	£4.99
☐ Unquenchable Fire	Rachel Pollack	£3.99
☐ Golden Sunlands	Christopher Rowley	£3.50
☐ The Misplaced Legion	Harry Turtledove	£2.99
☐ An Emperor for the Legion	Harry Turtledove	£2.99

Prices and other details are liable to change

ARROW BOOKS, BOOKSERVICE BY POST, PO BOX 29, DOUGLAS, ISLE OF MAN, BRITISH ISLES

NAME...

ADDRESS..

....

....

Please enclose a cheque or postal order made out to Arrow Books Ltd. for the amount due and allow the following for postage and packing.

U.K. CUSTOMERS: Please allow 22p per book to a maximum of £3.00.

B.F.P.O. & EIRE: Please allow 22p per book to a maximum of £3.00.

OVERSEAS CUSTOMERS: Please allow 22p per book.

Whilst every effort is made to keep prices low it is sometimes necessary to increase cover prices at short notice. Arrow Books reserve the right to show new retail prices on covers which may differ from those previously advertised in the text or elsewhere.

Bestselling Thriller/Suspense

☐ Skydancer	Geoffrey Archer	£3.50
☐ Hooligan	Colin Dunne	£2.99
☐ See Charlie Run	Brian Freemantle	£2.99
☐ Hell is Always Today	Jack Higgins	£2.50
☐ The Proteus Operation	James P Hogan	£3.50
☐ Winter Palace	Dennis Jones	£3.50
☐ Dragonfire	Andrew Kaplan	£2.99
☐ The Hour of the Lily	John Kruse	£3.50
☐ Fletch, Too	Geoffrey McDonald	£2.50
☐ Brought in Dead	Harry Patterson	£2.50
☐ The Albatross Run	Douglas Scott	£2.99

Prices and other details are liable to change

ARROW BOOKS, BOOKSERVICE BY POST, PO BOX 29, DOUGLAS, ISLE
OF MAN, BRITISH ISLES

NAME...

ADDRESS ....

....

....

Please enclose a cheque or postal order made out to Arrow Books Ltd. for the amount
due and allow the following for postage and packing.

U.K. CUSTOMERS: Please allow 22p per book to a maximum of £3.00.

B.F.P.O. & EIRE: Please allow 22p per book to a maximum of £3.00.

OVERSEAS CUSTOMERS: Please allow 22p per book.

Whilst every effort is made to keep prices low it is sometimes necessary to increase cover
prices at short notice. Arrow Books reserve the right to show new retail prices on covers
which may differ from those previously advertised in the text or elsewhere.

Bestselling Crime

☐ No One Rides Free	Larry Beinhart	£2.95
☐ Alice in La La Land	Robert Campbell	£2.99
☐ In La La Land We Trust	Robert Campbell	£2.99
☐ Suspects	William J Caunitz	£2.95
☐ So Small a Carnival	John William Corrington	
	Joyce H Corrington	£2.99
☐ Saratoga Longshot	Stephen Dobyns	£2.99
☐ Blood on the Moon	James Ellroy	£2.99
☐ Roses Are Dead	Loren D. Estleman	£2.50
☐ The Body in the Billiard Room	HRF Keating	£2.50
☐ Bertie and the Tin Man	Peter Lovesey	£2.50
☐ Rough Cider	Peter Lovesey	£2.50
☐ Shake Hands For Ever	Ruth Rendell	£2.99
☐ Talking to Strange Men	Ruth Rendell	£2.99
☐ The Tree of Hands	Ruth Rendell	£2.99
☐ Wexford: An Omnibus	Ruth Rendell	£6.99
☐ Speak for the Dead	Margaret Yorke	£2.99

Prices and other details are liable to change

ARROW BOOKS, BOOKSERVICE BY POST, PO BOX 29, DOUGLAS, ISLE OF MAN, BRITISH ISLES

NAME..

ADDRESS..

....

....

Please enclose a cheque or postal order made out to Arrow Books Ltd. for the amount due and allow the following for postage and packing.

U.K. CUSTOMERS: Please allow 22p per book to a maximum of £3.00.

B.F.P.O. & EIRE: Please allow 22p per book to a maximum of £3.00.

OVERSEAS CUSTOMERS: Please allow 22p per book.

Whilst every effort is made to keep prices low it is sometimes necessary to increase cover prices at short notice. Arrow Books reserve the right to show new retail prices on covers which may differ from those previously advertised in the text or elsewhere.